HEIR

OF

RAVENS

AND

RUIN

HEIR
OF
RAVENS
AND
RUIN

First Paperback Edition October 2022
First Hardback Edition October 2022
First eBook Edition October 2022

ISBN: 978-1-7397126-2-4 (paperback)
ISBN: 978-1-7397126-0-0 (hardback)
ISBN: 978-1-7397126-1-7 (eBook)

For you, Dad. I wish you were here to see that I did it.

<u>*Trigger warnings*</u>

This book contains strong language, sexual scenes, talk of sexual assault, intense fight scenes, violence, blood, death of a loved one, depression, PTSD.

PROLOGUE

Bathed in fire and ash was how the world would be cleansed, the songs of birds replaced by screeching and howling of creatures from the very depths of the darkest realms. Rivers would flow red with the blood of the innocent. Darkness would prevail, evil would conquer, and the sun would give way to the everlasting night.

But not all hope was lost. A beacon of light and power would be the world's only chance of survival, piercing the darkness and bringing a new dawn.

At least that is what the legends foretold.

I

It was the sound of birds singing their morning songs that woke Rexah from her nightmare. The winter sun shone into her room through the large windows to the left of her bed making the chandelier hanging from the ceiling sparkle.

Another dream filled with death and storms had plagued her sleep. Thunder roared so loud and real she felt the very earth beneath her feet tremble; lightning flashed across the sky so brightly it felt almost enough to blind her. Suddenly, with her back flat against the world, her last breath fading away, a raven landed on her bloodied chest. It looked her straight in the eye as its black wings stretched out behind its body, and before she found out her fate, she'd woken up, as she had done other countless times when she had the dream.

Sighing loudly, she ran her hand over her face. The nightmares were growing more frequent as the nights went on. They'd been happening for the last month or two at least, and she was getting fed up with them. It was the same thing every godsdamned time.

She threw off the covers and stood up stretching. Her room was huge, a little too big for any one person if she was being honest. White marble covered the floor, and a beautiful shade of purple coated the walls. That particular tone happened to be her favourite colour. Her room was a perfect impression of herself, she thought. She could decorate it any way she liked – with permission from her grandmother – and so she did. Rexah had designed every little detail, and she loved it – her own little sanctuary. A bookcase beside the large windows was her favourite part of the room. It stretched from the floor to the ceiling and was filled with her favourite literature that she loved to get lost in, especially when she needed to get away from royal life.

Rexah lived in the kingdom of Adorea and had been raised by her grandmother, Queen Aurelia. Her mother and father died not long after she was born. They were travelling back home from a trip to the south when their carriage was ambushed. They were robbed and killed by thieves.

Rexah was lucky to have been staying with her grandmother at the time of the attack. She never asked for any further details about her parents' deaths – she'd rather not know. Still, nightmares of the event often plagued her sleep. She would wake up in the middle of the night covered in cold sweat, her heart beating so fast she feared it might explode.

Growing up without a mother and father was difficult, so was being an only child, but being part of a royal family meant that she was always surrounded by people no matter where she went, and sometimes that could get a little overwhelming.

Adorea was beautiful. This part of the realm, Etteria, was mainly occupied by humans. Only a handful of fae resided here. A forest surrounded the kingdom filled with a variety of stunning trees and a lake within the heart of it. No matter the season, the flowers scattered in the forest bed, and forming meadows by the lake did not wither and die. The palace gardens, too, were filled with flowers the likes no other kingdom had ever seen. They changed colour in the winter – shedding bright shades of orange and yellows to take on the most stunning blues and indigos.

She loved walking through the forest and reading by the lake. Sometimes at night when everyone else in the castle was sleeping, she would sneak out of her room to go lay amongst the flowers and look up at the blanket of stars filling the night sky.

Stars were her most favourite sight of all. Laying underneath their watchful eyes, she knew no judgement and always felt calmed by the very presence of them. The assurance that they'd be back the following night brought her peace of mind. Each time her eyes fell upon them she wondered about the secrets and stories they held.

A soft knock at her bedroom door pulled her from her thoughts and she called out permission for them to enter. Nesrin stepped into the room and closed the door behind her.

Rexah had never known anyone else with such a soft complexion. Nesrin's copper hair was neatly pulled back into a braid, highlighting her skin tone even more. A delicate sprinkle of freckles dusted her pale cheeks, some spreading to the bridge of her nose. Sure, her own skin wasn't much darker, but Nesrin could almost be mistaken for a ghost. The young lady, who was around the same age as Rexah, bowed to her.

"Good morning, Your Highness," she said softly. "Her Majesty has requested that I get you dressed and prepared for today's guests."

Usually, Rexah would wear breeches and an under-shirt beneath a tunic but today was different. Today was especially important. It was all her grandmother spoke of these days. The king of Kaldoren, a kingdom that was a five-day ride away from Adorea, had come to visit the court. The prince and heir to the Kaldorien throne was accompanying him.

Kaldoren was the closest kingdom to Adorea – and almost rivalled it with its size. Mostly known for the castle built within the mountain side itself, the walls were the same colour as the rock and blended in perfectly.

What fascinated Rexah most was the mist that had settled around the kingdom. She'd been terrified of it when she was younger. She imagined monsters living within the fog and crawling out whenever anyone would get too close. It had been the prince himself who planted those very thoughts in her head in the first place.

She had visited many times together with her

grandmother, but it had been a while since their last visit.

Rexah smiled softly at Nesrin and nodded. "We best get started then."

The Queen expected her to be in her best dress and looking presentable for their royal guests. Rexah did not mind wearing dresses but given the chance she'd always choose the more practical option, a tunic and breeches, over heavy, suffocating fabrics.

After seeing to her needs in her bathing chamber, the next half hour consisted of ridding Rexah of her night clothes and being helped into a beautiful, dark purple gown with black trimming, courtesy of the royal seamstress. The dress hugged her waist before falling smoothly around her hips and down to the floor. Rexah tugged at the long, tight-fitted sleeves that stopped at her wrists.

Thank the stars it came without a corset.

She wasn't thin but couldn't be considered over-weight, either. Training helped her to keep fit and even gain some muscle mass. Despite the exercise, her hips were round and brought out the hourglass shape of her body. Her bust filled the decolletage. She knew she looked different than most of the girls her age, but she loved every single one of her curves and wouldn't change them for anything.

Nesrin fixed her hair whilst she sat at her vanity table, staring at her reflection in the mirror. She had to say, the woman was a miracle worker. Nesrin let it fall with the natural soft curls that she had been born with, and once she was ready, Rexah stood up and walked over to the full-length mirror. Her long black hair fell to just above her waist, curling slightly at the ends. The colour itself was striking, but in certain light flashes of purple shone through its length, perfectly complimenting the violet of her eyes.

There was only one other member of her family whose features had been the same as Rexah's, her great, great grandmother, Queen Riona. Rexah knew this only because she had spent many days in the gallery with the royal portraits studying the long dead queen for hours on end.

Queen Riona had been the fiercest in their family, loved by her subjects and feared by her enemies. Her life was taken from her at the age of thirty-six, two years after the birth of her daughter, Arius.

"Killed in battle, she'd been a true warrior," Rexah's grandmother had told her. She was the last one to fall protecting the kingdom she loved in the fight known as

the Battle of Adorea. Queen Aurelia liked to tell her granddaughter the tales of their family history as bedtime stories, and Rexah wondered on occasion if they had contributed to her nightmares.

"One last thing, Your Highness," Nesrin's gentle voice said behind her.

Rexah looked over to see her lady's maid holding out her tiara. She sat back down at the vanity table and let Nesrin place the jewel encrusted headpiece upon her raven-haired head, making sure it was perfect.

"Do you think I'm presentable enough to my grand-mother's liking?" Rexah asked, looking at her through the mirror.

Nesrin's green eyes lit up as a small grin played on her lips. "You look divine, Your Highness."

Both girls burst out into laughter. Even while being her lady's maid, Nesrin was Rexah's best friend. Since she had been assigned to her a few years ago, Nesrin had been there for her at times when she couldn't share her burdens with anybody else – even her grandmother – and since she was a princess, Rexah couldn't neces-sarily have normal friends, not like the girls living in the village below the castle.

She often wondered what it would be like to live a life where you didn't have the restrictions or responsibilities that came with royalty, a life where you didn't have servants and maids doing everything for you.

Rexah looked to the mirror, taking in her appearance one last time and smoothing out her dress. Yes, now she looked like the royal her grandmother expected to see every day, not the rebel princess who wore trousers and didn't act lady-like at all.

Today, for her grandmother, she would call upon her royal training; she would remember her table manners and show the King and the prince the respect she expected to have returned; for she was Rexah Ravenheart, princess and heir to the Kingdom of Adorea.

Winter sun shone in through the beautiful floor to ceiling windows and filled the corridor with light as the women made their way to the Grand Hall together. Stained-glass at the top, each window portrayed their own different story of how Adorea came to be and begun to flourish. Various suits of armour lined the wall; the sunlight reflected off the polished metal and the brightness stung her eyes as she passed. Rexah often wondered how anyone wore those things in battle, what with the heaviness of them and not to mention the amount of sweating they must have done underneath all that steel. She was glad that armour was different nowadays.

As usual, Nesrin walked a few steps behind the princess.

"Did you have another nightmare?"

Rexah looked at her, a small smirk on her face. "Is it that obvious?"

"You do look a little tired." She nodded softly with a smile. "But don't worry, you look beautiful."

"I don't know what I'd do without you." Rexah grinned.

Guards were stationed here and there along the corridor, their eyes watching anyone who walked by them. They straightened up when they saw her, some holding their spears tighter to show they took their post very seriously.

As she drew closer, they bowed to her. Some murmured "Your Highness" while others stayed silent. Rexah couldn't help the smile that spread across her lips, nodding her head to the guards as she passed. Two guards keeping watch over the entrance to the hall quickly opened the doors for her, before falling into a respectful bow.

The Grand Hall, that's what her grandmother liked to call it, and grand it was indeed. A floor laid from white and silver crushed marble and white painted walls decorated with paintings of Adorea – landscapes and a few other decorative pieces – greeted Rexah when she stepped into the wide-open space. During the daytime, the room was filled with light that spilled through windows adorned with cobalt blue drapes; in the evening, huge chandeliers that hung from the high ceiling would be lit regularly to create a breath-taking ambience. Many unforgettable parties had been held over the centuries in this very room.

The thrones were magnificent and always commanded attention more than any other object in the vast space; three of them sat on the dais. The two smaller thrones were identical, each emblazoned with a raven with a violet diamond eye, perched on top of a heart with two swords pierced through it – the Raven-heart crest. Smaller and less detailed drawings of ravens etched the woodwork around it until there was no space untouched by the masterful art.

Like the thrones on either side of it, the larger throne

in the middle had the royal crest emblazoned along with the etchings of ravens in the woodwork, but what made it stand out from the other two were the two black wooden raven wings protruding from the top of the throne and expanding wide. That's where her grandmother sat now.

Queen Aurelia's hair – once ash-brown, now dark grey – was pulled up into a braid. The crown on her head glistened in the sunlight and her grey dress brought out the colour of her bright blue eyes. Silver clips attached a matching cape onto her shoulders leaving it to flow down behind her in brilliant waves.

Rexah gave her grandmother a smile before she took her place on the smaller throne to the right of her. Nesrin stood off to the side in case she was needed.

"When do our honoured guests arrive?" Rexah asked the Queen as she smoothed out her dress slightly.

"They will be here any moment now," she replied before slowly tilting her head to her granddaughter. "You look beautiful my darling."

A smile played on Rexah's lips. "Thank you, Grand-mother, as do you."

It was then that the huge heavy doors to the Grand Hall were once again opened, groaning as they were, and in walked the King and the Crown Prince of

Kaldoren accompanied by a few guards from Adorea and a few of their own.

The King, Orland Crowfell, who was around fifty years of age – the years clearly showing on his face – had a warm youthful shine in his grey eyes. He was tall, around five foot eight with greying hair and beard to match.

The Crown Prince, Ryden Crowfell, bore many of his father's features, his grey eyes being one of them. Although Ryden's eyes were brighter than his father's and quite mesmerising if Rexah thought so herself.

It was one of the reasons why he had girls falling at his feet wherever he went. His short black hair was neatly brushed underneath his crown. He was a few inches taller than his father, around six foot two.

Those bright grey eyes were fixed to Rexah who gave him her most amazing smile.

Rexah rose to her feet in unison with her grandmother. "Your Majesty, it is an honour to have you in our home."

"The honour is all ours, Your Majesty," the King replied, bowing his head slightly in respect. King Orland was a dear friend to the Ravenheart family. The kingdoms having been allies since the start of recorded history and would continue to be so until the end of times.

"Prince Ryden, oh how you have grown. You were only in your early teenage years when I saw you last." Aurelia smiled at him. "What a handsome man you have become."

"Thank you for your kind words, Your Majesty," was his reply as he followed his father's lead and bowed his head to her slightly.

The King's eyes then moved to Rexah. "Your Highness, how wonderful it is to see you again," he said with a heart-warming smile.

Rexah returned the smile with a customary bow. "As it is you, Your Majesty," she replied before the prince caught her attention and they exchanged their delicate bow.

"Alright, now that the formalities are out of the way, why don't we catch up?" Aurelia smiled.

Orland grinned at her and held out his arm.

The Queen stepped down from the dais and took it before she looked at Rexah. "Why don't you take the prince for a walk around the gardens?"

"That sounds like a fantastic idea." Rexah nodded before looking at him. "What say you?"

A soft smile tugged on his lips. "I would love to, Your Highness," he replied.

Whilst the King and Queen got caught up on all things political and otherwise, Rexah walked out of the Grand Hall with the prince. Nesrin, who'd gone to retrieve her cloak – black with a purple trim to match her gown – waited outside the door for her. Rexah thanked her as she placed the cloak around her and fastened it with a silver raven-shaped clip at her shoulders. A playful smile stretched at Nesrin's lips, and Rexah narrowed her eyes in the same playful manner. She swore she saw Nesrin wink at her before she stepped back.

Rexah squared her shoulders slightly, pulling up her posture before she glimpsed at Ryden. He stepped up beside her holding his arm out. She couldn't help the smile that spread across her face as she took it and they walked out.

T he winter sun was her favourite. She loved the way its rays of light shone through the thin layer of fog that settled over the kingdom this time of year. It gave the grounds a hauntingly beautiful look.

The gardens were huge. Vast areas of the grass were covered with frost and scattered amongst the shades of green and white were stunning blue and indigo flowers, rippling back and forth in the gentle, cold breeze like waves in the ocean. On the far end of the gardens lay a labyrinth, a maze in which she'd wound up lost on many occasions when she was a child.

Rexah reached into the inside pocket of her cloak and took out her matching gloves. "My grandmother is right; you have turned out to be such a handsome man," she said as she pulled them onto her chilled hands.

"Were you expecting anything less?" Ryden asked her, a hint of sarcasm in his deep voice.

She grinned as she took his arm once again. "Well, it was debatable," she said, which caused him to chuckle. His laugh made her stomach flutter. It was nice to have him back at court.

"What have you been up to since the last time I was here?" he asked her.

"Reading, writing, fighting. You know, the usual," she replied.

Rexah had weapons training a few times a week with the royal trainer, Zuko. His father, Nikos, had trained her grandmother. He'd died when Rexah was ten, and Aurelia had given Zuko a home in the palace. In return he had offered to train Rexah; it was the only payment he could offer, not that her grandmother was expecting any, as she saw Zuko like a son.

"How is your training coming along?" he asked.

"Very well. Zuko told me in our last session that he's proud," she told him. Rexah was trained in most weapons, daggers and swords being her speciality.

"Wow, that's amazing coming from him." Ryden smirked.

Rexah gave him a playful prod in the side as they made their way through the garden and headed for the maze. "How have things been in Kaldoren?"

"Oh, you know, the usual." He beamed before his face became serious. "My father has been in a lot of meetings as of late, more than usual."

"And you? Have you been to any of them?"

Ryden shook his head. "I asked but he said it wasn't necessary for me to join him; said he'd let me know if anything changed. I've still not been asked to attend. I don't know whether to take that as a good or a bad sign."

"I'm sure it's nothing. He probably doesn't want you to be bored to death," she said.

Ryden wore a worried expression on his face, a look she didn't see very often. "I'm not so sure. I think something is happening. Something big."

"Has something happened in Kaldoren?" she asked as they stopped just outside the maze.

The hedges were tall, and the same blue and indigo flowers that littered the gardens and forest bloomed within them.

The maze had been terrifying for Rexah when she'd been younger; the hedges seemed to reach the sky compared to her tiny frame, and she swore one day she was going to grow taller than those hedges, but even now in her adulthood they still seemed to tower over her.

"I overheard my father speaking with the generals of the Kaldorien army after one of the meetings. They spoke of gathering more troops," he told her.

Rexah's stomach turned. "You think a war is starting?"

"Yes, or a war has already begun."

Her heart pounded as she looked behind them at the

castle, wondering how much her grandmother knew of this and what secrets of her own she held.

She opened her mouth to speak to Ryden but quickly closed it when she turned her head to see he was no longer standing beside her. She frowned and looked around, her eyes scanning the garden for him. "Ryden?" she called out.

"Come on Rexah! Stop dilly-dallying and get in here!" Ryden's voice echoed from somewhere within the maze.

A grin spread across her lips. "Are we really doing this?" she called back to him, taking a tentative step closer to the entrance of the maze.

"Yes! You're not afraid, are you?" he replied, his chuckle echoing through the air.

No, she was not afraid. Her grin spread wider across her face as she lifted the skirt of her dress slightly and ran straight into the labyrinth.

Both of their laughs spread through the hedges as they called to each other. Ryden told her when she was getting hotter or colder. Rexah laughed as she rounded a corner, expecting to find him. She came to a stop when she saw he wasn't there. She could have sworn he had been right there.

Her eyebrows knitted together in a frown as she slowly made her way forward. "Ryden? Are you there?"

He didn't answer.

It was quiet, too quiet. The silence made her heart begin to beat faster in her chest. She forced herself to take another few steps towards the corner before her. Taking a steadying breath, she rounded the corner only to find the path before her empty. Her throat became dry.

Suddenly she was tackled from the side, her back pushed up against the hedge. Feeling strong hands on her waist, she lifted her fist ready to strike when her eyes met Ryden's.

She glared at him, hitting him on the chest. "You fool! What do you think you're doing?!"

"Oh, come on, Rex. The look on your face was worth it." He laughed softly.

Rexah fought the urge to smile at him but failed miserably. "You're lucky I like you."

"I'm honoured, Your Highness." His perfect mouth uptilted into a smirk, and his eyes moved away from hers and down to her lips. Slowly, he leaned forward and captured her mouth with his in a soft kiss.

Rexah's eyes fluttered closed as she kissed him back, her hands resting on the tops of his powerful arms. The kiss was gentle and unhurried, as were his hands as they slid to her hips to pull her against him. Her fingers found their way into his dark silken hair as the kiss deepened, sending her heart into overdrive.

"Ryden," she whispered breathlessly against his lips after a few moments.

This wasn't the first time they had shared a kiss. The last time he had been here, when they were both in their late teenage years, they had shared a bed and been each other's firsts. The King and Queen knew nothing about it, no one did. This was something between the two of them, something that Rexah cherished.

"I'm sorry princess," he whispered back. "I just couldn't help myself."

Rexah smiled shyly at him. "Your kissing has improved."

He chuckled softly, shaking his head, and helped her out of the hedge. "I missed you," he said, removing some leaves from her hair.

"I missed you too," she said as she felt him fix the tiara on her head before he fixed his own crown.

Ryden held out his arm to her once more and they continued through the maze. It didn't take them long to reach the centre.

It was so beautiful: a white marble arch stood at the

very centre, a fountain flowing under it, and marble benches to match were placed around its circumference and separated by stunning flowerbeds.

They walked over to the bench closest to them and sat down. Neither of them spoke for a while as they enjoyed the sound of the fountain, the birds tweeting and singing, and each other's company. It was so peaceful and so quiet.

"One day you are going to be king," Rexah said, finally breaking their silence.

"And one day you will be queen," he replied.

Rexah turned her head and looked into his eyes. Those breath-taking swirls of grey that always turned her stomach into a fluttering mess. "Do you think we will be good leaders?"

He smiled at her. "I think I'll be the best. You, on the other hand…"

She laughed and shook her head. "I think you will make an excellent king. You are kind and understanding, but you can be firm when you need to be."

"You will be a fair queen. Compassionate and loving," he replied. "And when anyone crosses you or betrays you then you'll be as fierce as Queen Riona."

Rexah looked back to the fountain once again and considered the name she had to live up to, that legend.

"I will fight for what's best for my people and my kingdom. I will protect them, protect those who cannot protect themselves, because in the end it's what we all fight for."

"And what do we fight for, Rexah?"

Her head turned once again, her violet eyes shining as they connected with his. "A better world."

Ryden's eyes brightened, and a smile spread across his beautiful face as he repeated her words. "A better world."

Rexah couldn't help but smile back at him. "We should head back before my grandmother and your father have eaten all the breakfast food."

He chuckled and nodded as he rose to his feet. He held out his arm to her. "Let's go, Your Highness."

She grinned and stood up, taking his arm. They made their way back through the maze, chatting as they went, and soon arrived back at the palace.

2

"**M**ove your feet," Zuko ordered in her training session later that day. "Stop dropping your left elbow."

They trained in the garden situated in the centre of the castle. It was a square stone courtyard surrounded by lush greenery, flowerbeds, and a glass roof above. Lanterns hung upon the pillars and provided perfect lighting during the night; Rexah took this route for her nightly walks, passing through this very garden on her exit of the castle.

There was plentiful space as they completed their daily routine of warming up and sparring. Rexah loved these training sessions with Zuko as it granted her the opportunity to let off some steam and forget for a few hours that she was a princess. In these training sessions she could be whoever she pleased, and it was so freeing.

Zuko had been teaching her the art of sword fighting and helping her build strength since she was eleven. Aurelia had given Zuko all the time he needed to grieve his father, but the young man came to her six months later ready to begin Rexah's training, two months after her eleventh birthday.

She'd come a long way since that first lesson. Nothing would take away the memory of the day he'd first let her hold a sword in her hand, not the wooden one they trained with but a real weapon. Obviously, the blade hadn't been sharpened enough to do any serious damage – Zuko wasn't stupid – but from that moment he no longer went easy on her. She could keep up with him now, and so he didn't treat her like a beginner, he treated her like an equal – well, almost. She still had much to learn.

"Your enemy won't let you take a moment to catch your breath," he had told her many times.

This time was no different.

"Your enemy won't—"

"Won't let you take a moment to catch your breath, I know." She cut him off, breathing heavily, her hands on her knees as she bent forward trying to ease the burning in her lungs.

Sweat ran down her spine and covered her entire body, her clothes sticking to her like a second skin. She loved wearing the thick leggings the seamstress made for her, loved anything other than dresses if she was being completely honest. The leggings were less restrictive and less of a nuisance.

Her raven hair was pulled back into a braid which had fallen out slightly, a piece hanging in front of her face as she caught her breath. From the ray of sunlight shining down on them from the glass roof above, she could see a flash of purple in that strand of hair.

Zuko was then on her once again, not giving her the chance to rest and bringing the sword down with a cry. Rexah pulled up her own weapon to block the attack, and the sound of their blades clashing together sang throughout the garden as she only just managed to parry the blow. Her foot came down hard on his shin causing him to groan in pain and ever so slightly let his guard down.

Bingo.

Rexah latched onto the opportunity and brought her left leg up, her foot aiming for his chest, but her teacher was faster than she'd anticipated.

He grabbed her ankle tightly and twisted it. She dropped and spun her body, using the momentum to swing her right leg around. As planned, her foot connected with the side of his head.

Zuko fell to the ground in a heap as she twisted her body and landed on her feet in a crouched position, her sword out to the side, glinting in the rays of sunlight.

For a moment, all that could be heard was Rexah's heavy breathing. Zuko didn't move. She waited for him to sit up and praise her, but he didn't. Slowly, she rose to her feet and made her way over to him. Her heart began pounding in her chest, panic beginning to seep through her. Surely, she couldn't have knocked him out, she wasn't that strong, not yet at least.

"Zuko?" she asked, frowning as she reached down to touch his arm to try and rouse him.

As soon as her fingertips brushed his shoulder, Rexah's legs were taken out from under her and she landed hard on her back, gasping in surprise. Her sword clanged on the stone as it escaped her grasp and slid just out of reach. She looked up and her eyes met the blue ones of her instructor; he pinned her to the ground, the coolness of a smaller blade pressed at her throat.

"Do not let your guard down," he said, teeth bared and eyes stern. "*Ever.*"

Rexah didn't dare speak. The anger in his eyes alone sent a tremor of fear down her spine. He removed the blade from her throat before he stood up, offering his hand to her. She took it and got to her feet with his help, her legs shaking slightly.

"Let's take a break, go get some water," he said, sheathing the small blade back into his belt before picking up their swords from where they'd fallen.

Rexah walked over to the small table then lifted the jug of water filled with ice and poured herself a glass. "You know I'd never check to make sure an enemy was still alive, right? I'm not *that* stupid."

"I know but Rexah, letting your guard down even for a second gives the enemy all the time they need. If I were an enemy just now, you'd be bleeding out on the ground," he said, walking over to her after putting the weapons away, the sun dancing off his auburn hair.

She nodded softly, feeling a little guilty. "I understand, I'm sorry. It won't happen again, I promise."

"Oh, I know it won't," Zuko said, pouring himself his own glass of water, a hint of a smile on his face.

"You have to admit though," she said as a smirk

spread across her lips, "that kick to your shin caught you off guard and was inevitably your downfall."

He chuckled before drinking half of the glass in one go. "Yes, I'll admit, it was a good tactic. Your only undoing was checking to make sure I was all right, but we can work on that."

"Well excuse me for caring." She laughed before she drained her glass of water and set it down on the table beside the now almost empty jug. "I was worried I'd done some serious damage."

"It would take a lot more than that to take me down, Rexah," he told her.

It really would. Zuko was pure muscle. She remembered the first time they had engaged in hand-to-hand combat: she had successfully landed one punch to his chest, and she thought she'd broken her hand. Thankfully, it was only a sprain that needed a support bandage, but she never tried that move again. He was one of the strongest men she knew. Sure, the other guards were strong, but Zuko was another level.

"Do you think I will ever need to use this training? Do you think there will be another war?" she found herself asking him. Deep down she didn't want to know the answer to those questions, but her chat with

Ryden earlier about how his father had been in more meetings than usual had made her curious.

"There is always a chance of war. Your grandmother wants you to be prepared, even if a war doesn't happen in your lifetime," he replied. "It's still a good skill set and knowledge to have. Life is unpredictable."

Zuko had always been truthful with her. He'd never sugar coat anything just to ensure her feeling of safety. He had always been straight to the point and told things as they were. It was something Rexah always admired about him and was the reason she was asking him about this and not her grandmother.

She nodded slowly, picking up a towel from the table and wiping some of the sweat from her brow and the back of her neck. "I appreciate the time you take to teach me, Zuko."

His lips curled up into a smirk. "You are actually thanking someone for something? Are you feeling well?"

Rexah laughed and playfully rolled her eyes, putting the towel into the basket beside the table. "You make me sound like a spoiled brat, Zuko."

"We know that you're far from a spoiled brat. We'll end our lesson here. Despite your little hiccup, you did good today," he said, giving her a smile. "Your footwork needs a bit extra work, but your technique is improving."

She bowed her head to him. "Thank you, Zuko. I'll see you soon," she said, smiling before heading back into the castle.

The corridors were buzzing with the usual staff going about their daily duties, each bowing their head respectfully to her as they went by, and Rexah met their bows with a warm smile. Her legs were already starting to ache as she reached the top of the stairs and headed towards her room. She could hear a steaming hot bath calling her name.

Stepping into her room, she grinned when she saw Nesrin hanging up her freshly cleaned dresses in the wardrobe. "Good afternoon, Nes."

The copper-haired woman almost jumped out of her skin, and Rexah couldn't contain her laughter.

"By the Gods Rexah, you scared the living daylights out of me," Nesrin said, her palm flat on her chest. "I never heard you come in."

Rexah grinned. "I kept my footsteps as light as a feather, another thing Zuko taught me. It'll give me the upper hand and surprise my enemies."

"Well, you can tell him that it definitely works." She sighed as she calmed down before laughing softly.

Giggling, Rexah sat down on the edge of her bed and kicked off her shoes. "How has your day been? Busy?"

Nesrin nodded. "Just the usual. How was your session today?"

"It was good. I managed to catch Zuko off guard and took him down," she replied, a smug smile on her face.

Her best friend's green eyes widened. "You did?"

Rexah nodded. "He was completely surprised, but then I made the mistake of checking to make sure he was alright. I ended up on my back with a blade at my throat," she said, cringing at the memory.

Nesrin burst out into laughter, and Rexah soon joined her, pulling her hair out of the braid and letting it fall in dark waves down her back.

"I will run you a bath, just how you like it," Nesrin said, closing the wardrobe door.

Rexah grinned at her. "You know me too well."

Her lady's maid winked at the princess before making her way into the bathing chamber. Rexah shed her clothing, rolling her shoulders to release the tension already building up in her slightly aching muscles. The bath would soothe them before they could get too painful; Nesrin always used the best oils and soaks to help. She didn't know what she'd ever do without her best friend.

As the days passed, Rexah had her regular training sessions with Zuko, and she made sure not to check he was okay whenever she managed to knock him off of his feet, which was a considerable number times. Meals were had with her grandmother and their royal guests, which were filled with banter and reminiscing of the past.

She enjoyed walks and more kisses with Ryden, stolen kisses within the maze, within the library, and even in her chambers if they were daring enough. Rexah was shocked no one had seen them sneaking off, and maybe that added to the thrill of it all.

Both knew this thing they had, whatever it was, couldn't continue for much longer. They would both be married off soon and be expected to carry out their royal duties. In all honesty, Rexah was surprised her grandmother hadn't married her off yet, although the thought of it sent a shiver down her spine.

Rexah turned to the next page of the book she was

reading, her heart beating fast in her chest with anticipation of whether the prince would save the princess or not. The castle library was one of her favourite places to escape to. Of course, her most treasured books were kept in her room, but being surrounded completely by books was one of the most comforting feelings.

Thankfully, the chapter ended with the prince and princess being reunited; she was saved, and the ending would be a happy one. Closing the book with a sigh, she sank further into her chair, holding the volume to her chest as she looked around the empty library. The memory of Ryden running through the stacks with her when they were children flooded into her mind.

"The monster is chasing us!" Ryden cried as they ran through the tall bookcases.

Rexah giggled as she pushed her little legs to keep up with him. "It's huge! Did you see those sharp teeth?!"

Both children broke through the stacks and into the open space where a large circular table stood. Made from dark oak, the surface had a map of the realm, Etteria, etched into it.

The young boy picked up a large scroll from atop the table, wielding it like a weapon, before turning to her. "Fear not princess, I shall kill the beast!" he called, holding out his tiny hand out to her.

Rexah took Ryden's hand, grinning as he helped her climb a chair and up onto the table.

"Whatever happens, stay up there until I tell you it's safe to come down," he said before turning his back to her and fighting the invisible monster with his scroll sword. Ryden dodged and danced around as he evaded the beast's strikes. Rexah grinned as she watched him.

With one final swing of his scroll, the monster was defeated. Ryden turned back to her, his eyes shining brightly. "It's safe now! The monster is gone!"

The little princess cheered and clapped her hands as she celebrated atop the table, earning a giggle from the little prince. Their joy was short lived as the doors to the library were thrown open to reveal an unhappy Queen Aurelia and a disappointed looking King Orland.

"Rexah Ravenheart, get down from that table before you hurt yourself!" the Queen said as she walked through the door, her dark blue dress flowing behind her like a wave in the ocean. King Orland following her, dressed in grey like a storm.

The princess jumped from the table, her feet finding the floor with an echoing thump. "We were just playing, Grandma."

"Not on the furniture, Rexah. How many times do you need to be told?" she asked, her hands folding in front of her.

King Orland looked to his son. "You should know better, Ryden, and put that scroll down. It could contain important information. You know better than to touch that which isn't yours."

Ryden nodded slowly and set the scroll down carefully where he'd found it in the first place. "I'm sorry, Papa."

"Dinner is almost ready," Aurelia said. "It's time to make our way to the Grand Hall."

The King and Queen turned and made their way out of the library. Rexah and Ryden looked at one another, mischievous grins spreading across their faces as they walked out, nudging each other as they went.

The memory made Rexah grin. It was not the first time they had gotten into trouble with the King and Queen – sometimes it was Aurelia's lady's maids who lectured them.

"It's not ladylike to run around getting dirt on your dress," Rosa had once told her. Seven-year-old Rexah didn't care about getting dirt on her dress, she cared about defeating monsters at every opportunity with Ryden – that was much more fun.

Ryden was her oldest friend. Whether he was visiting Adorea, or she was visiting Kaldoren, they always had so much fun together. She possessed not one memory of them growing up where they weren't laughing together. He was the reason she didn't feel as lonely.

Groaning at the ache in her stiff muscles, Rexah stood from the armchair. As she went to slide the book back into its space on the shelf, she noticed something peeking out of the bottom of the book. Frowning, she carefully pulled out a neatly folded piece of parchment.

She slotted the book back into its place before she unfolded the note. Her heart went into overdrive as her eyes glided over Ryden's familiar handwriting.

Just in case I don't tell you enough, you are beautiful.

Ry.

Blood rushed to her cheeks as she grinned like a little girl, her heart pounding in her chest like a drum. *He sure knows the right words to say and how to put a smile on my face.* This was a book Rexah loved to read that was kept in the library, and he knew it.

With Ryden's note tucked safely into her cleavage, she headed out of the library. Dinner was only a few hours away and she needed to look presentable. Having royal guests meant Rexah needed to take extra care of her appearance, even more so than she did already; not a hair was to be out of place, not a wrinkle in her dress.

Queen Aurelia took pride in her appearance, and it showed with how immaculate she looked every day, so she expected the same from her granddaughter. Not that Rexah didn't take pride in her appearance, but she couldn't help but wonder if maybe her grandmother sometimes went a little overboard. Even so, it was one of the things she loved most about her.

Nesrin should be in my room getting everything set out now, she thought and pondered over what her choice of dress would be. Nesrin's taste was impeccable. Whenever Rexah thought she had the perfect dress to wear, Nesrin would suggest another that blew the other one out of the water.

Rexah climbed the marble staircase as she headed towards her room, Ryden on her mind.

Gods, I cannot wait to see him, she thought as excitement bubbled in her stomach. The words he'd written in the note played through her mind.

Dinner was going to be fun.

3

It was time for dinner and as usual Nesrin helped Rexah dress for the occasion. She had opted for a long-sleeved midnight-blue dress with black trimming that complimented her features. As she had predicted, Nesrin had chosen well. It wasn't her most dazzling gown, but it still earned her grandmother's approval as she sat down at the table in the Grand Hall.

Rexah nodded her head to King Orland and Prince Ryden as she brushed off her dress. Ryden gave her a quick wink, making her smile shyly and her insides turn to liquid. It took everything she had not to grab him and drag him off into a dark corner and kiss him silly.

The smell of various meats being carried in filled

Rexah's nostrils, pulling her from her inappropriate thoughts, and it wasn't until that moment that she realised just how hungry she was. Her stomach growled slightly, confirming her hunger. She watched as the servants set the large platters of food on the table, and she could feel her mouth water.

She thanked the girl closest to her as she filled Rexah's glass with wine. The blonde-haired servant, Sophia, bowed her head to her and smiled softly before she moved to fill the rest of their glasses.

Once the food had been served and the wine had been poured, her grandmother smiled at them. "Please, eat," she encouraged them.

Rexah didn't have to be told twice. She picked up her fork and began devouring the pork and potatoes smothered in rich gravy. There were vegetables on her plate, but Rexah would get to them later. The meals in the palace were always delicious and she was grateful to have the option of such delectable food. Not everyone was so lucky throughout the kingdom.

Rexah often visited the kitchen and had long conversations with the cooks and the servants. She knew all of their names, had taken the time to memorize them, and learned about their families and their history. The stories of their upbringings and ancestors always fascinated her. She enjoyed listening to how other families grew up.

Queen Aurelia treated all the staff in the castle with respect and kindness, and it was the reason Adorea was such a sought-out place to both live and work. The Ravenheart family were known for their compassion towards their people, but also the fierce way they protected them too.

Rexah had heard horror stories from various servants, and Nesrin, about other kingdoms who paid their staff next to nothing and provided unsanitary living quarters. They simply didn't care about the underprivileged people living within their territory. She found herself waking up now and again during the night thinking of those poor people, wishing there was something she could do to help them, but it wasn't within Adorea's jurisdiction.

"How is your weapons training coming along?" Orland asked Rexah. "Your grandmother tells me you have lessons almost every day."

Rexah smiled at him and nodded softly. "That's correct. I thoroughly enjoy my training. It means I can defend myself against anyone who dares take a swipe at me. You can never be too careful."

The King grinned. "Excellent, maybe you could teach my son a few things."

Ryden rolled his eyes. "I'm quite capable of wielding a blade, Father," he said, earning a soft giggle from the princess.

Rexah remembered the first time she'd seen Ryden training. It was something she would never forget in a hurry.

"Try not to get yourself into too much trouble, please?" Aurelia asked her granddaughter as she moved some of her raven hair from her face.

The sixteen-year-old princess smirked at her grandmother. "Me? Get into trouble?"

Aurelia sighed softly. "Go, before I change my mind."

Rexah nodded and headed down the corridor, grinning. Her shoes clicked against the stone floor as she walked, the skirt of her dress gathered in her hand slightly, so she didn't trip. The only thing she hated about visiting Kaldoren was that she needed to wear gowns.

It didn't take her long to arrive at the hall where the Crown Prince trained. As she rounded the corner and slipped in through the ajar door, Ryden came into view, and what a sight he was. His dark hair clung to his face, soaked with sweat. The muscles in his bare back shifted and moved with each swing of the sword, the blade whooshing as it swung through the air. Ryden's back was slick and gleaming with sweat, and it took everything in Rexah to stay where she was, back pressed against the wall next to the door.

Gods above, *she thought as she took in the glorious sight of him.* Calm yourself down, Rexah.

As if he'd heard her thoughts, Ryden gazed over his shoulder, his steel-grey eyes meeting hers. He turned to face her, his strong chest heaving, and he grinned. "Well, aren't you a sight for sore eyes."

"Hello Ryden," she replied, smiling shyly.

The prince walked over to the side of the room and placed the sword down before grabbing a towel. "I'd hug you," he said. "But I fear that I may ruin that pretty dress."

Rexah stepped further into the room. "I wouldn't mind, maybe if you did I could then borrow something a bit more comfortable."

Her eyes were glued to him as he ran the towel along his skin, across those muscles rippling down his abdomen, as he dried himself off.

Ryden chuckled softly. "How long will you be staying?"

"A few weeks," she told him. "Think you can put up with me for that long?"

His lips tugged up in a smirk. "Of course I can. Do you think you'll be able to put up with me?"

Rexah stopped a few feet away from him. "Hmm, that's debatable."

Ryden tossed the now damp towel to the side and pulled her into a hug. She didn't pull away; she wrapped her arms around his neck, leaned up onto her tiptoes, and hugged him back. His body was warm against hers.

"I missed you," he said into her hair.

Rexah smiled. "I missed you too."

Pulling away, Rexah gazed up into his eyes. He wasn't the little boy who chased her around the library in Adorea anymore – he was a man.

"Let me grab my shirt and we can go for a walk. I need to cool down after that session," Ryden said.

Rexah frowned. "Where is your trainer?"

"It's his day off, but I still continue with the exercises," he said, smirking as he pulled on his shirt. "Can't have all this muscle sagging now, can I?"

Rexah laughed and shook her head. "No, you certainly can't. Well, let's go."

Turning on her heel, she began walking towards the door, the skirt of her dress flowing behind her. She only took a few steps before Ryden's voice halted her.

"Rexah, wait."

She looked over to him. "Yes?"

"There's something I've wanted to tell you, something I've wanted to do, but I've just not had the confidence," he said.

She grinned softly. "I didn't take you for the shy type."

"Only when it comes to you, princess," he said, those grey eyes connecting with hers across the room.

Her heart began to beat faster in her chest with each step closer he took to her. "What do you want to tell me?"

"I don't know if I can tell you," he said, stopping in front of her, "but I can show you."

Before she could comprehend what was happening, Ryden gently cupped her face and leaned down, kissing her. Fireworks exploded behind her eyes as she slowly kissed him back, her hands moving to his wrists.

The kiss was unhurried and soft. Her heart was pounding against her chest like a drum as she melted against him. Too soon, he slowly pulled away, leaning his forehead against hers.

That had been their first kiss and Rexah's first kiss ever. Butterflies fluttered like crazy in her stomach every time she thought about it. After that first kiss, they'd shared many others during that particular visit.

"There is something King Orland and I would like to discuss with you both," her grandmother said, pulling her from her thoughts.

"Yes, Grandmother?" she asked as she wiped her mouth on her napkin.

"As you know, we've been in meetings these past few days, sorting out business in the kingdoms, and putting plans into place," the Queen said.

Rexah looked over to Ryden who was already looking at her with the same confused expression on his face.

As they'd discussed between kisses, both were under the impression this was just another one of their friendly visits; they hadn't realised it was so official meetings could take place. Why weren't Ryden and Rexah included? Now she understood why Ryden was so suspicious. Was this something to do with the gathering of soldiers?

Rexah turned her attention back to her grandmother, but it was the King who spoke next.

"You are almost in your twenty-third year, and we feel that both of you should have been married by now. Granted things in both kingdoms have been busy over the years and more pressing matters arose, but it's not an excuse for why your marriages haven't been carried out. It is our fault for not ensuring your marriages still went ahead regardless," he said.

"I am sorry Father, but you know how I feel about

arranged marriages. Being tied to a complete stranger for the rest of my life isn't how I imagined spending it," Ryden told him before shoving another forkful of food into his mouth.

"It will not be a stranger you marry, my son," was the King's reply.

Rexah felt the entire world shift beneath her, and for a moment that world existed entirely within that room. Her eyes met her grandmother's, and there she saw all the clarification she needed of what was being asked of her.

"The two of you will marry," the Queen said with a bright smile that made the creases around her eyes more prominent. "Each other."

The words echoed in her mind, playing over and over again but refused to sink in. Her eyes slowly slid to the prince across from her who looked just as shocked as she was, his steel-grey eyes as wide as hers were.

They want us to marry. They want us to become husband and wife. Surely, I must be dreaming.

She had pictured it though, being married to him. Ever since they were teenagers, since that first kiss they'd shared, she daydreamed about their wedding and how spectacular it would be. She imagined their whole life together; imagined their beautiful children, even going as far as knowing what their names would be; but she thought that's all it would ever be, just a fantasy.

"We believe it is best for both kingdoms if we unite them," Aurelia said. "The best way to accomplish that is by marriage."

"You … you truly wish for us to be wed?" Rexah asked, turning back to her. She was worried this was all a dream and she was about to wake up at any second.

The Queen nodded her head. "Ever since you were both young you've always been close and had such a beautiful connection to one another. It makes perfect sense."

The words boomed in her mind, blocking everything else out. They wanted Rexah and Ryden to be married, joined together.

Rexah turned her attention to the prince once again and found him studying her, the confused look no longer on his face. His grey eyes were soft as if he too were picturing their married life together.

"We know this might be a lot for you both to take in," Aurelia said, her attention shifting between the two of them. "We will give you both time to let it sink in before plans are put into place."

"When do you plan for our union to happen?" Ryden asked, his eyes now focusing on his father.

The King sat back in his chair, lifting his wine glass to his lips and taking a sip before he replied. "Two months from now. It will take a few weeks for everything to be organised."

"You will marry in the Meadow of Tella," the Queen said. "A shared and sacred place between both of our kingdoms."

Tella was one of many goddesses. She was known as the Goddess of Love and Fertility, and the meadow was a place of true beauty, filled with flowers and a shrine to honour her. Only the most sacred of rituals and events could take place there; the location was mainly used for the joining of two souls in matrimony or providing offerings to Tella, often to ask for her blessing when trying to conceive.

Situated between Adorea and Kaldoren, perfectly in the centre of the vast forest, it was the ideal place for them to be wed.

"Why now?" Rexah asked, turning her gaze to her grandmother. "Why so soon? Two months from now still doesn't provide a lot of time to let it sink in or prepare."

Aurelia sipped her wine before placing it down on the table. "As King Orland said, this should have been done years ago, and it will solidify our alliance agreement, unite our kingdoms. Whilst there is still peace in the realm, we think it's important to have your union."

There it is.

She moved her eyes to Ryden where she saw his mind was working just as fast as hers was.

"Whilst there is still peace in the realm? What do you mean by that, Your Majesty?" Ryden asked the Queen.

Rexah saw Aurelia's eye twitch ever so slightly. *She's been caught out. She let something slip that she didn't mean to.*

"Life is full of surprises, Prince Ryden. It's better to enjoy the happiness life can provide rather than dwell on the heartache it tends to throw at you."

Orland took the opportunity to chime in and cut the conversation short as he raised his glass, a grin on his face. "To the future of our kingdoms."

Aurelia returned the grin, a look of relief on her face that he'd interrupted when he did, and raised her glass.

Rexah lifted up her own, her eyes never leaving Ryden's. "To the future of our kingdoms."

4

The temperature of the bath water was almost scalding as Rexah settled down into the tub with a relaxing sigh. It was just the way she liked it, the heat seeping deep into her skin, soothing her tense muscles.

The rest of dinner had been a blur. She couldn't stop thinking about what was going to happen and what their marriage meant for both kingdoms and the realm.

What irritated her most was that both the King and Queen had spoken about and decided this behind their backs, not including them in their talks. Then again, that was how things were done most of the time at court. The only time Rexah would have to be included in any of the Queen's business was if war were on the horizon, otherwise it was at her grandmother's discretion if Rexah attended or not. Still, it hurt nonetheless not to be included in something as important as her marriage. The last war took place around a century ago, ending in the death of Riona, and she hoped to never be called to one of *those* meetings.

Rexah sighed and leaned her head back against the bath, her hair tied up so she wouldn't get it wet.

"We believe it's best for both kingdoms if we unite them." Her grandmother's words echoed in her mind. Closing her eyes, she willed her racing mind to stop so she might enjoy the peace and quiet whilst she could, but her brain had other ideas.

A wife. She was soon to be a wife, soon to have a husband. She should be happy, ecstatic that the man she would marry was a man she knew very well. She should be grateful it wasn't some stranger from a faraway land who would do nothing but use her for her kingdom and producing heirs – she would never let that happen, no matter the consequences. But Ryden, he was perfect; he would never use her in that way.

After an hour soaking in the tub, Rexah got out and dried herself. She was soon sat at her vanity table in her nightdress, pulling out the pins holding her hair in place; it came undone, sweeping down her back, and she ran her fingers through the strands, taming it, when there was a quiet knock at the door.

Rising to her feet, she crossed the room and opened the door slightly and was met with familiar stunning grey eyes.

"Hello," Ryden said gently.

Her eyes softened as she stepped back and let him into the room. She closed the door gently before turning to him, her future husband.

"Did you have any suspicions that this is what they were meeting to discuss?" Rexah asked him. "That this was one of the reasons for your visit?"

Ryden shook his head as he turned to her. "Of course I didn't. I was in the dark, just as much as you were. My father told me it had been far too long since our last visit here and that it would be good to catch up. I'm just as shocked as you are, trust me."

She believed him; she could see the truth in his eyes.

"I can't believe it's going to happen," she said as she walked over to him. "It feels like a dream, one I'm terrified of waking from."

Ryden's hands gently slid around her waist, bringing her closer to him, her body pressed against his so tightly she could feel the hard muscles of his abs and it sent the sharp feeling of need pulse straight through her.

"I can't either," he said, "but I believe everything happens for a reason and that this is a blessing to us from the Gods."

Rexah's hands moved up his strong arms as she looked up at him. Those gorgeous eyes of his were always her downfall; no matter how angry or upset she was with him, she could never stay that way for long, not after a mere glimpse of those eyes that reminded her of sunlight behind passing storm clouds.

"You are sure you want this? You are happy?" Rexah asked.

"We don't have a choice," he said, leaning his forehead against hers, those serene grey eyes connecting with hers. "But if we did have a choice, I would still choose you, Rex."

Rexah's heart began to thunder against her chest. She loved it when he used her nickname. "I would choose you too," she said.

Ryden's lips connected with hers. Her eyes fluttered closed as she kissed him back and slid her trembling fingers through his silky dark hair. He pulled her closer in response, so close her body was pressed firmly to his, and his hands moved down to her hips.

This kiss was different from all the others that they'd shared. This kiss was full of love and protection, and the promise of forever. She hadn't thought they could get any closer, but they'd somehow found a way.

Ryden's tongue slid along her bottom lip, begging for access. She opened her mouth for him gladly and they explored each other's mouths hungrily, eager to taste every inch of one another.

The moment passed her by in a haze; in one swift movement, Ryden lifted her into his strong arms and set her down on the vanity table, her personal effects falling to the floor and landing on the rug with soft thuds.

Rexah's fingers found the bottom of his shirt, and she pulled it up and over his head, throwing it away, not caring where it landed; all she cared about was this moment with him and making the rest of his clothes join his shirt on the floor.

Their lips connected again as Ryden's hand slowly slid up her bare thigh and under the fabric of her night-dress, coming to rest on her hip. His mouth moved to her neck causing her head to tilt back, the strap of her nightdress sliding off her shoulder. The heat pooling between her thighs felt almost unbearable, her need for release becoming too much. But it was clear she wasn't the only one who felt that way; the hardness of Ryden's length ground against her, sending another shudder of pleasure through her already aching core.

Rexah had to bite her lip to stop the noise that threatened to escape, her fingers finding their way into his hair once more.

"Ryden," she whispered breathlessly.

"Rex."

He groaned against her skin, sending another rush of heat flooding through her. This wasn't the first time they'd been in this position on her vanity table, and she prayed it wouldn't be the last.

Ryden's hand moved from her hip to the ache between her legs, his fingers brushing against her. A gasp left her lips as he eased a finger inside.

"Gods, Rexah," he whispered softly against her neck.

She tightened her grip on his arm as he began thrusting his finger in and out of her, soon adding a second that caused her to moan softly. A wave of pleasure rushed through her as her hips moved against his fingers, pushing him deeper.

Oh Gods.

A soft whimpering sound left her lips when he withdrew his fingers.

"Patience, princess," he whispered breathlessly. He

fumbled with the buttons on his trousers and Rexah helped where she could, her heart pounding with anticipation.

His clothes soon joined his shirt on the floor and his lips pressed to hers. Rexah cupped his face as she kissed him back. Her body shuddered as Ryden's hands slid up her bare thighs, pushing up her nightdress before gripping her hips and pulling her forward slightly.

"Off the edge a little, princess," he whispered against her lips, his eyes hooded with desire as he teased her entrance.

Her hips shifted forward with the movement of his hands, the bundle of nerves between her thighs brushing against his hard length. Rexah gasped and gripped his shoulder before he pushed himself inside of her.

His thrusts were slow and gentle until he was fully seated, his chest rumbling with a soft growl. Rexah bit her lip so hard she was surprised it didn't bleed, and when his hips began to move again, her mouth hung silently open as her legs wrapped a little tighter around his hips.

"So ... fucking ... beautiful," he groaned quietly into her neck, his hips thrusting a little harder with each word.

"Ry." His name fell breathlessly from her lips, and she threaded her fingers through his soft dark hair, tugging on it slightly as he moved within her.

Suddenly he lifted her from the vanity table, still buried to the hilt. She wrapped her arms around his strong shoulders as he turned towards her bed.

"Tell me," he whispered. "Are you still taking your elixir?"

"Of course," she whispered back.

Rexah began taking the contraceptive when her cycle became irregular. The healer advised her grandmother it would help balance it out, which it did, but it also came in very handy for moments like these with Ryden.

He lay her on her back, his forehead against hers. "Good," he said before his hips began to move once again, this time at a faster pace.

Rexah gazed into his eyes as she moaned softly.

Fuck, I've missed him.

He kissed her hungrily. "Quiet, my love, we don't want anyone hearing you. Although, I'd kill to hear those sinful noises that leave your mouth." He smirked, and his hips began to pound harder.

She turned her head and buried her face into the pillow as she moaned louder, muffling as much noise as she could in the soft fabric. Each stroke brought her closer and closer to the edge; the way his fingers dug into her hips, the way his hair clung to the sweat glistening on his skin; but most of all it was the hunger in his eyes that made her muscles tighten.

"That's it," he moaned quietly, his hips beginning to falter as he gritted his teeth, "come with me, princess."

His hand left her hip, and when his fingers found the bundle of nerves between her legs she fell straight over the edge. Arching into him, she cried out into the pillow, her body shaking as her orgasm barrelled through her. Ryden took the opportunity and buried his face into her neck, groaning against her skin as he slammed into her a few more times before spilling his release within her.

Rexah's body trembled with aftershocks, her legs feeling like jelly.

Gods, I could get used to this.

Ryden lay down beside her, holding her close as they both came down from their highs. His lips brushed hers in a soft kiss. "You're amazing."

She smiled at him. "No, you're amazing."

"We can argue about this all night if you want," he replied, smirking at her.

They lay in each other's arms for a short while

before Rexah got up and walked into her bathing chamber, fixing her nightdress as she went. Once she had freshened up, she made her way back into the room seeing Ryden had pulled his trousers back on.

I wish he didn't have to go afterwards. Soon he won't need to though, because he'll be my husband. The last thought sent her heart into a fluttering mess.

"We are to be married in two months' time," she said as she walked over to him. "I think we should wait until our wedding night to be with each other again."

He finished tying the laces on his boots and stood up. "You do?"

She nodded softly as she stopped in front of him. "I think if we waited it would make the day even more magical," she said, moving a piece of his dark hair from his eyes.

"Alright, then we wait until the night of our union to be intimate again," Ryden said, kissing her nose. "This means no more secret kisses in the library or in the gardens."

"Agreed. No more secret kisses, so don't come knocking on my door at all hours of the night," Rexah said, grinning.

He chuckled and kissed her forehead softly before he moved around her and picked his shirt up off the floor. She couldn't help but watch him pull it back on, those powerful muscles in his back shifting as he did. She pushed away the urge to tackle him to the floor and go back on her word and have him right there.

Rexah walked over to the door with him. He opened it as quietly as he could before peering out to make sure the coast was clear. He turned to her, smiling.

"Goodnight, prince," she said quietly.

"Goodnight, princess," he replied, winking at her before he made his way down the corridor towards his room.

Rexah closed the door quietly before she turned, leaning her back against it. She let out a breath, trying to calm her racing heart down. Ryden always had such an effect on her; he didn't have to do much, just a look from him turned her into a flustered mess.

After picking up her hairbrush and the hairpins that had fallen to the floor during their heated moment, she blew out the candles as she made her way around the room until the fire burning in the fireplace across from her bed was the only light source remaining. She slid under the sheets and lay back on her bed.

Never in a million years would she ever have thought that when she woke up that morning she would be going to bed that night betrothed to Ryden, that her life would be changing.

She got herself comfortable and closed her eyes, and for the first time, those fantasies she'd had about her life with Ryden were no longer that: they were coming true.

"Can you believe it's finally happening?" Nesrin asked beside Rexah as they strolled through the gardens the next morning. "You're getting married."

It had been three days since the King and Queen announced to Rexah and Ryden that they would marry, and already so much was happening behind the scenes.

The royal seamstress was currently collecting fabrics and gathering jewels and other little accessories she would need to make the dress perfect. Her apprentices were up to their knees in all different types and colours of material and running around like headless chickens trying to keep up with the strict deadlines. Rexah felt bad for them; they always looked so flustered.

Royal weddings were no small affair. Sure, the ceremony itself was sacred and therefore only a small number of people would be in attendance, but when it came to presenting the newlyweds, the Grand Hall would be full to the brim with guests from throughout the realm. All eyes would be on Rexah and Ryden.

"I'm surprised it's taken this long," Rexah admitted to her, trying to shove her panic back in its box.

Usually, princes or princesses were married a lot younger than they were, whether the prince or princess liked it or not, and that was something that had never sat right with Rexah but that was part of the package when you were a royal.

"The King and Queen have been awfully busy," Nesrin replied, nodding her head softly.

Rexah pulled her cloak closer around herself as an ice-cold breeze swept by them. "I know, but marriage is tradition. What could be more important?"

War was certainly more important, that was for sure, but her grandmother and King Orland hadn't mentioned anything about war or gathering more soldiers – she has heard nothing about what Ryden had told her – and that worried her.

Nesrin shrugged. "I'm not sure. I'm just a maid," she

said, making the two girls laugh as they rounded the corner.

They went on walks regularly, but Rexah really needed them now more than ever. She often found her head aching each night when she went to bed from the constant questions she was asked from her grandmother and the other staff members.

Every conversation was about the wedding, nothing else, and Rexah was already getting sick of hearing the word. She was growing tired of being asked which colour she preferred or which flowers she would like in her bouquet. At least these walks with Nesrin let her escape the hustle and bustle inside the castle, even if it was only an hour or so. She would take every second away from anything to do with the wedding she could get.

Nesrin seemed to realise that Rexah didn't want to talk about the wedding every minute of every day, as she never lingered on the subject for too long.

"One of the cooks found two of the servants in a very intimate situation in one of the storage closets."

Rexah's eyes widened. "Please tell me it wasn't the food storage?"

Nesrin laughed and shook her head, her soft copper curls faintly shining in the early morning sun. "Thankfully, no. It was the closet where all the spare chairs and other furniture is kept," she said.

Rexah laughed. "Well, good for them. They're human too and deserve to have some fun," she said. It wasn't news to Rexah that some of the staff were married to each other or relatives of some nature. Queen Aurelia didn't have any rules against it; all she cared about was that the work was done.

Nesrin nodded in agreement as they sat down on one of the many benches scattered around the gardens. This was their bench. They sat on it every time they went for a walk. It had the best view of the gardens, the maze, and the fountain that lay within it. The grounds were stunning but especially so this early in the morning: the soft glow from the sun, the thin layer of winter fog, and the light dusting of frost covering the grass was simply beautiful.

"What about you, Nesrin? Wouldn't you like to go out and have some fun rather than waiting around after me?" Rexah asked.

A soft smile appeared on Nesrin's face. "What makes you think I don't have fun with you?"

"You know what I mean, Nes. Wouldn't you like to go into the village and socialise?" asked Rexah as she studied her.

Nesrin was quiet for a moment, a sorrowful look in her eyes, before she spoke again. "I wouldn't like to go to the village or socialise with anyone else. I prefer it better within the castle. I feel … safer."

Rexah knew exactly why she didn't want to go into the village and socialise. Nesrin had experienced something awful before she was brought to the kingdom, something Rexah couldn't even begin to imagine happening to her.

When she was in her early teens, Nesrin and her mother were walking home from the tavern her mother worked at in a small village not too far from the castle. It was an hour or two after midnight when her mother's shift had ended, and they were attacked by three drunken men in the alley next to the tavern.

Nesrin was forced to watch as they beat and raped her mother, and when she tried to fight back, when she tried to pull them off her mother, one of the men smacked her so hard across the face she was knocked unconscious.

The Adorian guards who were patrolling heard the commotion and stopped the men, escorting them off to the dungeons within the castle, but by that point it was too late.

When Nesrin awoke in the infirmary the next

morning, she learned that her mother had died from her injuries not long after they were brought to the palace.

Gods, Rexah, you are an idiot.

"I'm so sorry, I didn't mean to bring up those memories."

When she shook her head softly, her curls fell to the front of her shoulders. "Don't be silly, Rex. You're only trying to help, and I appreciate it, but I prefer your company over anyone else's."

Rexah's eyes softened as she studied her. She remembered the day that Nesrin was brought to the castle. Queen Aurelia had made such a fuss over making sure the young girl was seen to right away that it had caught Rexah's attention.

Nesrin hadn't been allowed visitors for the first few days whilst the healers ensured she was all right but that didn't stop the curious little rebellious princess from sneaking out of her room and into the infirmary whilst everyone else was sleeping.

Rexah had spent the first night watching Nesrin for an hour or two. The thought of having a girl around the same age as her staying in the castle was so exciting, and she'd known from that day they would be the best of friends.

One night when Rexah went for her nightly visits to see Nesrin, the young girl was awake. They spoke for hours, Rexah cross legged on her bed, telling each other stories and talking about their favourite things. There was an instant connection between the two of them, and they'd been inseparable ever since.

"Do you remember when I used to sneak into the infirmary at night?" Rexah asked, a mischievous look spreading across her face.

"Of course, and when you were feeling adventurous you'd sneak to the kitchens and steal us a pastry to share," Nesrin grinned, her eyes brightening at the memory.

"I'll never forget that one time I was caught. I've never seen my grandmother so angry or disappointed. She was furious," Rexah laughed, shaking her head.

Nesrin nodded, laughing. "It was worth it though. Those pastries were absolutely delightful."

Rexah grinned, her violet eyes shining. "I'll make sure they have them at the wedding."

The wedding.

Rexah felt her stomach roll with nerves once again, threatening to bring up what she had eaten for break-fast. She knew she shouldn't be nervous; she had dreamt of this her whole life, after all, but now it was actually happening.

It was easy to daydream about it, easy to imagine what her dress would look like, the flowers and Ryden. He would be perfectly handsome – then again, he always was – but the thought of it becoming reality, of having to walk up that aisle and say those vows, it sent wave after wave of anxiety through her.

"Rex," Nesrin said, placing her hand on Rexah's knee. "Everything is going to be alright; I promise."

Rexah placed her hand on top of hers and gave her a small smile, nodding her head. "I know."

She didn't know what she would ever do without her, and she never wanted to find out.

5

The next few days went by so quickly that Rexah couldn't believe today was the day her grandmother hadn't stopped speaking about. Today was the first fitting of her wedding dress, and she was a bundle of nerves.

Never being one for dresses or pretty things, she didn't understand the big fuss over it, but her grandmother insisted that her dress be nothing less than perfection – the Gods help the royal tailor if it wasn't.

Rexah stood at the foot of her bed, fidgeting with her fingers as she watched the maids set up the mirrors so that when she stood before them, she would be able to see the dress from every angle.

She found herself wondering what they thought

about this whole wedding situation. There hadn't been a royal wedding in Adorea in years. Had any of these girls been here when that last wedding took place? Judging by how young they looked, some either the same age or a few years older than she was, it was doubtful.

Queen Aurelia stepped into the room with a few of her own personal lady's maids following closely behind. She recognised them both: Rosa, and Lizzie. Both women were in their mid-fifties and had served her grandmother for Rexah's whole life. She remembered when she was young both Rosa and Lizzie helped take care of her, gave her baths, and helped her dress until she came of age to have her own lady's maid.

The two women weren't empty handed; Rosa held a large oak box in her hands whilst Lizzie held what she could now see was the dress. A wave of anxiety rolled through her.

"Thank you for your help, ladies. You may return to your duties," Aurelia said to the other maids with a warm smile.

Each of them bowed to both Rexah and her grandmother before they walked out of the room, the door clicking closed behind them.

Aurelia nodded to her lady's maids who began to get

everything ready. The Queen then walked over to Rexah and gently took her hands. "I can't wait to see you in this dress. You're going to love it; I know you will."

Rexah gave her a small smile. "I'm sure the dress is beautiful, grandmother."

"Not as beautiful as the one who will be wearing it, my love," Aurelia said, gently moving a piece of her hair from her face.

After Aurelia helped her out of her nightdress and into a lilac slip, Rexah walked over to Rosa and Lizzie who were waiting for her, holding the dress open. She tried not to think too much as she stepped into the gown with care. The lady's maids began shimmying the dress up her body. She kept her eyes closed, letting them do what they needed to whilst she tried to calm the feeling of apprehension digging its claws into her.

The hinges of the wooden box creaked as Lizzie opened it, and Rexah saw it was filled with jewellery and other small trinkets. Aurelia confirmed which pieces of jewellery should be used; a beautiful tanzanite diamond necklace, bracelet, and earrings to match; and both women followed her instructions and began placing them on Rexah.

The final addition would be the tiara, and Rexah watched as Rosa lifted it from the box. The light from the sun shining in through the windows reflected off it, making the diamonds sparkle like stars.

A diamond graced the centre of the tiara, and small tanzanite gems surrounded it and formed the shape of outstretched wings. Once it was placed on her head, Aurelia's eyes were bright, a huge smile on her face as she took in the sight of her granddaughter.

"Absolutely breath-taking," she said, her palm flat on her chest with pride.

Rexah turned with the help of Rosa and Lizzie holding the bottom of the dress and walked over to the mirrors. The women gently let go of the bottom of the dress and smoothed it out before they stepped back.

"Gods" was the only word to escape Rexah's lips as she stared at herself in the mirror. The girl staring back at her was absolutely stunning, a true example of royalty. The tiara glittered on her head as did the diamonds of the necklace. The dress was made of richly gathered tulle which formed an A-line silhouette while the back descended into a V-shape with a button closure at the centre. The off-shoulder neckline was flanked with long, sheer draping cape sleeves, and glimmering embroidery appliques adorned the fitted bodice.

The gathered skirt gracefully fell to the floor. It was a magical shade of bluish lilac. Rexah had never worn such a gorgeous gown before. Yes, her other dresses were beautiful, but this dress was just flawless. Out of this world. Absolute perfection.

Aurelia appeared behind her with a proud smile and a heart-warming look on her face. "I wish your mother were here to see you," she said softly, her voice breaking slightly.

Rexah saw the sadness in her eyes. She wished her mother were here too, wished both of her parents were. She took another look at herself in the mirrors. "She is here, just like she will be there at the ceremony. They will both be there."

Aurelia's eyes were lined with tears as she nodded, her hands gently coming to rest on the tops of Rexah's arms. "They certainly are and will be. They would be so proud of the woman you have become, just like I am."

She often wondered if her mother and father would be proud of her. Of what they would think of her. She had seen their portrait in the gallery, but she always tried to imagine what they'd look like now.

It was difficult not having them in her life, but she was forever grateful to her grandmother for every single thing she did for her and for everything she continued to do.

"I hope so," Rexah said, placing her hand on her grandmother's.

Aurelia cleared her throat. "Anyway," she said as she walked round to the front of her, her eyes studying the dress, "the dress will need to be taken in just a little."

Lizzie stepped forward holding a smaller box with pins inside and began pinning the dress so it would be ready to be taken in.

Just as swiftly as they had helped her into the dress and jewellery, they helped her back out of it. Both Lizzie and Rosa bowed to Rexah and Aurelia before they exited the room with the box and the dress in tow after being instructed to do so by the Queen.

Aurelia took both of Rexah's hands in hers. "I know this wedding has been sprung upon you so suddenly, and I am sorry for that."

"It was a bit of a surprise, but I will admit I wondered why it hadn't happened yet. Don't get me wrong it is a bit of a shock, but I'm glad I will be marrying Ryden," Rexah said. "We are both glad it's each other and not someone who we don't know. I know other royals haven't been as lucky."

The Queen laughed softly and nodded. "That's true. Your grandfather and I didn't see eye to eye when we first met, but that all changed once we married. It was like something clicked. I loved him dearly."

Her grandfather, Henrik, was Aurelia's consort. She could not remember much about him. He died when Rexah was three years old in a hunting accident. All she could recall from that day was that her grandmother was very sad.

"What will happen once we are married? Will he remain here with me in Adorea or will I be joining him in Kaldoren?" she asked. It had been playing on her mind for the past few days, and if she was being completely honest, she didn't want to leave Adorea, but she was well aware she might not have a choice in the matter.

"King Orland and I have had a few discussions about it, but nothing has been set in stone as of yet. Once we have everything for the wedding in place, we will sit down with you and Ryden and discuss it with you both," Aurelia replied.

Rexah nodded softly as she studied her grand-mother. "Alright."

She wanted to ask her about the Kaldorien army gathering soldiers, why more men were needed, and how it would affect Adorea. Were they in danger? If so, was the realm too? The words hung on the tip of her tongue, but her grandmother spoke before she could.

Squeezing Rexah's hands gently, Aurelia gave her a bright smile. "I must go. The decorations for the temple arrived earlier this morning and I need to inspect them."

"Thank you, Grandmother, for everything," said Rexah.

The old woman's eyes softened, and she pressed a gentle kiss to her forehead. "Always, my darling," she said, before walking across the room and out the door.

Letting out a breath she hadn't realised she'd been holding, Rexah sat down on the ottoman at the end of her bed. Now she had seen herself in the dress and wearing the jewellery and the tiara, had seen how beautiful she'd looked, it was starting to feel all too real.

The night air was cool as Rexah walked through the forest. The moonlight shone through the canopy of the trees now and again aiding to light her way. The lantern in her left hand illuminated the areas the moon couldn't reach with a soft glow.

Apart from her breathing and the sound of the earth beneath her slippers as she walked, the forest was quiet save a few night calls of the wildlife. She hadn't been able to get out for one of her night walks since the arrival of King Orland and Prince Ryden.

Following the familiar path, she moved branches out of her way and stepped through. Her eyes brightened and she smiled seeing the lake glittering in the moonlight.

Rexah pulled off her slippers and walked towards the lake, the grass brushing her ankles now and again as she made her way through. She set the lantern down in front of her as she sat down on the fallen log she always used as a seat.

Rexah pulled her cloak closer around herself as the cold breeze grew a little stronger and washed over her, goosebumps spreading across her skin. She would admit, coming out here with nothing but her nightdress on underneath her cloak wasn't one of her best ideas, but she didn't care. She needed this walk, needed the night air to clear her head.

The forest was stunning at night; those indigo and blue flowers seemed to come to life, glowing in the gloom, and the moonlight made the lake glimmer like the sun catching a chandelier. She took a deep breath of the crisp air, letting it fill her lungs, and smiled before looking up at the sky full of stars.

They sparkled so brightly against the vast darkness. Something about them always calmed her down no matter what she was going through. Each star winked as if welcoming her back, and she couldn't help but grin. The feeling of relaxation was already flowing through her, filling her with much needed relief. She would stay here forever if she could.

The sound of the lake water rippling softly was soothing. An owl hooted off in the distance and on the other side of the pond, a fox drank from it. The animal's fur was a shade of brown so deep it was almost black, the perfect camouflage for hunting at night; the moon shining down on its fur was the only reason she spotted it.

The loud snapping of twigs behind her made the fox dart off into the bushes. Rexah twisted her head with a start, her wide eyes everywhere, searching for the source of the noise.

A shadow loomed in the undergrowth making her heart pound fiercely against her chest. Before she could rise to her feet, the shadow stepped out of the thicket and from the soft glow of her lantern on the ground Ryden's familiar features came into view, the warm flame shadowing some of his face, his grey eyes shining in the firelight.

Rexah's shoulders sagged with relief, and she let out a breath. "Ry," she said, willing her heart to beat at a steady rhythm.

"I'm sorry, Rex. I didn't mean to scare you," he said, his eyes softening.

"What are you doing out here?" she asked him.

"I could ask you the same thing," he said, making his way around the fallen log and sitting down beside her.

Her heart fluttered as his knee gently brushed hers. "I needed some air. I couldn't sleep. I had to get out of the castle for a bit."

She hadn't seen Ryden over the past few days. He'd been busy with his own preparations for the wedding. She had missed him. He still looked as handsome as ever of course, and the mere presence of him made her want to pull him to the forest floor and do all the inappropriate things that were currently going through her mind.

Flashbacks of them in her room flooded her mind: the way he'd lifted her onto the vanity table, his fingers moving against her bare skin, and the way he'd felt against her.

Gods help me.

"Is it the wedding?" he asked, his eyes studying her.

Rexah nodded softly, pushing those delicious memories to the back of her mind. "My fear has nothing to do with you; I want to marry you, of course I do. It's just the whole idea of it, everyone's eyes on us. Maybe if we'd been given more notice I could have had some extra time to let it sink in. It's a big thing."

She was used to having eyes on her, she was royalty, but this was different. Usually, she could pretend that everyone wasn't looking at her, that they were looking at the Queen – most of them were – but when it came to the wedding there would be no doubt that their eyes would be focused directly on her.

Ryden's soft hand slid into Rexah's causing her heart to flutter in her chest.

"I understand. I'm a little anxious about it too, but do you know what I tell myself?"

She looked up at him, those bright grey eyes shining in the darkness.

"Once those vows are spoken, once those rings are exchanged, and I kiss you," he said, gazing so deeply into her eyes that she felt like she was drowning. "It's all going to be worth it; I am going to be the luckiest man alive because you will be my wife."

Rexah's eyes softened, and her body melted into a puddle at his words. "Ry—"

Ryden's hand slipped into her hair and his lips gently brushed hers. Her eyes fluttered closed as she returned the kiss, and she rested a hand on his chest where she could feel his heart pounding just like hers was.

He was right, it would be worth it in the end; it would be him and her finally together, just like she had always dreamed of.

"Ry, I thought we said no more secret kisses?" she whispered against his lips, not wanting to fully break the kiss just yet.

He smirked against her lips before gently pulling away, much to her disappointment. "Sorry princess, you know I can't help myself around you."

Rexah giggled, biting her lip. "Well, I guess I can let you off this one time."

"How about this time?" Ryden whispered, his eyes darkening before he leaned forward and captured her lips again with his.

She melted into the kiss. She wouldn't stop him, no matter what they had promised each other before. She was surprised they had actually gone this long without kissing and without seeing each other. That didn't matter. All that did matter to her was this moment, kissing him under the blanket of stars.

6

The box in her grandmother's hands was beautiful; it was made of ebony wood with a silver clasp at the front, and the Ravenheart crest etched into the lid. Rexah was curious as to what lay within as soon as she saw it in Aurelia's grasp.

The Queen had taken time out of the busy wedding preparations and meetings with King Orland to spend some one-on-one time with her, and whilst she cherished it, she knew there was another reason for their walk through the gardens.

"How are you feeling? I know the wedding came as a shock to you, and I apologise for that," Aurelia said as they made their way through the winding paths amongst the flowers.

Rexah pulled her cloak a little closer. "I'm still trying to process it, but I'm okay, I think," she said, nodding. "If it were anyone other than Ryden I was marrying then it might be a different story."

"Since you were teenagers, I knew you were made for each other." Aurelia smiled. "The way he would look at you, the way your eyes lit up whenever he spoke, I knew."

They chatted about the wedding as they made their way through the labyrinth, and once they got to the familiar fountain, they sat down on one of the benches.

"Okay, what's in the box?" Rexah asked, her impatience getting the better of her.

Aurelia laughed softly. "It's something that has been in our family for as long as I can remember, passed down through the generations," she replied as she flipped the clasps open.

Rexah watched as she lifted the lid, the hinges squeaking slightly at the movement. The box was lined with purple silk and sitting inside was the most beautiful dagger she'd ever seen.

"Grandmother," Rexah whispered as Aurelia turned the box towards her.

Purple jewels adorned the black hilt, swirling up towards a raven with its wings splayed on the guard.

The blade itself was wicked sharp, ending in a deadly point.

"Go on, you can take it out," the old woman encouraged.

The dagger felt heavy in her hand, but it felt right. Rexah got to her feet and took a few steps forward before swinging her arm in a few practice strokes. The steel cut through the air with ease, soft whooshing sounds filling her ears. It was a stunning weapon.

"It's beautiful, expertly crafted," Rexah said as she examined the hilt closely.

"Consider it a wedding gift from me," Aurelia said. "It would have been passed down to you one day, and I thought now would be the best time."

Unease settled in Rexah's stomach as she looked over to her grandmother, the tone in the old woman's voice giving away the worry she had clearly been trying to hide. Rexah walked over and sat down beside her once more, gently placing the dagger back into the box. "What's going on?" she asked her.

A smile appeared on Aurelia's face. "What do you mean?"

"Enough, grandmother, tell me what's going on. I'm not stupid. Something is happening, something big, and you're not telling me," she replied.

Aurelia's smile slowly slipped, and she sighed, placing the box beside her on the bench. "I was hoping I wouldn't have to tell you, not if it wasn't necessary."

"Is it true? Is Kaldoren gathering additional soldiers?" she asked, her stomach turning slightly.

"How much do you know?" Aurelia asked, studying her.

Rexah shrugged softly. "Nothing beyond that. Ryden doesn't either. He said the King has been holding meetings without him, telling him he isn't needed."

"Reinforcements are being gathered as a precaution in Kaldoren. King Crowfell has come to ask for the aid of the Adorian army," the Queen explained.

"War is coming, isn't it? That's why King Orland is here asking for our help. It's why you've both been otherwise occupied, other than the wedding. You've been discussing the reinforcements," she said softly.

Aurelia met her gaze. "We are doing everything in our power to ensure war doesn't happen, but we'd be fools to rule it out."

Rexah's heart began to pound. "And the wedding? Is this the reason you're pushing for our union to happen as quickly as possible? Because you fear war will happen before you can unite our kingdoms?"

"Our kingdoms have been allies since the beginning

of time. We would always come to each other's aid no matter what. But, if we unite through marriage, then we can strengthen that bond further, show that we are a force to be reckoned with," Aurelia told her, the light breeze making her hair dance softly.

Rexah studied her. "Who is waging war on us?"

"It's not who, my darling, it's what," Aurelia said, her eyes filling with fear. It was a look she wasn't used to seeing in her grandmother's eyes.

What in the world?

"What do you mean?"

Aurelia took her granddaughter's hands in hers. Rexah squeezed her hands, so soft even though they were marked with age. "Evil is prowling, Rexah, wicked beasts. Darkness unlike anything you can imagine. I want you to work harder in your training with Zuko. I will sleep better at night knowing if it ever came to it, you'd be able to protect yourself."

"Beasts? What aren't you telling me?" she pressed, eager for more information.

There aren't many beasts that roam the forests of Adorea. Especially not beings of evil.

"The Dark Fae have been spotted throughout the realm, the Valfae with them," she replied, her hands shaking in Rexah's grip. "They haven't given any signs of attack yet, but our soldiers are prepared, and our spies are keeping a watchful eye on them."

Fear ran its claws down her spine. The Dark Fae were once normal fae who had been captured by the darkness, their souls and hearts corrupted by it and forever changing them into horrifyingly powerful beings of evil.

Those who were too far gone did not remain in their humanoid form; those poor souls transformed into horrifying creatures with batlike wings that protruded from their shoulder blades, claws so sharp they would rip anyone to pieces within seconds, and fangs that would tear your throat to ribbons before you knew they were even upon you. No one knew why some turned into Valfae and others didn't.

Oh Gods, this is bad, this is very bad.

"Please don't leave me in the dark. If I can do something to help, then let me," Rexah said, pushing her own fear back into its box. "I'm not a little girl anymore."

"No, you certainly aren't." Aurelia smiled and moved Rexah's hair from her face. "We are monitoring the situation, there's no cause for alarm right now, but I promise you, if anything changes, I'll let you know."

Always trying to protect me, let me protect you for once.

She wanted to say those words to her, but she didn't

want to argue and nodded. "Okay, but at least talk to me about these things. I can handle it."

Aurelia nodded. "I will. Thank you, Rexah, for being so understanding."

"Our conversation about this is far from over, but I appreciate that you opened up to me. If I can help, I will."

The Queen leaned forward and pressed a gentle kiss to her forehead. "So brave and so strong. You are a true Ravenheart, my darling."

Rexah moved closer and hugged her. "I love you."

Aurelia hugged her back, smiling against her hair. "I love you too."

The Dark Fae were not to be underestimated. She was lucky enough to have never seen one in the flesh, but she'd learned about them in her studies. The drawings she'd seen of the Valfae terrified her when she was younger.

When they pulled away from their hug, Rexah studied her grandmother. "It's okay to be afraid."

Aurelia's eyes softened. "It is, but when you are queen, and one day you will be, then you will understand that fear mustn't be shown, especially in front of your people. They look to you to keep them safe, to be that beacon of hope, and if you show them that you are afraid, then that fear will project onto them."

"You are forgetting one important thing," Rexah said, locks of her hair swirling around her in the light breeze. "We are all human, and if I know our people as well as I think I do, then they would not judge you for it."

Aurelia smiled softly, the skin wrinkling around her eyes. "I was truly blessed by the Gods to have you as my granddaughter. I am so proud of you, my darling."

"I'm the lucky one." Rexah blinked away tears she hadn't realised were building in her eyes.

The Queen gently patted the back of Rexah's hand. "You're going to be late for your training with Zuko. You should go," she said, picking the box up and handing it to her.

It was heavy in Rexah's hands as she took it from her. "Thank you again, Grandmother," she said, nodding her head in respect. When Aurelia nodded back, Rexah took her leave.

The princess's shoes clicked against the stone path as she headed back to the castle, her mind racing with everything she'd been told. The box dug into her skin as she gripped it tightly.

I'll do whatever it takes, she thought, squeezing the

box harder into her palm, *even if it's the last thing I do.*

"It's beautiful, isn't it?" Rexah said, a small smirk spread across her face as she watched her trainer examine the dagger.

Zuko smiled and nodded. "It's an incredible weapon. Would you like to train with it today to get used to the feel and weight of it in your hand?" he asked as he handed the dagger back to her and walked to the chest of weapons next to the table.

"Yeah, that's a great idea." She grinned as she walked to the centre of the training area, the sun shining down on them to provide the perfect amount of light.

Clanging sounds echoed as Zuko placed a few weapons onto the table. "How was your meeting with the Queen?"

"I finally got her to open up to me about what's happening," she said, rolling her shoulders as she warmed up. "The Dark Fae and Valfae are lurking. She said she hopes war will be avoided, but she's not ruling it out."

"I know," he said casually as he inspected the blades

he'd laid out.

Rexah's gaze snapped to him. "What? You knew and you didn't say anything?"

He looked at her over his shoulder. "I'm not only your trainer; I need to keep my own skills at their highest level, so I train with the soldiers." He selected a similar sized dagger as hers before he turned to her. "The Queen commanded the soldiers, and me, to not breathe a word of what was happening."

Rexah watched as he made his way towards her in the centre of the space. *Am I the only person in this castle who didn't know?*

"When my queen commands me to do something, I do it. Don't take it personally, Your Highness," he said, a hint of a smirk on his lips.

"I'm not taking it personally, Zuko. It's just a little frustrating is all," she replied, moving her neck side to side to stretch the muscles. "Let's get started, shall we?"

Zuko widened his stance. "Go ahead."

Taking a deep breath, Rexah readied herself before she shot forward, bringing her dagger down in a sweeping motion, the jewels on the hilt glistening in the rays of sunlight. Zuko was fast and easily dodged out of the way, his fist connecting with her side.

Rexah gasped in pain and stumbled back as the air

left her lungs, almost dropping her blade.

"You left your side exposed, *again*," Zuko said, twirling his weapon in his hand. "Stop slacking, it'll get you killed."

A growl left her lips as she gripped the hilt tighter and launched herself at him.

Zuko flinched and moved rapidly, scarcely avoiding her attack he'd obviously failed to anticipate, but he recovered quickly and grabbed her from behind, his arm pinning both of hers to her side. "Anger will get you nowhere," he said, panting. "Control your emotions and focus. Timing is everything."

Once she relaxed her body in his grasp, he let go of her and stepped back. Rexah turned to him, and her eyes widened in shock as she saw a trickle of blood run down his upper arm.

Shit.

"Oh Gods, Zuko, I'm so sorry," she said. "I'm used to using the blunt blades."

"Relax, Rexah. I've had worse." He chuckled softly as he walked over to the table and grabbed a cloth to clean the wound. "We will continue with proper weapons. I think it's time."

She huffed a laugh. "You trust me enough not to cut you again?" she asked.

He walked over and got into position again. "Of course I do," he said. "Now, this time I want you to focus and seek out any weak spots. They are key to taking down your enemy. Know their weak spot and they're easy prey."

She nodded and took a deep breath, studying him. Zuko moved fast and thrust the dagger towards her abdomen, but the princess was faster and stepped to the side, parrying his blade with her own. That's when she saw it, his weak spot. She brought the heel of her foot down hard on his shin, making his leg buckle, and she shoved him to the ground. Pinning him where he fell, she placed the blade to his throat.

Zuko grinned up at her, his blue eyes brightening. "Excellent, well done."

Rexah stood up and stepped back, letting him get to his feet. "This dagger feels amazing. I still can't believe it's mine."

"Good, the more you train with it, the better. You'll get to know the blade, learn the best way to wield it," he told her. "You'll become one with it."

"I don't know if I tell you enough, or if I've ever told you for that matter, but thank you," she said, softly.

"Thank you for what?" he asked, watching her.

"For taking the time to teach me. For putting up

with my tantrums and my silly mistakes," she replied. "I really appreciate it."

His lips tugged up into a smile. "No need to thank me. Your grandmother took me in, it's the least I could do, and besides, I enjoy training you, tantrums and all. I wouldn't change it for the world."

Rexah laughed softly and shook her head, the purple flashes in her hair shining in the daylight. "We should get back to it," she said getting back into position.

"Okay, just like last time," he said, widening his stance once again. "Show me what you've got."

Rexah grinned and took a deep breath before she attacked.

L ater that night, Rexah sat on her bed, on top of the covers, staring down at the dagger in her hand. It was so unbelievably beautiful, and it was hers. She still couldn't believe it.

Riona once held this very weapon in her hands, killed many enemies with it, she thought. *It's almost like there's power buried within the blade ... somehow, I can feel it.* Rexah shook her head and slid the blade under her pillow. *I'm being stupid now. I'm tired and my mind is playing tricks on me.*

She got up from the bed and padded barefoot over to the fireplace; she sat on the floor in front of it, the soft rug beneath her as she basked in the warm glow.

The Dark Fae being so close to the Adorian border made her uneasy. She wasn't naive to the fact that they existed, but she never expected them to come anywhere near her home, and maybe that was foolish of her.

Things are going to be tense for a while, or at least until the Dark Fae leave – if they leave.

That last thought sent an involuntary shiver slide down her spine. The possibility of them attacking was something that couldn't be ignored. The Valfae were different to the Dark Fae. They had next to no intelligence, only enough that they did what their masters commanded of them and only knew the taste of flesh and blood – they craved it.

The Dark Fae were the puppet masters, sending the Valfae as a first line of attack, but that didn't mean they didn't enjoy killing innocents; no, they relished in it just as much. Their main purpose was to destroy, and from what she'd learned about them, any place they visited they left in ruins, and she would be damned if she let them destroy Adorea.

Rexah knew how dangerous they were though, and if a war broke out she knew victory wouldn't be so easily achieved. Many would lose their lives, that was certain.

Can Valfae be killed with a sword? Can they be killed easily? Gods, there's still so much that's unknown about them.

The nightmares that had plagued her dreams surely couldn't be a coincidence. Were they a sign that war was coming, a warning to prepare? Should she have been paying more attention instead of dismissing them as meaningless nightmares?

Deep down she prayed to the Gods it wasn't, because in her dream, every damn time, she never saw her fate. She lay bloodied and unable to move, but before she found out what happened next, she would always wake up.

What about the raven though? Each time it would land on my chest and look me straight in the eyes. What did that mean?

She sighed and shifted her gaze to the fire. Staring into the flames, she prayed to any of the gods and goddesses who might be listening that it would all come to nothing, that war wouldn't come to their door.

7

Any moment she could get to herself she seized with both hands. Two days had passed since the kiss she'd shared with Ryden by the lake in the forest, and she couldn't stop thinking about it. She couldn't stop thinking about the feeling of his soft lips on hers, the way he held her close, the gentleness of his touch. Her heart fluttered in her chest when she recalled the way her name had fallen quietly from his lips. That strong, perfect man would be her husband so very soon, and she would be his wife.

The winter sun shone in through the large windows and touched the golden walls within, the many paintings that hung there alive with the light upon them. A few of the paintings depicted the battlefield on which

Queen Riona fought so bravely, and these were some of her favourites to look at. Others she favoured were of the many long-dead family members of the Ravenheart family, both single and group portraits.

Small benches were dotted around the room should anyone wish to sit and admire the artwork, and a golden chandelier hung from the middle of the ceiling catching the rays of the sun.

Her mind wandered to when her grandmother had made her sit for portraits; she had told her they were tradition, but it was also nice to be able to look at them and remember the years gone by. Her younger self hadn't fully appreciated the sentimental value the portraits held for the Queen, and it wasn't until she'd gotten older that she realised her grandmother was right, especially when it came to her parents' pictures.

Rexah stopped when she arrived at an all too familiar painting. The painting of Queen Riona standing tall and proud with her swords strapped to her back. She wore her black fighting leathers with the Ravenheart crest sewn into the breast, and her raven hair was pulled up in a half braid – the artist had captured the purple flashes in her hair perfectly.

She sat down on the bench behind her as she stared up at her ancestor, the woman who she most resembled, to whom she was compared. She did often find herself wondering why their eyes and their hair were the same despite no one else in the royal family having the same attributes since. What was so special about her above all the others? and why had it skipped generations?

"You have given me a lot to live up to," Rexah said softly. "I am a good fighter, but I will never be as powerful as you once were. Everyone says I am blessed to have your beauty, that I have been truly gifted."

Riona's violet eyes seemed to burn into Rexah so much so that she felt as though the Queen were standing alive before her in the room. The silence that filled the gallery was almost deafening, and goose-bumps covered every inch of her skin in response.

"Why?" Rexah whispered, her voice breaking slightly. "Why me?"

She paused, waiting as if the painting would come to life and Riona would answer her question.

After a few moments of silence, Rexah leaned forward, her elbows on her knees, and buried her face into her hands. She took a deep breath, in through her nose and out through her mouth, shoving the anxiety that threatened to creep over her back into the box she kept it in, buried in the back of her mind.

Taking that moment to gather herself and her thoughts, Rexah rose to her feet, her hand running through her hair as she looked up to the stunning painting once again.

"One day I know the responsibility of this kingdom will fall to me. It will be my responsibility to keep our home and our people safe, to give them a place where they can live their lives happily and bring up their children and earn a wage," she said. "When that day comes, I promise I will do just that. No matter how difficult or overwhelming it may be at first, I will do whatever it takes. I will make you proud."

Rexah bowed her head gently to the painting, sealing her promise with a respectful nod before she made her way out of the gallery.

Glad to be back in her room after another long day of being asked questions about the upcoming wedding, Rexah sighed as she kicked off her shoes. She left them where they fell, not really caring at that moment to pick them up and put them neatly away with the rest of her pretty shoes.

Her grandmother would have a heart attack if she walked in and saw the shoes just lying there in the middle of the room; on any other day Rexah would have put them away, but she was tired and all she wanted to do was get out of her dress and into her nightgown.

Her day had consisted of looking at several types and colours of material with her grandmother. Queen Aurelia insisted that Rexah choose which pattern and colour she liked best and that would be the material of the cloths that would cover each of the tables at the wedding feast.

Rexah didn't have the heart to tell her that she didn't mind what was on the tables, so she decided on a pale grey material with lilac swirls. Her grandmother had smiled brightly at her in response, and Rexah knew that meant she approved of her choice.

Rexah sat on the ottoman at the end of her bed and ran her hand down her face. She knew that when the day of the wedding arrived, when she stood with Ryden and said their vows, everything would be fine. All of this worry and stress would be long forgotten.

Part of her wished she could run away with him to Tella's Meadow and marry tonight, just the two of them. But they were royalty; weddings were a huge occasion of significant importance in the royal world, and they were never a small or private affair.

A knock at her bedroom door pulled her from her thoughts. "Come in," she called out.

The door opened and Nesrin stepped into the room closing the door behind her. "Your Highness," Nesrin said, bowing to her.

Rexah didn't like her using the royal formalities, but her best friend knew that and used her title regardless, even when they were alone. It was like their own private joke between one another.

Rexah couldn't stop the small smirk that spread across her lips. "Hello Nesrin."

Her eyes narrowed playfully as she stood straighter. "It's time to get you ready for bed."

"Gods, you make me sound like a child," Rexah said as she stood up, grinning softly.

Nesrin laughed, shaking her head as she walked to the wardrobe and opened its doors. "You know it's my job to help you, Rex."

She nodded. "I know," she said. "And I am forever grateful for you. The Gods know I'd have gone insane by now if it weren't for you."

"Oh, I can imagine," she said as she picked out a nightgown before closing the wardrobe doors. "What a tyrant you'd be." Nesrin walked over and lay the night-gown on Rexah's bed.

Rexah laughed softly as she turned her back to her. "I would be the worst of them all."

Nesrin grinned softly as she carefully undid the buttons on the back of Rexah's dress. She helped her step out of it and moved it to the side. "You will make a fine ruler one day," she said as she picked up the night-gown from the bed. "That is one thing I know for certain."

"I appreciate the faith you have in me," Rexah said.

The nightgown slid over her skin as she pulled it over her head, and Nesrin pulled it down from the bottom, making sure it was perfectly neat.

Rexah walked over to the vanity table and sat down. She watched Nesrin in the mirror as she began to remove the pins holding her hair in place.

"Your birth mark is so beautiful. I don't understand why your grandmother insists that it be covered at all times," Nesrin said.

She shrugged. "I don't understand either. I've asked her about it before, but she's never given me a definitive answer."

"Don't you find that a bit strange?"

"I do, but I know I'm only wasting my breath when I

try to ask about it again, so whenever she is ready to tell me the reason then I'll be here to listen," she replied.

Soon Nesrin was running a brush through the princess's raven coloured hair, once again covering the raven-shaped birthmark on the back of her neck.

Rexah found herself in a daydream, one she often had when Nesrin brushed her hair. In her daydream, it wasn't her lady's maid and best friend but her mother who ran the brush through her dark locks; it was her mother who smiled at her through the mirror and spoke to her, asking her how her day had been. Of course, Rexah's memories of her mother were pretty much non-existent, but there was a portrait in the gallery of her mother and father, the former holding Rexah as a baby in her arms, and she used it to form the image of her mother she kept in her head.

"Rex?" Nesrin's concerned voice asked through the daydream.

She blinked a few times and looked at her lady's maid in the mirror. She forced a smile on her face. "Sorry, Nes. I was away in a world of my own there for a second," she said.

"I was saying that I'm all done, that you can settle for the night now," she said, placing the brush down on the vanity.

Rexah nodded softly. "Before you go, I have a surprise for you."

Nesrin's eyebrow arched. "A surprise? For me? What are you up to?"

Rexah smirked mischievously as she got up from the stool and made her way over to her bed. She kneeled down and reached under it before pulling out a box. She stood up and walked over to her friend, opening the box to reveal four deliciously smelling pastries.

Nesrin's eyes lit up. "Are … are those what I think they are?"

"The very same." Rexah grinned at her. "I thought we might share them and chat for a bit. You know, like old times."

"I could think of nothing more perfect," she said, grinning back at her.

Both of them sat by the fire, Rexah in one armchair and Nesrin in the other, and ate their pastries.

"How did you even get these?" Nesrin asked before she took another bite.

Rexah wiped her mouth. "I spoke to one of the kitchen staff and they said an order had been placed for them for the wedding and that the bakery was sending some for tasting."

"So, what you're saying is that these pastries were

actually meant for you, your grandmother, the King and Ryden to try, and instead you commandeered them for us?"

Rexah grinned. "Precisely."

They both laughed loudly. "I will never tire of your antics, Rex."

Growing up Rexah was always up to no good in the castle. Playing pranks on members of staff and driving her grandmother crazy. Aurelia was visibly relieved when Rexah began her training with Zuko; the youngster could let off her energy in their lessons, and Aurelia could get some work done rather than disciplining the princess all hours.

"You've got to have fun. Life is too short to be serious all the time," Rexah replied as she broke off another piece of the pastry. "You never know when your last day is upon you."

"How insightful of you, Your Highness." Nesrin smirked softly.

Rexah grinned as she put the piece of pastry in her mouth. "I thought so too."

"Has it been difficult staying away from Ryden?" Nesrin asked.

"Well, we've both been kept terribly busy with the preparations for the wedding, so it hasn't been difficult to stay out of each other's company. It's such a stupid thing to say because he's in the same building as me, but I miss him," Rexah replied.

"It's not stupid at all," Nesrin told her, a smile spreading across her face. "Just wait until you are both wed. Then you won't be able to get rid of him."

Rexah laughed, shaking her head. "Indeed."

She would be bound to one man for the rest of her life, and she could think of no one better than Ryden. They would be wed, they would have children, one day they would rule, and they would grow old together. She couldn't imagine anything more perfect than that.

They talked for almost two hours about the past and whatever the future may hold for them. Rexah wasn't a princess and Nesrin wasn't her lady's maid, they were just two best friends reminiscing about old times and composing crazy destinies for one another. They had finished all four pastries and regretted nothing, but before long Nesrin had bid her goodnight and left her to it.

Rexah couldn't help the smile that spread across her

face as she stood up from the armchair. She blew the candles out as she made her way over to her bed. The sheets were cool against her skin as she got under the covers, and a happy sigh left her as she lay back getting comfortable.

A thought then made its way into her mind. Soon she wouldn't have the luxury of spreading out in bed, taking up as much room as she wanted and not needing to give space to anyone.

Soon she would be sharing a bed with Ryden, and stomach rolled at that image. They had shared the same bed before, but he'd never slept the full night next to her.

Taking a deep breath, she closed her eyes.

Everything was going to be fine.

The sound of birds singing filled the air, the sun shining brightly in the blue, cloudless sky above. The soft grass beneath her bare feet tickled her skin with each step she took, and Rexah's white dress blew gently in the cool breeze, as did her long, dark hair.

The meadow was beautiful and familiar.

Tella's Meadow.

Colourful flowers littered the grass that surrounded the shrine to the goddess, and a limestone statue of Tella had been placed in the centre of the alter. The goddess wore a long gossamer dress, one hand placed over her heart, the other resting on her abdomen, and her face angled down to her body: the representation of love and fertility.

Rexah stopped before Tella, bowing her head to her, her hands finding her own chest and stomach as the tradition expected when visiting the meadow to speak with the goddess. Her eyes closed as she whispered her silent prayer.

"Such a peaceful place," a soft, delicate voice to her right said.

Rexah's eyes snapped open, and her head turned to see another woman standing beside her. No, this was not just any woman. Brown hair flowed in soft curls down her back, gently swaying in the breeze, and her deep brown eyes met Rexah's as she smiled softly.

"Mother," Rexah said in quiet realization.

Amelia smiled deeper before she looked back up at the statue of Tella. "Everything is going to be all right, my sweet girl."

"You have a head fit for a crown, a heart made to rule," another female voice said, this time to her left, and the voice was unfamiliar.

Rexah's heart almost exploded out of her chest when she saw Queen Riona standing beside her.

It was eerie how similar they looked; they stood with the same dark hair with flashes of purple and violet eyes that *shone brightly. It was almost like looking into a mirror, only Riona was older.*

"Your destiny lies before you," Riona said.

Rexah moved her gaze back to the statue.

Her destiny: Marry Ryden, produce heirs and rule as king and queen. Yet, something didn't feel right; that future seemed to slide further and further away the more she tried to picture it in her mind.

A sour taste filled her mouth. "My...my destiny?"

"All you need to do is wake up, my love," said her mother.

Before Rexah could ask her what she was talking about, the sun disappeared, giving way to dark, ominous clouds. Lighting crackled across the sky and thunder roared causing the very ground beneath her feet to tremble.

"Rexah," Amelia said.

She looked at her mother and saw the panic and worry in her eyes. Her heart began to beat uncontrollably in her chest as another loud boom of thunder shook the ground violently.

"Rexah!" Riona said loudly.

When she looked at the dead queen, her eyes widened. Riona's violet eyes burned into her as she watched blood seep through the front of Riona's leathers, staining the material a deep red. Her ancestor's skin rapidly paled as her blood left her body from the wound that she'd received in the Battle of Adorea, her violet eyes no longer full of life.

The earth rocked beneath them again, the sound of the ground tearing filled her ears, and she looked down to see the earth fracturing underneath her feet.

"REXAH!" Her name was cried, and when she looked up, she was no longer in the meadow. Her mother and Queen Riona were gone, and in their place, hovering over her, was her grandmother.

Rexah glanced around the darkness quickly, and as her eyes adjusted, her bedroom came into view from the lantern Aurelia had set down on the table beside her bed.

Still a little dazed from being woken up, Rexah looked back up at her grandmother. "W-what's wrong?"

The Queen did not answer her. Instead, she grabbed the bedcovers and pulled them before hauling Rexah out of the bed. Aurelia moved to the wardrobe and pulled out the first piece of clothing her hand fell to and helped her granddaughter into it.

Rexah stood half-asleep, slowly processing the fear spread across her grandmother's features, a look of terror she had never seen before, and it sent a chill down her spine.

"Grandmother," Rexah said as she pulled on the dressing gown. "What's happening? You're scaring me."

"We don't have a lot of time. We need to move

quickly," she said as she moved back to the bed and blew out the lantern.

Rexah frowned at her. "Move? Move to where? What's going on?"

That's when she heard it, the cries and screams that echoed from outside. It sounded as though a battle was taking place on the castle grounds. Rexah rushed to one of the windows and pulled back the curtain. A sight of absolute horror greeted her: the village was on fire, as well as parts of the castle; huge pieces of rubble from the castle structure were scattered everywhere, crushing the surrounding buildings and homes; and thick black smoke filled the sky. In the distance, she could just make out the small figures of their people running for their lives.

Rexah slowly turned to her grandmother as Aurelia spoke.

"They are here."

8

"They?" Rexah asked, her heart pounding in her chest. "Who are *they*?" As soon as the words left her lips, Rexah realised she didn't have to ask. She knew exactly who and what her grandmother spoke of. "The Dark Fae," she whispered.

Aurelia grabbed the shoes that Rexah hadn't bothered to put away earlier and helped her put them on. "Yes," she said, "they have set the Valfae loose. They are chaos and ruin; death and destruction."

Rexah shook her head, denial quickly setting in. "No, this can't be happening."

"We don't have time to argue, Rexah, we must go," Aurelia said as she rushed to her granddaughter's side.

"No! You said there was nothing to worry about,

that our soldiers and spies had everything under control!" Rexah yelled.

Aurelia looked her straight in the eye. "Our spies are dead, five hundred of our soldiers fell along with them. The Dark Fae are smarter than we anticipated. We were watching them, and they were watching us, waiting for any sign of weakness in our defences, and they found one."

"How do you know that?"

"Because I received a shadow message from the head of the Night Witches. Her clan saw them, slinking out of the darkness and slaughtering our soldiers. They did what they could to help but had to retreat," Aurelia replied, her voice shaking.

The Night Witches lived deep within the Adorian Forest. Most people feared them due to their wraith like appearance, but they were not evil; they drew their power from the moon and shadows, building to their strongest during the dark hours of night. Judging from the height of the moon, Rexah reckoned, the darkest hours were still far off.

There was a loud boom, and the castle shook. Books fell from the bookcase, little trinkets crashed to the floor from her vanity table, and a small bottle of her favourite perfume smashed on impact with the hard wood, filling the room with its beautiful scent.

Aurelia grabbed Rexah by the arm and dragged her across the room. "Come on, there is no time. We must make haste. We cannot stay here a moment longer."

Rexah had never seen her grandmother in such a state before and it made her own fear escalate. The older woman's eyes held a panic that she was failing to conceal, her face serious as though she were calculating every step they were about to take, trying as ever to be ten paces ahead of their enemy.

"Wait!" Rexah called out, pulling her arm free from Aurelia's grip. Rexah rushed over to the bed and lifted the mattress, pulling something free. When she straightened, the blade of her dagger glinted in the candlelight. Gripping the hilt tighter, she rushed back to her grandmother. "Okay, let's go."

The Queen grabbed the handle of the door, after checking it wasn't too hot to touch with the back of her hand, and pulled it open, stepping out into the corridor with Rexah.

It was a scene of absolute chaos: thick black smoke filled the air around them, fire crackled close by as curtains and furniture burned, and the walls and floor, down at the end of the corridor to the left of her room, were rendered charred and ready to crumble into non-existence at any moment.

Screams and the sounds of choking could faintly be heard over the roaring of the blaze. Staff members tried to flee for their lives, and Rexah's eyes widened when she saw Sophie crawling on her hands and knees trying to get away from the flames and smoke.

"Rexah, come on!" Aurelia shouted over the roaring flames.

She tore away from her grandmother and rushed to Sophie's side, helping her away from the flames, trying not to let the smoke emanating from them smother her. Sophie was shaking as they returned to Aurelia.

"It's okay, we're going to get you out of here," Rexah told the frightened girl as the smoke clung to the back of her throat, her fear momentarily smothered by the adrenaline running through her veins.

Before Rexah could say anything else, they were being hurried down the corridor to her right, away from the intense heat of the flames but straight through the dense smog. She placed the sleeve of her dressing gown over her mouth as she coughed, the smoke stinging her eyes and burning her lungs.

The women rushed down the hallway as quickly as they could, descending the stairs two at a time as they made their way down to the ground floor. They manoeuvred around charred pieces of wood and, to her horror, bodies of her people, of those who hadn't escaped in time before the smoke had filled their lungs.

Her heart ached; they'd been so close.

The foyer was in ruins. Parts of the ceiling and walls had crumbled and littered the floor. It looked nothing like it had when she last saw it a few hours ago, and her heart ached to see it in such devastation.

Coughing caught their attention. Rexah looked up to see one of the guards stumbling towards them, the back of his hand covering his mouth. "Y-your Majesty, Your H-highness."

"Take Sophie and get her to safety," Rexah told him as she gently urged the girl forward. "Don't look back."

His brow furrowed. "But…"

"No buts; you heard the princess, get the girl to safety," Aurelia commanded.

The guard nodded before bowing quickly. Sophie looked at the Queen and Rexah. "U-until we meet a-again," she said, her voice trembling.

Rexah squeezed her hand before the guard guided her away, and she prayed to the Gods to keep them safe before she followed Aurelia.

Broken glass crunched underneath their feet as they

made their way towards the main entrance to the castle. Paintings that had once hung proudly on the walls were now nothing but ash on the floor. The marble floor was crumbling and cracking here and there, forcing them to change direction to avoid falling through the unstable floor.

The main door had been completely destroyed; it lay in pieces on the floor amongst all the other debris and rubble, and Rexah's heart sank when she saw that the way out was blocked by huge pieces of broken stone.

"Fuck," Aurelia cursed, earning a look of pure shock from her granddaughter. "We must find another way out, and quickly."

Rexah had never heard her grandmother use any foul language in all her life. "The … the servant entrance. We can get out that way."

The Queen nodded and hastily took her hand. "Good thinking, lets—"

Rexah turned to head in the direction of the servant entrance when she felt a sharp pull on her arm from her grandmother. Rexah turned, her eyes widening as she viewed the petrifying sight before her. A creature as dark as night stood behind Aurelia with its claws protruding out of her chest, blood staining the front of her dress crimson.

"NO!" Rexah screamed.

Aurelia's face twitched with pain, blood from her mouth running down her chin. "Go to ... Dorasa ... you will find all your answers t-there," she said between painful breaths. "Rexah ... run m-my darling ... RUN!"

Rexah reached out for her, but all she could do was watch in horror as the Valfae flew back, pulling her grandmother with it into the thick black smoke.

She felt numb. She couldn't move. Her feet felt as though they had been welded to the floor. Her whole body trembled as tears cascaded down her face.

This can't be happening. This can't be happening. This isn't real. This can't be happening.

It had to be a nightmare, and she would wake up any moment now with her grandmother by her bedside soothing her, telling her everything was going to be fine.

Wake up, Rexah.

But no, she didn't wake up. This wasn't a dream, and she had to get out of there. As much as her heart broke at the thought of what had just happened to her grandmother, there was only one thing she could do now: carry out her grandmother's final command.

Run.

Glass crunched and wood splintered under her feet as she raced through the room. The Great Hall wasn't so great anymore; the arched windows had been smashed, the cobalt curtains shredded, and a few beams snapped in two lay scattered across the cracked marble floor.

One sight in particular made Rexah stop dead in her tracks.

Oh Gods.

The two smaller thrones were nothing but piles of smoking rubble, but what made her heart ache most was the main throne. Three claw marks tore through the Ravenheart crest on the back of the throne, and the once magnificent raven wings at either side of it were now nothing but ash on the ground.

Hot tears fell down her face, but she quickly wiped them away. She couldn't fall apart, not now. Falling apart could wait until later. She had one goal: run.

Growling pulled her gaze from the ruined thrones, and standing a few feet away was a huge, terrifying shape: a Valfae. Rexah gripped her dagger tighter in her hand as she faced the beast, rage unlike anything she'd ever felt coursing through her veins.

The Valfae watched her, it's lips almost tugging up

into a smirk before it launched itself at her, fangs and claws reaching for her. Centring herself, just as Zuko had taught her, she waited until it was close enough and dodged out of its reach before sweeping her blade across its forearm. Sticky black blood spurted onto her dressing gown as the creature howled in pain.

Spinning, Rexah faced the Valfae's back, lifting the dagger high before plunging it down towards the beast's flesh. Before the tip of the steel could pierce its target, the Valfae spun to face her, its wing smacking into her right side and sending her flying into the wall.

The wall cracked slightly at the force, and she groaned as she slid down to the floor, her dagger surprisingly still in her grip. Pain spread through her back as she watched the monster stalk towards her. Ignoring the ache, she shoved herself to her feet in time to move out of the way of its claws.

Before the Valfae could have another strike at her, she planted her foot on its stomach, and with all the strength she could muster, she kicked it, sending the creature stumbling backwards. Pushing off the wall, she threw herself at the Valfae and thrust her dagger through its chin up to the hilt, angling it the way Zuko had taught her.

As soon as the steel made contact with the Valfae,

the handle began to vibrate in her hand. Her eyebrows knitted together in a frown before her eyes widened as lightning crackled from the hilt, through the blade, and into the creature. The Valfae roared and shook as the lightning surged through its body before it went limp.

Rexah yanked her dagger from the beast's chin and watched as its skin turned grey, cracks appearing in its flesh before it fell to the floor as nothing but a pile of ash. Her hands shook with adrenaline as she gazed down at the blade still sparking and spitting; fae runes glowed along the steel as the lightning danced along it.

What the hell?

The lightning soon died down and the dagger returned to normal. She'd never seen a weapon do that before, but she had felt something in it when her grandmother had gifted it to her.

I need to get out of here, whatever this blade is, it can wait until I'm safe.

Rexah had never killed anything before, and she'd just taken down a Valfae singlehandedly. A heavy breath escaped her as she tried to calm down. Once her body had stopped shaking enough, she rushed for the door at the opposite end of the room, dodging the broken beams as she went. Looking over her shoulder, she watched as the ashes of the Valfae swirled in the breeze, blowing in from the shattered windows.

Her foot caught on something, sending her straight to the floor, and she groaned as pain spread through her. Easing herself onto her elbows, she looked down to see what she tripped over, and another heart-breaking jolt of shock ripped through her.

His auburn hair was caked in blood, black and red, and three deep claw marks began grimly at his cheek and tore right down to his chest. His once bright blue eyes were vacant of life as they stared up at the ceiling.

"Z-Zuko?"

9

Time itself stood still. Her throat went as dry as the desert, and she swore she stopped breathing as she stared down at her teacher, lifeless on the floor.

"No … no … NO!" she roared. She shot forward and grabbed him. "Zuko?!"

There was no answer from him, no response whatsoever, no matter how hard she shook him. He was gone. Grief tried to pull her into its embrace once more, but before it could, the hair on the back of her neck suddenly stood up on end. A feeling of dread washed over her like a wave, and as she slowly looked up, she understood why.

Two glowing red eyes studied her through the black

smoke pouring in from the smashed windows. There was only evil and hunger in those eyes; they promised pain and a slow death.

Fuck.

She shot to her feet, stumbling slightly as she took a few steps back. The creature followed and matched her step for step.

Another Valfae.

This one seemed bigger than the others, more intelligent in the way it prowled towards her, copying her, its eyes taking in every detail. It's claws and fangs were sharper too.

Turning quickly on her heels, Rexah bolted towards the kitchen and closer to the servant entrance. Her heart was beating so fast in her chest she could hear her blood pumping in her ears.

Focus Rexah. One foot slightly out of place and you're dead.

Another thought found its way into her mind. What would she do if she managed to escape? Where would she go? These beasts wouldn't simply just let her flee if she managed to escape the castle grounds, they would tear after her, hunt her down until they had her in their claws.

After throwing the kitchen door open and slamming it against the wall, Rexah flew through the room. Relief flooded through her for a second when the door to the servant's quarter came into view just up ahead.

The Valfae was close enough she could hear it grunting and growling behind her. Her legs were already screaming at her to stop, but she couldn't – not when the door that would grant her freedom was within reach.

She pushed her legs to go that bit faster and the burning sensation of muscle fatigue intensified. Only once she knew she was safe would she deal with the consequences her body suffered. Five more steps and she would be at the door; each step seemed like an eternity to take, the door feeling as though it was moving further and further away from her the closer she got.

Finally, she was there, her hand outstretched, fingertips brushing against the brass door handle when she felt the full weight of the Valfae crash into her from behind, smashing her through the door.

Rexah slammed into the ground face first, her cheek scraping along the concrete of the path. Her dagger slid away from her, escaping her grasp, as pieces of the now shattered door rained down on her. The pain that spread through her head and cheek was intense, and she rolled onto her back, groaning at the aching protest of her body.

The Valfae was quick and wasted no time. Rexah had no chance to move out of the way, and all she could do was watch the creature raise its razor-sharp claw and swipe it down with wicked speed, slashing her.

The sound of her dressing gown and nightdress ripping was almost lost under the horrifying scream that left her mouth, a noise she'd never herself make before, as the talons shredded the skin of her shoulder and clavicle.

White hot pain flashed through her, stunning her as she watched the beast lift its claws to its mouth and taste her blood. Rexah swore she saw its red eyes brighten for a moment.

She had to put some distance between them.

Somehow, she began to drag herself backwards, away from the monster before her, and grab her dagger with a trembling hand. But the Valfae didn't follow her; it was completely enraptured by the taste of her blood that it didn't appear to take notice of her movements.

Rexah took the opportunity to look down at her shoulder and she instantly regretted it. Her clothing had been ripped to shreds and was stained red with her blood. From what she could see through the strips of material, her skin was in ribbons. The contents of her stomach threatened to rise; this wound was serious, and the pain grew worse as each second went by.

A low growl pulled her eyes away from her injury, and she looked up in time to see the creature stalking towards her once more, ready for another taste. The look in its eyes was one full of hunger and pure evil. She didn't have any energy left to get to her feet, or to run, or to fight.

This is it, she thought.

She had always thought she would leave this world how Queen Riona left it, on the battlefield protecting her people and her kingdom. The Gods clearly had a different end for her.

I'll be damned if I let this creature take me down without a fight, she thought as she gripped her blade a little tighter.

The unthinkable happened next as the beast came within a few feet of her; the clouds darkened, and the loud rumble of thunder filled the sky. Rexah's eyes widened as she watched a huge lightning bolt shoot down from the clouds, illuminating the area like that of a firework, and strike the Valfae directly in the centre of its chest. It let out a howling scream, and the Valfae shook violently before it fell to the ground with a loud thump, its chest smouldering from the bolt.

Rexah stared at the Valfae in complete shock; she was sure to meet her death when a bolt of lightning shot down from the sky and killed the creature. She watched it for a few moments to make sure it wouldn't rise again; it didn't, but the danger was far from over, and she knew it.

With the last of the adrenaline that coursed through her blood, she forced herself to her feet, swaying as her wound screamed in protest. The servant entrance was situated at the back of the building so they could enter and exit closest to their nearby living quarters. It was also the section of the castle that was closest to the woodland, and for that, she was grateful.

She returned to her senses only after she'd started running, unaware of her advancement into the forest until she tripped over some fallen branches. She managed to catch herself before she fell, but in turn knocked herself directly into the trunk of a tree. The pain that shot through her almost buckled her knees, but she managed to shove it to the back of her mind and stay on her shaking legs.

Keep moving, that's all you have to do, keep going. It was easier said than done but if she had any chance of getting out of there alive, she had to keep moving.

Rexah didn't know how fast or slow time was moving; she didn't have any sense of direction or know where she was, and the pain in her shoulder only intensified with each step she took. She'd managed to take her dressing gown off and hold it against the wound as best she could, but the bleeding remained heavy, and she clung desperately to consciousness.

A familiar sight came into view, those beautiful blue and indigo flowers, and the glimpse of it made her heart ache. As she passed through them, drops of her blood stained their vibrant petals.

Further along the path, she came to a cliff edge to the left of the trail. Memories flooded her mind of being here with Nesrin when they were younger. Sometimes they would come out here to look out at the view whilst eating those famous pastries, gossiping about the castle staff members or talking about what they had been through together.

Other times she would be here with Ryden; they would sit on a blanket and hold each other as they watched the stars, fantasising about how their lives would be and what the future held for them, how many children they would have, and where they would lead their kingdoms.

Rexah moved closer to the cliff edge, her heart breaking as she took it all in. It was no longer a breathtaking view. Smoke filled the sky so thickly she could hardly make out those sparkling stars.

The castle, her home, was almost completely gone – destroyed. Fire raged, and she could still just about hear the screams of her people and the roars of those beasts. Darkness had truly descended, and what had she done? She'd fled from her home and people like a coward. Her grandmother had told her to do so, but she should have stood her ground and done what she'd always promised, to protect those who couldn't protect themselves.

A thought then entered her mind that almost made her heart explode out of her chest.

Where were Ryden, King Orland, and Nesrin?

She had been so focused on getting herself and her grandmother out of there that no one else had crossed her mind. Even if they had, it was clear her grandmother wouldn't have let her stop for anything or anyone.

Tears built up in her eyes as pain and guilt spread through her like the flames had spread through her home and kingdom. She knew the odds of any of them surviving this attack was slim to none. She didn't know how she had managed to escape, and even so, she hadn't escaped unharmed.

The tears flowed freely down her face as she cried and mourned for her kingdom, her people, and those dear to her she had lost. Her best friend who she had grown up with, the boy who had been her first kiss – her first everything, who was to be her husband – they were gone.

They were all gone.

Families from the village had been completely wiped out; men, women, and children all slaughtered by the Dark Fae and their monsters.

Ripping her gaze away from the place she once called home, she looked down at the wound on her shoulder. No matter how much pressure she'd put on it, the blood kept seeping through. Her skin felt as though it was burning and freezing at the same time; the pain was like nothing she'd ever felt before, and she knew she would never feel anything like it again.

Rexah's legs began to give way beneath her. In an attempt to keep herself upright, she staggered backwards a few steps before her heel caught on the root of a tree, and she went plummeting to the ground.

The force of her back hitting the ground sent a new shock of pain rush through her body causing her to groan weakly. It was then Rexah noticed she had fallen back into a bed of those gorgeous flowers.

A sob escaped her lips. This was it now. She couldn't get back up no matter how hard she tried, no matter how many times she willed her heavy limbs to move. Her dagger lay at her side, her fingertips brushing the hilt. All the adrenaline was gone, all her energy was gone. The pain she felt in her shoulder, her body, had slowly numbed.

A small blessing, she thought.

She knew that wasn't a good sign, but she didn't care anymore. There was nothing left for her in this world, nothing but darkness; the kingdom had fallen and everyone she loved and cared for were gone – soon she would be too.

Her eyes moved to the sky above her. Surprisingly, the smoke hadn't reached this part of it, not yet at least, and the dark night sky was blanketed by shining stars.

They were her most favourite thing in the whole wide world.

As they twinkled, they seemed to glow a little

brighter as if comforting her, inviting her to join them in the heavens. And that's all she wanted. But before her eyes saw no more, before death took her in its eternal embrace, the last thing she saw was a huge, bright bolt of lightning shoot across the sky.

10
KALEN

There was a shift in the air; he felt it in his bones, his magic tingling in his veins. Something had changed enough for him to stop in his tracks. An owl hooted high up in the trees, insects buzzed, and bats clicked as they hung from branches. Thanks to his fae senses, he could hear it all.

"Kalen, what's wrong?" Torbin asked beside him.

Kalen shifted his gaze to his best friend, his brother in all honesty. He knew Torbin wouldn't feel it yet, not until they were closer; Torbin's power was flame, after all. Kalen, however, could manipulate wind and the energy in the air, and the energy surrounding them in that moment was filled with death.

"Something is wrong, I can feel it. The Valfae are

close. We have to keep moving," Kalen said as he began to walk again, this time in the direction his magic pulled him.

Their footsteps were silent, another benefit of their fae heritage, as they moved through the woodland. Kalen's eyes scanned their surroundings, the feeling of unease building with each step he took until the coppery scent of blood filled his nose.

Torbin sniffed into the air around him, his shoulders stiffening as he looked at Kalen. "Blood."

Kalen slid his dagger out from its sheath at his hip, the heavy weight familiar in his hand. "Be on your guard."

Both Fae moved forward, Torbin clutching his own dagger, and followed the coppery scent. The stench grew stronger as they approached, but now it was mixed with the smell of smoke. Crackling of flames filled Kalen's ears as they broke through the trees and onto the dirt path. In the distance, the kingdom of Adorea was in ruins, flame destroying the once magnificent palace.

"Shit," Torbin cursed as they watched from the cliff edge.

Kalen looked around trying to find the source of the blood, and when his dark blue eyes landed on a shape on the ground a few feet away, he darted towards it. As he drew closer, he saw the shape was a woman. She lay bloodied, her clothes shredded, and she was deathly pale.

"Torbin! Over here!" he called out to him as he kneeled to her.

Torbin rushed over and knelt beside him. He peeled back the torn fabric of her clothing, revealing a gruesome injury, and a curse fell from his lips.

Kalen got to his feet and stumbled back as a feeling washed over him, one he'd never felt before. The scent of her surrounded him, not only her blood, but *her* scent. His heart pounded so hard against his chest he thought it might explode through his ribs at any moment. Every inch of his skin tingled as his magic hummed in his blood.

Torbin held his hand over her wound, hovering just above it as his fingertips began to glow, green swirls dancing through his fingers. Along with his fire magic, Torbin was blessed with fae healing power, and Kalen never tired of watching him pull the injured away from death.

"A Valfae did this to her. I can feel the poison in her blood," Torbin told him. "My power can only do so much. We need to get her to a witch."

When Kalen didn't answer, Torbin looked up at him with a frown. "Kalen?"

Kalen blinked a few times before he looked at him. "Let's patch up her wound and get going. She doesn't have long." He could hear her heartbeat, and it was barely there.

"I know that look in your eyes, I've seen it too many times before in our people. You do know who she is, don't you?" Torbin asked, his amber eyes studying him.

Of course he did. She was Rexah Ravenheart, princess and heir to the Kingdom of Adorea, or at least she was.

"I know fine well who she is. The colour of her hair alone gives her away."

Torbin pulled bandages from his bag and wrapped her wound as best he could. "How she managed to get here from the castle is beyond me, especially with a wound like this."

Kalen spotted something glistening in the moonlight beside her. He reached down and picked up a beautiful dagger. It had been stunningly crafted and ended in a wickedly sharp point. He put his own dagger back in its sheath before tying hers to his belt.

"It was fight or flight and by the looks of things she

did both," Kalen said as Torbin finished securing the bandages. "I'll carry her."

Torbin stood up and stepped back as Kalen pulled off his cloak and wrapped it around the dying princess. He lifted her as carefully as he could into his arms, and she didn't make a sound or movement in protest.

That is not good.

"Oakhaven is closest. Merin can help," Torbin said as he rose to his feet. "We must go, now."

With a population of around fifteen, possibly twenty at a push, Oakhaven was one of the smallest villages in the realm, half a day's ride southeast of Adorea. It was the closest village to the edge of the Adorian territory than the castle was or had been. The settlers consisted of mostly farmers, but Merin was a highly skilled witch who had every single known herb in the realm, and she would have what Rexah needed to survive.

Their footsteps were hurried but silent. They would reach their destination quicker than any human on foot, but without a horse it would still take hours. Kalen knew his cloak would mask the scent of her blood long enough for them to reach Oakhaven, he only prayed to the Gods and Goddesses that she would survive the journey.

Every second, every minute, every hour seemed to last an eternity, but at last, Oakhaven came into view, much to Kalen's relief. Torbin had offered to carry Rexah to give him a rest, but he refused, too focused on getting to Merin as quickly as they could.

The soft tones of yellow and orange in the sky revealed sunrise was afoot. They'd covered a good amount of ground in a short space of time, but Kalen was glad it was still dark enough for them to keep hidden in the shadows. The last thing they needed was someone to spot the Adorian princess in his arms.

Merin's home was close to the treeline, situated between a grove of young pine trees. A handwritten sign had been nailed to the little brown gate:

No refunds. No returns. No time wasters, and please close the gate behind you.

The gate creaked slightly as Torbin pushed it open, holding it as Kalen walked through. Magic shimmered in the air around the sowed area, protecting it from thieves. *Very smart,* Kalen thought as he stopped at the front door. Merin was clearly proud of her garden; after all, it was where she grew most of her herbs.

Torbin knocked the red door, looking up at Kalen. "How are we going to pay her for this with no coin?" he asked him quietly.

"We'll figure something out. We always do," Kalen replied as the sounds of numerous locks clicking could be heard through the door.

The door groaned as it was pulled open just enough for them to see a pale blue eye staring back at them. "Well, I'll be damned," a soft female voice said as the door was slowly pulled further open. "Of all the people I was expecting to see today, it wasn't either of you."

"It's nice to see you too, Merin," Torbin replied.

"What brings you to my door at this hour?" she asked as her gaze shifted to Kalen and the woman in his arms.

"May we come in? It's rather urgent, and I don't think it's wise to discuss this on your porch," Kalen told her.

Merin studied the woman in his arms, recognition instantly filling her eyes, taking note of the injury on the girl's face before she stepped back. "Come in."

Both fae stepped inside, the warmth from the fireplace surrounding them, fighting away the cold. The walls were painted a soft shade of cream. Herbs hung plentifully from the ceiling above a table to the right which was filled with an assortment of candles, jars that held only the Gods knew what, and a pestle and mortar. The fireplace was situated next to the table, fire crackling softly within, and a cot was laid out before it.

"Lay her down there," Merin instructed, pointing to the cot as she rushed to the kitchen and collected the things she needed.

Kalen lay her down gently, arranging her posture delicately to make sure she was comfortable. "She was attacked by a Valfae."

The witch walked over carrying a small basket filled with jars and bandages. "How long has it been since she was injured?"

"It's hard to tell. We came across her on our travels and she was already unconscious. Gods only know how long she'd been there," Kalen said, leaning his shoulder against the edge of the fireplace.

Merin pulled Kalen's cloak away, handing it to Torbin, before she carefully peeled back the blood-soaked bandages. "Oh dear."

"Can you help her?" Kalen asked.

Merin nodded, her light brown locks falling forward. "I can, but I don't know how she's still alive.

This wound is severe, I can see right through to the bone."

Kalen and Torbin shared a look. "The castle is in ruins," the former said.

"She was extremely lucky to escape by the sounds of it then," Merin said softly. "A resilient one, our princess."

The jars clinked together as she pulled one out of the basket; she unscrewed the lid and discarded it before scooping out a small amount of an ash-like substance with her fingers. Merin placed her other hand above the pile of ash-like herbs, closing her eyes as she took a deep breath.

White energy began to dance along her fingers as she twisted and twirled them. Kalen and Torbin watched in amazement as the ash lifted, swirling like a storm in her palm. Merin opened her eyes and guided the herbs to Rexah's wounds, letting it fall into them like snow.

Rexah's body jolted, but she didn't wake up as Merin's magic worked with the herbs inside each of the claw marks. The witch's lips moved as she whispered words in a language neither Kalen nor Torbin understood: Witch Word.

It was unknown how long it would take to heal a

wound as severe as that, but they didn't disturb her work to find out. Torbin sat down on the sofa in the corner as Merin worked, and Kalen warmed his hands on the fire. Being outside in the cold without his cloak had left him chilled, not as badly as a human would have been, of course.

"It is done," Merin said half an hour later, sitting back on her heels. She looked up at Kalen, the crow's feet at the sides of her eyes showing she was nearing her elder years.

"Will she survive?" Kalen asked.

Merin rose to her feet. "She will. Like I said, a resilient one our princess. You got her to me just in time. Ten minutes more and she would have passed to the other life."

Kalen's stomach tightened at the thought. *She is of royal blood, it's a miracle she survived, that's all.* He tried to convince himself that's why he felt this way, but he knew fine well that wasn't the reason.

"I will keep her comfortable," Merin told them. "In the meantime, I suggest you both get some rest. You're welcome to stay, but I'm afraid you'll need to sleep on the floor."

"We have slept in worse conditions, thank you for allowing us to stay," Torbin replied, standing up from the sofa.

Merin smiled softly. "I'll make some tea. It will help you relax."

When the witch moved to the kitchen area, Kalen pulled up the armchair from the corner of the room and placed it at the foot of the bed Rexah lay in, but still close enough to the fireplace so he could keep warm. The armchair itself was small for his size, but he wasn't complaining.

Torbin smoothed out his bedroll along the floor, getting himself settled. "What are we going to do now?" he asked Kalen quietly.

"I haven't thought that far ahead yet," Kalen replied, sliding his concerned gaze to his friend.

Torbin's eyes almost mirrored the flames dancing in the fireplace; when he was born, the magical flickering in his irises was a sign he had been blessed with the fire gift, just as Kalen's blue eyes showed he was blessed with the air gift. Sometimes the legends of the fae mistook blue eyes as a sign of bearing the water gift: lighter shades of blue represented water, while darker tones of blue represented air.

"We are going to have to think about what comes next," Torbin said as he sat down on the bedroll.

Kalen sat back against the armchair, no matter how

uncomfortable it was. Torbin was right, they couldn't expect Merin to take her in. But what were they going to do with what looked like the last remaining heir to the Adorian throne?

"What if Queen Aurelia survived?" Kalen suggested.

"You saw the damage, the flames, the ruin. No one survived, no one but her," he said, nodding his head to the princess. "We cannot take her with us, Kalen."

"I know," he replied through gritted teeth. The feeling that had blossomed within him when he'd first saw her, first inhaled her scent, swelled in his chest so much so that he had to take a deep breath to ground himself. "I'm sorry."

Torbin studied him for a few moments. "No need to apologise. We all know what happens when you—"

"Don't say it, Torbin," he said quietly. "Don't even go there."

Merin placed a small tray with three steaming cups of tea upon it onto the small table. "Drink up."

Kalen reached forward and lifted one of the cups. "Thanks, Merin. We need to discuss payment for your services."

The older woman shook her head. "Absolutely not. She is royalty and the Ravenheart family have been nothing but kind and generous to me and Oakhaven. I will take no coin for helping her."

Kalen nodded softly before sipping his tea. "As long as you're sure."

"I am," she replied, drinking her own tea. "Poor girl, only the Gods know how she will get through this."

The road to recovery won't be an easy one, he thought as he studied the sleeping princess. *But the feeling brewing inside me won't let her go on the journey alone, despite the fact that Torbin is right, she cannot come with us.*

"If she's as resilient as you say she is then she will get through it. It'll take time, but she'll get there," Torbin said before taking a long sip of his tea.

"I'm sorry about Vellwynd," Merin said.

Kalen frowned. "How do you know?"

Her lips curled up in a soft smirk. "Witches talk," she said, her smirk slowly falling. "The war has begun it seems."

Vellwynd, Kalen and Torbin's home, had been destroyed a few weeks ago by the Dark Fae and their monsters. The ache in Kalen's chest for his home, his people, and his family still broke through no matter how hard he tried to shove it away.

"It's not just Adorea and Vellwynd," Torbin replied, "the Dark Fae are scattered all across the realm. Every day there is news of another kingdom being brought to its knees, of armies being torn apart in the blink of an eye."

Kalen finished off his tea before setting the cup down on the small table. "Their numbers have grown significantly. They outnumber every army in Etteria."

Merin's face paled. "So, you're saying there's no hope? That all we can do is go into hiding? What about the witch clans? Is there nothing they can do?"

"What we're saying is, as things stand, witches or no, there's no chance in hell anyone can stop them," Torbin replied, his eyes dark.

Kalen shifted his gaze to his fae companion as Merin whispered, "We're doomed."

II

REXAH

Voices echoed in the air around her now and again, both male and female from what she could tell, and they were not familiar to her. She felt as though she were floating in a calm sea, both body and mind surrendering to the feeling of weightlessness.

Pure and absolute tranquillity.

The peacefulness in her soul was nothing like she had ever experienced before, and she welcomed it with open arms. Nothing mattered anymore. Not the kingdom. Not her people. Not even her life.

Is this what death feels like?

She wanted to stay in this blissful feeling for eternity, but that eternity was short-lived. The voices she

153

heard as she drifted in and out of consciousness sounded like they were far away, but she knew they were close to her, whoever they were.

She couldn't make out what they were saying, only the tones of their muffled voices. As hard as she tried to listen, the peaceful feeling once again pulled her under in its comforting embrace.

The sound of movement pulled Rexah from her slumber, enough this time for her eyes to open. Blinking away the stinging sensation in them, she took a moment to wake up and gather her senses. Warmth spread through her from a fireplace to her left, and the blanket covering her was soft and comforting.

Where am I?

Rexah looked down at her wounded shoulder to find it expertly bandaged. Scanning the room, she realised she wasn't alone. An older woman with light brown hair stood in the kitchen area preparing delicious smelling food.

As if feeling eyes on her, the woman looked up and her eyes softened. "You're awake. Thank the Gods."

The woman poured what Rexah could only imagine was soup into a bowl, lifting a cup of water with her free hand, before she hurried over.

"Who are you?" Rexah asked. "Where am I?"

"I am Merindah, but you may call me Merin," said the older woman as she placed the steaming bowl onto the small table. "You are in Oakhaven."

Rexah spotted jars of strange looking liquids, herbs, and candles on a nearby table, and when her brain finally caught up to connect her surroundings with her knowledge, she realised that this woman was likely a witch.

Merin kneeled by Rexah's bedside and handed her the small cup. "Don't drink this too fast. Sip it slowly. The smoke from the fire damaged not only your lungs but your throat too."

The water cooled her throat as she drank it. She coughed a few times as she handed the cup back to her. "How did I get here?"

"That is an interesting story, my dear. Two fae stumbled upon you and brought you here to me," she told her.

"The kingdom, my people – what is left of them?" Rexah asked the witch, afraid of what her answer would be.

The look on Merin's face said it all. Rexah's heart sank; she knew there was no chance of anyone surviving that attack, but she'd had a tiny bit of hope, and now that hope was lost. Her eyes burned with tears that she refused to shed.

"You were in extremely bad shape when you were brought here. You were a breath away from leaving this world, Your Highness," Merin said.

"Please … don't call me that," Rexah mumbled.

Royal blood still flowed through her veins, but she did not want the title anymore. She had no kingdom; her people were gone as were those closest to her. There was nothing left in this life for her. The Gods certainly were cruel.

"I have been taking care of you and tending to your wounds," she told her.

Rexah slowly looked down at herself seeing her nightgown had been removed and replaced with a clean unripped one, the white bandage peeking out from the strap of the gown. "How bad is it?"

"It was bad, but I managed to stabilise you. I'd feared the poison in the Valfae's claws had gotten to you before I could. The Gods were watching over you and have been watching over you ever since," Merin said. "You are tremendously lucky that you did not lose your arm, or your life."

It felt as though she could still taste ash in her mouth. "Can I please sit up?"

Merin rose to her feet and moved behind the princess. Carefully, she placed one hand between Rexah's shoulder blades and the other took Rexah's outstretched hand. "Easy now."

Rexah slowly eased herself into a sitting position with Merin's help. A slight ache spread through her shoulder but thankfully it was nowhere near as excruciating as the wound had been before. She took a few deep breaths to ground herself. "How can I repay you for saving my life and caring for me?"

A smile appeared on Merin's face. "I require no payment from you Your— Rexah."

"There must be something I can do."

Merin sat down on the stool next to Rexah's bed. "Knowing that one member of the royal family survived is enough for me. There is still hope."

"Hope?" Rexah's head snapped to her. "All hope is lost. Those monsters, the Dark Fae, will not stop until they have consumed this entire planet and every living soul on it."

"I am well aware of what the Dark Fae are capable of, but whilst you still breathe there is always hope," Merin said.

"There is nothing I can do. I was helpless against them," Rexah whispered, her chest tightening.

Merin reached over and gently took her hand. "You may have not been strong enough to fight them, but you live, and whilst you live not all is lost."

"You say that as though I have an army hidden away with weapons and the power to defeat our enemies with one swing," Rexah said. "There is nothing left; no weapons, no army, no kingdom; and I think it's best everyone thinks I perished."

It was the truth. Not only was her family gone, but she knew in her heart that King Orland and Prince Ryden had also perished. Another royal family broken. The Adorian army had also been wiped out.

"You're right. I think putting yourself out in the public eye again might not be such a clever idea right now. I think you should try and keep a low profile," Merin said. "Rest and recuperate here for as long as you need to. Whatever happens after that can wait until you are back to your full health and strength."

"The Dark Fae will not wait for me to recover. They will not wait for anyone with my eyes and my hair colour. It's going to be extremely difficult not to be noticed," Rexah replied, lifting a strand of her dark locks that shone with a flash of violet.

"I can make potions that will help you to disguise yourself. They will change any part of your appearance that you want it to. In this case the colour of your hair and your eyes." Merin got to her feet and walked over to the table with all the jars atop it. "All you have to do is picture what you want to look like as you drink it."

Rexah watched as she rummaged through the jars until she lifted a small vial. It was filled with a shimmery silver liquid. "Are you sure it's safe?"

Merin grinned at her. "Perfectly. It lasts for a full day."

She slowly began to push herself up to her feet from the bed. "I'd like to use your bathing chamber if that's all right?"

Merindah's eyes softened, and she nodded. "Of course," she said before guiding Rexah towards a door to the back of the room. They walked at a pace that Rexah had set for herself. Her legs were stiff and sore, and aches and pains littered her whole body.

"I will be right here. Call for me when you are ready," Merin said softly.

Once she was alone in the bathing chamber, she sat down on the edge of the bathtub, catching her breath and willing her heart to stop beating so fast in her chest.

Merindah was right when she said she had to build up her strength again; she felt so weak and defenceless;

but she had to remember that no matter the horrors that she'd experienced, she had survived.

The bathing chamber walls were coated a deep green. It wasn't terribly small; it was functional but nothing like her private bathing chamber at the castle. Her eyes closed at the thought of what she had lost, who she had lost, and grief threatened to grip her tightly with a promise to crush her.

Somehow, she found the strength to push herself to her feet. Leaning her hands on the small sink before her, she looked into the little mirror that had been hung on the wall. The person looking back at her was a stranger. This wasn't her – it couldn't be.

Her hair fell limply by her shoulders, tangled in areas, it's usual shine dulled. It was clear Merin had given her a bed bath as her skin was clean from dirt but not free from the discoloration of bruises. Several of them covered her arms in patches, and her right eye was a nasty shade of black and blue with a gruesome looking graze that went from the side of her forehead down to her cheek.

Flashbacks of the Valfae crashing into her and sending her flying to the ground played in her mind, making her grip the edges of the sink tighter. The feeling of the concrete scraping against the soft flesh of her face was all too raw, the sound of the beast's roar still echoing in her ears.

Pulling herself from those horrific memories, her eyes trailed down once again to her bandaged shoulder. She had to look; she had to know what was under there.

With trembling fingers, she pulled the strap of the dress down and slowly unwrapped the bandage. The material fell from her hand as she took in the sight. Much to her surprise, the gruesome wound was now almost fully healed. All that remained were three pinkish claw marks that she knew would leave her skin scarred.

"It's all going to be worth it; I am going to be the luckiest man alive because you will be my wife."

Rexah's eyes burned with tears once more as Ryden's voice filled her mind.

"Sorry princess, you know I can't help myself around you."

She would never hear his voice again, see that perfect smirk, or be his wife; Nesrin wouldn't help her throughout the day or eat pastries with her; Zuko would never correct her for dropping her left elbow again; and Queen Aurelia would never fuss over

Rexah's unladylike activities, never see her grow into the woman she was supposed to become.

No, I refuse to believe they're gone. This can't be how the story ends, it can't, she thought as she stared at the stranger in the mirror, the girl who somehow survived.

Once Rexah pulled herself together and saw to her needs, Merin helped her sit down on the edge of the cot. The bowl of soup was still warm in her hands when Merin gave it to her, and Rexah whispered her thanks. Just as she lifted the spoon to her lips, the door to the hovel was pushed open and two tall figures stepped inside.

Rexah's heart began to thunder in her chest as she took in the sight of them. These were her saviours, their sharply pointed ears giving them away. Both were dark haired, but one had stunning amber eyes where the other had mesmerising blue ones.

"Oh, you're awake," Amber Eyes said as he closed the door behind him.

"Did you get what I asked you to?" Merin interjected.

Blue Eyes lifted his hands, containers in both. "Yes, milk and honey as requested," he said, his voice deep and husky.

Involuntarily, her toes curled at the sound of him, and she shifted uncomfortably in her seat. Merin nodded to him and walked over, taking the containers from him before heading to the kitchen.

Rexah set her bowl and spoon down on the table, trying to ignore the way his voice affected her. "I believe a thank you is in order. Merin told me it was both of you who saved my life."

Amber Eyes walked closer. "No need to thank us. We wouldn't have left you there. I'm Torbin. It's an honour to meet you."

"Likewise, Torbin," she said before her gaze shifted to his friend who had walked to the fireplace and leaned his shoulder against it.

"I'm Kalen," he told her.

Rexah's eyes lingered on him, taking in the white scar that ran from just above his left eyebrow, through the eyebrow itself, and ended just below his eye. His black hair stopped at his shoulders, half of it pulled back into a small braid, the other half left in loose soft waves.

Quickly, she tore her gaze from him as Merin returned from the kitchen.

"They've been rather helpful to me these last twenty-four hours. I might just keep them." Merin smirked as she sat down next to Rexah on the cot, earning a chuckle from Torbin.

"As much as we'd love to stay and be at your beck and call, we do have somewhere to be," Kalen said, folding his strong arms across his broad chest.

"If you have somewhere to be then why have you lingered?" Rexah asked.

Torbin warmed his hands on the fire. "Because we wanted to make sure you were okay. I know everything is still so raw, and you won't know what your next step is, but we can help you."

Rexah shook her head. "No offence, but I don't need any help. I'll figure something out."

"At least think about it. We leave first thing in the morning," Kalen told her. "It's up to you if you want to come with us or not."

"I don't even know you," Rexah said, her eyes narrowing slightly. "You might think you know me, but you don't."

Rexah swore she saw Kalen's eyes darken slightly as a small smirk spread across his lips.

"You're right, but we mean you no harm. If we did then we would have left you there to die," Torbin said softly.

She was quiet for a moment, her eyes moving to Merin who smiled at her. She looked to Torbin. "Where are you going?"

"Unfortunately, that's a secret," Kalen replied before Torbin could.

Rexah arched an eyebrow. "So, you want me to go with you, but you won't tell me where you're going?"

It was Merin who spoke next. "Gentlemen, give the lady some breathing space. Remember how you felt when your home was destroyed by those monsters."

Rexah's heart pounded as she looked from Merin to her saviours. *Their home was destroyed by the Valfae too.*

"I'm so sorry," Rexah whispered to them.

Torbin's eyes softened. "We are so sorry for your home too. We want you to know that you're not alone in this."

Rexah swallowed the lump in her throat before continuing to eat the soup. "The last thing I need right now is anyone feeling sorry for me."

She could feel Kalen's eyes burning a hole into her soul, but she didn't look at him. If she let herself feel the grief, even for a split second, then there would be no coming back. So, she made sure it was in a box, locked up tight, and shoved it deep within.

"There's no need to make any decisions right now," Merin said softly beside her. "You've been through a trauma, let yourself process."

Rexah set the half empty bowl on the table before rising to her feet. "Excuse me."

She slowly made her way towards the door, grabbing a spare cloak from the hook beside it, before walking out into the chilly evening air. The cloak was soft against her skin as she pulled it carefully around her, a slight ache pulsing in her shoulder. Stars began to twinkle in the darkening sky.

How did this happen? My grandmother told me everything was under control, that the Valfae were being monitored, she thought as she searched for an explanation. *The monsters were being watched, but so were we.*

That last thought sent an involuntary shiver sliding down her spine like wet paint on a wall. *This whole time we weren't the hunters, we were the prey.*

12

The next day, when the two fae left to explore the village and stock up on a few things for their journey, Rexah stood with Merin at her witch table, watching as the older woman talked her through how to make the disguising potion. Rexah took a mental note of the ingredients that went into the mortar. Bloodroot, rosemary, and lemongrass was all that was required. *I thought it would be more complicated than that,* she thought as she peered into the mortar.

"I know you won't have a pestle and mortar with you whenever you feel ready to go back out into the world, so crushing the ingredients up with your hands will do just fine," Merin told her.

Rexah nodded softly. "What about the ingredients? Will I be able to source them easily?"

"Of course, I'll make sure you're stocked up before you leave, but yes, all the components are easy to buy and find in the woodlands," she replied. "But there is one ingredient that you won't be able to obtain."

"And which one is that?"

"Magic," Merin said. "I will need to gather some of my magic into a vial. The potion won't work without it."

Rexah's eyes followed her as she went to the kitchen to grab some vials from one of the cupboards before she flicked her gaze back to the table, studying all the different herbs. Witches always fascinated her growing up – in all honesty, everything outside of royal life did.

Merin made her way back to Rexah's side and placed the small containers on the table, keeping hold of one of them tightly. Taking a deep breath, she closed her eyes, her lips moving as she whispered in the language of the witches. White energy emanated from her fingertips and flowed down into the glass vial like a waterfall of starlight.

"Wow," Rexah whispered as Merin placed the lid on the container. "That's amazing."

Merin smiled at her. "For the potion to work, all

you need is one drop of magic. Nothing more and nothing less."

She nodded as she watched her add one drop of magic into the mortar. The crushed ingredients bubbled and liquified into a shimmering silvery substance.

Magic is incredible.

"The potion is now ready for use," Merin told her as she filled the other empty vials on the table with it. "Like I said before, it lasts for a full day. The bloodroot will keep your disguise safe; the rosemary will ensure the magic within is kept calm, and the lemongrass will magnify the power behind whichever changes you make to your appearance."

"Thank you, Merin. I appreciate everything you've done for me," Rexah said quietly. "I wish you would let me repay you."

The wrinkles around Merin's eyes became more prominent as she grinned. "Nonsense. Your family have done more than enough for our little village. I'm honoured to help you."

Oakhaven was one of the smallest villages in Adorea, mostly occupied by farmers who sent milk and other necessities to the castle. Her grandmother paid them generously for the produce in addition to a bonus at the end of the year – a thank you for all their hard work.

"Can I try and make more of the potion? I want to know I can do it correctly," Rexah said.

"Of course, on you go."

Rexah cleaned the mortar before she picked up the jar labelled 'bloodroot' and picked out a few of the small flowers. After dropping them into the bowl, she repeated the same steps with the rosemary and lemongrass. Rexah set the last jar down on the table once more and lifted the pestle.

"What happened to the castle?" Merin asked softly beside her. "How did it happen?"

Rexah swallowed the lump in the back of her throat as she slowly crushed the ingredients together. "They attacked during the night; all I know is that it was before midnight because the Night Witches were forced to retreat, not yet at full power. I've never seen anything like it."

"Did anyone escape?" she asked.

"No, not that I know of," Rexah replied, her stomach churning and chest tightening. "The castle was in ruins, fire swept through it like a hurricane. The Queen told me everything was under control and they were being monitored. It was a trap; I see that now. Whilst we focused on the monsters they drew our attention to, others came at us whilst our backs were turned."

"An ambush," Merin said. "If that's the case then the Valfae would have killed the soldiers before they knew what was happening."

The sound of cracking stone filled the room, and Rexah looked down to find the mortar cracked in half. Her eyes widened. "Forgive me."

Merin's eyes softened as she gently took the mortar and pestle from her. "It's okay, a smart witch has more than one of these," she replied with a sympathetic smile.

"My grandmother told me to go to Dorasa. She said I would find all the answers to my questions there," she told her. "I've never been there before, so I'm confused as to why she'd tell me to go there of all places."

South of Oakhaven, Dorasa was a five-day ride on horseback. From the map in her mind, she remembered that it was a fairly big town with its own port. She'd read that not many ships could be anchored in the port, four ships at most could sit comfortably together at one time, but that was about as much as she could recall of the place. She needed to get there as soon as possible and find out why it was so important.

"Go to Dorasa, you will find all your answers there."

Tears built up in her violet eyes once more. *"Run, my darling."*

Shoving the tears back, Rexah cleared her throat. "I must find out. I need to go to Dorasa."

Merin placed her hand on Rexah's upper arm. "You don't need to make any hasty decisions. Take all the time you need to process, to heal."

Rexah studied her pale eyes. "I don't need time to process or heal."

"That's your grief talking. Trust me, taking a few days to let everything sink in will help you in the long run," Merin replied.

"I'll make some tea," Rexah said, moving to the kitchen.

Deep down she knew at some point she would need to let herself feel the full force of her grief, but now wasn't the time. She didn't want anyone's pity; she didn't want anyone's help. All she wanted was for things to go back to the way they were.

An hour later, the door to the hovel creaked open, and Kalen and Torbin stepped in; the latter carried a neatly folded pile of clothing in his hands, a generous pile of garments in a variety of colours and fabrics, indeed.

"We thought you might need new clothing. We spoke to one of the farmers whose daughter passed to the other life a few months ago, and he kindly provided some of her clothes for you," Torbin said, holding out the pile to her. "We gave him some coin of course."

Rexah rose from the armchair and took them from him, her eyes soft. "Thank you, Torbin."

Kalen pulled his cloak off and hung it up, the powerful muscles in his back shifting under his shirt as he did. Rexah tore her gaze from him, trying to ignore the feeling blossoming in her stomach at the sight.

Rexah sat back down, placing the clothes on the table before settling back. "When do you leave?"

"We've managed to acquire some horses from the stables down the road, but they won't be ready until tomorrow," Kalen replied, his voice washing over her like a wave of warm water.

"I'll make another pot of stew for dinner," Merin

told them. "It's been nice having company these last few days."

"I'll give you a hand." Torbin smiled at her before following her to the kitchen area.

Rexah and Kalen were left alone, and for a few moments neither of them spoke.

"I'm truly sorry for what happened to your home, your people, and your grandmother," Kalen said, finally breaking their silence.

Rexah looked up at him but didn't reply. Her body felt numb whenever she thought about it. It still felt so surreal, and she wondered if she'd ever come to terms with it.

"How did your potions lesson go earlier?" he asked, thankfully changing the subject.

"It was fine. The potion isn't as complicated as I anticipated," she replied. She couldn't help noticing the way the firelight from the fireplace danced along his strong jaw, licking up his cheek bone. She shifted in her seat, blinking aggressively in attempt to get a grip of herself.

Gods Rexah, what's wrong with you?

Kalen didn't seem to notice as he said, "I'm glad to hear it."

They sat in a few moments of surprisingly comfortable silence before he spoke again. "The offer still stands: if you'd like to come with us, you're more than welcome," he said. "It's your choice."

"I appreciate it, but I think I'll be just fine on my own," she told him even though she didn't believe her own words.

His deep blue eyes studied her. "What's your plan? Where do you think you'll go next?"

No way am I telling him about Dorasa. Sure, he and Torbin saved my life, but that could have been for their benefit, for their own agenda. She shrugged softly. "I haven't decided yet."

Kalen nodded, his dark hair falling into his eyes. Shoving it back with his long fingers, he said, "We leave at first light tomorrow, if you change your mind."

Rexah moved her gaze to the flickering fire. As tempting as their offer was, Dorasa was her main goal.

Rexah didn't speak much during dinner, instead she opted for listening to the conversation flowing freely between the other three. Once they finished eating and the dishes were washed and dried, they settled down for the night. Rexah watched the fire dancing in the fireplace as she lay on the cot. Merin was in her bedroom at the back of the hovel next to the bathroom, and the fae had opted to camp out in the garden. Merin's home wasn't big, so the previous night had felt a little crowded.

She felt her grief pushing against the box she kept it in, like a monster scratching at its cage, desperate to be released. It was times like this, when she was alone, that her own thoughts were too loud in her head. Shoving the blanket off herself, Rexah stood up from the cot. *I can't take this anymore. I need to get out of here.*

The clothes from the farmer fit her like a glove; she donned a deep red tunic, black breeches, and a pair of black boots that Merin had kindly given her. The witch had also prepared a bag of potions and ingredients for whenever she was ready to leave.

I wish I didn't have to leave like this, but I can't stay here a moment longer, she thought as she picked up the bag and lifted her dagger from its hiding place in one of the drawers before securing it on the belt at her hip.

Rexah moved silently into the kitchen and grabbed a few food items for the journey, shoving them in beside the vials. It wasn't until she moved by the mirror leaning against the wall next to the window that she remembered about her appearance.

Shit.

Reaching into the satchel, she pulled out one of the potions and quickly drank it down. It didn't taste great, but she soon forgot about it as she concentrated on what she wanted to look like. Her eyes widened as she watched her black hair almost melt off, being replaced with a beautiful shade of golden brown. Her once violet eyes now hazel. It was a shock to see herself like this, but it was necessary for her survival.

Moving to the door, she pulled the black cloak she'd now claimed as her own off the hook and wrapped it around herself, clipping it closed. She looked back over her shoulder, taking a few moments to memorise the hovel. She had a feeling she wouldn't be back for a while, if at all.

The door made no noise as she slowly pulled it open and closed it behind her. Scanning the area, she spotted the two fae camped within the forest next to the hovel, both curled up around the small fire, fast asleep.

I have to be extra careful, any noise I make, no matter how slight, they'll pick it up with their fae hearing, she thought as she cautiously headed for the gate at the end of the garden. The hooting of owls and the insects chirping would help muffle her sounds a little, but she'd studied the fae enough not to underestimate them.

Once she was out onto the main road, she looked over her shoulder and felt her body relax seeing both fae hadn't moved. Wasting no time, she hurried down the dirt road towards the stables. It wasn't huge but it was enough to hold five horses from what she could see.

"Can I help you lass?" a rough voice asked to her left. Turning, she saw a short man with a round belly stood in the doorway watching her – the stable owner.

"Apologies, I'm here to collect a horse," she replied.

"Which one?" he asked. "Has it been paid for?"

Rexah nodded. "Yes, I'm travelling with two fae, and they secured two horses with yourself. We've decided that I'll ride on ahead."

She felt awful for lying, but technically they'd offered for her to go on the journey with them, and the horse had been paid for, so it wasn't stealing either.

"Aye, I remember them," he said as he stepped into the stable and walked over to one of the pens. "This is one of yer steeds."

Rexah watched as he opened the gate and urged the horse out. "Do you need a hand up lass?"

Without a reply she pulled herself up onto the horse

with ease. To her surprise, no pain erupted through her shoulder. She took the reins in her hands, the leather of them only slightly cracked. These reins had hardly been used.

"I guess that answers my question then." He chuckled. "He will keep ye right lass. He's one of the best. Just make sure you treat him good, and he won't steer ye wrong."

"I will, thank you so much," she replied softly. "Tell my fae companions I said thank you."

He grinned and nodded before his face fell into a look of pure confusion. "What?"

Taking a deep breath, Rexah dug her heels into the side of the horse, and she was off, leaving the stable hand behind. It had been so long since she'd last ridden a horse; she'd grown used to riding in the royal carriage. The broken cobblestone street gave way to the dirt path of the surrounding forest as Rexah headed into the unknown.

13

Brywen was Rexah's next destination. It was the nearest town to Oakhaven, around a two, maybe three-day ride depending on the weather and resting. It had a population of around five thousand, livelier than Oakhaven that was for sure. Brywen was a town mostly known for supplying a bed and a warm meal for any passing travellers, as well as it's shady dealings – but that was no matter, Rexah did not plan to stay for long, even one night was too long for her.

Rexah was moving quicker than she expected; the weather was fair, and it thankfully hadn't rained. She always ensured she found the perfect spot to rest overnight, out of sight with plenty of cover from the canopy. The last thing she needed right now was to be spotted and robbed of her possessions – or worse.

On the first night, she lay on her back in the grass staring up at the canopy willing herself to fall asleep. A small gap in the trees let the moonlight shine through, and she could see the beautiful night sky above, the stars twinkling their greeting to her like an old friend, comforting her.

"We don't have a choice." Ryden's voice suddenly echoed in her mind. *"But if we did have a choice, I would still choose you, Rex."*

Tears built up in her eyes as she remembered that night. *"I would choose you too."*

She closed her eyes and let the tears flow down her face. She didn't try to stop them. Rolling onto her side she silently wept for Ryden, for the Queen, and for her people. None of what had happened felt real, and if it wasn't for the wound on her shoulder as proof then she wouldn't have believed any of it occurred. She could try and pretend, even if only for a short while.

The events of that night haunted her, and she had a feeling they would for the rest of her life. Had there been signs clear as day that there was going to be an attack? Should she have been more vigilant?

Of course, she should have. Instead, she let herself

get lost in the planning of her wedding, eating pastries with Nesrin, and fooling around with Ryden. She let herself think everything was under control, and her grandmother let her think that too. She should have worked harder in her training with Zuko, maybe she wouldn't have been so weak against the Valfae if she had. He would have been so disappointed in her.

A small blessing that he wasn't here to see my cowardliness, she thought.

Soon she finally drifted off to sleep, surrendering into the nightmare of her kingdom falling all over again.

After two days of travel, through the darkness Rexah could see the lights of Brywen flickering in the distance, and her shoulders sagged slightly in relief.

"Almost there, boy. You've been so good. I'll ensure they give you extra hay," she said, leaning forward to the horse's ear. "Maybe even a carrot."

The huff of approval from the horse made Rexah grin, and she urged him to move forward. The sound of his hooves was soft on the dirt road. She had never been to this town before, but her grandmother had told her stories about it when she was younger, and they had given her more than a few nightmares. She had vowed never to visit it, but here she was now about to break that vow.

Rexah wasn't the best at judging distances, but if she had to make a guess, she'd wager they would reach Brywen in around half an hour. The thought of being inside where it was warm, the mere idea of sleeping in a bed, made her want to get there faster. She knew it wouldn't be the comfiest of beds, but she wasn't going to argue after sleeping on a bedroll out in the cold for two days.

Twenty minutes later, a clearing up ahead in the trees came into view. So close. *Thank the Gods,* she thought, taking a deep breath of the crisp night air into her lungs.

A twig snapped to her left sending her heart into a fluttering mess. *It's just the wildlife,* she told herself. But when the sounds of footsteps grew louder, she no longer believed that to be the case at all, and the hairs on the back of her neck stood on end.

With only her dagger, she knew she was in trouble, but that didn't mean she wouldn't go down without a fight. She'd put Zuko's training to good use if need be. Willing her heartbeat to steady itself, she urged her horse to keep going and maybe pick up the pace a bit. The footsteps faded, and she looked back to make sure no one was there. Thankfully, the road was empty.

A sigh of relief left her lips, but the reassurance she felt was short-lived; she turned her gaze forward once more and saw a man standing in the middle of the road with seemingly no intention of getting out of the way. Her hazel eyes widened as she pulled on the reins, and her horse halted a few feet away from the man.

He was scruffy looking, and his clothes were nothing more than dirty rags covered in holes. The moonlight shone off his hairless head. "Look what we have here," he taunted, his voice sounding like he'd swallowed rusty nails. "The Gods have been very gracious to us tonight boys."

Boys.

Another man appeared a few feet away to her right; he was in similar attire to the bald fellow in front of her, only this man had hair, a deep blonde that was likely bright before a lack of care and personal hygiene caused it to lose its shine.

Rexah turned her attention forward once more. "I

urge you to use your better judgement, to step aside and let me pass, sir."

Both men let out a roar of laughter. "Did you hear what she just called you Dean?"

The man, Dean, grinned at Rexah, showing he was missing more than a few teeth, and the ones he still had, were not in the greatest of shape. "Oh, sweetheart."

"I mean it." She warned him, her grip on the reins tightening slightly. "Let me pass and no harm will come to either of you."

"Feisty. I love it when they talk back. It gets the blood pumping," Dean said as he smirked, nodding his head.

Suddenly a hand clasped Rexah's left forearm and she was yanked off the horse. Another man who she hadn't noticed before now stood far too close for comfort, and when he grinned at her, only a handful of yellow-brown teeth appeared – she didn't know how she didn't vomit in his face right there and then.

"Come on, lovely. We will ensure you enjoy it as much as we will." The almost toothless man snickered.

"Hurry up, Sid!" the blonde one whined impatiently.

Dean chuckled as she was dragged further under the trees and off the dirt road, struggling against Sid's surprisingly tight grip the whole way. "Patience, Zak.

Besides, I get the first shot. You can have your turn when I'm done with her."

Rexah could taste the vomit now in the back of her throat. Pain spread through her back as she was shoved roughly against the trunk of one of the trees. She gritted her teeth. "You're making a huge mistake. If you value your lives, you will let go of me!"

She winced in pain when Sid ripped her hood back, catching some of her golden-brown hair in his grip too.

Thank the Gods for Merin's potion.

Sid moved to her right side and Zak moved to her left, sadistic grins spread across their dirty faces. Both men held her arms tightly in their grip whilst Dean prowled forward towards his prey. It was clear that they had done this before, and they enjoyed it.

Gods, he smells awful.

The smell that emanated from Dean was almost enough to make her pass out. Then again, when was the last time he had the opportunity to bathe? When had any of them for that matter?

"You still have time to walk away. Don't do this."

That stupid smirk spread across Dean's face once again as he grasped her chin with his fingers, making her look at him. "I'm right where I want to be, or at least I will be in a few moments." That earned a chuckle from the other two.

A gasp left Rexah's lips as Dean took hold of her cloak and ripped it from her shoulders. It fell to the ground in two separate pieces. The look of complete hunger and lust that filled Dean's eyes made her shudder. She tried to swallow down the bile that rose in her throat as she felt his other hand slide up her waist to cup her breast.

"I can't wait to taste you, to feel you. Don't fight it. You might enjoy this sweetness, I know I sure will," Dean grunted as he leaned down.

Rexah waited until he was close enough, squeezed her eyes shut, and thrust her head forward, smacking her forehead into his face. A satisfying crunch sounded as the bone in his nose broke. Quickly she brought her foot up and kicked him hard in the stomach, sending him flying back onto the ground.

Wasting no time, she gathered all the strength she could muster in her arms and pulled Sid and Zak towards each other. The cracking sound their skulls made when they collided with each other was sickening, but Rexah didn't have time to dwell on that as she focused her energy on ignoring the burning pain that shot down her still healing shoulder.

The unconscious men crumpled to the ground in a heap giving Rexah the chance to straighten herself and assess her surroundings: Dean was still on the ground, clutching at his stomach and his bleeding nose, Sid and Zak were not waking up from their slumber any time soon, and she spotted her horse huddled underneath a few of the trees on the other side of the road.

Thank the Gods.

Adrenaline coursed through her veins as she ran as fast as she could away from her attackers and towards her horse. Her lungs burned and her legs ached, pleading with her to stop, but she pushed them to go faster. All she had to do was get into town.

One foot touched the dirt road before someone's fingers gripped the back of her hair from the roots and pulled her backwards. A cry left her lips as fiery-hot pain spread across her cheek caused by the back of Dean's hand, and she was thrown to the ground.

"You stupid bitch!" he roared, kicking her in the stomach. The lust was no longer present in his eyes; it had been replaced with a burning psychotic rage.

"Now, that's really no way to talk to or treat a lady, is it?" a new male voice said from behind him, a *very familiar* male voice.

Dean had no time to react whatsoever, and all

Rexah could do was watch as he suddenly went limp and collapsed to the ground beside her. Wide-eyed, Rexah stared at the now snoring Dean next to her, an egg-shaped lump on the back of his bald head.

Slowly her gaze made its way from the comatose man to her saviour, and she was met with the most striking and familiar dark blue eyes. Every inch of her tingled as she took in the sight of Kalen; the sharp points of his ears peeked out of his dark hair, and the white scar that ran from his left eyebrow seemed more noticeable and beautifully majestic in the moonlight.

"Rexah?" he asked quietly.

The humiliation set in quickly; she had been staring at him for only the Gods knew how long. She also realised that he was now kneeling, a concerned look in his beautiful eyes.

"Sorry," she whispered breathlessly, trying to stop herself from blushing.

"Here, let me help you up," he said, reaching for her. He was gentle as he wrapped his arm around her and helped her to her feet, his arm stilling around her waist to steady her. She watched as he undid his cloak, and once she found her footing he wrapped it around her shoulders.

"Won't you get cold?" Rexah asked.

He gave her a ground shaking smile. "I'll manage."

His scent surrounded her. Cedarwood and berg-amot with … was that a hint of sage? It took everything in her not to deeply inhale that gorgeous combination. What in the world was wrong with her?

Kalen studied her, searching for injuries. His eyes lingered on her cheek which she was certain was already bruising. "Are you hurt anywhere else?"

Rexah shook her head softly. "No, no I'm fine."

He then looked into her eyes. "You stole my horse."

"I … the horse had been paid for, so technically it wasn't stolen," she replied.

"Yes, with my coin."

Rexah watched him. "I merely borrowed it, then."

Kalen's face was serious for a few moments before his lips tugged up into a smirk. "You're lucky we were passing by when we did."

She looked around and she spotted Torbin standing by their horses, keeping hold of the reins. "It didn't take you long to find me."

The smirk grew on his face. "We're fae, darling. We were born with natural tracking abilities far more superior than that of a human. I followed your scent."

Rexah's traitorous heart stumbled in her chest.

Darling.

She cleared her throat as she walked around him and towards her horse. She rubbed her throbbing cheek. "I must be on my way," she said, trying to calm her erratically beating heart.

"Where are you headed?" Torbin asked her. He sounded a little tired. *Possibly due to trying to catch up with me,* she thought.

"Brywen," she replied, taking the reins from Torbin and gently patting the horse's neck.

"Any particular reason you chose Brywen of all places?" Torbin asked her.

Rexah shrugged her uninjured shoulder. "It's the closest town, and I'd like to sleep in an actual bed for a night."

"It just so happens we are also headed that way. Can we escort you?" Kalen asked as he drew closer.

She groaned internally. "You both saved my life, twice. I'll be forever grateful for that but forgive me if I still don't trust you."

"It's understandable but going into Brywen alone at night isn't the safest course of action," Kalen said.

Rexah shifted her gaze to him. "I can take care of myself."

Kalen rolled his eyes. "Oh, I can see that darling, but sometimes everyone needs help."

"How long would it take to get there from here?" she asked.

"Around fifteen minutes, give or take," Kalen answered. His voice was deep and did things to her that would have made her blush if she hadn't forced herself not to.

"All right, fine. You can escort me to Brywen, but after that we go our separate ways." She swung herself up onto the horse before she could change her mind, her body slowly calming down from her attack. "Let's go. I don't want to be out here any longer than necessary."

Kalen and Torbin were silent as they mounted their horses great ease – thanks to their fae strength – and Rexah was almost certain she saw a grin on the former's face as he did so.

They set off down the dirt road, Kalen to her right and Torbin to her left. Companionship was unexpected, but all she cared about was getting off this dirt road as quickly as she could and arriving at Brywen in one piece.

14

They'd left their horses at the stables which were situated just inside the main gate, and Kalen had given the stable hand a few extra coins to ensure the horses were properly taken care of.

Two guards had been stationed at the main gate and another two stood ahead at the inner gate. None seemed to care who entered the town and who left; they hadn't given Rexah and the others a second glance and were more interested in the card game they were in the middle of.

Reliable guards, indeed.

The town was alive with people as they entered through a second set of gates, and it wasn't a surprise to Rexah that the streets were filled to the brim; from what she could remember from her studies there weren't many rules here. If you were robbed or attacked no one would help you; none of the guards would come to your aid and throw your attacker in jail. You had to be overly cautious in this town and keep a tighter grip on your coin bag.

The lack of security was blatantly obvious as they made their way down the lantern lit cobblestone street: revellers from the taverns poured out onto the street; some had their arms around each other's shoulders, singing and laughing, whilst others were gathered around those who had decided to engage in a fist fight, betting their coin on who would win.

When the crowd got a little too excited, Rexah felt a strong, steadying hand on the small of her back guiding her out of the way, and she looked up to find that it was Kalen. His lips lifted in a small smile, and they continued walking.

Turning right at the bottom of the street, they came face to face with an open square. Various buildings surrounded it: an inn, a blacksmith, and of course a few more taverns. Rexah was beginning to notice that this place had more taverns than anything else.

"There are other inns around the corner, but – and I mean this with no offence to you – those are places that

aren't meant for ... people who are ... sensitive ... or ..."
Kalen trailed off as he saw the look on Rexah's face.

Her eyebrow lifted as she waited for him to finish his sentence, curious as to what his next choice of words would be.

"What my friend is trying to say is that this inn right here is the best one in town," Torbin interjected, pointing to the building closest to them.

"I will take your word for it," Rexah said, smiling softly at Torbin. The only sources of light were the lanterns scattered around the square and the lights emanating from the inn and two taverns nearby, but she was absolutely certain she saw Kalen's cheeks redden ever so slightly.

"I'm sorry if I've offended you," he said quietly to her. "I didn't mean to."

"It's fine, Kalen. I'm not sensitive." She smiled at him before she walked to the inn.

The sign hanging above the door read, 'The Rusty Nail'.

What a charming name.

The door groaned and creaked as she pushed it open, and Kalen and Torbin followed her in.

The smell of food and ale, along with some other questionable scents, hit her instantly. The serving lounge wasn't huge, but it was a lot bigger than it looked from the outside. Tables were spread out around the room, most of them occupied by drunk men; some were playing cards, a few had fallen asleep still clutching their tankards, and others were sat at tables in the corners of the room, where the shadows seemed to gather, with half naked women on their laps.

Good Gods.

She quickly turned her gaze away when she realised what was happening at those tables.

If this was the best inn, she hated to think what went on in the others around town. She wasn't a prude, but what she had just seen that woman doing in a public space made her blush.

The bar stretched along the length of the far wall, and two barmaids stood behind it, serving a few customers who were seated there. No one batted an eyelid at them as they walked over to the bar. Rexah purchased a room for herself with the coin Merin had put in her bag, and the two fae bought a room to share. Torbin also bought drinks for them.

"Thank you, for everything," Rexah said, picking up what she assumed was a tankard of ale.

"We wouldn't have rode by and left you with those assholes," Kalen replied before taking a sip of his ale. "I don't take kindly to those who think it's acceptable to prey on anyone like that."

Rexah watched as a muscle twitched in his strong jaw. Her heart fluttered when she heard him curse. "I appreciate everything you've done to help me."

"Have you decided where you are headed from here or is this the last stop?" he asked her.

Did she want to share that information with them? She was trying to keep a low profile, and so far, she'd already been close to either being killed or raped or both.

"I haven't decided yet." The lie rolled off her tongue easier than she thought it would. It was a small lie, one that she had to tell.

Torbin's amber eyes softened. "That's under-standable."

"Will you be okay on your own?" Kalen asked.

"I'll be perfectly fine, no need to worry," she replied. "I was caught off guard before. That won't happen again."

Kalen didn't push her any further and nodded. "Well then, I guess this is farewell."

She nodded and looked to Torbin who flashed her a smile, and with a nod of his head he walked to one of the empty tables closest to the wall.

"Safe travels, and if you do decide to stay here then be cautious." Kalen smiled. "People from all sorts of backgrounds like to visit here."

"I will, and safe travels to you too," she replied, returning the smile.

Rexah forced herself not to watch him walk off to join Torbin. She turned back to face the bar, both hands wrapped around her tankard. She'd never had ale before. It didn't look nice, but everyone drank it so it must be delicious, right?

Rexah had been about to take a sip of the horrible looking liquid, but the tankard stopped halfway to her lips when she heard a conversation nearby.

"Yeah, the castle is in ruins now. Heard it was the work of a dragon," said one of the men next to her.

The other male with him scoffed. "A dragon? No, I heard the princess finally lost it and burned the place to the ground. Heard she was all kinds of crazy. A right mouth on her too, a rebel princess."

"Shame she burned with the rest of them. I would have loved to have put that mouth of hers to good use."

Both men chuckled as they clinked their tankards together and said, "cheers".

Rage unlike anything she had ever felt before enveloped her and shot through her veins like lightning. The tankard in her now trembling hand slammed down hard onto the bar with a loud thud causing both men to look at her. She wasn't looking at them, but she felt their eyes on her.

"All right there sweet?" the one furthest away asked her.

An arm snaked its way around her waist and the stench of ale washed over her. "You need a shoulder to cry on love?" the man closest to her said into her ear. "I can put a smile back on that beautiful face of yours."

The boiling rage within her exploded, and it all happened so fast. Rexah turned to the bastard, grabbed him by the nape of his neck, and brought his face down onto the bar. He let out a cry of pain before he collapsed to the floor and did not get back up.

"Gods, what is your problem?!" the other man yelled. He got up, ready to have his turn at her, but the look in her eyes was enough to make him reconsider his actions. He grabbed his friend under his arms and began dragging him out of the inn. "Crazy bitch!" he yelled.

A familiar, gentle hand touched the small of her back, and she quickly looked up at Kalen.

"Are you hurt?"

Rexah didn't say anything. Everyone in the room

had turned their attention to her, and she didn't like it one bit. She walked by him and headed for the staircase. Her heart thundered in her chest as she rushed up the stairs, the steps creaking and groaning as she stood on them. Once at the top, she turned to head down the hallway when someone grabbed her hand, pulling her gently to a stop.

"Wait, please," Kalen pleaded with her.

She stopped walking and leaned her back against the wall. *Gods give me strength.* She had seen red when she'd heard their words. Nothing was stopping her from doing what she'd just done.

"Breathe," he whispered to her.

Rexah looked up and was captured by his dark blue eyes. She could see sincere concern shining in them, so she did as he said and took a few slow deep breaths, calming herself down.

Once her heart and breathing had settled, she looked up at him again. "Why do you care? You don't even know me."

"Like I said before, I hate those who prey on others. What did they say that made you so angry?"

"I don't want to talk about it," she replied bluntly.

Kalen slowly let go of her hand. She hadn't even realised he had still been holding it. "Whatever it was, it was enough to make you knock a fully grown man out with little to no effort," he said.

Rexah's stomach fluttered madly when his fingers gently caressed her cheek.

Gods, was this happening right now or was she dreaming? This had to be a dream.

Kalen's lips tugged up into a heart-stopping smirk and his dark blue eyes brightened. "You're a vicious little thing, aren't you?"

The muscles low in Rexah's stomach tightened and her blood began to sing in her veins. She should have shoved him away, should have knocked him out too for touching her, but she didn't.

"Enjoy the rest of your evening and have a safe journey, wherever it leads you," she said once she found her voice and senses again. She moved away from him, her heart pounding so hard in her chest. She didn't look back; she wouldn't be in control of her actions if she did. Although, with what was happening below her feet with some customers she was sure no one would care.

She looked at the numbers on the doors as she made her way down the dimly lit hallway. She stopped when she got to number eighteen, the number on the key the woman behind the bar had given her. Once she unlocked the door, she walked inside and closed it behind her, locking it quickly. She stood with her back against the door, leaning her head back on it as she took long deep breaths.

Her chest began to tighten as she thought of Ryden. His laugh, his scent, and the way his eyes brightened when he smiled. She'd not been so close to anyone since the last time she'd been with Ryden, and how close Kalen had been to her just now, how he'd touched her cheek, it was all too much.

She didn't realise she was crying until the hot tears slid down her face. Sinking to the floor, she lifted her knees to her chest and buried her face in them.

What she would give for Nesrin to rush in and sit beside her, cry with her, and then tell her to fix her crown and pull herself together; her friend would tell her that she was Rexah Ravenheart and that nothing could keep her down. But what she wanted most of all, what she would give up anything for, would be her grandmother by her side to tell her everything would be all right.

The tears finally stopped after what felt like an eternity. She slowly pushed herself to her feet and looked around the room. It was small, and the only furniture in the room was the double bed, a small table beside the bed with a few candles atop it, and a wardrobe that looked like it was ready to collapse at any moment. To the left, a small mirror hung on the wall above a table, a wash bowl and jug of water placed upon it, and the window to the right of the room looked out onto the empty square. Altogether, the room and atmosphere within it was bleak.

Rexah stepped further into the room, undoing the clip of her cloak. She froze, her hand on the silver clasp.

Shit.

It wasn't her cloak. Her eyes moved down to the dark material that surrounded her; she had forgotten to give it back to Kalen.

Cursing herself again, she pulled the cloak from her shoulders and hung it up on the small hook on the back of the bedroom door. She would return it to him in the morning if he wasn't already gone by then.

After she quickly cleaned herself up as best as she could in the wash bowl, she sat down on the edge of the bed and slowly peeled off the support bandage around her shoulder.

She cleansed her shoulder before applying the salve Merin had made for her. The soothing coldness of it spread through her shoulder as she applied it, and she sighed softly. Merin had told her it would help the scarred tissue and her shoulder joint; it didn't look nice, but the witch had been correct as it had done wonders on her wound.

The fresh bandage was awkward to apply, especially since she had to do it by herself, but she managed it before retiring for the night.

The bed wasn't the comfiest, but after everything that had happened to her that day, she didn't care one bit. All she cared about was the fact that she was indoors and able to sleep in a bed, at least for the night, with no need to worry about wolves or bears eating her or her horse whilst she slept.

She rolled onto her side, her uninjured side, and sighed softly. The moonlight shone in through the window, illuminating the room. The silence was almost deafening, and the walls felt as though they were closing in on her.

Her chest tightened and tears built up in her eyes again. The grief creeped over her once more, slithering from the cage she'd kept it in like a snake, inviting her to fall completely into its embrace. The realisation of just how alone she truly was threatened to overwhelm her, and like a child she pulled the cover over her head, curled up into a ball, and let the tears flow freely until sleep took her.

15

KALEN

The lounge wasn't too crowded, much to Kalen's delight. Small groups of patrons clustered around tables: some ate their breakfast, chatting quietly amongst themselves, others began the daily task of drowning their sorrows, and a few rowdier customers sang drunkenly near the front door, disturbing Kalen's peaceful breakfast.

"I can't wait to get out of this shithole," Kalen murmured to Torbin who sat across from him at the table.

Torbin's lips lifted into a soft smirk. "After we've eaten, we will be out of here."

Kalen had a restless sleep. His dreams were filled

with a certain princess who he couldn't seem to get out of his mind. The chair creaked slightly as he sat back in it. *Get yourself together Kalen. Stay on task.*

"I saw the menu on the chalkboard behind the bar. The variety of food provided here is really good," Torbin told him.

Kalen chuckled. "Your love of food will never cease to amaze me, Tor."

His best friend grinned. "You've got to enjoy the little things in life, Kal. Food is a blessing from the Gods."

Goosebumps flooded Kalen's skin. His blood began to tingle in his veins as a familiar scent drifted towards him on a phantom breeze. Shifting his gaze, the princess who'd filled his dreams stood at the bottom of the staircase next to the bar, her eyes scanning the room until they fell on him.

The rest of the inn disappeared as she walked towards the table; his surroundings blurred and faded until there was nothing left but her; and when she spoke, it took everything in him not to get on his knees before her.

"Good morning, I'm sorry to bother you, but I wanted to give this back to you," she said quietly, holding out the cloak to Kalen.

"Thank you," Kalen said once he found his voice again and took the cloak from her. "Why don't you join us for breakfast?"

"Oh, no thank you. I really should get going," she replied.

"It's not wise to travel on an empty stomach," Torbin commented.

Kalen pulled out the chair next to him. "The food here is really good, I promise." He could feel Torbin smirking at him, but he didn't look away from Rexah.

She hesitated for a moment before she sat down beside him. Food and water were brought to the table. The smell of warm bread and eggs filled the air, and it wasn't until he inhaled that beautiful aroma that he realised just how hungry he was.

"So, you've decided to leave Brywen then?" Kalen asked as he picked up a slice of bread and broke a piece of it off.

Rexah tensed for a moment before she replied, "Yes, it doesn't seem wise to settle down in a town so …"

"Shady?" Torbin suggested as he poured himself a cup of water from the large jug. His amber eyes brightened slightly, seemingly pleased with himself for the suggestion.

"That's one word you could use to describe it," she

said as she helped herself to a slice of bread and a boiled egg.

"There are plenty of towns like this one spread throughout Etteria. The realm isn't full of sunshine and rainbows princess," Kalen said, smirking softly.

Rexah's hazel eyes moved to meet his own. She gripped the fork a little tighter in her hand before she continued eating. "I agree," she said. "But not every town or village is … shady."

Kalen noticed the way she tensed when he'd called her princess. Was it because she liked it, or because it brought those memories of Adorea burning back to her?

Kalen broke off another piece of bread. "Where do you think you'll go from here?"

Rexah shrugged her shoulders softly. "I'll figure that out on the road."

Torbin sipped his water before he said, "We've seen some beautiful places."

"I've always wanted to see the world," Rexah said.

"What's stopped you?" Kalen asked her before shoving another forkful of food into his mouth.

"A lot of things," she replied, sipping her water.

Kalen studied her. She hid her feelings well, he'd give her that, but her eyes betrayed her. They were filled with conflict and worry.

"Fair enough," he said, not pushing her any further.

"What brought you so close to Adorea?" Rexah asked as she ate.

Kalen took a drink from his cup before setting it back down on the table, a sombre look in his eyes. "Our home was attacked and destroyed a few weeks ago, as you know. We're on our way to a safe haven where the rest of our people who managed to flee are waiting for us."

Torbin cleared his throat. "We had no warning," he said, "and they had already destroyed most of our homes before we knew what was happening. We had no time to prepare."

Kalen watched Rexah get lost in her own thoughts once again, her eyes sad and distant.

Before he could stop himself, he placed his hand on hers. "Are you okay?" he asked quietly.

She jumped lightly at his touch, and her gaze shifted to his face. "Yes," she whispered, blinking a few times. To his surprise, she didn't pull her hand away.

"The Valfae have been sweeping through Etteria like a sickness. Their numbers are growing by the day it seems," Torbin said, a calm rage in his voice.

Kalen slowly pulled his hand from Rexah's. "Something needs to be done, but first we must get to our destination."

"Where is the safe haven?" she asked.

"Like we said before, and I mean you no offense, but we are sworn to secrecy. No one can know the location for the safety of our people," Kalen told her.

She nodded her head. "I completely understand. Where are you from?"

"Vellwynd," Torbin answered.

Located East of Adorea, Vellwynd was known for its warriors. The fae who resided there were a force to be reckoned with. One fae equalled the strength of ten human men.

"You are warriors?" she asked.

"We were, until those monsters came," Torbin replied. "The Valfae are ruthless, and stronger than I've ever seen them before. It's like they're evolving."

Kalen grunted his agreement before shovelling more food into his mouth.

The rest of their meal was filled with small talk. When she was finished eating, Rexah pulled out her coin purse and reached into it.

"There's no need for that," Kalen said, a small smile on his face. "This inn provides breakfast as part of the cost of a room."

"Oh," she said, surprised.

"You've never stayed at an inn before, have you?" Kalen asked as he sat back in his chair, a playful gleam in his blue eyes.

"I really should get going," she said as she stood up from her seat, the chair scraping along the floor slightly.

"I know that you don't know us that well, but we're leaving today, and the roads aren't safe," Kalen said.

She sighed. "Please don't give me the speech about how some people are sensitive."

Her comment earned a deep chuckle from Torbin who was finishing off the last of his bread. "You deserved that one, Kal."

"I won't, but we could leave together and go our separate ways when the time comes. Travelling in a group is better than being alone," Kalen said, sitting back in his chair.

She studied him for a moment. "Why are you so concerned for my wellbeing? Like you said, we are strangers."

"Forgive me for trying to be helpful," he replied, that playful look in his eyes again. "But the look on your face betrays you, not to mention the fear rolling off you in violent waves."

The smell of fear radiated from her; it was so strong it was like he could taste it in the back of his throat. It was difficult to lie to a fae when their heightened sense of smell gave everyone's true feelings away, and Kalen wished she would simply be honest about how scared and lonely she was.

"Why don't you travel with us to the safe haven?" Torbin suggested. "There you can rest and replenish your supplies before you continue on your journey."

Kalen nodded. "You are more than welcome to join us. No pressure though."

"I thought this safe haven of yours had to be kept a secret. What would your people think if you come waltzing in with a stranger?" she asked, folding her arms across her chest.

There it is, Kalen thought. *That fire within her. Gods help me.*

Torbin sat back in his seat. "Our destination does need to be kept a secret, but our people don't turn anyone in need of aid away."

"I'm not in need of any aid," Rexah replied. "I told you my plan, and I want to stay on track."

"Of course, I understand, but you'd be able to replenish your supplies, and you'd be safe," Torbin said, sympathy in his eyes now. "The safe haven is protected by magical wards that keep beings of evil from entering."

"Are you evil, darling?" Kalen asked her, his voice deep.

Rexah looked Kalen dead in the eye. "Of course I'm not."

Torbin watched her. "It's up to you, but the option is there."

She was quiet for a few minutes before she sighed. "All right fine, we leave together and go to this safe haven you keep talking about, but if either of you try anything, anything at all, I'll cut your balls off, got it?" she asked, looking between the two of them, moving her hands to rest on her hips. She raised an eyebrow as she waited for one of them to speak. "Well?"

Both sat in stunned silence for a moment.

"I didn't expect those words to come out of your mouth," Kalen said, finally breaking their silence. "But you have a deal. If we try anything, anything at all, you cut our balls off."

Rexah nodded. "Very well, then it's settled."

"One last thing before we set off," Kalen said. "You've changed your appearance; I think you need to change your name too."

"I agree. You are royalty, and your name is very

unique. It wouldn't be wise to continue using it whilst you're still in danger," Torbin said.

"Gods, I didn't even think of that," Rexah replied, her hazel eyes widening. "Okay, how about Nes?"

Kalen's eyebrow raised. "Nes? Why that name?"

"It was my best friend's name," she said, her voice thick with grief.

Kalen's stomach sank like a stone in the ocean. "It's a beautiful name, I like it."

Torbin watched them, his eyes soft. "Let's get going then, shall we?"

The three of them soon walked out of the inn and into a busy marketplace, set up in the early hours on what had been an almost empty square the night before. The whole atmosphere was different now than it had been at night. Stalls were set up all over the square selling a variety of goods; as Rexah walked by them, Kalen watched as she sniffed at delicious smelling spices, ran her hand along gorgeous silks, and admired beautiful trinkets. Vendors engaged with potential customers, showing them their wares with great enthusiasm and answering their questions. A small group of children ran by, giggling as they chased one another, their feet splashing through small muddy puddles as they went.

They made their way through the stalls. Kalen walked on Rexah's right side and Torbin was on her left, just as they were when they had ridden into town.

Kalen watched as Rexah politely refused a few vendors until they reached one that sold numerous fabrics, shirts, and cloaks. Rexah handed the woman the coin for a simple black cloak.

It's not a cloak fit for a princess, but it'll do the job.

Their horses had been moved to a different stable located on the opposite side of town. They had been well taken care of; Kalen noted Rexah's obvious joy and relief with the smile spread across her face as she walked to one of the horses. Kalen had seen how worried she'd been about leaving them the night before due to the reputation of the town, but it looked well rested and ready to go.

Rexah gently stroked the nose of her horse, and he nuzzled into her palm and whinnied in response. Kalen watched her strap her bag to the saddle, ensuring it was secure before she swung up into it.

Kalen was impressed by how easily she mounted

her horse as he got onto his, moving his gaze to his belt as he secured his weapons. He'd needed to purchase another horse thanks to Rexah commandeering the other one, and Torbin lifted himself onto his new, slightly agitated horse with the natural grace that the fae possessed.

"Are you ready to go, Nes?" Torbin asked Rexah, using her fake name for the first time. When she didn't answer, he spoke again. "Nes?"

Kalen looked over to her, seeing she was off in a daydream.

She blinked a few times, and her cheeks went pink when she realised they'd been speaking to her. "I'm sorry, did you say something?"

Kalen smirked at her. "Are you ready to go?"

Licking her lips, she nodded. "Yes, let's go."

Gods fucking save me, Kalen thought as he watched her tongue swipe over her lips.

The inner and outer gates groaned and creaked as they opened. Kalen could feel the eyes of the guards of the gates on them as they passed through, watching them with an annoyed look on their faces that they had to momentarily pause their card game to open the gates for them. Ignoring their stares, they set off down the dirt road.

16

REXAH

Conversation flowed easily between them as they made their way through the forest. They talked about their favourite foods, their hobbies, and even their favourite books. She'd learned that Torbin enjoyed the same books that she did. It was nice to have company on her travels. It was a most welcome distraction from the thoughts that constantly filled her mind. Anything that would take her mind off the horrors she had experienced was a blessing.

Even when Rexah didn't join in the conversation she enjoyed listening to Kalen and Torbin as they spoke to each other. They were extremely close to one another, that was clear; the way they joked with each other and how relaxed they were in each other's company was refreshing, and in a painful way, reminded her of how she and Nesrin once were. With the information they'd shared with her back in Brywen about their home, she knew they'd die for each other if they had to. The weapons they carried didn't go unnoticed by her either.

Sunlight gleamed off the hilt of the sword strapped to Kalen's back, most of it hidden by his cloak, and the dagger on his left hip. Torbin had twin short swords strapped to his belt. She hadn't got a good look at them before they left, but she knew they had them and it calmed her knowing that if they ran into trouble, they weren't completely defenceless.

"How far is your safe haven from here?" Rexah asked a few hours into their journey.

"Around a three-day journey," Torbin replied. "If the weather continues to be this clear, then I reckon we can make it in two."

"Hold on, if you are from Vellwynd, why were you so close to Adorea?" she asked, going back to that mental map in her head once she'd worked out the distances between their home, Adorea, and their destination. "Surely it would have made more sense to go to your destination directly?"

Kalen nodded. "It would have been the best course if we hadn't started on that path only to be met with a nest of Valfae blocking our route. There were too many of them for us to fight, so we had to double back and go the long way around to throw the beasts off our scents."

Well, if Rexah didn't feel bad before, she sure did now. "I'm sorry," she said softly.

"It's all right. If we hadn't of gone the long way round then we wouldn't have met you," Kalen said. "I think it was fate that made our paths cross."

Fate was something she wholeheartedly believed in. When she was younger, in her teenage years, one of her favourite lessons had been about fate – and she'd become a little obsessed with it.

"That may be," she said, her grip tightening on the reins slightly. "Fate has a mysterious way of changing your destiny. You may think you're on one path, and the next fate swipes it from under your very feet."

It was then she realised she hadn't been thinking and had said it aloud. Both Kalen and Torbin looked at her for a moment, but thankfully didn't ask her to elaborate.

Rexah was curious to see this safe haven. How many fae would be there? Would it be fae only or would there be humans there too? Would they be welcoming to a stranger? So many questions swam around in her head.

As they rode through the forest Rexah couldn't help but take in every single detail: the smell of damp moss, the multitude of colours of the wildflowers, and how tall the trees seemed to get as they moved deeper into the woodland.

She'd never been to this part of the realm before. The furthest she had travelled was Kaldoren to visit King Orland and ... Ryden. She felt her throat begin to close up at the thought of him.

"Are you sure you're all right, darling?" Kalen asked her, his voice full of concern as he studied her.

Clearing her throat and willing the grief to slacken its grip on her, she nodded. "Yes, I'm fine. I just got lost in a daydream for a moment there." She didn't know if he believed her or not, and quite frankly, she didn't care.

They rested their horses for an hour and were back on the road again. The sun soon gave way to the moon, and night descended upon them. From what she could tell, they'd covered a decent number of miles.

"There's a good amount of space under the roots of a large tree over there," Torbin said, pointing to the left and off the road. "It will be good to cover us if there is any rainfall during the night."

Rexah couldn't see a godsdamned thing. She wasn't as blessed as her two fae companions who could see in the dark as clearly as they could if the sun were shining in the sky.

"Lead the way," Rexah said.

She followed Torbin as he took the lead, Kalen riding behind her, and she soon saw what Torbin had been pointing out to them now that they were closer.

They had walked through the forest at a fair incline for some time, and another dirt road spiralled up off the main road they'd been taking and wound further up what she could now see was the side of a hill. The space underneath the tree was massive, just like the tree itself, and the thick roots had formed an arch around the space beneath the tree, looking to Rexah like the entrance to a cave.

"Good spot, Tor," Kalen said as he swung down from his horse, his feet silent as they hit the ground.

Torbin grinned softly as he too got off his own horse, and his feet touched the forest floor.

Rexah swung her leg back over the horse. She was halfway off when she felt strong hands grip her hips, helping her down onto her feet. Her heart hammered against her chest. Turning, she was met with Kalen's deep blue eyes. "Thank you," she whispered.

Kalen gave her that ground shaking, knee trembling smile, and grabbed the reins of her horse. He took the horses off to the side to secure them, ensuring they were fed and watered before walking off to gather some wood.

Rexah turned her attention back to Torbin who'd made his way under the tree and lit torch in his hand which illuminated the space. It looked like a small cavern, but where you'd find rocks there was soil and more roots.

As she drew closer, she realised Torbin wasn't holding a torch – his hand was on fire. Her eyes widened as she watched the flames dance in his palm.

"Does it hurt?" She found herself asking him.

What kind of stupid question is that?

Torbin looked over to her and smiled softly, the flames brightening his amber eyes. "Not one bit."

Torbin set the wood ablaze with ease, much to Rexah's fascination. It was well known that the fae possessed many different powers from birth. Some humans were born with these powers too, like Merin, and the lore fascinated her. She had read many books on the history of magic and the Gods, and as with the topic of fate, magic was another one of her favourite subjects in her studies growing up.

The Gods of the Light created the world because their own was destroyed by the Gods of the Dark. The war that had been raging between them ended; so long it had been since peacetime that nobody knows when the war had begun, too early perhaps to have ever been documented; and the world was created.

For the world to be made, each of the Gods of Light combined what remained of their powers; to replenish their light magic, some created the humans and the rest created fae.

This world would blossom, and with it so would the power of light, and the Gods would soon be able to step foot on the world they created. Until then, they would remain in their crumbling dimension.

The Gods of the Dark learned of this secret world and destroyed their way through dimensions until they found it. Like the Gods of the Light, they also couldn't step foot on the planet. Instead, they sent their own dark and terrible power and thus the Dark Fae were created.

It did not stop there. Innocent fae were captured by the Dark Fae, their very souls corrupted by wicked magic, turning those pure fae into something darker.

The Light Gods quickly realised that in order for them to fight back they needed soldiers, and so they chose both human and fae creations to possess their magic; those chosen were then known as Power Blessed.

Power Blessed humans were hence known as witches and warlocks. The magic was proclaimed to pass down through the bloodline, occasionally skipping a generation for reasons still unknown.

They'd settled in beneath the tree, and they gathered around the fire for warmth once Kalen returned. Rexah was glad to be off the horse, as her legs were aching from riding for so long.

"I'm sorry if I was staring at you, it's just, I've never met someone who is Power Blessed before," Rexah admitted as she gently massaged her legs, trying to soothe the dull ache.

Torbin sat back against the wall of solid soil. "No need to apologise. You wouldn't be surprised to hear that I'm used to the stares of others, we both are."

Rexah's eyebrows knitted together in a frown. "Why?"

"Fae are different from humans, that's a fact, and it's only natural for them to be wary. It's happened for centuries, and when we use our power it can cause panic or uncertainty," Kalen explained. "We don't let it affect us, it's human nature."

"I'm not afraid of either of you, or any fae," she said. "Well, apart from the Valfae."

"It's all right to be afraid sometimes. It's what makes you human," Torbin said, his eyes soft.

Rexah was afraid. She would never admit it to them, but she couldn't deny it. If the Valfae ever found out she was still alive they would hunt her down and wouldn't stop until she was killed. That thought alone absolutely terrified her.

"When I was younger my grandmother always told me that fear could either render you helpless or you could take that fear and crush it with courage and bravery," she said, gazing into the fire. "Do not let the fear devour you, let it do nothing but strengthen your will to survive."

"Your grandmother sounded like a very wise woman," Kalen said.

"Yes," she whispered. "She was."

"I'm so sorry this has happened," Kalen said sympathetically.

Rexah shook her head. "It's all right."

She was a liar. She was getting good at lying to everyone, including herself. None of this was all right;

the whole situation felt like a nightmare that she couldn't wake up from.

Torbin rummaged through his bag and pulled out some rations. He held out some to Rexah. "Here, we need to eat before we rest."

Rexah thanked him quietly and took it. She hadn't even thought about restocking her supplies before they left Brywen.

"So, do you prefer book shops or libraries?" Rexah asked Torbin, trying to take her mind off everything.

Kalen snorted a laugh before he tucked into his rations. "Yeah, Tor, which do you prefer?" Kalen looked smug whilst Torbin glared at him.

Rexah looked between the two of them. "Okay, clearly I'm missing something here?"

"Torbin was once thrown out of the library in Vellwynd and banned from ever entering again," Kalen told her, the grin on his perfectly sculpted face never faltering.

Torbin narrowed his eyes at him before turning his gaze to her. "One day, I was at the library, and I was lost in a book. I'd been there for a few hours reading when something exciting happened in one of the chapters and I ..."

"And you what?" she asked, leaning closer to him.

Torbin's cheeks pinked. "My fire ignited in my fingertips, and I accidently turned the book to ash in my hands."

Kalen burst into laughter, causing her traitorous heart to flutter madly in her chest. Rexah also couldn't help the laughter that escaped her.

Torbin looked away, embarrassed, but she caught a glimpse of the smile spread across his face. "It was one time, and it wasn't a rare book, thank the Gods," he said.

"I'll never forget the look on the librarian's face, Tor. It was priceless," Kalen laughed.

Rexah's laughter slowly faded as she smiled at him. "At least it was only one book. Imagine what would have happened if it had been a whole bookcase."

"That's true," Torbin chuckled. "I can laugh about it now, but when it happened, I was horrified."

Once they finished eating, Rexah settled down to go to sleep. Using her bag as a pillow and her cloak as a blanket, she ensured to stay close enough to the fire to keep herself warm.

"Goodnight," she said softly to the fae.

Torbin flashed her a smile. "Sleep well, Nes."

Kalen studied her for a moment before a smile spread across his face. "Sweet dreams, darling."

She ignored the explosion of butterflies in her stomach at Kalen calling her that again and closed her eyes. Surprisingly, it didn't take her long to fall asleep as she listened to Kalen and Torbin's quiet conversation.

It was another beautiful day, the air crisp and the sky clear. They'd set off from their camping spot a few hours ago; Rexah had taken another potion and the effects took place rather quickly, allowing them to set off in good time.

"I've read a lot about Vellwynd," Rexah told them as they made their way through the trees.

"You have?" Kalen asked, falling back to ride beside her while Torbin remained a few feet ahead.

She nodded. "I love reading. Any chance that I can get my nose stuck in a book, I take."

"I hope it's all good things you've read," Kalen smirked softly.

Rexah found herself smiling shyly at his smirk. "From the drawings in the books, Vellwynd looks beautiful."

"Descriptions in books don't do it justice," Kalen told her. "When the sun has almost disappeared, the sky turns a beautiful shade of purple, and when the stars come out, they're so bright and magical."

Her eyes lit up. "That sounds incredible."

"It is. Well, it was. I don't know if we will ever be able to go back," he said, sadness coating his voice.

The sorrow in his words hit her deep inside. She could understand how he felt. Her own home had been burned to the ground before her eyes by the same monsters who'd destroyed his.

"I believe you'll go back. The Valfae won't win; they can't, not whilst we have courage left in us. Not whilst we fight for the same thing," she said.

"And what do we fight for?"

"A better world."

Suddenly she was in a memory, back in Adorea, sitting at the fountain in the gardens with Ryden.

"And what do we fight for, Rexah?"

"A better world."

A warm hand on hers pulled her from the memory. She blinked a few times and Kalen came into view.

"Are you sure everything's all right?" he asked, concern in his eyes.

She did her best to give him her finest smile. "Of course. Sorry, I'm a daydreamer."

He nodded slowly. She wasn't convinced her lie had worked, but she was glad when he didn't push any further.

Rexah knew they were nearing the edge of the forest when the density of trees that surrounded them began to thin out with each hour that passed. They ensured to take a quick break to take care of the needs of themselves and the horses, but they never lingered for too long, one of them always on the lookout for danger.

The sun was soon beginning to make its decent, making way for the approaching moon.

"We should set up camp," Torbin said. "We don't want to be setting up during nightfall."

Rexah frowned. "We set up during nightfall last night."

"Correct, but we were further in the forest last night. We're slightly more exposed here, easy to spot by the nightlife," Torbin replied.

They found a sheltered area where two large trees had grown entwined with each other. Rexah had never seen anything like it before; it was like the trees were twirling in dance as they raced for the sky.

Torbin saw to the horses, securing them and giving them some more water.

"I'll go and collect some wood for the fire," Rexah said.

"Don't go too far," Kalen told her, pulling something out of his belt and pressing it into the palm of her hand. "Take this."

She looked down at the beautiful dagger; the blade was wicked sharp and stunning fae scripture, of which she could not decipher, had been etched into the steel. The handle was dark blue and fae runes had been carved into it.

"It's beautiful."

Kalen smirked softly. "It is. It's also extremely sharp, so be careful."

Her gaze met his and she smiled at him. "I've already got a dagger, remember?" she asked, motioning to the blade secured at her hip.

"I know, but two daggers are better than one," he replied, urging her to take the weapon.

Rexah laughed softly and nodded as she took the blade from him. She turned and walked a little further into the forest, feeling Kalen's eyes burning into her back until she was out of his sight.

It didn't take long for her to gather enough wood,

and she smiled as she picked up the last few branches. As she straightened back up, she heard the unmistakable thumps of running footsteps.

Frowning, she began to turn in the direction of the sound, but before she could see who it was, she was tackled to the ground. The wood she'd collected went flying in every direction. She groaned in pain when her body slammed into the ground and another body landed on hers.

"Get the hell off—" She was quickly silenced by a hand over her mouth, and her wide eyes met familiar dark ocean ones.

Kalen's finger came up to his lips, urging her to remain silent. The seriousness in his eyes made her comply without question. Once he knew she was going to remain quiet, his hand left her mouth and his focus turned to scanning the area around him.

Rexah was pinned to the ground by his body. The only person she'd been in this position with before was Ryden, and the thought of Kalen in this position made her cheeks burn. She craned her neck, trying desperately to see what he was looking for, but it was useless. She turned her gaze back to him and saw a dark, concentrated look on his face. He had seen someone, or something. A horrible sinking feeling settled in the bottom of her stomach. *This is not good.*

Kalen's eyes met hers once more as he whispered to her. "Be as quiet as you can. We are not alone."

Rexah didn't dare speak, she only nodded her head in response. Once she was back on her feet with Kalen's help, she scanned their surroundings. She spotted Torbin standing around forty feet to their right, his twin swords in his hands. He wore the same dark look on his face that Kalen did.

A sound then tore through the forest that chilled the blood in Rexah's veins. She felt the blood drain from her face, and her heart almost stopped dead inside her chest. Her eyes slowly moved to where the deafening roar emanated from, and her shoulders sagged in disbelief when she saw their huge forms, dark batlike wings, and blood red eyes.

There was no escape.

The Valfae were here.

17

R exah backed up a couple of steps, a few twigs snapping in two beneath her feet.

The last time she'd come face to face with these monsters it had been nightfall, but with the sun still in the sky she could see them more clearly, and they were utterly terrifying.

"Stay behind me, or behind one of the trees. Keep one of the daggers in your hand at all times," Kalen told her, his eyes never leaving the Valfae. "Don't come out unless we tell you to, do you understand?"

"Y-yes," she stuttered quietly, pulling out her dagger. Her heart was beating a million miles an hour in her chest as she fought to calm herself.

Kalen looked down at her for a moment before his

gaze moved to Torbin who nodded to him, and they both moved forward.

Rexah stayed where she was, taking cover behind one of the trees. Peering around it, she watched as they both advanced towards a small clearing in the trees.

The Valfae, five in total, stalked forward once they saw the two fae approaching. From her previous experience she knew not to underestimate them; one Valfae alone could do unspeakable damage.

Kalen and Torbin showed no fear as they prepared themselves, the latter twirling his blades expertly in his hands as if he'd done this countless times – and from the look of hatred in his eyes, Rexah was sure he had encountered evil before.

A feeling came over her in that moment, one that made her question why she was hiding. She couldn't conceal herself behind a tree hoping Kalen and Torbin killed the Valfae every time they encountered one. She couldn't expect them to be her knights in shining armour to protect and save her from the monsters. She wouldn't; she was Rexah Ravenheart, descendent of Queen Riona, and she would not bow down; she would not hide, not anymore.

Gripping the dagger in her trembling hand she moved out from behind the tree and walked towards

Kalen and Torbin. Her stomach turned with each step she took, and adrenaline coursed through her. There was no turning back.

Kalen and Torbin looked over to her, watching as she approached. She knew Kalen wouldn't be happy that she disobeyed his commands, but she didn't care. This was her fight.

"No. Go back. Run," Kalen told her, slight panic rising in his voice.

Rexah stopped once she got to them, standing between them, her eyes never leaving the Valfae. "No, I'm done running. I'm done hiding in the shadows. I've already killed one of these monsters, and I can do it again. They want me, so here I am," she said, lifting her chin high. Her hands were no longer trembling.

The Valfae's eyes seemed to glow brighter when they saw her and smelled her scent. Two of them growled in hunger, and the other three screeched with excitement before they launched themselves at Rexah and the fae, unable to hold back any longer.

Kalen didn't hesitate. He shoved Rexah back before he swung his sword towards the first Valfae that dared approach. A moment later, the Valfae's head was rolling along the forest floor, its body falling in a heap at Kalen's feet. Black blood spurted from the stump and oozed onto the forest floor.

Rexah's eyes widened. She'd never seen one of these beasts be taken down so easily. When fleeing from her home, she'd seen a few of the guards battling the Valfae, and they'd been torn apart the moment they got close enough to fight. She never thought it possible for these creatures to be killed with one swing of a sword.

But you killed it with one strike, right through its chin.

Rexah looked down at her dagger. She had killed one just as easily. She quickly shoved down the memories that were beginning to surface from that night.

Torbin muttered something beside her in a language she didn't understand, but she recognised it as the language of the fae. As soon as the words left his lips, orange runes began to glow along the steel of his swords, and seconds later fire roared to life down the blades, burning a vibrant orange and red.

This was no ordinary fire: this was fae fire. She'd only read about the magic of fae fire in her lessons growing up. This was the first time she'd seen it in person with her own eyes, and Gods it was magnificent.

Torbin moved with speed as he slashed one sword down the chest of the Valfae that had charged him, his amber eyes glowing like the fae fire that engulfed his blade. The Valfae roared in pain and anger, and the monster swiped its claw towards him. Torbin was faster though and brought his other blade back, cutting clean through the Valfae's claw. The amputated limb fell to the ground at their feet, and the creature growled with rage. Torbin dealt the killing blow to the brute before engaging fearlessly with the next.

A screeching howl tore Rexah's gaze from Torbin to that of another Valfae heading straight for her. Her grip on the dagger tightened as she readied herself. The Valfae swiped at her with its razor-sharp claw. She ducked out of the way before she stretched out her arm and swung the blade towards the creature with all the momentum she could put her weight into; the blade sliced through the creature's side like a knife through butter, and Rexah could have sworn that the steel of her dagger sang as it tore through the beast's flesh. It almost vibrated with power in her grasp, much like it had before, back in Adorea.

Black blood spilled from the wound as the creature howled in pain. Rexah spun away, making some space between her and the beast. This time it swung its outstretched wing round to hit her. She backflipped out of the way before it could touch her, earning a growl of annoyance from the brute.

The Valfae staggered slightly; the wound she had inflicted on its side was a nasty one, a laceration so deep that the blood flowed like a waterfall. It was hurt.

Good.

That meant she'd slowed it down at least.

Rexah flipped the dagger in her hand, the blade now pointing down towards her inner arm. She took a deep breath, taking those short few seconds of time to remember her training with Zuko before she ran at it.

The creature roared and reached down to engulf her in its arms. But Rexah was quicker as she ducked out of its reach and blocked its attempt to strike her. She rose once again, the Valfae now behind her on its knees. Rexah didn't turn to face it though; instead, she gripped the dagger, blade out in front of her chest, before she swung it out and to the side, letting the movement drive her upper body around to face the monster. The steel sank deep into the back of its neck causing it to shriek in pain. As soon as the dagger made contact, lightning shot down the knife and into the beast. With a twist of the blade, and the sickening crack that followed, the Valfae went limp. She pulled the dagger from its neck and kicked it to the ground for good measure.

Her eyes were wide as she watched the monster's body twitch from the shock of lightning before it stilled completely. Rexah looked down at her hands. *Where the hell is this lightning coming from? The dagger?*

"Stop!" a new voice called out, and the remaining two creatures came to a halt as commanded.

The three of them looked over to find another fae – a Dark Fae, and he wasn't alone. Just behind him were two more Valfae, but they looked bigger than the others.

Rexah's stomach twisted as she remembered the monster that attacked her in Adorea. It had seemed bigger and more intelligent than the others, and now *two* of them were here. If they weren't in deep trouble before they certainly were now. Facing Valfae was one thing, but the Dark Fae? They were relentless.

"Enough of this pointless fighting," the Dark Fae said, his voice smooth and soothing. He began walking towards them, the Valfae following closely behind him like his own personal guard – not that he needed them. His black hair fell to just below his ears, and the sharp points of them poked through. He was tall, maybe a few inches taller than Kalen. Small black veins leaked from his eyes, passing over his temples before running down to the top of his cheeks, like rays of sunlight penetrating the cracks of an old wall.

"That's close enough, scum," Kalen almost growled at him, his chest heaving as he caught his breath.

The Dark Fae stood his ground at Kalen's request, and the being of evil and darkness had his eyes locked onto him. "That's not a polite way to address someone."

"Then what should we call you?" Torbin asked, glaring at him.

When the fae smiled, two sharp canines became visible. "My name is Venrhys, General of the Dark Army. Well, one of them at least."

Oh Gods.

She noticed that the two Valfae who'd originally attacked them had backed off and were now standing closer to the others, awaiting further instruction from their master.

"We were on our way to meet up with another general when a scent hit us, a sweet, familiar, delicious scent. One I thought I'd never smell again, and curiosity got the better of me," Venrhys told them, his eyes holding a far-off look for a moment as if he were caught up in the memory.

Rexah shifted slightly, uncomfortable with the tone

of his voice. The handle of the blade felt slick in her sweating hand, and she gripped it a little tighter, trying to pull herself together. She would not show this monster any fear even though she knew that would be pointless – they could practically smell it.

Do not let the fear devour you.

Venrhys grinned. "I couldn't let the opportunity pass me by, not when that scent was destroyed around a month ago, or so it was supposed to have been. We followed it through the forest, and low and behold, here we are," Venrhys said, his black eyes fixing on Rexah. "Alive and well it seems, isn't that right, Little Raven?"

She didn't recognise him. She didn't recall seeing him as she fled from the kingdom, but he could have been there in the shadows watching her for all she knew, relishing in her fear and the death of her people.

"I will say this, you don't look the same as before. Have you done something with your hair?" Venrhys asked her, a playful smile lifting the corners of his mouth.

Kalen stepped in front of her protectively. "You want her, you'll need to go through me first."

Venrhys smirked at him. "Oh, I don't need to do anything."

"I am not your enemy, Little Raven," Venryhs's voice echoed in her mind. *"These fae you travel with do not care for you; not like I do. Be rid of them and come with me. I will protect you. I will guide you.*

"Kill them, Little Raven."

She had no control over her body or mind. No matter how hard she fought she couldn't push him out. Did she want to push him out though? This was wrong, wasn't it? He was lying, wasn't he?

"Do it now before it's too late. Do it now before they kill you first. Set yourself free."

Her muscles itched, begging to obey.

"Fly!"

Before she could think about what she was doing, her arm raised, and she thrust the dagger forward to stab Kalen in his side.

Thankfully he was quick enough to spin away from the attack. He faced her and grabbed her wrist, stopping the blade just centimetres from his body. "Stop, it's me. Don't listen to him! He's inside your head and feeding you lies!"

Torbin stepped forward to intervene but was thrown back with force into one of the trees with a flick of the Dark Fae's wrist. He hit the ground with a loud thud and didn't get back up, his swords lay scattered nearby.

Rexah swung her fist around and smacked Kalen in the jaw. He stumbled back, but his grip on her wrist still held tight like a vice. She let go of the dagger, catching it in her other hand. Kalen cursed loudly and grabbed her other wrist, but she was relentless.

She had to kill him. She absolutely had to, and she wouldn't stop until both Kalen and Torbin were dead. They had to die before they killed her.

"That's it. Come on, you can do it," Venrhys encouraged her excitedly.

Rexah brought her knee up into Kalen's stomach, causing him to double over. His grip on her wrist slackened as he tried to suck the air back into his lungs that she had kicked out of him, and it was all she needed to regain her advantage; her hand shot out and grabbed him by the throat, squeezing tightly.

"N-no ..." he choked.

She didn't let him go, didn't react to his pleas. She only squeezed his throat harder. She didn't know where all this strength was coming from, but that didn't matter – all that mattered was that his heart stopped beating.

"D-don't … don't make m-me … do this d-darling," he croaked, still trying his hardest to get through to her.

Her face was blank of expression, her usually vibrant eyes now glazed over. She wouldn't let go until he was no longer breathing, and nothing would stop her before then.

Kalen's eyes begged her to snap out of it, but he knew this was the only way.

"I-I'm sorry," he rasped.

His fist swung round and struck Rexah's temple hard. As soon as his fist connected with the side of her head, her whole world went dark.

18

It was the pounding pain in her head that woke Rexah, pulling her from the strange dream she was having about a Dark Fae general. She could hear his soothing voice in her head, urging her to *kill*; she could feel her fist connecting with Kalen's jaw and her hand wrapping around his throat.

That wasn't a dream.

Her eyes snapped open, and she shot up into a sitting position. A small groan escaped her lips as a shooting pain spread through her head. She frowned as she took in her surroundings. *How did I get here? Where am I?*

She was in a tent reasonably spacious for one person, that was for certain. The fabric rippled slightly in the wind. A small table was placed to the right of the cot she lay in, an unlit lantern sat on top of it. The grey blankets kept her surprisingly cosy considering how thin they looked.

Pulling the blankets off, she swung her legs over the side of the cot and her toes touched the soft grass below. She looked down at herself seeing she wore a white dress that she didn't remember changing into. She didn't remember how she got here in the first place, wherever here was.

As she went to stand up, her heart jolted in her chest when she caught sight of the ends of her hair, now it's natural colour. The potion had worn off.

Cursing, she shot to her feet. Black spots blocked her vision for a moment, but she soon shook the dizziness off and rushed over to her bag that had been left for her on a fold away chair in the corner. She shuffled the items around in the bag in search of the vials of shimmering silver liquid, and her pulse quickened when she couldn't find them.

"Looking for these?" a familiar voice asked from behind her.

She whirled round to find Kalen standing there, the vials in his hands.

"Yes, how did you get them?"

"They fell out of your bag when I had to knock you unconscious," he replied.

Rexah stepped forward and took the vials. "Thank you," she said softly.

"You don't need to use the potions here," he told her. "Everyone already saw your true self. The magic wore off before we got here."

"Here?" she asked.

He studied her for a moment. "We're at the safe haven."

"Oh, how long have I been out?"

"Two days," he replied, a flash of worry in his eyes.

Her eyes widened. "Two days," she repeated as she sat down on the edge of the cot. It only felt like a moment ago that Venrhys was in her head, making her do things she didn't want to.

Kalen walked over and sat down beside her. "He can't get to you here. We have the wards. You're safe."

To her surprise, anger built up within her and she looked at him. Her heart fell into a fluttering mess at how close they were to each other. She could feel the heat from his body. His thigh gently touching hers.

"For how long? They could sense the magic in the wards, they could tear them down and kill every single living soul here! You don't know what they're capable of!"

Kalen gave her a moment to settle before he spoke. "You've been through a lot, Rexah. More than anyone should have to endure, but don't think for one second that you are the only person this happened to."

The anger in her violet eyes melted, a startled look filled her features. "I … oh Gods, I'm so sorry, Kalen. Please, forgive me. I-I shouldn't have said that."

Kalen reached up and his fingers gently stroked the soft skin of her cheek making her flinch in surprise, his eyes never leaving hers. "You're grieving. Never apologise for grieving, darling. You need to feel it. As much as you don't want to, you need to. Let yourself feel it a little bit every day, and you'll get there."

Why was she letting him touch her like this? She'd only known him for about a week. Yet she made no move to push him away. It felt like her blood was beginning to sing in her veins. *What the hell is this feeling?*

"I can't," she whispered. "I have things to do, places to be, and I can't crawl into a corner and let my grief tear me apart."

Kalen slowly removed his fingers from her cheek. "Where are you headed?"

Gods, should I tell him?

Kalen and Torbin had saved her life, twice. They could have left her to die in Adorea, could have ridden straight by her that night on the outskirts of Brywen, but they didn't. They had been nothing but hospitable. Her own instincts had been guiding her to trust the fae, and they hadn't let her down this far.

She needed to talk to someone about what happened, someone who had been personally touched by the Valfae, who knew exactly what she was going through, before the grief consumed her.

"I'm going to Dorasa," she began, her voice trembling slightly and her throat becoming dry. "Before my grandmother died, she told me to go there."

"What's in Dorasa?" he asked.

Rexah shrugged her shoulders. "I don't know. I've tried so many times to think of what could be so important about it, but nothing comes to mind."

Kalen studied her. "Maybe once the shock wears off a bit, you'll remember."

She looked at him. "Maybe, or maybe it's just a dead end."

"You really believe your grandmother would send you to the other side of the realm for no reason at all?"

Running a hand through her hair, she sighed. "Of course not. I'm just trying to process it all."

Kalen nodded. "Give yourself some time. You'll get there, I promise."

She nodded. "Thank you, Kalen."

"It was a Valfae that gave you that injury," he said, nodding to her shoulder.

The sounds of screeching filled her head, the growl it made as it tore through her flesh, the way its eyes lit up at the taste of her blood. "Yes, it was."

"A wound like that should have killed you almost instantly. Someone is watching over you," he said softly.

"Maybe," she whispered, her throat closing up as she thought of her grandmother.

Kalen's warm hand took hold of hers. The contact of his skin against hers made her heart slam against her chest. "I am so sorry, Rexah. We have lost some of our people, yes, but you lost everyone."

Her eyes burned with tears. She refused to let them fall and shoved them back. She swallowed the lump in her throat and nodded, not trusting her voice. Kalen's hand left hers, his finger moving underneath her chin and gently tilting it up, her eyes meeting his once more.

"Your eyes are absolutely stunning," he whispered, his own eyes moving from hers to her lips.

She could have looked away. She could have pulled away from him. She could have stood up and walked away – but she didn't. She stayed where she was and watched as he slowly leaned in, closing the distance between them.

"Sorana said food will be ready in ten minutes," Torbin said excitedly as he entered the room.

Rexah jolted away from him and wiped her eyes. Kalen took a deep, shaky breath in and slowly looked over his shoulder to look at his friend.

"Am I interrupting something?" Torbin smirked, folding his strong arms across his chest.

She couldn't be certain, but Rexah was sure she heard a low growl escape from Kalen's lips, and she would be a liar if she said she didn't like it.

"Fuck off, Torbin. Tell Sorana we will be there in a few minutes."

Torbin looked pleased with himself that he'd hit a nerve, and he nodded, looking to Rexah. "It's good to see you awake. This one here wouldn't leave your side without being forced to."

Rexah fought the urge to blush as she watched Torbin walk out of the tent. She silently thanked the Gods that he'd walked in on their moment, whatever it was about to be. Did she want to kiss him?

Unequivocally, yes. Of course she did, but now wasn't the time.

Would there be a time? Do I want there to be?

"Sorry about that," Kalen said as he turned his attention back to her.

Was he sorry Torbin interrupted them or was he sorry for his attempt to kiss her? The latter strangely made her stomach twist. "No, it's fine. I should be the one who is apologising."

Kalen frowned at her. "Apologising for what?"

"Did you forget that I tried to kill you? I heard his voice in my head and I couldn't stop myself. I couldn't do anything other than what he forced me to do."

"Don't. I know exactly what he did. It wasn't you who tried to kill me. It was him," he replied.

Rexah sighed softly. "It doesn't matter, I'm sorry all the same."

"He seemed to know you. Have you ever met him before? Was he there the day your kingdom was attacked?"

She shook her head. "I've never seen him before. He could very well have been there, but I was too busy running for my life to notice, you know?"

Kalen's eyes were soft as he studied her. "Of course."

She looked up at him and before she could get lost

in his eyes again, she stood up. "I'm guessing Sorana won't be happy if we are late to breakfast?"

"You would be correct." He chuckled as he rose to his feet. "There are some fresh clothes for you in the trunk over there."

She looked to where he pointed and saw the trunk at the bottom of the bed. "Thank you."

"I'll leave you to get dressed. I'll wait for you outside. Remember, you don't need to use those potions whilst you're here; my people already saw you without the glamour, but if it makes you feel more comfortable by all means take it," he said softly, smiling at her before he made his way out of the tent.

She thanked the Gods when she opened the trunk and saw a dark green shirt and a pair of black leggings. The leggings fit her like a glove and the shirt was a little on the larger side, but she made a quick fix of that and tucked it in.

After pulling on her boots, she smoothed down her hair. Nerves began to build up in her stomach. This was the first time she'd be stepping out into the public eye, so to speak, since before the attack on Adorea, as well as herself. She had never felt so vulnerable before.

Deep breath, Rexah. You've got this.

Allowing a few moments to compose herself, she

took a deep breath before she walked out of the tent. Kalen was exactly where he said he would be.

His smile made her warm and fuzzy inside. *What in the world?*

"Ready to go and have some breakfast?" he asked her.

She nodded. "Lead the way."

"You're going to love Sorana's cooking," he said before he guided her away from the tent.

As expected, everyone looked their fill of her as she made her way through the camp with Kalen, but to her relief, the looks seemed more related to curiosity than judgement or hatred. Surprisingly, the haven wasn't occupied only by fae; she'd spotted a few humans, not many, but they were definitely human.

"They have also been unlucky enough to have been visited by the Valfae," Kalen told her when he followed her gaze.

Rexah looked up at him and saw the pain in his eyes, like he was reliving the horrors of what the

Valfae had done to his home and the people who perished.

"It wasn't your fault," she whispered to him.

He looked down at her as they walked. "You should listen to your own advice, darling."

There was that godsdamn word again, her heart doing its little skip when he said it. It was doing that a lot lately, and the smirk that spread on Kalen's face told her that he'd noticed too.

"How much further until we reach Sorana?" Rexah asked, swiftly changing the subject.

"Meals are served in that tent just ahead," he said, pointing.

Rexah looked up and her eyes widened. The tent was huge and reminded her of the tent that the circus used when they had visited Adorea. It was Rexah's tenth birthday, and her grandmother organised for the best circus and performers in the realm to attend and put on a show. It had been magnificent. This tent, however, lacked the vibrant colours of a circus tent and the joy of her grandmother's presence.

Kalen pulled back the cover, motioning for her to go first. She thanked him and stepped inside, hearing loud chatter and laughter as she did so.

Tables that looked to be handmade and carved from

pieces of wood from the surrounding forest lined either side of the tent, unlit candles atop them. Fae occupied most of them, some laughing with each other, others in deep conversation as they ate.

A familiar fae waved to them from near the back of the tent. Rexah smiled at Torbin, and they made their way over to him, but before they got to the table a tall fae woman stepped towards them.

"I'm glad to see you are awake," the woman said, her voice soft and warm.

"Sorana, this is Rexah." Kalen introduced them with a smile.

"It's a pleasure to meet you, Sorana. Thank you for allowing me into your safe haven," Rexah replied with a small nod of her head.

She grinned. "The pleasure is all mine. Welcome to Savindeer."

Sorana wasn't as tall as Kalen, but she was still taller than Rexah. Her half-braided hair was a light shade of pink, and it was stunning. She'd never seen anyone with pink hair before, and Rexah adored how it complimented Sorana's almost-white eyes. Her skin was a shade paler than Rexah's, and her sharply pointed ears were covered in various piercings. It was difficult to tell her age due to the fact that the fae aged so slowly, but the way she held herself told her that Sorana was definitely older than Kalen.

"Please, make yourselves comfortable. I'll bring over some food shortly," Sorana said, gesturing to the table where Torbin sat.

Rexah thanked her once more before she followed Kalen over to the table and sat down. "I love her hair."

Torbin grinned softly. "Everyone does."

"This place is incredible. Your people are doing amazing work here," she said.

"They are hardworking people. Just wait until another week has passed, you'll be amazed at what they'll have done." Kalen smiled.

"She called this place Savindeer," Rexah said. "I've never seen that name on a map."

"That's what our people decided to call this safe haven," Kalen replied. "So, I must ask you never to repeat it to anyone else. We can't risk any curious people hearing that name and looking into it."

Rexah nodded softly. "I understand. Don't worry, my lips are sealed."

Sorana soon came over with plates filled with delicious smelling food. "Enjoy," she said before walking off.

Rexah wasted no time and dug in. She couldn't help herself; she was so hungry.

"What happened after I was knocked out?" Rexah asked.

"Venrhys grew angry that I'd taken you out of play and looked as though he was ready to strike me down, but then the most bizarre thing happened," Kalen replied.

Setting her cup down on the table, she looked at him. "What happened?"

"The sky grew dark, and thunder began to rumble. Venrhys looked uneasy as a storm began to roll in, and he ordered the Valfae to retreat. Before I could take a swipe at him, he was gone," he explained.

A storm. Thunder. That had to be a coincidence. The flash of lighting that had killed the Valfae who attacked her had been pure coincidence.

Or had it?

"That is strange," was her reply.

"How are you feeling?" Torbin asked her before he ate a forkful of his food.

"Now that Venrhys isn't in my head, I feel better. I also feel like I slept well, so that's good," she replied.

Torbin smiled. "Good, I'm glad to hear it."

Lowering her fork to the plate, she looked at Kalen. "That reminds me. How hard did you fucking hit me?"

Kalen's eyes widened when she cursed, but then a small playful smirk spread across his face. "I had to hit you pretty hard; you would have stopped at nothing to kill me. I tried to get through to you, but nothing was working, and the only solution I had was to knock you unconscious. It was the only way to break Venrhys's control of your mind."

"Thank you for getting him out of my head, but don't ever hit me again. Also, sorry for cursing. My grandmother would have had a fit if she'd heard me just then," she said softly.

"Don't apologise, it's fine," he said, picking up his fork again. "Besides, I find you extremely attractive when you're angry, and the cursing only adds to it."

Rexah coughed, almost choking on her food. She managed to swallow what was stuck and take a drink of water from her cup. Once her food had settled, she looked up and saw Torbin chuckling to himself while Kalen sat with his eyes fixed on her, that gorgeous smirk on his face.

"That was very inappropriate of me," he said softly.

"Yeah, sometimes he speaks before he thinks. You'll get used to it though," Torbin told her.

She couldn't stop herself from smiling. Kalen was right. It was a very inappropriate thing to say, especially to royalty – if that's what she still was – but that didn't stop her stomach flipping with excitement, like a thousand butterflies fluttered within, bursting to be let free.

19

During their meal Rexah spoke of her plan to go to Dorasa. She'd never been before, and she didn't know what to expect once she got there. It's not like someone would be standing by the gates waiting for her, holding a sign with Rexah's name on it.

"We've been there a few times. It's one of our favourite places to visit," Torbin told her before he ate another forkful of food.

"Really? Port towns are known for their dodgy dealings and thieves," she said.

"Dorasa is different. Everyone is welcoming and business, as far as we could tell, is clean," he replied. "Don't believe all the rumours you hear."

Her anxiety eased a little at his reassurance that Dorasa was one of the good places in the realm to go to.

Once breakfast was over, Kalen took Rexah on a tour of the camp. She still couldn't believe this place was here. They had set up in the thickest part of the forest, and the trees hid their location well. She had also met some of Kalen's people who welcomed her with open arms. A few others, as expected, were a little hesitant of her.

I don't blame them, she thought as she watched a human woman gently pull her toddler closer and away from Rexah's path. There was a heart-warming sense of community throughout though, something she hadn't felt for weeks. She'd be lying if she said it didn't hurt or remind her of how Adorea once was.

The village just outside the castle walls thrived on the spirit of the community, and Rexah's family often joined them in their celebrations and provided anything they needed. Their families were one.

She missed Adorea terribly.

As the day went by, Rexah helped the Vellwyndians with their day-to-day tasks, whether that be collecting wood for their fires, bundling hay together for their horses, or hanging up their clothing to dry. It was the least she could do to say thank you for their hospitality, and she loved every second she spent with them.

She learned of their family history, of their customs, and she was fascinated by each and every one of them. They didn't have much, but they had each other and that was enough after everything they'd gone through.

"You don't need to help," Elly, a young fae woman told her.

Rexah smiled as she picked up another wet item of clothing from the basket. "I know, but I want to," she replied, hanging the shirt over the washing line, securing it with two pegs.

Elly returned Rexah's smile. "It's much appreciated. We've so many clothes to wash that it takes so long to hang them up to dry."

"It's my pleasure," she said. "I'm sorry for what happened to Vellwynd."

Elly's eyes softened. "I'm sorry about your home too."

Rexah looked around at everyone going about their business. "What you've all achieved here is amazing, truly brilliant," Rexah told her, picking up another freshly washed shirt.

"It was difficult in the beginning, but we got there. We're still getting there," Elly said, her smile widening.

The conversation flowed easily as they worked, and it didn't take long for their large pile of clean laundry to be pegged on the line, rippling softly in the gentle breeze.

Helping out the people of Vellwynd with their tasks made the day go by quickly, and before she knew it, she was back in her tent getting ready for dinner.

She changed out of her mud and hay covered clothes and had a quick wash in the basin she was provided with. Fresh clothing had been left on her cot by Sorana; the fae had told her it was her way of saying welcome one more time; and Rexah smiled seeing a pair of black leggings – a little thicker than the previous ones she'd worn – and a dark purple shirt. Her smile grew as she couldn't help but wonder if Sorana had colour co-ordinated her clothing with her hair on purpose or not, but she appreciated it all the same.

Once she had dressed in her new clothes and laced up her boots, she walked out of the tent. The camp wasn't huge, so it was easy to navigate on her own. A few of the fae waved to her or said hello as she made her way through.

Everyone was incredibly friendly and kind; it came as a shock to her – a stark contrast to the horrors and attacks she'd been subjected to over the last few weeks – but it was a nice and welcomed change.

"Rexah?" a female voice called to her.

She turned to her left to find one of the fae she'd helped earlier. "Vega. Is everything all right?"

Vega smiled as she walked over to her, carrying a bundle of folded towels in her hands. "All is well. I was just wondering if you could take these towels to the bathing tent?"

"Of course, I can," she said, taking them from her. "Can you point me in the right direction?"

"It's the light green tent to the right of the dining one. Thank you so much, I owe you one!" she said before rushing off, her mane of dark curls bouncing as she went.

Rexah continued walking, following Vega's directions, before she came to the bathing tent. Kalen hadn't told her this was here on their tour, but she wouldn't hold it against him; he'd done a good job introducing her to everyone and telling her their journey's and how their experiences had led them here.

She loved hearing about the history of others, especially from the people themselves; it made their stories more personal. Often Rexah would find tears in her own eyes as she saw first-hand the emotion in their faces as they spoke of years gone by and those who were no longer here.

The tent was larger on the inside than it looked from the outside. It was lined either side with wooden bathtubs separated with sheets for privacy. She spotted the doorless cabinet which had other fresh towels stored within it and placed the ones she carried into the empty spaces.

As she turned to leave something caught her eye. The sight made her stop dead in her tracks, and the world itself felt as though it had stopped turning. Time stood still and everything around her seemed to disappear.

Everything, apart from *him*.

Kalen stood on the opposite side of the tent wearing nothing but a towel around his waist, facing away from her. The powerful muscles of his back and shoulders moved as he ran his long fingers through his wet hair.

How on earth did I not notice him when I first walked in?

"Like what you see, darling?" he asked, his voice deep.

"Uh ... I ..." she trailed off, her heart pounding fiercely in her chest.

Kalen turned to her, and it took everything she had to not shudder out of complete appreciation for him and his body – one that had clearly been sculpted by the Gods themselves. His shoulders were broad and strong. To her surprise, his muscled biceps were covered in tattoos, but he was too far away for her to make out the details. Excess water ran down his chest, over the toned muscles of his abs, down over the trail of dark hair, and underneath the V-shape that disappeared below the towel, the towel that hung so dangerously and deliciously low on his hips.

Rexah swallowed the lump in her throat. "I'm sorry, I didn't see you. I didn't mean to disturb you."

That stunning smirk of his spread across his lips. "I'm not complaining."

She felt her knees shake slightly, and not in a bad way. "I should go, give you some privacy."

"It's all right, Rexah. I'm sorry if I've made you feel uncomfortable. I'm just about to get dressed if you want to wait outside for me and I can walk with you to the dining tent?" he suggested.

Not being able to form any further words she gave him a sharp nod and swiftly exited the tent. Once outside, she leaned against the nearest tree and let out a long breath, one she didn't realise she'd been holding.

Gods help me.

A few moments later Kalen emerged fully dressed,

his dark damp hair falling into his blue eyes. His eyes brightened when he saw she'd waited for him. "Ready to go?" he asked her.

She nodded, and they began walking.

"I didn't know anyone was in there. I thought everyone would have been at the dining tent by now."

"Don't worry about it, princess," he said. "I'm not embarrassed or anything, and I hope you aren't either."

A smile spread across her face. "I just don't want you thinking I was intentionally watching you bathe."

"I wouldn't be embarrassed about that either." he smirked.

"So, it must be an amazing feeling to be with your people again," she said, swiftly changing the subject.

Kalen's smirk grew slightly, but he nodded. "It is. We might not share blood, but our bond is just as deep. I've spoken to a few of them, and after what happened in Vellwynd I have a feeling that we are going to become even closer."

Her eyes softened as she listened to him. She loved his voice. He could talk all day long and she would never tire of listening to him.

"The Valfae and the Dark Fae want nothing but death and destruction, but they will never tear us apart, no matter how hard they try," he said, almost growled.

"I won't let them harm my people ever again. Even if I must give my life to ensure it."

"You are a credit to your people, Kalen," Rexah told him.

"As are you, Your Highness."

"I wish you would stop calling me that," she replied, her stomach twisting with sorrow.

He frowned. "Why not? That's your title, is it not?"

"Your Highness, princess, heir. To what exactly? Ash and smoke? Ruins?" The ache of grief filled her chest, gripping tightly at her heart. "My days as a member of the royal family of Adorea are over. The sooner I come to terms with that, the better."

The warmth of Kalen's hand on hers made her look up at him. His walking slowed, and his eyes grew full of sadness and sympathy as he came to a stop.

"Don't look at me like that, Kalen," she said, her voice breaking. "Please."

"Like what, Rexah?"

"Like you pity me. Like you're scared at any moment I'm going to shatter into a million pieces, leaving fragments nobody would ever be able to put back together again."

"You are the sole survivor of a horrific attack. You should have died, you almost did, but you didn't. I've only known you for a few days, but I know the look of grief when I see it. I bare it every single day too," he said before his other hand came up and cupped her cheek. "You are so brave and so strong, but darling, you can't keep that grief buried inside you."

It wasn't until the tears slid down her face that she realised she was crying. Kalen gently wiped them away with his thumb.

"Don't be afraid to let go," he whispered.

Rexah could see Kalen's own pain and suffering in his eyes. She knew that he would understand. Sure, everyone here would understand too, but Kalen's grief ran deeper than theirs.

They were both broken.

"I can't," she whispered. "Not right now. If I do that, if I do let go, then I won't be able to stop myself from breaking beyond repair; there will be nothing left to fix."

"That's where you're wrong, darling," Kalen said. "One day you will let go, and when you do, I'll be there by your side. I'll pick up your broken pieces, and I'll mend them with my own."

Rexah felt like she was floating in the clouds. Her heart pounded something fierce in her chest as she watched Kalen's eyes move to her lips, only for a moment before he leaned in, and just as his lips were about to touch hers, she stepped back.

Kalen studied her face, his eyes soft and full of sadness. "I'm being too forward."

"No ... no. I-it's me," she stuttered, suddenly feeling too hot in her own skin. "I-I can't. I'm sorry."

Turning quickly on her heel, Rexah raced off. She heard Kalen calling her name, but she never looked back.

Rexah never went to the dining tent. Her appetite had diminished the moment she'd decided to step away from Kalen and run from him. She'd found herself at the edge of the camp where the stream ran into a small lake. Her back rested against one of the tall trees, her knees tucked into her chest and her face buried in them.

Did she want to kiss him? Of course, she did. He was drop dead gorgeous and she couldn't help but gravitate towards him. No matter how much she tried to resist, her body always threatened to betray her – if she wasn't careful, it would be her undoing.

The one thing, or rather one person, stopping her was Ryden. As stupid as that seemed to her, Ryden was still in her heart. He was gone, but it still felt like he was here. If she kissed Kalen, it would be breaking her promise to Ryden.

He's gone, Rexah.

She sighed and shoved that little voice to the back of her mind. Right now, the last thing she should be thinking about was kissing anyone. There were important things she still had to do and the first on her list was to get to Dorasa in one piece. The danger was far from over.

"Rexah?" a soft familiar voice asked to her right.

Lifting her head from her knees she saw Sorana standing there, a soft smile on her face and a plate of delicious smelling food in her hand.

"Mind if I join you?" she asked.

Rexah stretched her legs out and sat up a little straighter. "Of course."

Sorana sat down next to her and held out the plate. "I didn't see you in the dining hall. I thought you might be hungry."

"Thank you," Rexah said quietly as she took it from her.

"He means well," Sorana said.

274

Rexah looked over to the fae, picking at the delicious food in silence as she waited for her to elaborate.

Sorana smiled. "Kalen. I'm sure whatever he did to upset you, he didn't mean it."

"He's done nothing wrong. It was my fault. I have a lot of things to deal with and get through right now, and I know Kalen is only trying to help make me feel better, but I need time."

"That's completely understandable," Sorana replied, nodding her head. "You've both been through a lot. You're still going through a lot. It's not something you can easily get over in a few days."

Rexah continued to eat. "He saw his home destroyed just like I did."

"Kalen has always been kind and respectful. I watched him grow into the man he is today. Nothing prepared any of us for what happened in Vellwynd, but it completely ruined Kalen," she said. "He has never shown it, but I can see it in his eyes. Every time he thinks no one is paying attention to him, his eyes betray him."

"What happened in Vellwynd?" Rexah asked her. She felt awful for asking, but if she was ever going to fully understand Kalen then she needed to know.

"It was like any normal day. Everyone went about

their business until the storm rolled in. We've had storms before, of course, but this one carried a promise of death," Sorana said, a haunting look in her eyes.

Rexah set the almost empty plate down on the grass next to her, her appetite waning as the image of thunder and lightning on the night Adorea was attacked entered her mind.

"At first it was the wind, then the thunder began to rumble, and then they came. I've seen a few Valfae in my lifetime, but I've never seen so many in one place before, and I will never forget the terror that washed through me," Sorana told her, her fists clenching slightly.

"The Valfae thrive on fear," Rexah said. "Even the bravest warriors have cowered before them."

Sorana nodded softly. "Everyone was in a panic. Mothers grabbed their children whilst their husbands grabbed their swords, and then the slaughtering began."

Rexah could still hear the screams of her people; she still heard the horror of her own scream in the edges of her mind, the shriek that had escaped her lungs when her grandmother was ripped away.

"Kalen made sure the women and children got to safety, killing any Valfae that got in the way. Torbin was there by his side, both fighting and protecting with all their might. It wasn't until the storm grew stronger that things really took a turn for the worst. A Dark Fae general, not the one you met, appeared with two stronger Valfae."

Rexah's stomach was rolling. It was taking everything in her not to throw up on the grass. "What happened next?"

"One of those monsters held Kalen's mother, the other one held his younger brother, Niken," Sorana told her. "Kalen and Torbin were mind controlled by the General, and no matter how hard they tried, no matter how hard they tried to resist, they couldn't move."

Rexah slowly looked up at her, dreading the words she was about to hear.

"The General ordered the Valfae to kill them, and they did. They killed Kalen's mother and younger brother right in front of his eyes whilst he could do nothing but watch."

Rexah's heart broke, and tears filled her eyes. "Oh Gods."

"The General seemed satisfied with the destruction and misery he and his beasts had caused, and they left as quickly as they'd come. Torbin managed to get Kalen out of there before the fire completely consumed them," she said. "Since then, he's sworn revenge on them, not just for our home, but for his mother and brother."

"He will get his revenge," Rexah replied.

Sorana nodded softly. "You both will."

It had begun to rain shortly after their conversation, so Rexah had picked up the plate, pulled the hood of her cloak up, and walked with Sorana back into the camp. Sorana took the plate from her and bid her goodnight before she left.

Rexah's mind was racing as she headed for her tent. She knew what had happened in Vellwynd was terrible, but she hadn't realised the full extent of it. Her heart ached for him, for his people, and for his family.

A figure standing outside her tent made her stop in her tracks a few feet away. Kalen stood in the rain, seemingly unfazed by it. He'd been standing there for a while given how wet his hair and clothes were.

"Kalen," Rexah said softly.

He looked up and those gorgeous blue eyes connected with hers. "I know I'm the last person you want to see right now, but I had to make sure you're all right."

"Come inside," she said as she walked over and into her tent.

Rexah took off her cloak and hung it up as Kalen

followed her inside. She turned to him as he cleared his throat.

"First of all, I want to apologise. I don't know what's come over me. I'm not like that. I don't go around trying to kiss every woman I meet," he said. "I'm sorry if I've overstepped and made you uncomfortable."

Rexah didn't speak; she didn't know what to say, not because of what had almost happened between them, but because of what Sorana had told her.

She removed her boots and placed them to the side of her bed before making her way over to him and wrapping her arms around his waist. She rested the side of her face against his chest without a care that his shirt was wet against her cheek. She could hear how fast his heart was beating in his chest, and after a few long moments of complete stillness, she felt his arms slowly wrap around her, holding her close as he leaned his cheek on top of her head.

20

Rexah sat on the edge of her bed lacing up her boots, unable to stop thinking about the night before.

They'd hugged each other for a long time. Neither one of them spoke, they didn't need to. They held each other without judgement, without need of explanation, and it felt like the most natural, most right thing in the world. It was something she was sure they'd both been in great need of for a while.

When their embrace was over, Kalen had seen how tired she was and bid her goodnight. He'd kissed her forehead before he'd left, and it had taken every effort possible to not ask him to stay.

Later, when she had managed to fall asleep, her

dreams were filled with Kalen, and when she woke up from those dreams, she still thought of their embrace. She'd given up trying to stop thinking about it just before the sun began to rise.

Moving to her feet, she picked up her bag and placed it on the bed before gathering her things. No matter how safe she felt here or how badly she wanted to stay, she couldn't. Answers were waiting for her in Dorasa, according to her grandmother. Answers to what questions? She didn't know, but she had to find out.

Once her bag was packed and securely fastened, she grabbed her cloak and pulled it on, clipping the clasp together. She didn't know what Dorasa held for her, but it was important enough for her grandmother to tell her to go, so she would.

Before she stepped out of her tent, she took one of the potions Merin had made for her – she couldn't leave without her disguise. A cool breeze swept by that made the ends of her now golden-brown hair dance lightly around her shoulders.

Rexah made her way through the camp looking for Kalen and Torbin. She had to say goodbye to them. They'd done so much for her, and it would be unfair to leave without a word. She also wanted to say goodbye to Sorana.

It didn't take her long to find them. The three fae were sat around the unlit bonfire in the centre of the camp. Sorana was chatting with Vega whilst Kalen and Torbin laughed at something they were talking about. Kalen's laugh made her heart skip a beat, and when his eyes met hers, it felt like her heart had stopped all together.

She walked over to them. "Good morning."

"Good morning, Rexah. Did you sleep well?" Torbin smiled at her.

"I did, thank you." She smiled back at him.

"You're leaving," Kalen said, his eyes on the bag on her shoulder.

Rexah nodded. "I am. It's time for me to go. I've already stayed too long. I must be on my way."

Torbin's eyes saddened, and he looked at Kalen.

"Come to say goodbye then?" Kalen asked her.

She could hear the hint of sadness in his voice that he was trying so hard not to show. "Yes, I wanted to come and say my farewells. I wouldn't have felt right if I hadn't."

Torbin lifted his cup to his lips and held it there. "You know we're coming with you, right?"

Her eyes widened. "What?"

"I'll let you explain this one, Kal," Torbin said to Kalen before he sipped his drink.

Kalen stood up and walked over to her. "We are coming with you, to Dorasa."

"But ... but you're with your people now," she said, frowning. "I don't understand."

"Our people are safe, albeit for the time being, but the thought of you out there alone kills me ... us." He corrected himself quickly. "It kills us. Not that we don't think you're more than capable of taking care of yourself, but you know how vicious and dangerous the Valfae can be. Three of us together is better than one of us alone."

Rexah looked at Torbin before she looked back up at Kalen. "I can't ask you to leave your people."

"Good thing you aren't asking then, darling." Kalen smirked.

"There's no way I'm going to change your minds, is there?" she asked.

"Nope," Kalen replied, his smirk growing.

Torbin stood up after finishing off his drink. He lifted a bag over his shoulder that he'd had tucked away at his side. "We're ready to go when you are."

"You've packed already?"

"Yeah, we technically didn't unpack. We didn't

know when you'd be heading off, so we made sure we were packed and ready to go at all times," Torbin replied.

Rexah couldn't help but smile. "And your people are all right with you leaving right away?"

"They understand," Kalen said, picking up his own bag.

Nodding softly, Rexah smoothed out her cloak. "Well, let's get going then, before I change my mind."

"You will come back, won't you?" Sorana asked from behind her.

Rexah turned and her eyes softened. "Of course, I will. Thank you again, for everything you've done for me."

"No need to thank me," Sorana said, pulling Rexah into a hug. "You will always be welcome among the Vellwyndians. You are never alone."

"I will never forget this," Rexah whispered as she hugged her back.

Sorana slowly pulled away, her hands on Rexah's upper arms. "Go and find the answers you seek. Be brave and keep your chin up. It may seem dark, but lighter days are coming."

Rexah slowly bowed her head to her. "Until we meet again."

The fae smiled at her and returned the gesture. "Until we meet again, Rexah Ravenheart."

Rexah turned to Kalen and Torbin who were finishing saying their goodbyes to their people. She felt awful that they would be joining her, but she knew there was no use in trying to get them to stay, and soon they were making their way out of the camp.

It would be around a four-day journey to Dorasa on foot; their horses had gotten spooked by Venrhys and the Valfae and had run off. Kalen and Torbin had carried her the rest of the way to Savindeer. There were a few villages on the way to Dorasa that they hoped would have horses for sale to make their journey a little quicker, but for now they would walk.

"Thank you," Rexah said as they walked.

"For what, darling?" Kalen asked.

Her heart fluttered in her chest as usual when he called her that. "For coming with me. I really appreciate it."

Torbin grinned. "We're very fond of your company."

"I'm very fond of yours too." She grinned. Rexah didn't know what awaited her in Dorasa, but with Torbin and Kalen by her side, she wasn't afraid anymore.

"We'll keep moving for as long as possible. The

quicker we get to the next village, and hopefully access to horses, the better," Torbin said. "I don't want us to be out in the open any longer than we need to be."

Rexah nodded. She liked how Torbin took charge, like he was the planner of their group.

Their group.

That made her smile once more.

They travelled for most of the day. Rexah's legs felt as though they might fall off at any moment; they'd stopped now and again for short rests, but they only helped her aching muscles for so long. When Kalen announced they should find a place to camp for the night, Rexah almost let out a groan of relief.

Torbin found a dense group of trees that created the perfect amount of cover, and he wasted no time clearing some of the brush, sweeping away dead leaves and twigs to give them more room.

Rexah thanked Kalen when he gave her a spare bedroll, and she lay it out before sitting down, her legs screaming out in thanks to her. She gently massaged her aching limbs, trying to ease the pain in them as she watched Kalen walk off to collect some wood for a fire.

"So, what do you think is waiting for you in Dorasa?" Torbin asked as he sat down on his bedroll beside her.

Rexah shrugged her shoulders softly. "In all honesty, I don't know. My grandmother told me I'd find all my answers there. For all I know there could be nothing, but I have to go."

"I'm sorry about your grandmother, about what happened in Adorea," he said quietly.

"Thank you," she said, kicking the grief back into its box when it tried to escape. She would deal with it later, whenever later would be.

They sat in a comfortable silence for a few moments before Rexah broke it. "You were incredible during that fight with the Valfae. I've never seen anyone use magic like that before."

Torbin smiled at her. "Thanks. Although, I wish I hadn't been knocked unconscious," he said, his cheeks growing a little pink.

Rexah couldn't help the grin that spread across her face. "How do you use your power?"

"Fae blood is magic in itself when it comes to our fast healing and our aging, but the raw power within me is different. I've learned to tap into the magic I was born with by speaking the ancient language of the Gods, and thus my power awakens," he told her.

"What happens to those who aren't Power Blessed?" she asked.

"Well, you met a few of them at the haven," he said, smirking softly. "Vega, being one – just because they don't have power doesn't mean they're any less important."

Rexah nodded. "Sorana, is she Power Blessed?"

"She is. She can conjure light. I know it sounds unimpressive, but she can make it as dim or as bright as she likes. She's blinded our enemies in the past," he said, a look of remembrance on his face as he recalled the memory.

"That's incredible," Rexah said, her eyes wide. "It's so fascinating what your kind, The Chosen, can do."

"I'll take that as a compliment." He chuckled.

She couldn't help but wonder if Kalen was Power Blessed. She hadn't seen him use any magic during the fight, but that didn't mean he didn't possess any power.

"We'll need to keep the as fire low as possible," Kalen's voice said to their left as he approached their small camp.

Rexah nodded and helped him get the branches and

twigs he'd gathered into place. She sat back once they were done and watched with fascination as Torbin curled his fingers and flames appeared, licking up his long fingers. He stretched forward, and with the flick of his wrist he directed sparks of fire magic onto the wood which soon came to life with the flames.

Kalen sat on his bedroll to the left of Rexah. "We leave at first light."

Torbin settled himself against the large tree behind them, folding his arms across his chest.

Rexah looked over to Kalen who had also gotten himself comfortable, so she did the same, leaning back further into the tree. "Do you have power?" she asked him quietly.

His lips spread into a knee-shaking smile. "I do, yes."

Rexah found herself licking her suddenly dry lips. "What can you do? Or is that a really personal question?"

Kalen's eyes met hers, amusement dancing in them. "It's not like you're asking my age, darling, now *that* would be personal."

They both stared at one another for a moment before they laughed softly.

"I can manipulate the energy in the air, bend it to my will," he told her.

"So, you can move things without touching them?" she asked.

"Precisely," he said, nodding his head.

Something moved out the corner of her eye, and she shifted her gaze to a flower now floating in front of her. The rapid beating of her heart made her a little dizzy as she reached up and gently took hold of the stem. In the firelight she could see its petals were a beautiful mix of lilac and pink.

"You do that trick for all the girls?" she asked.

"Only the ones I like," he replied, smirking.

Rexah looked over to him again. "Is that so?"

"No." He grinned.

Her heart felt as though it was about to explode out of her chest at any second. She licked her lips again. Godsdamn it, why were her lips so dry?

"Stop licking your lips," Kalen commanded her, his ocean eyes fixed on her lips.

"W-what?" she asked, clearing her throat.

"Stop licking your lips or I'll not be responsible for my actions," he said with a seductive roughness to his voice.

Swallowing the lump in her throat, she nodded softly. "Thank you for the flower."

Kalen took a deep breath and his expression softened. "Sorry."

"It's all right." She smiled at him even though all she wanted to do was jump on him and let him do what the look in his eyes had promised.

Gods help me. No one in their right mind would think like that about a stranger. Well, he wasn't a stranger, but she hadn't known him long. One thing was for certain though, she couldn't deny the feeling in her heart, the feeling in her soul when she was around him, when he looked into her eyes, and when he looked at her like she wasn't a broken princess with no kingdom. She couldn't dismiss those feelings – not anymore.

21

The next day went by fairly quickly. They were making good time and only stopped now and again to eat and gather their strength. Conversation flowed with ease the whole time, and Rexah hadn't felt so at peace in what felt like a long time.

Kalen and Torbin engaged in friendly banter now and again, much to Rexah's amusement. She felt so secure with them, and she'd noticed how much she'd relaxed in their company. The constant tension in her shoulders had lessened to an occasional anxiety-fuelled stiffness, and she took that as a positive sign.

She was no fool though. She knew danger still lurked at every turn, and the grief buried deep within her chest never let her forget; its claws scraped at the edges of the cage she'd shoved it in, reminding her it was there, but she would never let it show on her face.

As the sun began to set, they found an area to set up camp. Rexah was starting to get used to camping, and she liked it.

"On your feet," Kalen said, the sharp point of one of his daggers aimed at her.

Rexah frowned. "What?"

"You heard me, on your feet," he replied. "Let me see those fighting skills again."

"You want to fight me?" she asked, arching her eyebrow.

"I want to keep up your strength. The road ahead is growing increasingly perilous. I need ... I want to make sure you can handle yourself," he said, correcting himself.

Rexah rose from her bedroll and looked him straight in the eye. "I'm more than capable of handling myself, and I'm happy to show you exactly what I can do."

Her dagger sang softly as she pulled it from her hip. Kalen's dark blue eyes seemed to grow darker, a look of challenge and hunger in them. Torbin sat back against one of the trees, folding his arms as he watched them, amusement dancing in his amber eyes.

"I won't go too hard on you. At any point if you want to stop—"

Rexah's dagger swiped milometers from his chest, cutting off his words as he stumbled back slightly. "If I was a little faster, you'd be dead right now," she said.

Kalen was speechless for a few moments before a grin spread across his face. "That's how you want to play, darling?"

"Bring it on." She smirked at him.

Kalen wasted no time and began his attack. His arm swung towards her, his blade reaching dangerously close to her neck, or at least it would have if she hadn't brought her hand up to block his wrist. Rexah spun and drove her elbow into his stomach, and when he doubled over with an *oomph*, her fist flew up and connected with his perfect jaw.

Kalen stumbled back, holding his nose. Rexah gave him no time to recover, the adrenaline running through her veins and boosting her confidence as she took another strike at him. This time he was fast and blocked her blade with his own, knocking her wrist away. Before Rexah knew what was happening, Kalen had grabbed her and spun her around so her back was against his chest. As he lifted his dagger to her throat, her hand shot up and her dagger blocked his just in time.

"Good." He panted, his hot breath on her neck.

Rexah breathed heavily as she said, "You've forgotten one thing."

When he chuckled, she felt it vibrate through his chest and against her back. "And what's that, darling?"

"You left your side exposed," she replied.

Rexah drove her elbow back into his right side. Kalen stumbled back and had no time to react as she knocked his weapon from his hand and spun, kicking his feet from under him. Kalen hit the forest floor with a groan, and she went with him, pinning him to the ground. The cool metal of her dagger gently dug into the skin of his throat. She watched as his eyes took in the way she straddled his hips, the fingers of her left hand splayed across his chest as she held him down, the hunger she knew was in her own eyes as she stared down at him. Her heart began to pound like a drum against her chest as Kalen's hands slowly slid up her thighs to rest on her hips. Instinctually, Rexah's hips dipped to meet resistance, and her breath hitched as she felt something hard beneath her.

"I'm going to go ... get some more firewood,"

Torbin said quietly before he walked off into the forest, the shuffle of his footsteps growing quieter as he went.

The hilt of the dagger began its familiar hum in her hand, and lightning crackled down the blade towards Kalen's throat. Rexah's eyes widened, and she shot to her feet before it could do any damage. She watched the lightning fizzle out before securing her dagger at her hip once again. Her blood sang in her veins, her skin tingled as she turned away from Kalen. *Calm down Rexah. Get a hold of yourself. Deep breaths.*

A gentle hand on her shoulder pulled her from her thoughts and she flinched from it. Looking up, she met Kalen's worried gaze.

"I'm sorry," he whispered to her.

Rexah took a few deep breaths, trying to calm her erratic heart. "It ... it's not you. I just ... I still have a lot to process, and I ..."

"It's okay. You don't have to explain, I get it," he replied, softly. "Just breathe, darling."

Rexah took a few deep, steadying breaths, her body slowly relaxing as she did. She pretended not to notice Kalen turn around, trying to sort the problem in his trousers that was standing to attention. She fought back the blush that threatened to spread across her face. Once he calmed himself, he sat down on his bedroll.

"What just happened? Where did that lightning come from? Do you have magic?" he asked softly.

She dropped back down onto her bedroll and shrugged her shoulders. "I don't know where it came from. It happened during the attack on my home. I was fighting one of the Valfae when the dagger began to vibrate, and before I knew it lightning was shooting down the blade and into the beast. I'm human. I don't possess any magic."

Kalen studied her. "Maybe the dagger is magical then."

Running her hand through her hair, she sighed. "I don't know."

"Get some rest, darling. We can talk about this tomorrow or whenever you feel up to it," he said.

Rexah nodded slowly and lay back, looking up at the blanket of twinkling stars. Her heart hurt, and each beat of it was a painful thump that spread throughout her body.

The strap of her bag dug uncomfortably into her shoulder as they made their way through the forest. She'd tried to ignore the ache, but it was becoming more difficult as time went on.

"You all right there?" Kalen asked her, suddenly appearing at her right side. His eyebrows were knitted together in a frown and his eyes shone with concern.

They hadn't talked about what had happened the night before; there was no need for words. He'd wrapped his blanket around her when she'd started shivering, and they'd given each other a look of apology and forgiveness.

She couldn't deny that it melted her heart when he worried about her. "I'm fine. It's just the strap of my bag digging into the wound on my shoulder," she told him as she adjusted it to a more comfortable position.

He nodded. "I can take it for you if you'd like?"

"Thanks, but I've got it," she said, smiling at him.

"Okay, well the offer still stands if you change your mind." He grinned as they continued down through the dirt road that led through the forest.

Rexah had a newfound love of being outdoors. She didn't know if it was due to growing up in the castle. Sure, she was able to go outside into the gardens, but as a member of the royal family, her safety was priority above anything else, above her ambitions and her dreams. So, being out here in the middle of the forest, far from Adorea and without the feeling of royal responsibility, for the first time in her whole life she felt free.

The sun was starting to set, turning the sky stunning shades of orange, pink, and purple. Her grandmother used to tell her that if the sky turned purple as the sun went down, it was a sign the Gods were happy and your luck was about to change for the better. Rexah sure hoped that was true, especially now.

The earth crunched softly beneath their feet as they walked, and Rexah felt peaceful and calm as she took in the colours of sunset. The serenity didn't last for long as she was yanked to the left, pushed through the forest brush, and shoved back into a tree.

"What the—" She was cut off by a hand covering her mouth.

"Quiet," Kalen ordered quietly.

Rexah frowned up at him and started to struggle against him. That was until she heard the loud snapping of twigs. Her body instantly froze when she realised why Kalen had suddenly thrown her against the nearest tree he could find. The sound of growling and the occasional snarl filled the air, and there was only one creature, one monster, that made those gods-awful sounds.

The Valfae.

Rexah felt her blood chill in her veins as the growling grew closer, and out the corner of her eye, she saw it slowly stalking its way up the dirt road they'd just been walking on like it was hunting its prey – and its prey was them.

The Valfae stopped in its tracks, its nose twitching as it sniffed at something in the air, and a growl of hunger emanated from its chest.

Kalen pressed his body further against Rexah's, and her heart almost leaped out of her throat. She felt every hard muscle in his abdomen, the pure strength of his body, and the heat from him made her legs shake. It was then she realised what he was doing: he was masking her scent with his own.

Rexah slowly looked up into his eyes. He didn't look as scared or as terrified as she felt and probably looked, instead he was cool, calm, and collected, and she could feel herself getting lost in his deep blue eyes, his scent enveloping her.

The Valfae was getting closer and closer to them. Suddenly, a loud noise caught the beast's attention on the other side of the woodland, and it tore away into the direction of the sound, growling and roaring as it went.

Rexah's eyes slowly moved from Kalen's to the other side of the road where Torbin was hiding behind one of the trees. He looked over to them and nodded his head, telling them that it was safe to come out.

Kalen removed his hand from Rexah's mouth. "Sorry, darling," he whispered to her.

"No, don't apologise," she replied quietly as they stepped out of the brush and back onto the dirt road. "You saved me. Again."

"I'll always save you," he told her, and she heard the sincerity in his voice.

"Are you both okay?" Torbin asked in a hushed tone as he approached them.

Rexah nodded softly. "Yes, are you?"

"I'm good. That was far too close for comfort," he said as he looked behind him in the direction the Valfae had gone before turning back to them. "We should get going before it comes back."

Both Rexah and Kalen nodded, and they set off again. This time they were quieter and on higher alert.

"What was the noise that caught its attention?"

Rexah asked softly when she felt they were far enough away.

"I threw a rock." Torbin smirked at her.

Rexah stared at him for a moment before she covered her mouth with her hand and giggled as silently as she could.

"They may be vicious and dangerous, but they can be so fucking stupid." Torbin chuckled lightly.

Considering how close they'd come to being Valfae food, Torbin sure knew how to lighten the mood.

Both Torbin and Kalen had shown no fear for those monsters, maybe it was the warrior in them, but like Rexah had told Sorana, even the bravest warriors had fallen to their knees in fear before them. Maybe what happened to their home, their families, was enough to make their need for revenge overshadow their fear.

A small part of her wished she could be like them. She wished she could channel Riona and let her bravery overshine the grief and terror she felt. Maybe one day that would happen, but it wasn't today.

"They're getting closer and closer," Rexah said.

Kalen's warm hand on the small of her back sent a calming wave through her body. "They won't get to you. I promise, Nes."

"I don't want either of you to feel like you have to

put all your time and effort into keeping me safe. You should be doing that back at the camp for your people," she replied, the use of her best friend's nickname waking up the grief inside her for a brief moment.

"We don't feel like we have to," Torbin said. "If we didn't want to then we would have stayed at the camp, but we wanted to come with you. Whether you like it or not, Nes, you are in a serious situation and without a few helping hands I fear it won't end well."

"Like it hasn't already started badly? My kingdom is destroyed. My people slaughtered. My…" Rexah trailed off feeling bile rising in the back of her throat.

Kalen gave Torbin a sharp look telling him not to push it. "Come on, let's keep going. It's going to be dark soon and I don't want us out in the open when the sun is gone."

Torbin gave Rexah an apologetic look before he went on ahead to scout for the perfect spot for them to settle down for the night. She knew he didn't mean anything bad by what he'd said. Every word had been the truth.

"Once Torbin has his heart set on something there's no telling him otherwise," Kalen told her, his arm now wrapped around her waist.

Rexah tried not to think anything of it. He was

comforting her. That was it. "It's okay, really. I know he means well, and I appreciate it. I appreciate everything you're both doing for me."

"I wouldn't have been able to sleep knowing you were out here by yourself," he admitted to her. "Not knowing if you were alive or if you were dying in a ditch somewhere, crying out for help."

The visual that his words had put in her head was a stomach wrenching one, but the pain in his voice sent her heart racing. "In all honesty, I didn't want to leave the camp without you."

They didn't stop walking but Kalen shifted his gaze down to her. His eyes were full of surprise and something that looked like hopefulness.

"And Torbin," she quickly added. "You...you and Torbin."

The look in his eyes never left as a soft smirk spread across his lips. "All right, Nes."

T t was the next afternoon by the time they made it to the nearest village. The village was small but still a little livelier than Oakhaven had been. The inn was pleasant; despite its name, The Bloody Rose was welcoming, and as far as Rexah could tell from her quick glance around, it was clean. After acquiring keys to a room and scoffing a bowl of their surprisingly tasty stew, Rexah excused herself and dragged her ever-aching legs upstairs.

She walked into her room, pulled the strap of her bag over her head, and set it down on the floor at the bottom of the bed before locking her room door – you could never be too careful. She pulled off her cloak and hung it up before she sat down on the edge of the bed. A small groan of relief left her lips as she slid her boots off her aching feet.

The bed squeaked softly as she lay down on her side and curled up. She sighed in bliss; the mattress was comfortable, better than any bedroll that was for sure; and she closed her eyes as she let herself relax.

Sleep began to fog her mind, and just as she was about to give into it, a knock on the door jolted her into a sitting position.

Carefully getting up and pulling out her dagger, she

made her way to the door. Her grip on the blade tightened as she opened the door slightly.

"Sorry to disturb you, can I come in?" Kalen asked her.

Relief flooded through her seeing it was him. Nodding, she stepped back and opened the door wider for him and he stepped inside.

"Everything okay?" she asked as she closed the door be.

"Yeah, everything's fine. I was actually coming here to ask you the same thing," he said.

Rexah nodded. "I'm fine. Well, as fine as I can be considering."

Kalen eyed the dagger in her hand. "Were you going to stab me?"

"Only if you were evil," she replied, setting the blade down on the bed.

Kalen chuckled softly before his features turned serious. "That night before we left the safe haven, I can't stop thinking about it," he told her.

The night they'd almost kissed. The night they'd held each other in silence. She couldn't stop thinking about it too, and she would never forget it.

"You've already apologised, Kalen. There's no need to do it again," she said.

"I wasn't going to, and I know we've spoken about it already, but I need you to know that I would never force you to do anything you don't want to do. There are plenty of scum in this world that wouldn't care, but I do," he said.

Rexah nodded her head. "I know, and I really appreciate it, and I appreciate you taking the time to reassure me."

"You are so incredibly brave, Rexah. We have both been through similar things, but you lost everything," he said, his eyes full of sadness.

"You lost your mother and your brother," she replied quietly. "Sorana told me what happened back in Vellwynd, and Kalen, I am so sorry."

A muscle ticked in his perfect jaw as the memory replayed in his mind, his hands clenching into fists at his sides as he tried to shove it away, much like she did with her own grief.

"We are both damaged," Rexah whispered.

Kalen moved closer to her, so he stood only a few feet away. "We are, but we won't be forever."

"You can't know what the future has in store for me or for you. My grandmother used to tell me that if things were bad then they couldn't get worse, they could only get better, but I don't see how any of this gets better." She sighed.

"Maybe the answer to that question is in Dorasa," he suggested.

Rexah shrugged her shoulders. "I don't know what awaits me there. Sure, it could be something life changing that fills my life with sunshine and rainbows, but more realistically, there could be nothing there for me, and I won't know where to go from there."

"Torbin and I won't leave you there alone unless you want us to. We won't abandon you; I won't abandon you," he whispered.

Rexah met his gaze, and it wasn't until she did that she realised he'd moved closer, much closer. She could feel the heat radiating from his body and her stomach fluttered madly.

"Kalen ..." she whispered but trailed off when he slowly leaned down and pressed his lips to hers.

Rexah didn't move. Her mind was full of thoughts travelling a million miles an hour through her head, but once her brain had registered what was happening, she slowly kissed him back.

The kiss was slow, gentle, and full of tenderness. His mouth moved against hers as he slowly backed her into the door, and her blood began to sing in her veins. His hands gently slid to her waist, and her hands found their way up to cup his face.

Kalen's strong body pressed against hers as the kiss began to deepen, and Rexah's fingers pushed into his dark hair. When his tongue brushed hers, a quiet moan escaped her, and the sound of it brought her back to her senses.

Rexah pulled away from the kiss, her breathing heavy.

"Wow," Kalen whispered, his own breathing ragged.

She thought she would feel remorse for kissing someone else, but she didn't. The feeling that coursed through her was the exact opposite; she felt like something deep inside her had stirred.

"My thoughts exactly," she whispered back as her eyes connected with his once again.

"There are those stunning eyes," he said, a soft grin spreading across his face.

She frowned and looked down at her hair; the potion had worn off, and that meant her eyes were back to their natural shade of violet.

Kalen stepped back, letting go of her waist. "I should go. We need all the rest we can get."

Rexah nodded and stepped away from the door, but just as he pulled the handle and opened it, she opened her mouth and the word escaped her before she could stop it. "Wait."

Kalen paused and looked down at her.

"Will ... will you stay with me?" she whispered.

Gods, you're making yourself look like a fool.

Kalen closed the door and locked it before he gently took her hand in his. "Forever."

Rexah walked over to her bag and pulled out the nightdress that she'd been given back at Savindeer. She looked over her shoulder to find Kalen had turned his back to her to give her privacy whilst she changed. Her clothes soon joined the boots in a pile on the wooden floor. Once her nightdress was on, she picked up her clothes and folded them neatly before putting them on the side.

Kalen had taken his own boots off, and Rexah frowned softly when she watched him sit down in the chair in the corner of the room.

"No," she said as she walked over to the bed. "I ... I meant stay with me, here."

Kalen's gaze fixed on her. "Are you sure?"

"I am," she replied before she could change her mind. "I'm sure."

Yes, she was sure, but that didn't stop her heart

beating furiously in her chest as she pulled back the soft covers and slid into the bed.

The mattress dipped slightly as Kalen got in beside her. They got comfortable, laying on their sides facing each other.

"If you get too uncomfortable, just let me know," he whispered. "I don't mind sleeping in the chair."

A small smile spread across her lips; she loved how caring and gentle he was with her. "Thank you, but I'm quite content with you right here."

"I meant what I said earlier, I won't abandon you, not when you need someone more than anything," he told her.

"I won't abandon you either," she said, her voice quiet.

Kalen slowly reached for her and pulled her to him, his arms circling around her. She didn't resist and didn't pull away. She snuggled into the warmth of his body, her head fitting perfectly under his chin, and with the side of her face pressed against his shoulder, she smiled.

For tonight, she was safe.

22

It was the best sleep she'd had in so long: no nightmares plagued her dreams, she didn't wake up in a cold sweat with her heart almost beating out of her chest, and her dreams were pleasant. Her body and mind felt more rested than it had ever been, so when she did wake up the next morning, she didn't want to get out of the bed or out of Kalen's arms.

Rexah slowly looked up at him. He was still sleeping, his arms wrapped around her. At some point during the night, their legs had become entangled with each other, and she didn't mind one bit.

Before, she would recoil at the thought of another man touching or being this close to her, but for once that little voice inside her head was right. Ryden was gone and he wasn't coming back. He would always be a part of her, she would never forget him, but he wouldn't want her to live her life in misery, and neither would her grandmother.

However, just because Kalen had agreed to stay with her last night didn't mean he saw it that way. He was being supportive. He was her friend…

Yes, Rexah, a supportive friend who kissed you, who you kissed back.

She closed her eyes. She had to stop being so stupid; there were more important things going on than what was happening in her confusing, non-existent love life. Romance of any kind could be put on hold until she sorted through her heartache and grief.

"You know, it's not polite to stare at someone whilst they sleep," Kalen mumbled, pulling her from her thoughts.

Rexah's eyes moved to his face, and she saw his eyes were still closed. "Well, technically you're awake, so I'm not being impolite."

His eyes opened slightly, a small smirk playing on his lips. "I guess you're right."

She grinned up at him. "I guess I am."

Kalen reached up and gently moved a piece of her dark hair from her face. "How are you feeling?"

His touch made her heart stumble in her chest. "Better than I was last night. Thank you for staying with me."

"Always." He smiled at her.

They lay in each other's arms for ten more minutes before they got up; no matter how much Rexah didn't want to let go of him, she had to eventually.

Kalen went back to his own room, giving her a gentle kiss on the forehead before he left. She couldn't tell if she was wary or exhilarated by whatever was happening between them. Whatever it was, she shoved the feeling away for now and got dressed.

Once her bag was packed and her cloak was on, and she had made sure the potion took effect, she walked out of the room and headed downstairs. Kalen and Torbin weren't there yet, so she sat down on one of the stools by the bar and waited, her bag secured over her shoulder.

It was still very early in the morning; the sun had only just started to rise, so the main area of the inn was almost empty. A man sat at one of the tables at the far end of the room, slouched over on the table, and the sound of his snoring echoed throughout the space. It was clear from the tankard still in is hand that he'd drank until he'd passed out.

"There's no way it'll ever be the same," a voice to her left said quietly.

Turning her attention to where the voice had come from, she saw another two men at a table in the far corner of the room looking like they were ready to pass out from the amount of alcohol they'd consumed.

"No one has managed to get near Adorea after the attack. It's infested with those beasts," his friend replied.

It felt like someone had reached into her chest and squeezed her heart tightly.

"It's a damn shame. I bet the loot left behind would make us rich," the first man sighed.

"You really are an idiot. The castle was destroyed. It's nothing but rubble and ash. You really think there would be anything of value left?" the second man said, shaking his head in disbelief at the stupidity of his friend.

"Well, when you put it that way, I guess not," he said, taking a sip from his tankard. "I tell you this though, if I lived in that castle and those beasts attacked, I'd never have lay down to them. They'd never have destroyed it. I'd have destroyed them."

Rexah couldn't sit there any longer. She felt bile rise to the back of her throat, so she stood up and hurried outside.

She took a deep breath, filling her lungs with the crisp morning air as she tried to stop the nausea.

People talked; people always loved to speculate and gossip; but when it was about your own home, your own people, and your own family, it cut deeper. Especially when they never knew your loved ones. Especially when they didn't witness the horror first-hand.

People always thought they knew better.

A gentle hand on her shoulder made her jump in fright and take a steadying step back.

"Darling? Are you okay?" Kalen asked her, his eyes filled with worry.

Rexah relaxed as she felt the familiar squeeze of his hand on her shoulder. "Yeah, I'm fine."

Torbin stepped beside Kalen. "You sure?"

"A few of the drunkards were talking about Adorea," she whispered to them. "I couldn't listen to it any longer."

Torbin's eyes softened as he nodded his head in

understanding. "We're ready to go and see about horses if you are?"

"Let's get going," she said, not wanting to talk about it any further.

The stables were small, but they had a fair number of horses; Rexah counted at least six. She'd left the haggling to Torbin, who was a man of many talents it seemed. He'd managed to get two horses for a good price, though Rexah had no idea how much a good price for a horse was. In her days as a royal, horses were gifted more often than they were purchased.

It occurred to her in that moment just how sheltered and privileged her life had been. Looking around at the villagers, it was evident that they didn't have much, but what was plain to see was that they had each other, and that was worth more than anything coin could ever buy.

Having three people in their party and only two horses meant Rexah had to buddy up with someone, that someone being Kalen. He moved forward to help her, but she kindly refused him.

"I can do this. I'm trained, remember?" she asked, smirking softly before she pulled herself up onto the horse with absolute grace. When Kalen made no immediate move to get on behind her, she looked down at him to find a look of pure admiration on his face. "What?"

"Nothing," he said, clearing his throat before he swung up onto the horse.

Rexah felt those powerful muscles of his body against her back, his strong thighs resting against either side of hers as he settled himself on the saddle. She willed her pounding heart to calm down, and with a quick nod to Torbin after he took the reins in his hands, they set off.

Gods, this part of the journey is either going to be torturous or interesting.

Thanks to the horses, their travel time was reduced by a day. They had rested overnight, and as soon as the early morning wildlife began to wake the forest up with their songs and calls, they set off again. Time was a precious thing, and they couldn't waste a single second of it.

According to Torbin, they would reach Dorasa by midday, and the closer they got the more Rexah's stomach twisted with nerves. She'd gone through so many scenarios in her head of what would happen when she got there. The most ridiculous one her damaged mind had conjured up was that her grandmother would be there waiting for her with open arms. If only that was true. A girl could dream.

They kept their conversations as quiet as possible as they made their way through the forest. Rexah could hardly focus on the conversation as her mind raced at the feeling of Kalen's body against hers. It didn't help when he slid his arm around her waist to secure her in the saddle, his chest pressed firmly against her as he did so. Torbin was talking, but she couldn't hear him; his words were echoes as her body began to react to Kalen's touch. Swallowing the lump in her throat, she gently placed her hand on his arm – something firm she could hold onto better than the saddle.

Rexah's blood began to hum once again in her veins, something it seemed to do every time he touched her, and her skin tingled.

"I wonder if that cake shop is still there," Kalen said, pulling her from her thoughts.

Torbin grinned. "I hope so. Nina's cakes are the best in the realm."

"Well, if the shop is still there then *I'm* buying us

some cakes," Rexah told them. "You've both paid for more than enough for me."

"I'm sure we can make an exception." Torbin chuckled.

Rexah smiled. "Good, because I'd have bought them anyway. I hope you know I've got high hopes for these cakes now, so they better not disappoint."

"Oh, don't worry about that, darling, I promise you won't be disappointed," Kalen said, his breath tickling her ear. It would have sent a shiver through her if she hadn't anticipated he would do something irresistible and squashed her body's response before it could surface.

An hour or so later, Rexah felt her eyes begin to droop. She was trying her hardest to stay awake; the last thing she wanted was to fall asleep and fall off the horse, though with Kalen's supportive arm around her waist, she knew the likelihood of that happening was very slim. The thought of being safe in his arms eventually led to her giving in and letting sleep take over.

It felt as though she'd only closed her eyes for ten minutes when she woke with a start. A change in the sound of the horse's hooves on the ground had woken her.

"Shh, it's okay," Kalen's soothing voice said into her

ear. This time she couldn't stop the slight tremor her body gave in response.

Shifting her gaze to the ground, she saw that it was no longer the forest floor but a light grey stone. It was then she realised how far back she'd sank into Kalen in her sleep. Quickly, she sat up straighter and looked behind them to see the forest fading further and further away.

"We've just left the forest," Kalen said softly to her. "Look ahead."

Following his instructions, she moved her gaze back in the direction they were heading, and her eyes grew wide.

There it was.

She could only make out the distant shapes of buildings made of grey brick or stone – from the distance she couldn't know for sure which it was – that stood scattered along the horizon. Behind it, the Edarian Sea stretched out for miles, disappearing into the distance.

Dorasa.

She couldn't believe they'd made it. They were here. Their horses continued their approach as she stared in wonder. *At any moment I'm going to wake up to find this is all a dream.*

The fear of the unknown suddenly gripped her tight, suffocating her as the town drew closer.

"Darling, breathe," Kalen whispered to her. "Everything will be all right. You're safe with us. You're safe with me."

The ache in her chest began to ease at his words. "I can do this," she whispered. She didn't know if she spoke to Kalen or herself, but it was the truth. She could do this.

The pounding of her heart didn't ease as they drew closer and closer. The town was alive with people; she could hear them as they approached the stables situated on the edge of the town. Torbin dismounted his horse and Kalen followed suit, turning to Rexah and holding is arms out to her.

Rexah didn't need help getting off the horse, but she wasn't about to turn down his offer. She swung her leg round and held onto his shoulders as his strong hands gripped her hips and gently lowered her to her feet.

After nodding her thanks to him, she looked over to the stable hand; he was an older man with a bald head, and his light green eyes were friendly.

The stable hand gave the three a warm smile before greeting them, and soon the horses were settled in the stables for a small amount of coin. Yet again, neither

Kalen nor Torbin would let her pay. *I really hope that godsdamned cake shop is still open.*

A surreal feeling washed over her as they made their way into Dorasa. She wasn't sure why she felt that way; she'd never been here before, nothing of sentimental value remained. Since the fall of Adorea she'd been so fixated on getting here that it didn't feel real now that she was walking through the streets, now that she walked by the market stalls and the residents of Dorasa.

A woman to their left called out to passers-by, encouraging them to purchase her wares of handmade candles and beautifully scented incense. To their right, a man did the same, except he was selling exotic trinkets. She was tempted to go over and have a look at what he had to offer, but a look from Kalen made her reconsider. He was right: they had more important issues to be dealing with right now.

"So, what are we looking for? Is there someone you're here to meet up with?" Kalen asked her as they reached the main square around twenty minutes later.

Rexah had been keeping an eye out for anything or anyone that stood out to her, but she'd had no luck. Nothing jumped out at her. She sighed and shook her head. "No, I have no idea who or what I'm looking for here. My grandmother didn't exactly have the time to elaborate on her order to tell me to go to Dorasa."

Kalen cringed slightly. "Sorry, darling, I didn't mean it like that."

"No, it's okay, Kalen. I'm just starting to wonder if it was a huge mistake coming here with no knowledge of who or what I'm actually looking for," she said, defeated.

"Let's take a look around the town. If we don't find anything then we can rent some rooms at an inn and rest, start afresh tomorrow," Kalen suggested.

"Okay," she said quietly, nodding her head.

Torbin and Kalen began walking, heading towards the other side of the square. Rexah moved to join them when suddenly something caught her eye, and she halted. At the end of the row of shops to her right, there was a smaller shop with walls of a darker grey than the buildings surrounding it. Her eyes narrowed as she tried to make out the details of the shop, but she was too far away.

Her feet began carrying her towards the shop before she could even think. She could vaguely hear Kalen calling for her, using her fake name, but she didn't stop – she had to see what made this building so special. Why had it caught her eye?

Rexah soon stopped outside the shop. The door was held open by a metal bucket, and a medium sized window to the left of the open door allowed anyone walking by to see in. From what she could see from her position, it looked like a carpenter's shop, and as she backed away from the window and looked up, she read the name embossed on the sign above the door: Wylan's Woodwork.

"Nes, are you okay?" Torbin asked from behind her.

She didn't answer him. Her gaze was fixed on the sign, not on the name of the shop but on the symbol etched into the wood beside it.

The head of a raven.

The hair on the back of her neck stood on end as a chill worked its way through her body. This was the sign she'd been looking for, quite literally. It was too much of a coincidence to simply ignore it. She tore her gaze away from the sign overhead and looked at the open doorway.

"This is it," she whispered. "This has to be it."

"You're sure? Do you want me to go in first?" Kalen asked her.

Rexah shook her head. "No, I'll go first, but you'll both come with me, won't you?"

Kalen's deep blue eyes softened. "To the ends of the earth, darling."

She could have kissed him right then and there, but she didn't. Taking a deep breath to ground herself, she slowly stepped inside the shop.

It was much bigger on the inside than it looked on the outside. The smell of wood shavings filled the air, and various tools littered the shelves around the room, as well as jars filled with liquids, some labelled wax, polish, and resin.

An unlit fireplace sat to the right of a large wooden workbench placed in the centre of the space. A man stood there with his back to her, engrossed in the task of smoothing out the edges of a plank of wood.

The sound of their shuffling feet on the floor made him pause for a moment before he spoke. "Hold on, I'll be right with you."

"I'm sorry we've disturbed your work. We can come back later," Rexah said.

A moment later, the man set the equipment down on the workbench. He reached up and pulled off his protective glasses before setting them down beside the tool. "All right, how can I help you today?" he said as he turned, giving them a warm and welcoming smile, wiping his hands on the dust covered apron he wore.

The world shifted beneath Rexah's feet as she took in his familiar features, the way his dimples appeared when he smiled, and the small scar on his left cheek. Her heart felt as though it had stopped beating when she looked in his familiar eyes – her eyes.

When she managed to find her voice, there was only one question, one word that left her lips in a broken whisper.

"Father?"

23

There was absolutely no mistaking it, the man standing in front of her was her father. She had stared long enough at their only family portrait to know that this was him. His hair had some grey streaks through it, his skin a little wrinkled, but other than that, he didn't look any different to that portrait.

No one spoke for what felt like an eternity. Rexah couldn't find any other words to say. Her father wasn't dead; he was standing right in front of her, alive and well. She knew she wasn't dreaming because Kalen and Torbin could see him too. The look of pure shock and surprise on her father's face told her that he hadn't been expecting a visit from her. Not today, not ever.

"Rexah?" he whispered in disbelief, breaking the silence.

Her head was spinning as she tried to process every thought swirling around in her mind, tears burning in her eyes. Kalen's strong hand on the small of her back grounded her once again.

"My little girl," he whispered as he took a step forward but stopped when Rexah stepped back, moving further into Kalen.

"Give her a minute," Kalen said to her father.

He looked at both fae before his eyes settled back on Rexah. "I'd heard of the attack on Adorea and I ... I thought you'd perished," he replied, his voice thick with grief.

"A lot has happened," Kalen said. "She's still trying to process it all."

"Forgive me," her father said. "Who are you?"

"I'm Kalen, this is Torbin," he replied, motioning to his friend.

He nodded softly. "I'm Oliver Wylan."

Rexah's mind was moving at a million miles an hour. Her knees trembled and her stomach rolled. "I ... I don't understand," she barely managed to whisper.

"I'm sure you have a lot of questions and I'm more than happy to answer them," Oliver said, looking at his daughter with sympathy in his eyes. "But I think it would be best if we went back to my home where we can have a proper discussion. You can never be certain who might be listening; you can never be too careful."

Torbin nodded. "We will go to the nearest tavern and wait until you are finished here."

"No, it's okay. I can close up the shop for the day. This piece I'm working on is going to take me a few months anyway," he replied.

Once the shop was closed Oliver guided them through the town. He explained what certain shops sold along the way, trying to make small talk, and trying to lighten the mood. *Or it could be down to how nervous and in shock he is too,* Rexah thought.

Rexah walked beside Kalen, practically stuck to his side as Torbin walked behind them. They made their way through the streets, past a butcher' shop, an apothecary hut, and a glorious bookshop that on any other occasion she would not hesitate to enter. He led them away from the busy main square, and Rexah was surprised when he guided them down a dirt path that led away from the town and into the forest. It made her feel a little uneasy, but that feeling was soon diminished when a beautiful wooden cottage came into view. The sun bounced off the elliptical windows and drew Rexah's attention to a willow tree that grew a stone's throw away from the home.

"Did you build this?" Rexah found herself asking her father.

A smile appeared on his face. "I sure did. I built it with my own two hands. It took me a while, but it was worth it."

They made their way up the stone path towards the cottage. Oliver stopped them once they got to the front door, which was painted a deep violet colour – Rexah didn't think it was a coincidence.

"Deep breath, okay?" her father said.

Rexah frowned in confusion, but she nodded. Her stomach fluttered with nerves as she watched him open the door and head inside. She glanced quickly over her shoulder; Torbin gave her a firm nod and Kalen offered an encouraging smile. With a deep breath, she followed her father inside.

The interior of the cottage was just as beautiful as the exterior. They walked immediately into a living and kitchen area; the floral fragrance from the bunch of lavender on the windowsill mixed with the earthy scent of basil from the kitchen screamed comfort, safety, and belonging. The feeling that washed over Rexah in that moment was one she hadn't felt in a long time: the feeling of home.

"Is that you, Oliver?" a female voice asked from down the hallway.

"Yes, it's me," he replied as Kalen helped Rexah take off her cloak.

"You're home early," the woman called back to him.

"I am, something came up," Oliver said, looking down at Rexah.

Rexah watched as Kalen collected her and Torbin's cloaks and hung them on the pegs fitted to the wall.

"What do you mean something came up?" the woman asked, her voice louder now. "I hope it's nothing to worry about?"

Rexah looked over in time to see her appear from the hallway, and for the second time that day, her heart felt like it had stopped dead in her chest as she took in the softly curled brown hair and deep brown eyes of her mother.

Her mother gave her the same shocked expression she was sure Rexah was giving her back. Rexah felt her body begin to shake with adrenaline as her mother took a few tentative steps towards her.

"Rexah, my sweet Rexah." Her mother began to sob quietly.

Surely this was all a dream, it had to be. There was no way this was real life. Her mother and father were dead, they had been since she was a baby. Yet here they were, flesh and bone and breathing.

"I ... I don't understand," Rexah whispered again.

What is going on? This is a trick, a cruel trick. It has to be.

"There is so much we need to talk about, my love. Take a seat, and I will make us some tea," her mother said before she spotted the two fae by the front door.

Both Torbin and Kalen bowed their heads slightly to her in greeting.

"Well met. I am Kalen," he said softly. "This is my friend, Torbin."

"Welcome to our home. I'm Amelia," her mother replied with a smile on her face – Rexah's smile. "Would you like some tea?"

Kalen nodded. "Please, thank you," he said, his hand returning to the small of her back, rubbing in small, supportive circles.

Rexah's eyes softened, and her heart melted. She knew all he wanted to do was hold her close, she could almost feel his want rolling off him in waves. She felt the exact same way but shoved the feeling away, for now.

"Please, make yourselves comfortable," Oliver said as he walked over to the armchair and sat down.

Rexah turned and walked over to the dark blue settee, covered with beautifully embroidered gold flowers, and sat down with Kalen and Torbin either side of her. Her heart was still beating fiercely in her chest, anxious to hear their side of the story.

Amelia set a tray on the table that held steaming cups of delicious smelling tea before she sat down in the other armchair to Rexah's right.

"Here you go, sweetheart," Oliver said, handing her one of the cups.

Rexah thanked him quietly as she took it. "You have such a beautiful home."

"Thank you. Your father did an amazing job. It's exactly what we dreamed of." Amelia smiled.

"It took a such long time to build, but like I said, in the end, it was worth it," Oliver said, sipping his tea.

Amelia studied her daughter. "Forgive me, Rexah, but, your hair and eye colour are different to what I'd imagined."

Rexah explained how the potion Merin had made for her worked, which her mother seemed utterly impressed with.

"I think it's time we explained what happened," Oliver said, setting his tea back down on the tray.

Rexah's stomach twisted. Did she really want to know? This is the reason why her grandmother sent her here; she had known her parents were still alive, and they would give her the answers she needed.

My grandmother lied to me my whole life, she thought as another stab of grief and betrayal coursed through her.

"I need you to answer me something first," Rexah said, her throat suddenly dry. "Why did you abandon me?"

The look of pain on her parents' faces told her that was not the reason why they hadn't been in her life, and she felt a little guilty for asking, but she had to know.

"We didn't abandon you, Rexah," Amelia said.

"My grandmother," she said, swallowing the lump in her throat at the mention of her, "Aurelia told me that on your journey home from the south, your wagon was attacked by bandits, and the reason why I survived was because I wasn't with you at the time, I was with her. How much of that is the truth?"

There was a long pause of silence, longer than Rexah was comfortable with, and it ultimately answered her question.

Oliver cleared his throat softly. "None of that is the truth."

Rexah had expected that to be the case, but that didn't stop the aching pain that spread through her chest at the lies her grandmother had told her all her life. However, she knew there had to be a godsdamn good reason for it, and she needed to know what that reason was.

"This isn't going to be an easy conversation," Amelia said. "We didn't abandon you, not through choice, at least."

Rexah frowned as she set her tea down on the tray with trembling hands. "What do you mean 'not through choice'? Did someone force you to leave?"

Oliver took a deep breath. "You know the history of your ancestor, Queen Riona. Your grandmother told you, yes?"

"Yes, she told me everything. The history of our family were my bedtime stories," she replied, clasping her hands tightly in her lap to stop them shaking. "Riona was a fierce warrior who defended our home to the very end."

"There is a part of that history that we asked your grandmother not to tell you," Oliver said.

A chill ran down her spine. "And what part was that?"

"Riona Ravenheart wasn't human," Oliver told her. "She was fae."

Rexah's eyes widened. "That … that's impossible. If she was fae then we all would have fae blood in our veins. I've seen her portrait many times, and she didn't have pointed ears."

"When her portrait was taken, she was human. She became fae a year after her daughter, Arius, was born. That's why the rest of our family don't have fae blood," Amelia said.

Rexah could see in her mother's eyes that it wasn't easy to tell her this, just like it wasn't easy for her to hear. Riona wasn't human when she died; if that was true, then that was of huge importance.

"No; a human cannot turn into a fae," Rexah said, shaking her head refusing to believe it. "That's the most ridiculous thing I've ever heard."

"Please listen to what we have to say, and then you can do and say what you wish once we're done," Oliver said, his voice gentle. "We have no reason to lie to you, Rexah."

Kalen gently took her hand in his and squeezed it softly.

Rexah took a steadying breath and nodded. "I'm sorry, go on," she said.

"The Dark Fae and their beasts descended upon Adorea with only one goal: death. Riona rallied the Adorian Army, humans and fae together," Amelia continued. "Her army had an advantage though, not the battlefield or number of soldiers, no – the advantage they had was the sword Riona wielded, The Shadow Star."

"The Shadow Star was a weapon of incredible power," Oliver said, continuing the story. "A blade crafted by the Gods themselves. It was the sword that turned Riona into a fae; as soon as she lifted it, the power within it coursed through her and changed her."

"Why did it turn her into a fae? Where did she find the sword?" Rexah asked. There were so many questions swirling in her head and those were the first she clung to.

"No one knows," Oliver replied. "The history of the sword itself is mostly unknown, as is its current location. When Riona died the sword disappeared without a trace."

Rexah sat in silence for a few moments as she let the information sink in. It sounded like a tale from one of her story books, but it was a part of her history that had been kept from her, and she still didn't understand why.

"What does any of that have to do with why I've been lied to all my life?" she asked them, anger edging her voice.

"The sword can only be awakened by the power of the Chosen, and it can only be wielded by those who are blessed by the Gods – the Raven God specifically," Amelia said.

Oliver took a deep breath. "The power is known as the Blood of the Raven. Riona has been the only person, as far as the history books go back, that was chosen to possess this power."

"At least that was until you were born," Amelia said quietly.

Rexah was sure her heart had stopped dead in her chest. The room began to spin as she felt her throat begin to close up. Oliver reached out and gently put his hand on her knee in a comforting gesture, but Rexah instinctively moved away as far as she could on the settee, almost sitting on Kalen's lap.

"You honestly think I am the next *chosen one?*" Rexah asked, not completely believing their story.

"We don't *think*, Rexah. We *know*," Oliver replied.

It was Torbin who spoke next, much to Rexah's surprise. "And how do you *know* this exactly?"

"Her hair and eyes are the most obvious giveaway; her physical resemblance to Riona is uncanny. No one else in our family possessed those features, and the significance of this cannot be understated," Amelia said softly before turning her attention back to her daughter. "Also, you have the birth mark, the same one Riona had."

Rexah's hand self-consciously went to the back of her neck, her fingers touching the raven-shaped birth mark. Next to no one knew it was there; the only people who did were her grandmother, Nesrin, and Ryden, and they were all gone.

This is the reason why; this is the answer she failed to give me whenever I asked about it.

"We know this is a lot for you to take in, my love." Her mother's soothing voice comforted her. "We are so sorry it was kept from you. We know it's not easy to hear any of this."

"You know nothing of what I've had to go through this past month or so," she whispered. She knew that was a low blow, and she regretted saying it the moment the words left her lips. "Forgive me, I'm just trying to process a lot of new information as well as everything that happened in Adorea. It's been a terribly difficult few weeks."

"No need to apologise. We don't have to talk about everything right now. Let's leave it for later tonight, or maybe tomorrow, give you time to process it and let it sink in," Oliver suggested.

"I'd like that," Rexah replied, nodding her head.

Oliver nodded and gave her a small smile before he rose from his seat. He picked up the tray with the cups on it and took it into the kitchen.

"You are so beautiful," Amelia told her.

Rexah looked at her mother, her eyes softening. "I know this must be a shock for you too, me being here."

"A welcome shock." Amelia nodded as her eyes saddened. "We feared you were dead. When we heard about the attack, how violent it was, we were heartbroken. The sorrow we already felt turned into a new kind of grief. Not only did I lose my mother, but I lost my daughter for a second time."

Rexah could see the pain in her mother's eyes, and it sent an ache through her. *Yes, they lied to me – everyone lied to me – but at the end of the day, they're my family.* Rexah reached over and gently took her mother's hand in hers, squeezing it softly.

The front door of the cottage swung open suddenly, letting in a blast of cold air.

"I need to get a new job. I'm sorry, but I cannot work in that tavern any longer. The customers are rude and absolutely stink of ..." A male voice trailed off.

Rexah looked up to see a man around the same age as her standing by the door with a look of pure surprise on his face. She didn't know him, of course she didn't, but that's not what made every inch of her body lurch forward, standing with the wave of shock that passed through her.

She stood frozen, staring at what seemed like a mirror image of herself – a male version of herself.

"I didn't think you'd be home so soon," Amelia said, her voice laced with nerves as she rose to her feet too.

Rexah stared at him, unable to form any words. He was staring right back at her with a confused look on his face.

"What the hell is going on here?" he asked when he found his voice once more.

"I was going to tell you, I swear," Amelia said, gently turning Rexah to face her.

Rexah studied her mother's face. She still couldn't find her voice, and she knew her eyes told her mother how disorientated she was, how fast her mind was racing. Another family secret she was about to learn.

Amelia looked over to the male. "Xandyr, this is Rexah," Amelia told him in a calm, quiet voice before looking back at her. "Rexah, this is my son, Xandyr – your twin."

24

Your Twin.

Rexah heard the words leave her mother's lips clear as day, but they just wouldn't register in her mind. Her gaze shifted back to Xandyr – her brother, her *twin*.

They were identical. The only difference between them was that his hair didn't have any flashes of purple in it, his hair was solid black, and his eyes weren't violet, they were a stunning shade of light blue. He was taller than Rexah, not by much though, and from what she could tell from the muscles in his arms and shoulders, working at the tavern wasn't his only pastime.

Xandyr didn't move a muscle. "I ... I have a sister?" he whispered in disbelief.

Rexah swallowed the lump in her throat. She didn't know what to say, so she said the first thing that popped into her head. "Hello, Xandyr."

Amelia looked between the two of them. "Let's sit back down and take a moment to let this sink in."

Xandyr hesitated for a few moments before following his mother's instructions and took his father's armchair.

Rexah sat back down on the settee just as her father walked back out from the kitchen.

"Xandyr," he said in surprise.

"It's okay, Oliver, they have been introduced," Amelia replied to him.

Oliver walked around the settee and sat down on the arm rest beside his son. He looked over to Rexah and gave her an apologetic look.

Kalen's hand pressed comfortingly against her lower back. Both fae had been quiet, from shock or politeness Rexah wasn't sure – possibly a bit of both – but Kalen's touch relieved some of the tension in her shoulders.

"So," Rexah said quietly, trying to get it through her head that she had a sibling. "Who is older?"

Their parent's faces lit up at the question.

345

"Xandyr is a minute older," Oliver said, grinning softly.

"He was born screaming and crying, but you, Rexah, you came into the world quiet and content," Amelia said. "You were both our little miracles, and we were so blessed to have you. We still are."

Oliver smiled as he remembered the day as if it were yesterday. "It was one of the happiest days of my life."

Xandyr hadn't stopped looking at Rexah; he studied her in wonder as though at any moment he was going to wake up from a dream and she would disappear. "All of this must be a shock for you."

Rexah looked to her brother and nodded. "It is. It must be for you too."

"I didn't think that when I stepped through that door I'd have a sister waiting for me," he said, nodding his head before looking at his parents. "Why didn't you tell me?"

Oliver sighed softly. "We wanted to. There were many times when I almost told you, but we wanted to keep you safe, and knowing about Rexah would put you in danger."

Her father's words stung, and she found herself blinking back the tears that had rapidly filled her eyes.

Xandyr's light blue eyes softened as he saw her reaction. "Protecting me or not, I deserved to know I have a sibling," he replied, anger coating his words.

"I'm so sorry, love," Amelia said, sadness filling her eyes.

Xandyr stood up and walked to the other end of the cottage, looking out of the windows. His hands were balled into fists at his side. Rexah understood his anger, her own simmered beneath the surface, waiting to be unleashed.

"I need some time, we all do, to process all of this," Rexah said, fighting to keep that anger in check. "We should go to the inn and rest."

Her mother nodded. "Take all the time you need, sweetheart. It's been a shock to us all."

That's the godsdamned honest truth, she thought as she rose to her feet with Kalen and Torbin. "Thank you for your time, we will be back soon, and we can talk more."

Oliver and Amelia stood up. Both looked ready to step forward and hug her, but much to her relief, they didn't.

"You know where we are when you're ready. Our door is always open for you," Oliver replied, his eyes full of sympathy and remorse.

"I can cook breakfast for us tomorrow if you'd like?" Amelia asked with hope in her voice.

Rexah looked up at Kalen before moving her gaze back to her mother. "I'd like that; it gives us a chance to talk more."

Amelia smiled at her and nodded. "I agree."

As they made their way to the front door, Rexah stole a glance at her brother. He hadn't said a word, didn't look their way, and from the tension in his shoulders, she could tell he was still angry, and rightly so.

They'd managed to secure a few rooms at the inn in the centre of town. They'd also walked around town to familiarise themselves with it again; it had been a while since Kalen and Torbin had last visited Dorasa, so it had been a good opportunity for them to see it again and relive some of their better memories, and Rexah had enjoyed listening to their stories of their times here. It helped take her mind off everything for a little while.

The silence was deafening in her room at the inn. After changing into her night clothes, Rexah sat at the end of the bed, her elbows on her knees and her head in her hands. Thoughts and questions flooded her head and prevented her from properly processing any of them.

This is madness. A brother, I have a brother. Not only a sibling, but a twin, her thoughts swam. *My mother and father are alive, have been all this godsdamned time.*

A soft knock at the door thankfully pulled her from her thoughts before they could drag her under too deeply. Her bare feet padded over to the door before she unlocked it and opened it slightly. Her shoulders sagged with relief seeing Kalen on the other side. She didn't speak as she stepped back, opening the door wider to let him in.

He walked inside, looking around. "Sorry if I'm disturbing you. I just wanted to make sure you're okay. Well, as okay as you can be."

The door clicked as she closed it. "To be honest, I don't know how I feel, how I should feel," she replied, walking over to the window and looking out at the busy nightlife of Dorasa.

Everything that had happened in the last few hours still felt so surreal to her. The family she'd been told were dead all her life weren't. They had been alive this whole time and to top it off she had a twin. It would take time to properly sink in, but she couldn't shake off the fear that this was all a dream and any moment now she would wake up.

Kalen's strong arms gently wrapped around her waist from behind, and his familiar intoxicating scent surrounded her. She found herself leaning back into his embrace, feeling the softness of his lips against her temple as he gently kissed her. The fear was quickly washed away by the feeling of complete security that grounded her.

"That's completely natural, darling" he said in a calm, quiet voice. "It's been a tough day."

Rexah gently lay her hands on his arms around her waist. "I don't understand why my grandmother kept them a secret from me. Maybe she was trying to keep me safe, but I wouldn't have told anyone. Knowing that I did have parents and a brother somewhere in the world, alive and well – I would have been so happy."

"I can only imagine what's been going through your mind, what you've been feeling," he said.

"Nothing prepared me for what I found here today, for who I found. My grandmother should have told me. She had no right keeping something like that from me," she said, peeling herself from his embrace and walking to the middle of the room.

Kalen watched her. "Rexah."

She began to pace back and forth. "I spent my whole life thinking they were dead. Watching the children in the village running to their mothers, being embraced by them, and playing in the streets with their fathers, knowing that would never be me. It killed me inside, and I hated them for having what I so desperately wanted, so desperately needed."

The cage she kept her grief in exploded and it gripped her like a vice, coating every word with anger and pain. "I had no right to be jealous. I lived in a fucking castle; I had what they would have given everything up for. Selfish – that's what I am. Selfish that I wasn't satisfied with what I had, with what most people never would have."

Kalen took a step towards her. "Don't say that."

Her eyes, wide and wild, met his. "Why not? It's the truth. The castle, the parties, the jewellery, none of it compared to what I craved most, a mother and a father, and my grandmother deprived me of that my whole life! So don't stand there and tell me not to say that!"

Kalen watched her silently and made no effort to interrupt her. His face gave away nothing as he watched her unravel in front of him.

"I watched whilst the Valfae reduced my home to ruins. Whilst they tore my people apart, what did I do?

I ran. Did I stop to fight the beasts off and save as many lives as I could? No. Sure, I killed one of them, but that wasn't nearly enough." Rexah's chest heaved with anger. "I promised to keep my people and kingdom safe; it's what I trained with Zuko to do for most of my life!"

"You cannot put the blame of what happened in Adorea on your shoulders," Kalen told her. "It wasn't your fault."

"Riona would never have let any of this happen. Gods, she would be so disappointed, so ashamed," she whispered, her voice cracked with grief.

He wasted no more time and closed the space between them, pulling her into his arms and against his chest. She fought against him, her fists thumping against his chest, but he didn't let go. Twisting and turning in his grip, trying to break free, she felt that wall she'd built within herself begin to tremble.

Kalen let her pound her fists on his chest, let her curse and shout, and when he felt her body begin to shake he said, "Let it out."

Rexah tried to refuse; if she let it out her grief would win, but her body wasn't giving her the choice. Her knees gave out and she collapsed to the floor, Kalen going with her. Gripping the front of his shirt, burying her face into his chest, she cried.

Kalen's fingers threaded through her hair; his other arm wrapped tightly around her. "Let it all out, darling."

She finally broke. That wall within her was now nothing but rubble. Her body shook, her heart shattered, and the sobs that escaped her felt like razors in her throat. Kalen didn't let her go. He let her cry in his arms, soothing her all the while.

When she couldn't cry any longer and her sobs slowly quietened, Kalen said, "Gods, I'm so proud of you."

His words made her heart flutter. She slowly looked up at him, her eyes puffy from crying. "Proud of me? For what?" she asked, her voice broken.

"Surviving," he said, looking into her eyes and gently wiping the tears from her cheeks. "You've not only survived life-threatening violence, but you've survived through your grief, through the emotional trauma. I know it might not feel like it right now, but you have gone through so much horror and come out the other side so strong. Not many would have the strength or the willpower to do that."

Rexah's heart was beating faster in her chest. He was completely right. No matter how hard every single breath had been, how hard every single step had been, she'd survived.

"I wouldn't have made it if it weren't for you and Torbin," she whispered.

Kalen shook his head softly. "No, your determination was what got you here. We just tagged along."

A small smile tugged on her lips. "Well, I'm glad you did."

"I'm glad we did too," he replied, returning her smile. "We were meant to find you on that dirt road."

"It's not just about your help getting me here; you kept me from tipping over the edge, kept my head above the water and saved me from drowning," she said, and her eyes connected with his gorgeous deep blue ones.

Kalen's hand gently cupped her cheek, the touch igniting a fire within her. "I will always save you, darling," he whispered before he leaned down and pressed his lips to hers.

Rexah didn't hesitate this time and closed her eyes as she kissed him back. It was full of love and compassion; it was a promise of protection. Her arms slowly found their way around his neck as his hand moved back to her waist and pulled her against his strong body. A rush of warmth rushed through her chest, spreading downward as she felt with her fingers every single one of his powerful muscles.

Before the kiss could become heated, Kalen slowly pulled away and leaned his forehead against hers. "I'm sorry, I just can't help myself around you. If you're uncomfortable with this, please tell me."

His words melted her insides, and she smiled at him. "It's perfectly fine, Kalen. I enjoy your kisses. You're a good kisser."

That perfect smirk spread across his face. "You're not a bad kisser yourself."

Rexah felt her cheeks flush. Gods, he always knew how to lift her spirits and put a smile back on her face. For that she would be forever grateful to him.

Suddenly, exhaustion hit her; the day had finally caught up with her. Kalen seemed to sense it and lifted her into his arms as he rose to his feet. She held onto him, resting her head against his shoulder as he walked to the bed.

The sheets were cold as she slid under the cover. Kalen's lips were soft against her skin as he kissed her forehead. "Get some sleep, Rexah. You'll feel a bit better in the morning if you get some rest."

He straightened up, and as he turned to walk away, her hand shot out and grabbed his wrist, halting him. "Stay with me," she whispered.

His dark blue eyes softened, and he kicked off his

boots. Rexah watched as he tugged off his shirt and discarded it on the floor. Her eyes drifted to his chest, to those abs that went on for days, to the v that disappeared beneath his waistband along with the trail of dark hair.

Kalen disturbed her ogling as he pulled back the covers and slid in beside her. His body was warm and welcoming as she moved closer.

Now that he was close enough, Rexah could make out the beautiful designs of the tattoos decorating his upper arms. A dove in flight with two roses beneath it covered his right arm, both in black and grey. On his left arm, a dagger wrapped in vines marked his skin, fae runs carved into the blade. The artwork was absolutely stunning.

"Your tattoos are incredible," she whispered as her fingers gently traced the wings of the dove. Rexah swore his strong body shuddered slightly under her touch but didn't comment on it. "Why did you choose these designs?"

Kalen studied her as she continued to trace the outline of the wings. "The tattoo on my left arm represents my people, the warriors."

Rexah nodded softly, listening as she inspected the designs further.

"The dove represents my mother, her name was Doveline, and the roses are for my brother, Niken. Roses fascinated him," he told her.

Sorrow swept through her as she moved her gaze to his. "It's a beautiful tribute to them, Kalen. I'm sure they would have loved it as much as I do."

"They're always with me," he said in a broken whisper.

Rexah rested her forehead against his, swallowing the lump in her throat. "They are."

Kalen placed a gentle kiss on her forehead.

"Thank you for checking on me, for staying," she whispered as she looked up at him.

"No need to thank me, darling, your wellbeing is all I care about," he replied quietly, moving a strand of her hair from her eyes.

No more words were needed. Rexah snuggled into him, her head resting against his chest as he held her in his arms. Sleep soon took her to the sound of his beating heart.

25

The smell of the food her parents were making hit her as soon as she opened the cottage door, and her mouth instantly watered. Rexah pulled off her cloak and hung it up as she watched Xandyr setting the table towards the back of the room, his dark hair hanging over his eyes as he leaned down.

"Good morning," Rexah said softly so not to frighten him.

Xandyr looked up, seeing her and her fae companions. "Good morning. Breakfast is almost ready, please take a seat and make yourselves comfortable."

He's certainly in a better mood today, she thought, glancing over her shoulder to Kalen and Torbin. She walked over to the table, and Kalen, being the gentleman that he was, pulled out the chair for her. She thanked him as she sat down.

Xandyr disappeared into the kitchen as the fae took their seats; Kalen took the chair beside Rexah and Torbin sat opposite Kalen.

"The food smells so good," Torbin said.

"That's because it's not tavern food." Kalen chuckled softly.

Rexah smiled softly. "Nothing will ever be better than homecooked food."

A few moments later, Amelia walked in from the kitchen holding a large clear jug of orange juice, and her eyes lit up when she saw them at the table. "Good morning, everyone."

"Good morning," Rexah said. It was still strange seeing her, but it was something she would get used to, and something she was blessed to be able to do.

"Morning, Amelia. Thanks again for inviting us." Torbin smiled and nodded to her in thanks. He was incredibly polite, and Rexah knew by the look on her mother's face that she thought it refreshing.

"The more the merrier." Amelia's grin widened as she carefully placed the jug in the centre of the table. "I hope you're hungry; we may have gone a little overboard with how much food we've prepared."

"Like you said, the more the merrier. Don't worry; we will make sure the bowl is empty, I promise," Kalen replied, smirking softly.

"I like the way your mind works, Kalen," Amelia replied.

Oliver and Xandyr walked in; they each carried a tray filled with food, and the mouth-watering smell they'd sniffed at before intensified. Rexah's stomach growled as she watched them set the trays down on the table, the jug of orange juice between them.

"Please, dig in," Oliver said.

No one wasted any time, and everyone was soon seated with plates filled with freshly baked bread and an array of finely cooked meats. She couldn't deny it: her parents were excellent cooks. Rexah could get used to this.

Amelia studied her daughter. "Your hair and eyes are a stunning colour."

Rexah looked over to her. "I know I should have taken my potion," she said, looking down at her dark locks, "but I feel safe here. Also, no one even looked at me as we made our way here which was nice."

Amelia's eyes softened. "Everyone here lives in

harmony. That's the reason why your father and I chose to live here in Dorasa instead of Adorea – well, one of the reasons," she said as she looked over to her husband lovingly.

Oliver smiled. "The other being the fact that I'm not of royal blood. Your mother decided she didn't want to take the throne after your grandmother, so they officially agreed that your mother wouldn't stake her claim to the Adorian throne, so long as we moved away," Oliver smiled.

"And before you say anything, I don't want the throne either," Xandyr chimed in, then frowned. "Well, I wouldn't want it if it still existed. Gods, I'm sorry."

Rexah shook her head. "No, it's okay. I understand what you mean. The whole situation is up in the air at the moment. Who knows what will happen in the future?"

He nodded softly and gave her an apologetic look before taking another forkful of food.

She could tell he was mentally kicking himself. No one knew what the future held, if there would ever be a future for Adorea again, and that was a lot to step lightly around.

"How did you sleep?" Oliver asked her.

"It was one of the best sleeps I've had in a while," she replied.

Kalen had stayed with her all night, holding her close. She'd never felt more secure in her life, and knowing he was there made everything that had happened seem so small, even for a short time.

Oliver smiled and nodded. "Good, I'm glad to hear it."

"I still can't believe I have a sister," Xandyr said. "I don't mean that in a bad way, it just feels so surreal, and I bet it feels like that for you too."

"It is, but now that I've had some time to think about it all, I feel a little more relaxed and ready to talk about it," she said, moving her gaze to her parents. "If that's okay with you?"

Amelia nodded. "Of course, my love."

"Do you want us to give you some privacy?" Kalen asked quietly beside her.

Rexah shook her head as she looked up at him. "No, I want you both to stay."

"Are you sure?" Torbin asked her.

"Yes, I want you both here. I want you both to hear what's left to be said," she said shifting her gaze to meet Torbin's amber eyes.

Torbin gave her a smile and a nod and settled back down into his seat.

"Okay then, let's pick up where we left off," Amelia said, taking a sip of her juice before continuing. "The Shadow Star, it's being sought after by the Dark Fae, and it's why they're attacking villages, towns, and kingdoms."

"No one knows where the sword is like we said yesterday," Oliver said, "but that's not stopping the Dark Fae. They know the last person to have it was Riona, that's why they attacked Adorea so brutally." His eyes grew sad. "They were convinced it was there, and when they didn't find it, they started their attacks on other towns and villages."

"There was a prophecy that another Chosen One of the Raven God was on their way. No one knew who it would be or which bloodline would be chosen this time. I gave birth to Xandyr and knew straight away it wasn't him, and then a minute later, you were born, and my heart sank a little," Amelia explained. "Not because I didn't love you, but because I saw the colour of your beautiful eyes; I could already see the violet in your hair, and I knew then the danger you were already in."

Rexah's eyes saddened as she listened to her. She could feel the heartache and loss oozing from their words; this was just as hard for them as it was for her, if not more.

Oliver gently put his arm around his wife in a comforting gesture. "Your grandmother was here for the birth. We talked – well, more like argued – for days about what we were going to do, about how we could make things work, and two weeks after you were born the decision was made that you would go to Adorea with her."

"I was born here in Dorasa?" she asked softly. "I thought I was born in Adorea?"

Oliver set down his glass of orange juice. "Shortly after we left Adorea, your mother found out she was pregnant. As soon as we arrived in Dorasa, we married."

Ryden then appeared in Rexah's mind. She pictured him standing before the statue of Tella looking devastatingly handsome as he waited for her to walk up the aisle. Before her grief threatened to rise, her mother's voice thankfully pulled her from her thoughts.

"It was one of the hardest decisions of our lives to let you go with your grandmother, and not one we made easily. We tried so hard to keep you with us, but we knew that in the end we couldn't protect you," Amelia said. "In Adorea you would be surrounded by guards sworn to protect you with their lives, and you would be kept safe by the castle's strong walls, by your status."

"And the choice to tell me you were dead? Who came up with that idea?" Rexah asked as she took another bite of food.

"We thought that if you found out about us you would come here, and for your safety, for your brother's safety, we couldn't risk it," Oliver replied.

"And here I am, regardless." Rexah sighed deeply, internalising her sorrow. "Why not tell me the truth? I would have understood and maybe I ... maybe I could have saved Adorea."

Kalen's hand moved to rest on her leg under the table, and the touch sent her heart into a fluttering mess. "Even if you knew the truth, darling, there would have been absolutely nothing you could have done to stop that attack."

Rexah looked up at him. "Maybe not, but I would have been more vigilant. I'd have trained harder with Zuko, and I would have fought harder."

Kalen gently squeezed her leg in comfort. "Those beasts are ruthless, Rexah. No one blames you for what happened."

Torbin set his glass of orange juice on the table

before he looked over to her. "There was nothing you could have done for the kingdom; it was already gone. You got yourself out of there and that took so much strength and bravery."

Rexah swallowed the lump in her throat and took a tentative sip of her own orange juice.

"Do you want us to continue?" Amelia asked quietly.

"Yes, please." Rexah nodded.

Oliver finished off the food on his plate and wiped his mouth before he spoke. "The Dark Fae are after the sword because it holds raw power. Their master is weak; Riona wounded him badly with The Shadow Star, and he retreated into the hole he crawled out from. If he rises, the power within the sword will restore him to his full strength, and some."

The food in Rexah's stomach turned sour as she looked at him. They had a *master*.

"But that's not all," Amelia said, her voice calm. "The power within the sword must be activated in order for it to transfer ownership to that of their master."

"And how is it activated?" Kalen asked when Rexah couldn't form the words.

"With blood," Oliver answered before he looked at his daughter. "With your blood."

Rexah hadn't realised she had her fork in a death

grip until Kalen pried it from her hand, set it down on the table and replaced it with his hand. Chills ran deep through her body and into her bones.

"The Dark Fae … they … they attacked Adorea because … because they wanted me?" she asked, her voice trembling as she stuttered. "They destroyed Vell-wynd and other towns because of me?"

Amelia's eyes filled with tears, but it was Xandyr who spoke next. "They did, but they also attacked Adorea and all those other places because they are animals. They enjoy death and destruction. Don't keep putting the blame on yourself, sister. I know it's difficult, but none of it is your fault."

When she looked over to him, she could see the anger in his eyes, a look of protection for her that made her eyes soften. She tried to convince herself that he was right, but it was hard when that little voice in the back of her mind told her otherwise. Her heart ached for her people, for all those families across the realm who didn't survive.

Once she took a few moments to calm herself down, she looked to her parents again. She didn't want to know the answer to this question, but it was one that needed to be asked: "What would happen if their master gained the power within the sword?"

Amelia shifted uncomfortably in her seat and averted her eyes. Oliver gently ran his hand up and down her back supportively.

Xandyr wiped his mouth after finishing off his juice. "If he gets his hands on the sword then we can kiss goodbye to a world without darkness; we can kiss goodbye to our freedom. What happened in Adorea will seem like child's play. I know it's harsh, but it's the truth."

Rexah tried to remember if she'd read about their master; she'd learned about the Dark Fae during her tutoring, but she couldn't recall anything about a master. "I don't know what happens next, but I do know we can't let him be set free. I won't let that happen. I don't care what it takes. These monsters have had their fun, now it's time for them to be sent back to the hell they came from."

26

Once breakfast was over, they'd spent the day talking with her family. Everyone taking the time to get to know each other, to ask the questions that had been swimming around Rexah's mind since last night. Questions about how her mother and father met and how they'd made a normal life for themselves. Unsurprisingly, Xandyr and Rexah had so much in common.

Afterwards, Rexah felt she needed time to let all the new information sink in properly, and her heart melted when Kalen had asked to join her on her walk. Torbin had parted ways with a wink, going back to his room at the inn to bathe.

Rexah now sat on the edge of the dock with Kalen

beside her, his leg gently resting against hers. The cool breeze had her dark hair dancing around her shoulders as she watched the sun descend in a sky of orange, yellow, and red.

"Are you sure you still want to be here?" Rexah asked him after more silence than she could bare.

"What do you mean by that?" Kalen asked.

Rexah kept her eyes on the small ripples and waves of the water. "You heard what my parents said about me. My blood is the key to freeing the Dark Fae's master. Do you really want to stay with me and put not only yourself in danger, but Torbin too? I wouldn't judge either of you if you decided to go back to your people."

"Nothing will ever send me away from your side, not even death itself," he replied softly.

Rexah could feel tears building up in her eyes, but she refused to let them fall. Crying was something she'd done far too often lately. There was absolutely nothing wrong with it, but she was sick and tired of it. Her skin began to tingle when she felt him move a little closer to her.

"All my life I thought I had everything that I needed. I trained hard to become a warrior, did what I could to provide for my mother and my little brother, but nothing I ever did made me feel complete. All my life I've searched for my purpose in this world," he said, his fingers gently lifting her chin up so that her gaze met his. "And now I've found it."

Rexah searched his eyes but all she found was truth and the undiluted raw emotion of love. She opened her mouth to speak but he silenced her and spoke before she could.

"Don't deny it, darling. I know you feel it too. I can see it in your eyes," he whispered. "I can't deny it any longer either. You are my purpose."

Kalen's words sunk through her skin, deep into her bones, and found her soul. His words made her blood sing in her veins. She had promised herself that she wouldn't deny her feelings for him any longer, and she would keep that promise.

"And you are mine," she whispered back. The sincerity and conviction in her voice surprised her a little, but it was the truth, and it was what she felt wholeheartedly.

Kalen gently wrapped his arm around her shoulders and pulled her in close, her head leaning on his shoulder as they both watched the waves.

"Whatever happens, it's going to end in a fight,"

Rexah said. "A dark, bloody fight that not all of us will survive. The journey ahead won't be easy."

"You want to know what I think?" he asked her.

Rexah nodded against his shoulder, his scent surrounding her. "What do you think?"

"I think that's tomorrow's problem," he said. "I think for the rest of tonight we should put it to the back of our minds and just simply ... be."

Rexah couldn't stop the smile that spread across her face. "I like the sound of that."

Kalen lay a gentle kiss to the top of her head. "I know we don't know each other very well, but I feel like I've known you my whole life. Is that stupid?"

Rexah pulled away to look up at him as she grinned. "No, it's not stupid. What do you want to know?"

Kalen thought for a moment. "What's your favourite colour?"

"Purple," she answered. "You?"

"I should have known." He chuckled. "Mine is blue or grey."

"What's one of your favourite childhood memories?" she asked him.

"The day my little brother was born," he said quietly. "He was so small, and I promised him that I would be the best big brother in the world to him. I promised that I would protect him."

Rexah's eyes saddened. "You did everything you could for him and your mother."

He scoffed slightly. "No, I was helpless and weak when they needed me most. I failed them."

It might have been the look of pain in his gorgeous blue eyes or the grief in his voice that made her do it, she wasn't sure, but she straddled his lap, her legs either side of his hips. She cupped his face gently in her hands. "You didn't fail them. You fought your hardest and did everything you could," she said, looking deep into his ocean eyes. "Those monsters will pay for what they did to your family, for what they did to my home, and for all the pain and death they've caused throughout the realm, not just in the last few weeks, but throughout their entire existence. We will make them pay, together."

Kalen didn't reply, not with words anyway. He leaned up and kissed her passionately, his hands gripping her waist.

Rexah kissed him back without question, her fingers threading through his silky dark hair. She was losing herself in him, and in that moment, being lost was the perfect place to be.

Kalen's tongue slid along her bottom lip, begging for access which she gladly granted. As the kiss deepened, and his tongue explored her mouth, his hands slid to her hips and gripped them tightly, and Rexah responded with a soft moan. Her grip on his hair tightened as her hips instinctively rocked against him, feeling the hard length of him straining against his trousers. The low rumble of a growl vibrated deep within Kalen's chest, sending heat flooding through Rexah's core and filling her with intense need.

The overstimulation of her body jolted Rexah back to her senses. She pulled away, keeping her eyes closed as they both breathed heavily. "I-I'm sorry."

Kalen gently moved a piece of her hair behind her ear. "No need to apologise, darling. I won't push you into anything you don't want to do. We take this at your pace."

She gently lay her forehead against his as she calmed her breathing, willing her erratic heart rate to slow.

"What was his name?" Kalen asked after a few moments.

Rexah opened her eyes. She realised she hadn't said his name in … well, only the Gods knew how long now.

"Ryden," she whispered. "His name was Ryden."

"Was he good to you? Did he treat you right?" he asked.

"Yes, he was … he was amazing," she said quietly. "He was my first kiss, my first everything. We were due to marry before … before the attack."

Kalen nodded softly, his hand rubbing those gentle, comforting circles over her lower back as he listened. "Did you love him?"

"I did, I truly did. But even when I was with him, something was always missing, and I didn't know what. It was something that I refused to acknowledge, and I always pushed the feeling to the back of my mind, telling myself I was being silly," she replied. "I've grieved for him; I've shed my tears and … maybe … I think I'm ready to let him go. Oh Gods, I'm a horrible person for thinking that way. I shouldn't have said that, should I?"

"Rexah look at me," he said, making sure her eyes connected with his before he continued. "You aren't a horrible person. You loved him, a part of you always will, because those memories you made will always be in your heart. Just because you're ready to move on with your life doesn't mean you are letting him go or insulting his memory. It means that you're keeping him there, in his space in your heart, so that when you do have days where you feel down, he's there."

Tears were flowing freely down her face. "I don't deserve you; you know that?"

Kalen smiled softly at her. "You deserve the world, darling." He reached up and gently wiped her tears away.

Rexah found herself leaning into his warm touch. "So do you, Kalen."

Kalen landed a soft kiss on her nose, and she blushed in response.

Her finger gently traced down the scar on his forehead. "How did you get this?" she whispered.

"When I was younger, Niken was only a baby, we were on our way back to our home from the market when bandits tried to take our food from us," he explained. "I went into warrior mode and fought them off. I hadn't had much training at that point, but luckily what I did have was enough."

Rexah's eyes softened. "You got it whilst protecting your family."

Kalen nodded. "One of the bandits got a lucky swing with his blade. I thought I'd lost my eye there was so much blood."

She leaned forward and pressed a soft kiss to his

scarred skin, and she swore she felt him shudder slightly beneath her.

Moving back to sit beside him again, she said, "When I was fleeing through the castle ruins, I found my trainer. I was far too late. He was already dead."

Kalen's eyes saddened. "I'm so sorry."

"He was the best trainer I could have asked for. If it weren't for all the things he taught me I'd have perished that day along with everyone else," she said quietly, hugging her arms.

"He would have been so proud of you," Kalen said, tugging her closer to him.

Rexah nodded softly. "He would have. I wish he could have seen me take down that Valfae. I surprised myself at how easily I took it down. That's when the lightning first appeared."

"It never happened before then?" Kalen asked.

"No. I think maybe the power is within the dagger. Maybe my parents know more about it," she replied.

With a gentle kiss to the top of her head, Kalen said, "We can ask them about it. You've all got a lot of catching up to do."

Rexah snuggled closer into his side, her head resting against his shoulder. "I should tell my mother how my grandmother died. She deserves to know how brave and selfless she was, right to the very end."

Kalen gently ran his hand up and down her arm. "What happened to her?"

Rexah let the memories flow back into her mind, every agonising second. "We were fleeing. Our escape route was blocked by fallen stone and rubble. I remembered the servant entrance, but it was too late. A Valfae tore it's claw through her chest. She told me to go to Dorasa, and before I could grab her the beast dragged her into the shadows."

"Her last act was to save you," Kalen said softly.

Rexah nodded. "It was. She firmly believed that everything happens for a reason, but she knew that my parents were alive; she knew all about my brother and the Raven God."

"She knew you were destined for great things."

"Despite all the lies and all the secrets that she kept from me, I miss her so much," Rexah whispered.

Kalen lay his cheek on the top of her head. "We all miss those we have lost, but they are never far away."

They both stayed there, sitting on the edge of the dock, holding each other close as the sun made way for the moon which was almost full in the night sky.

Over the next few days Rexah spent time with her family. Kalen and Torbin joined often but knew when to give her privacy; they seemed to understand that she needed space to be with them alone without her having to ask for it, and she greatly appreciated their blossoming friendship. It was still a lot for her to digest, but she was getting there, albeit slowly.

Every time she saw Xandyr she was always taken aback. It was so strange seeing someone else with almost identical features to herself. It was a strange feeling, but not a bad one. It was one she welcomed with open arms, because she had a brother; she had a sibling that she hadn't realised until now she so desperately wanted.

Rexah sat on the edge of the steps connected to the porch in the back garden of her family's cottage, watching as Xandyr and Torbin sparred. She had been right regarding her initial thoughts about her brother: he'd had weapons training and knew how to fight, and it showed as he fought with Torbin.

The steaming cup of tea in her hands kept her a nice

temperature in the cool evening. The sun hadn't gone down yet, but it was making its slow descent.

Torbin knocked the wooden stick from Xandyr's grasp and took his legs from under him. He pointed his own stick at Xandyr's neck. "You left your right side exposed, *again*."

"Bullshit!" Xandyr protested.

"Xandyr!" Amelia said, her voice raised as she walked out of the cottage.

Rexah smirked softly, looking up at her mother as she sat down beside her.

"The curses that come out of that boy's mouth," her mother said, shaking her head. "Boys will be boys, I guess."

Xandyr swiped Torbin's hand away as he got to his feet and picked up the stick. "Again. Let's go again."

Torbin twirled his stick effortlessly in his hand, smirking at his opponent. "As you wish."

"How long has he been training?" Rexah asked her mother before she took a sip of her tea.

Amelia held her own cup close. "Since he was around ten. His friends were all learning how to fight, and he begged us to let him join them. Ten years old may seem too young to learn, but your father spoke to the instructor, and it was mainly exercising to build strength and learn all the different ways to stand."

"I started my training when I was ten too," Rexah told her before taking another sip of the sweet tea.

Amelia looked at her. "You were taught how to fight?"

"Yes; Grandmother thought it was a good idea, believe it or not," Rexah replied, a soft smirk on her lips. "She said she wanted me to be prepared for anything."

"I'm glad you've been trained," Amelia said. "That eases my mind."

"The night Adorea was attacked I had a dream about you," Rexah told her.

Amelia looked at her daughter. "You did?"

Rexah nodded softly. "You and Riona."

"What happened in the dream?" she asked.

"We were all standing in Tella's temple looking up at the statue. You told me everything was going to be okay, and Riona told me that my destiny lies before me. I didn't know what she was talking about, but now I do," she said. "Then Riona started bleeding from the wounds that had killed her, and you began screaming my name. I woke up then to realise it wasn't you screaming my name, it was Grandmother."

Amelia's eyes saddened. She moved closer and wrapped her arm around her daughter's shoulders. "My sweet girl."

Rexah looked into her mother's eyes. She could see sadness and guilt within them, and she knew what she was about to say. "Mother …"

"I should have never let her take you from us. I should have put my foot firmly to the ground and said no. Then none of this would have happened; you wouldn't have had to go through any of this," she said, tears slipping down her cheeks.

Seeing her mother cry made her chest tighten. "No; this isn't your fault. No matter what happened in the past, the Dark Fae would have come after me one way or another."

"All we ever wanted was to keep you safe." She sniffled, wiping her eyes.

The words that fell from Rexah's lips left a sour taste in her mouth. "I was never safe, Mother."

27

Rexah always kept her promises, no matter what, and this time wasn't any different. She'd made a promise to Kalen and Torbin that once they arrived in Dorasa, she would visit their favourite cake shop and buy for them whatever they wanted. She wanted to thank them for everything they'd done and continue to do for her, but she also just wanted to pay for something for a change.

Amelia had wanted to accompany her on the trip, but Rexah politely declined her offer. She wanted to explore the town on her own. She couldn't remember the last time she'd had time to herself, and right now it was exactly what she needed. Everything was still so raw, and the fresh air helped.

She enjoyed the walk from her parents' home to the main part of the town. It was quiet and provided her with a most welcome sense of calm that helped her gather her thoughts. Birds sang their morning songs, and calls from other wildlife echoed throughout the forest. Beams of the soft early morning sun shone through the small gaps in the trees, lighting her path. Taking a deep breath, she filled her lungs with crisp air. Feeling oddly hopeful, she left the path that led from the cottage and took the main path into town.

The town was alive with activity: children ran excitedly across her path, chasing butterflies, and streams of people went about their daily tasks, greeting her with a friendly smile as they walked by. Rexah returned the welcome, and a warm feeling spread through her chest at their kind gestures. Even in a world that held such evil and darkness, good and beautiful things could still be found – and Dorasa certainly was a beautiful town.

At the centre of the main square, a large fountain flowed with crystal-clear water that fell graciously down the bodies of two limestone statues: a man and woman, locked in an embrace as they gazed into each other's eyes. The man held a compass covered in dirt in one hand, and the woman held a ship covered in seaweed and barnacles in hers.

Rexah recognised the depiction immediately: they were Arentious, the God of Earth and Adventure, and Nadvika, the Goddess of Water and defender of the sea.

Looking around the square, Rexah realised that she couldn't remember where the cake shop was.

Godsdamn it.

Luck seemed to be in her favour though as a young woman around her age walked by holding a box with 'Nina's Cakes' written on the lid.

"Excuse me," Rexah said softly, stepping forward.

The young woman stopped and turned to her. She smiled. "Yes?"

"I'm sorry to bother you, but I see you've been to Nina's cake shop. Could you be so kind as to point me in the direction of it?" Rexah asked, feeling every bit of the tourist she was.

The woman grinned softly and nodded. "Of course. Go down that street over there, and once you get to the bottom, take the left turn. If you make your way down that street, you will see the shop ahead of you."

"Thank you so much." Rexah smiled at the woman before she set off in the direction she was given.

From the smell of the cake rising from the woman's box, Rexah knew they were going to taste as good as they smelled.

Rexah made her way down the street, passing a few more shops. One sold fine clothing displayed in a variety of stunning shades and fabrics, and she couldn't help but stop and admire the clothing in the shop window. Before long, a light breeze swept by and carried with it the scent of sugar and sweets. Turning her head in the direction the of the delicious smell, she saw the cake shop just up ahead. Before she knew it, her legs were taking her towards it.

The shop was tucked away at the dead end of the street. A wooden sign above the entrance was carved into the shape of a cloud, a rainbow curving over the top of it. There were no pots of gold at the end of this rainbow, but there were stunningly illustrated cupcakes.

The building itself was painted a shade of soft lilac. It stuck out like a sore thumb nestled amongst the grey buildings that surrounded it, but Rexah loved it, none-theless, and she didn't need a sign to know this was the right place.

A small bell rang when she pushed the door open, and the smell that engulfed her when she stepped inside was one of pure sugary bliss that she would happily let herself get lost in.

A counter ran along the left side of the shop in an L-shape. The glass cabinets were filled with all different types and flavours of cakes, cookies, and pastries.

Rexah stopped in her tracks when she saw the pastries. They looked just like the ones she'd shared with Nesrin the last time they'd spent time together. An ache filled her chest at the memory.

"So, what you're saying is that these pastries were actually meant for you, your grandmother, the King and Ryden to try, and instead you commandeered them for us?"

Nesrin's voice played in her mind so clear it was as though her best friend was standing by her side.

"I will never tire of your antics, Rex."

"Good morning, welcome to Nina's Cakes, how can I help you today?" a woman's voice asked, pulling her from her grief.

The woman's deep blue hair was pulled back into a braid, loose strands hanging down the sides of her face. Flour dusted her chin and one of her cheeks, and she watched Rexah with her honey-coloured eyes, a welcoming smile stretched across her lips.

Rexah blinked a few times. "Forgive me, I was lost in my thoughts for a moment there."

"That's okay. What can I get you? A cake? A pastry?" she asked.

"Can I have a box of your best cupcakes?" Rexah

asked, pulling out her coin purse.

"Of course, coming right up!" she grinned before pulling out an empty box from the shelf under the counter. "I haven't seen you around town before."

"Yes, I just arrived not too long ago. My name is Nes," she replied. She may have neglected the potion, but she was reluctant to drop the name.

"It's a pleasure to meet you, Nes. Welcome to Dorasa. I'm Nina, but I'm sure that wasn't too difficult to guess." Nina laughed softly as she picked random cupcakes from the cabinet and placed them inside the box.

Rexah loved Nina's positive energy; she lit up the room without even doing anything. It was a refreshing feeling being around someone like that after everything that had happened, and everything that was still happening.

"What brought you to Dorasa? Trading or adventure?" Nina asked as she prepared her order.

"Family actually," Rexah replied. "It's been a long time since we've seen each other."

Nina's eyes softened. "Oh well that's so much better than trade or adventure."

Rexah smiled and nodded. "My friends talk about

your cakes all the time; they say they're the best cakes in the realm."

"Not to toot my own horn or anything, but your friends aren't wrong." She grinned. "I've never had a complaint."

"I'm looking forward to trying them," Rexah said, her smile growing.

It was no secret that she loved all things sugary and sweet. The best part of the royal parties her grandmother held in Adorea was the desert table. Rexah's mouth watered just thinking about all the cakes, pastries, and other puddings that would line the table. *Not to mention the food coma I would get myself into at the end of the night. Totally worth it though.*

Nina placed the box on the counter. "That's three silver."

Rexah gladly handed over the coin, happy that she was finally getting to pay for something for a change.

"I've added a few extra cupcakes in there for you, Your Highness," Nina said, lowering her voice at the last part.

It was no surprise that Nina had recognised her hair and her eyes, but that didn't stop a jolt of shock rushing through her.

"Thank you," Rexah said quietly.

Nina reached forward and gently placed her hand on Rexah's arm. "I see the worry in your eyes, but there is no need for it, not in Dorasa. Do not hide who you are here, and do not be ashamed of it either."

"I'm not ashamed, but you're right, I am worried. I fear that someone might alert the Dark Fae of my whereabouts," she admitted to her.

"That will not happen; Dorasians stick together no matter what. We aren't just a community, we are family. We look out for each other," Nina replied. "If someone were to alert the Dark Fae they would have been here by now, don't you think?"

Rexah nodded softly. "Of course. I just can't be too careful."

Nina squeezed her arm before letting her go. "Of course not, and that is the best attitude to have. Like I said, don't worry about anything whilst you are here. Go home, make yourself a cup of tea, and dig into my delicious cupcakes."

Rexah laughed softly and nodded. "I will, and I'll be sure to let you know what I think of them."

"Oh, please do! I look forward to it!" Nina grinned at her.

Picking up the box filled with sugary goodness,

Rexah said her farewell to Nina before she walked out of the shop.

Rexah retraced her footsteps and made it back to the main square. There was one more stop she wanted to make before she headed back to the cottage; when they'd first arrived in Dorasa and she'd been reunited with her father, on their way to the cottage she had spotted a book shop.

As she made her way towards it, an almost overwhelming feeling washed over her: she didn't want to leave Dorasa, ever. Everyone was friendly, no one passed any judgement, and it was the only other place other than Adorea where she felt like she belonged.

'Bernard's Books' was etched into the sign fixed above the shop window, and she took not one moment longer to head for the door, caring only for what she'd find inside.

The door creaked as Rexah pushed it open, the bell above the door jingling softly as she did. The smell of the ink and paper was what hit her first; it was a glorious smell she hadn't met for a while, and it was certainly one she had missed. She might have been strange, but she loved the scent of books, old and new.

Lanterns littered the stone walls filling the space

with a soft glow. Warmth from a small fireplace on the far wall spread through Rexah's body. It was cosy and inviting.

An older man stepped out from the curtains behind the counter and smiled. "Welcome, I'm Bernard. Are you looking for a particular volume or are you browsing?"

He had a light dusting of silver hair on his head and stubble on his face to match. His brown eyes were kind and sparkled as he waited for her answer.

"Good morning, I'm browsing at the moment." Rexah smiled back at him.

Bernard nodded. "If you need any assistance I shall be right here."

Rexah thanked him before she approached the closest bookcase. The shelves were filled with a wide variety of different genres and books from different ages. A few titles were familiar and jumped out at her, ones she had in her own bookcase in her room, and there were other titles she hadn't heard of before.

She was in her element as she made her way along the bookcases, scanning each book as she went. She was like a child in a sweet shop. Books hit a different level with her –they always had – and getting lost in a story, real or imagined, was one of her favourite things to do.

A loud thud sounded to her right, and she whipped her head around to find a book had fallen from one of the shelves and onto the wooden floor. Frowning, she walked over to it. No title decorated its spine; the cover didn't have the title etched into it either, only the picture of a giant star with a sword in its centre graced the front cover.

The Shadow Star.

Rexah reached down and picked it up, its weight heavy in her hand. As soon as the book connected with her skin, her vision went white, blinding her. She blinked rapidly and willed her eyes to adjust. As they did, a figure appeared in front of her.

The figure before her was cloaked in shadows, stars twinkling and rippling within them. Their face was obscured by the dark swirls surrounding them, but when they spoke, it was a deep male voice that sounded.

"War is coming," he said, his voice echoing. "The sword must be found."

Rexah's heart was pounding against her chest. "I … I know. Where can I find it?" she asked. To her surprise, she wasn't afraid of him.

"It calls to you; all you need to do is listen," was his reply.

Taking a step forward, she asked, "Who are you?"

"We are running out of time. Find the sword, my one, my Chosen," he said before two black wings shook and spread wide, an extension of his lofty silhouette.

Rexah stood awestruck, her mouth hanging open. *This ... this can't be,* she thought. *It's not possible.*

"Interesting choice," a voice said over her shoulder, pulling her from the vision.

She flinched and turned to see Bernard standing there; she was back in the shop. She turned her attention back to Bernard. "I'd like to purchase this one," she said a little breathlessly.

"For you, my dear, it's yours for one gold piece," he said.

Rexah fished a gold piece from her coin purse and handed it to him. "Thank you."

"The pleasure is all mine. Is there anything else I can help you with?" he asked, smiling.

She shook her head softly and barely managed to return his smile. "No, thank you. Enjoy the rest of your day."

"You too, my dear. Please do visit again!"

Rexah hurried outside, tucking the book under her

arm. It was awkward to do whilst balancing a box of cupcakes on her other hand, but she managed it.

As she made her way through the town, she couldn't stop her knees from shaking or her heart's thunderous beat in her chest. Her steps were quick as she hurried down the dirt path through the forest, and it wasn't long before the cottage came into view. She wanted to see what Kalen, Torbin, and her parents thought of the book; she wanted to know what they thought of the vision she'd had.

Amelia's laughter was the first thing Rexah heard as she walked through the front door.

"Rexah," Oliver said, smiling. "What's that you have there?"

"Is that ... is that something from Nina's?" Torbin asked as his eyes zeroed in on the box in her hand.

Rexah didn't reply; she couldn't find the words. Her body trembled like an earthquake and her breathing quickened. In a flash Kalen was by her side, his hands resting on her waist.

"Come sit down," he said softly as he guided her to the sofa where he'd been sitting.

Torbin took the box and the book from her as she sat, and Kalen kneeled before her, his hands on her knees.

"What happened?" Kalen whispered.

"I ... I saw him," she croaked.

Kalen studied her face, frowning. "Saw who?"

Rexah's eyes connected with his, her voice barely a whisper. "The Raven God."

28

The silence in the room was deafening as Rexah's words hung in the air. She knew how ridiculous it sounded, knew how impossible it was, but it happened.

"Where did you see him?" Kalen asked as he lightly pressed his hand to her shaking knee.

Rexah took a deep breath. "In Bernard's, the book shop in town."

"He appeared to you?" Torbin asked as he set the book and the box of cakes down on the coffee table.

"I'm not sure if he was actually there in the shop or not. The book fell from one of the shelves, and when I picked it up, when I touched it, I saw him," she explained, her hands resting on top of Kalen's. His touch helped calm the anxiety and adrenaline rushing through her.

Amelia watched her daughter, concern shining in her eyes. "What did he say to you?"

"War is coming. Time is running out. I need to find the sword," she told her.

"Did he by chance tell you where to find it?" Oliver asked as he leaned forward, his elbows resting on his knees.

Rexah shook her head. "He said it calls to me, that I need to listen. Whatever that means."

"I'll go make some hot coco," Oliver replied before he rose to his feet and headed into the kitchen.

"I've been in Bernard's many times. I know every book on every shelf, and I've never seen this one before," Amelia told her, baffled as she lifted it from the table to inspect it.

"It has no title, but that's the Shadow Star on the cover, there's no mistaking it," Rexah said.

"May I?" Torbin asked Amelia, gesturing to the book.

"Of course," Amelia said, handing it to him.

Torbin held the book in his hands, his eyes scanning every inch of it, a concentrated look on his face. His amber eyes began to glow.

"What is he doing?" Rexah whispered to Kalen when he sat by her side.

"He's trying to see if the book is enchanted or has been touched by magic," he explained to her. "The Power Blessed are able to sense other magic."

Rexah watched, fascinated as Torbin's magic lightly danced down the edges of the book, sparking here and there as it went.

"There's a faint hint of magic, divine magic," Torbin said.

"The Raven God wanted you to have this book," Amelia said, surmising its significance almost immediately.

Xandyr got up from his seat on the settee and opened the box of cakes. "What is the book about? Have you opened it yet?"

Rexah shook her head, taking the book from Torbin when he handed it to her. "No, I haven't yet. I wanted to wait until I got back before I did."

The book was old, its pages creased and discoloured. The thick black font was thankfully still legible, and illustrations broke up the dense pages of writing.

"It's a book on the history of the Dark Fae and the Shadow Star," Rexah said as her eyes ran over the words. She looked at her mother. "I thought you said there was nothing written about the sword?"

"There wasn't, at least not until now, it seems," Oliver replied as he walked back in from the kitchen with a tray of steaming hot cups filled with hot coco.

"The Gods work in mysterious ways, my love," Amelia said. "You were meant to have this book, and only you. That's why it hasn't been found by anyone else."

Rexah closed the book. "The Shadow Star can only be found by the Chosen One. Surely its location won't be in this book?"

"It won't be," Torbin said. "But clues to its whereabouts might. The information in this book will certainly help in the search for it, and it may help you better understand who and what you are. With the right training you'll be able to sense the sword's power."

"We can help you with that," Kalen said, his hand rubbing the small of her back comfortingly. "It won't be easy, but we will help you in any way we can."

Rexah nodded softly as she looked up at him. "Thank you."

Xandyr took his spot back on the settee, a cupcake in his hand. "I haven't had one of these in so long."

"Well, enjoy," Rexah said softly. "Everyone, please help yourselves. There's plenty to go around."

Amelia reached forward and picked out a cupcake as Oliver sat back down, lifting one of the cups.

"Are you okay?" Kalen whispered to her whilst the others helped themselves to a cake.

Rexah looked up at him and nodded softly. "I think so. As much as I can be. This book could change everything, or it could do nothing."

"We'll all take turns reading it. If it helps then great, if not then we move on. We will find it, I promise," he said. His hands had grown bold; he no longer took those gentle circles on her lower back, and instead his fingers navigated her back more freely, exploring as they drifted up her spine – if he didn't stop, she would have to excuse herself to avoid doing something inappropriate.

"I have a question," she said, trying to distract herself from her crude thoughts.

"Ask away." He smiled at her.

Rexah ran her fingers through her dark locks. "If those who are Power Blessed can sense other magic, why can't you or Torbin find the sword?"

Kalen's brows knitted together in a frown. "I'm not sure. We've never tried to focus on it before. We could try, but I don't have much hope in us finding it. Neither of us are the Chosen One of the Raven God."

"Of course, my mind is all over the place right now," she said, shaking her head softly.

Kalen's lips touched her forehead in a gentle kiss. "It's okay, darling. I'll get you a cake. There's nothing better than a warm drink and cake."

Rexah nodded and sighed, sinking back into the cushion just as her mother handed her one of the cups. She thanked her and lifted it to her lips, taking a small sip of the sweet liquid within.

The cupcake Kalen handed her looked absolutely delicious; chocolate icing swirled on top, and when she peeled back the casing, she was greeted with chocolate sponge. Wasting no more time, Rexah bit into the cupcake, and she almost groaned at the taste. Hidden within the sponge was rich melted chocolate.

"Okay, you were right," she said, picking up a napkin and wiping her mouth. "Nina makes the best cakes in the realm."

Torbin and Kalen chuckled softly.

"We used to come to Dorasa specifically for Nina's cakes," Torbin told her.

Kalen sipped his tea. "Not only the cakes; her chocolate chip cookies are out of this world."

"Nina was the baker who made our wedding cake." Oliver grinned. "We wanted something simple, a single tiered cake, but Nina being Nina went all out for us."

"It was three tiers, each one containing a different filling. To this day it's been the best cake I've ever tasted," Amelia said as she stirred her hot coco.

Rexah's eyes softened as she listened to them reminiscing, and the look of joy on their faces filled her chest with warmth.

"When you named Xandyr, why didn't you give him a name beginning with R or A? Why did you break that tradition?" she found herself asking them.

Oliver sat back on the settee. "Well, we wanted to do something a little different than the others before us."

"There had never been twins born before in our family, on the Ravenheart side. It had also been generations since a male had been born into the family, and we wanted to give him a different name to mark the special occasion.

"Alexandyr was my father's name," Oliver said. "He was a good man, and I wanted to pay tribute to him. I wanted his name to live on, but like your mother said, we didn't want another A in the family, so we shortened it to Xandyr."

"That's amazing," Rexah whispered. Tears had built up in her eyes, but she quickly blinked them away.

"With you we wanted to pay tribute to Riona, that's why the tradition continued with you," Amelia told her.

"The defender of men, and royal or queenly: that's what our names mean." Xandyr smiled at her. "Quite fitting if you ask me."

Rexah grinned at her brother and nodded. "Quite fitting indeed."

Conversation flowed with ease, and connecting with her family calmed Rexah's worrying mind. Oliver and Amelia reminisced more about their wedding day, and to Rexah it sounded absolutely perfect. It had been the two of them along with two witnesses from the town who went on to become their closest friends. A small wedding was what they had wanted; with little coin they possessed, they couldn't afford a lavish ceremony even if they'd wanted one.

As it had before, Rexah's mind drifted back to Ryden and the wedding fantasy she'd had in her head since she was young. For a short time that fantasy was becoming a reality, but now it was nothing more than the fairy tale in her mind once again.

"I was to be married," she said quietly.

Amelia's eyes widened. "You were? Who was the lucky man?"

"Prince Ryden Crowfell of Kaldoren," she replied with a heavy heart. "We were to marry in two months' time, but then the attack happened."

"You would have made a stunning bride," Oliver said softly. "I'm so sorry, love."

She gave them a weak smile before sipping her drink. It hurt to talk about it as much as it felt to think about it, but when she opened her mind to try, something unexpected happened; in her head, as she walked down the aisle towards Ryden, something had changed. When he spun to face her, it wasn't Ryden waiting for her at the end, but Kalen. His beautiful deep blue eyes brightened when he saw her, a life-affirming smile spread across his face.

A warm hand on her arm jolted her from her daydream. Blinking a few times, she turned her head to be met with those stunning blue eyes, but they were filled with concern.

"Sorry," she whispered to him. "I was off in another daydream there."

He gave her arm a gentle squeeze before letting her go, sitting back in his seat.

A few hours later, Rexah sat on the porch in the back garden. The book she'd purchased from Bernard's open in her lap. She'd spent the last hour combing through the pages, looking for any useful piece of information.

Details about the history of the Dark Fae were mentioned in the first few chapters, everything that she'd either learned in her studies or her parents had told her – nothing new. The following chapters on the history of the Raven God had been most interesting. The pages detailed how he'd helped in creating the realm, and how he'd blessed Riona with his power. What caught Rexah's attention was how he'd forged the Shadow Star into one of the most powerful weapons in history.

The Raven God plucked several stars from the night sky, banded them together with raven feathers, and solidified them with a strike of lightning, and thus the Shadow Star was born. He'd added the final touch by fusing the blade with his blessing so that only his Chosen may wield it.

"Find anything interesting?" Kalen asked as he sat

down beside her on the porch.

"I know how the sword was made," she said. "Also, I know why only the Chosen One can find it."

"Go on," he said, listening intently.

She took a deep breath. "The Raven God lay within the blade his power, but also a vow that no evil shall ever wield it; only his Chosen, only those he gifts with his power, can seek it out."

Kalen nodded, wrapping his arm around her waist. "Only you can find it."

Rexah nodded softly. "But that's not all. I had been wondering why the Dark Fae's master wants the sword so desperately if I'm the only one who can wield it. I found my answer in the book."

"What did it say?" he asked, studying her.

Taking a deep breath, she looked into his eyes. "The only way their master can access the power within the blade is if it is activated with my blood, we know that already, but in order for him to wield it he has to … I have to …"

Concern shadowed his features. "Have to what darling?"

"I have to die," she whispered.

She'd never seen Kalen pale until that moment. The blood drained from his face. "That will never happen. I will keep you alive even if it takes my last breath."

Her heart pounded as she saw the truth in his eyes. She felt it rolling off him in waves.

"I've gone through every page, and nothing in this book gives any clues as to where it might be," she said, sighing softly as she tried to steer the conversation in a different direction. "I don't know where to start."

Kalen wrapped his arm around her tighter, tugging her close. "You're not in this alone, darling. You've already begun your search; this is just another stop in the road."

Rexah leaned into him, inhaling his familiar scent. "I'm glad you're here with me. I don't think I'd be able to go on without you and Torbin."

Kalen smiled softly and lay the side of his face against the top of her head. "We're always going to be here for you, no matter what. I promise."

"There is still time for you both to go back to your people," she said. "I won't be offended."

"Venrhys already knows who we are. If we go back to Savindeer we risk our people's lives more than they already are," he replied. "I won't lead the wolves to their door."

Rexah moved and looked up at him. "You are amazing."

His lips tugged up into a smirk as he looked down at her. "Thank you, darling."

"I mean it. Your people are extremely lucky to have you," she said. "I'm extremely lucky."

Kalen's eyes softened as his fingers gently stroked her cheek. "You deserve the world, Rexah, and I will give it to you."

Before she could reply his lips captured hers in a gentle kiss. Her heart pounded fiercely in her chest as her stomach fluttered with a million butterflies. She knew that with him by her side nothing was impossible.

29

It was Xandyr's task to collect wood for the fireplace and Rexah had offered to go with him. Kalen and Torbin were back at the inn, so this would give her a chance to speak with her brother alone.

"What was it like living life as a royal?" Xandyr asked her. "Take me through a normal day for you."

Rexah took a deep breath. "Well, I would read or go for walks in the garden. Nesrin, my lady's maid – my best friend – would accompany me. She would also help me dress for parties that members of the surrounding royal families would attend. But that doesn't really scratch the surface of what Nes did for me."

"Wow, never a dull moment then? It must have been good having someone do pretty much everything for you," he replied.

She wondered if he was jealous of her life. In all honesty, she was the jealous one; he'd gotten to grow up with their parents.

"Actually, it was a pretty boring life," she admitted. "At first, yes, it was great having someone dress you and cook your food. It was great having someone at your beck and call."

"I can sense a but coming," Xandyr said as they stopped so he could pick up some pieces of wood.

"But I wanted to do all those things for myself. I'm not stupid, I know that there are lots of people throughout the realm who would give anything to have the life I had, but I didn't have friends; I couldn't go out and play with the children in the village," she told him. "I couldn't do the things I really wanted to."

Xandyr placed the pieces of wood into a large sack he'd carried into the forest over his shoulder before he looked at his twin. "When you put it like that then, yes, I can see why living a privileged life can still lead to a lonely one."

He didn't mean anything bad by his words, and she

knew it, but that didn't ease the sting of the tone in his voice.

They held so many similarities, not just their looks, but their personalities too. She'd noticed so many of his mannerisms matched her own. The way his dimples appeared when he smiled even the slightest, or the way he gripped his thumb in his hand when he was nervous. They were all things she did too.

Rexah looked up at the sky. The pines were tall here, and from this angle it looked like the treetops touched the clouds. She made her way over to a bush dotted with light blue flowers and inhaled the beautiful scents of them.

"You deserved everything that happened to you," Xandyr mumbled as he picked up another log, tossing it into his bag.

Rexah turned, straightening as she pulled her face away from the bushes.

What an odd, and quite frankly hurtful thing to say.

"What makes you say that, brother?"

Riona's dagger sheathed at her hip suddenly vibrated and sparked. The sensation sent a shock through her, and her stomach turned to lead as fear took over. Rexah frowned again as she looked down at it. *What the hell?*

"If you'd have just surrendered that night of the attack ... innocent lives needn't have been lost. So much destruction and death – all because of you," he said in a voice that wasn't his.

Rexah whirled around to face him, and her stomach sank. It was still her twin standing before her, but those eyes weren't his. She would recognise those haunting eyes anywhere. His light blue eyes were now completely black, and familiar dark veins shot out from his eyelids like slithering serpents.

Venrhys.

"Gods, these human bodies are a tight fit," he groaned rolling his neck from side to side. "It takes a while for them to stretch."

"Let go of him," Rexah growled.

"Not until you and I have had a little conversation," he said, stepping closer. "Don't worry, your brother is safe. He won't come to any harm whilst I'm in his body."

Rexah took a step back. "I don't care. I'm not having a conversation with you. Let him go! Now!" she yelled at him, her hands balling into fists at her sides, her nails digging into the skin of her palms.

"Careful, Rexah," he said, hissing her name like an

angered snake. "I can quite easily make sure dear Xandyr doesn't come back. It's your choice."

Rexah's mouth snapped shut. She watched as he rolled his shoulders and as he approached with a step, she retreated with a step of her own.

"You are a slippery little thing, but I do have to admit, I rather enjoy the chase," he said, his black eyes focused on her. "I enjoy the hunt."

Her skin crawled with disgust at his pleasure. "You can chase me all you want. I won't go down without a fight," she promised him.

An evil grin spread across his face. "Oh, I would expect nothing less. In fact, I look forward to it," he said as he took yet another step closer to her. "I look forward to hearing your cries of pain as I kill your family and fae protectors in front of you."

Rexah backed away from him, further as each word left his lips. Her heart jumped into her throat when she tripped on an overgrown root, and she stumbled back into the trunk of a tree. Venrhys took the opportunity to pin her against it; she struggled against him, but his strength overpowered hers, rendering her helpless.

"I look forward to watching you on your knees before me, begging for death," he said as he moved her hair from her neck, his fingers gently tangling themselves in the dark strands. "And I especially look forward to watching the light leave your eyes."

Rexah shivered as his breath caressed the skin of her neck. *No, no this can't happen. I can't let this happen, I won't.*

Gathering up what strength she could, Rexah placed her hands on his chest and shoved him back with everything her muscles would give her. He staggered enough for Rexah to regain a more comfortable distance. "If you've come here to frighten me with talk of my demise, then I suggest you give up now and give me back my brother."

Venrhys took a few more steps back. "I love the fire within you. It's a pity I'm going to have to extinguish it."

"You mistake me for someone who is weak and afraid. Maybe I was once, but not anymore. The next time we meet there will be death, and it shall be yours."

Rexah held her head high but winced at her words, taken aback by a threat she never thought she'd hear herself deliver.

A deep rumble of laughter emanated from him; a laugh that made every hair on her body stand on end.

"Your enthusiasm warms my heart, but you are so incredibly naïve if you think I will die by your hand."

"I guess we will have to wait and see." She glared at him. "Or are you afraid I might actually be right?"

"We will see indeed, but now I must leave you. I have a lot of ground to cover, but I don't think it will take long. Before I go, here is the answer to your question, Little Raven," he said. "You be the judge of whether I'm afraid or not." A devilish grin spread across his face, across her brother's face, and a wickedness gleamed in his eyes as Rexah caught sight of something glinting in his grasp.

Time itself felt as though it had come to a complete stop when she saw a dagger in his hand. She didn't know when her legs had started to move or how she got to him, but she moved so godsdamned fast, but it still wasn't fast enough.

Rexah grabbed his wrist and pulled it with all her might, but the blade swept around to its target regardless, the steel slicing his skin clean open.

They both fell to a heap on the ground, Xandyr letting out a sharp cry of pain.

Rexah grabbed the dagger from his hand and tossed it away. "Xandyr? Xandyr look at me!" she said as she cupped his cheek.

Her brother's eyes connected with hers and relief washed through her when she saw they were back to their sky-blue colour. Her relief was short lived when she looked down at his side where his grey shirt was quickly turning crimson. The adrenaline already coursing through her intensified as she grabbed the bottom of her own; she ripped a large section of it off before she peeled back Xandyr's shirt revealing a deep, heavily bleeding laceration.

"Keep your eyes on me, brother. I've got you," she said as she pressed the scrap of clothing to his wound. As she applied pressure, another yell of pain left his lips. His skin was paling rapidly, and he was breaking out into a cold sweat.

"Don't you dare close your eyes," she warned him.

"R-rex ..." he stuttered, breathing rapidly.

Rexah looked around for signs of anyone who might be passing through, and her heart sank with the realisation that no one was coming.

They were alone.

"You're going to be okay. I'm going to get you back to the cottage," she said, turning her attention back down to him. His eyes were now shut, and she began screaming for someone to help her, to help her brother, but no one answered. No one came running; they were too deep in the forest for anyone to hear her screams. Rexah kept the pressure firmly on Xandyr's bleeding wound. The blood quickly seeped through the fabric in her hand and her skin became sticky with it. His eyes fluttered slightly but refused open.

She couldn't lose him; she refused to let another member of her family die. But what could she do? She didn't have the knowledge to heal him.

"Xandyr? Please … Xandyr, open your eyes." She begged him, her voice raw from her cries for help. "You can't leave me; I won't let you. I just found you."

It was then she heard the most beautiful sound fill the eerie silence. Someone's voice was calling her name. She looked around, scanning the area to decipher the direction of the voice. Who was it? Had Venrhys caught up with her already? The thought sent a shiver through her.

Footsteps fast approached her, and her body tensed, ready for another confrontation. But it wasn't confrontation she was met with.

"Rexah?!" the voice yelled louder, closer now. It wasn't just anyone's voice, she realised.

It was Kalen.

Snapping her gaze behind her shoulder, she desperately tried to catch sight of him. "Kalen!" she cried out, not caring if danger was lurking.

The footsteps grew louder, and a few moments

later, both Kalen and Torbin crested the hill and skidded to a stop, their eyes wide as they took in the scene before them. Relief washed over her like a tsunami.

"Help him ... please," she pleaded, her cheeks wet with tears she hadn't realised were falling.

Wasting no time, the fae were at her side in an instant.

Torbin looked at Rexah, his hand gentle on the small of her back. "I need you to take your hand away so I can take a look at his wound."

"N-no it's bleeding heavily. If I remove my hand he will bleed out in seconds," she replied, her voice trembling.

Torbin gave her a sympathetic look. "He won't. I promise you; I won't let him die. Do you trust me, Rexah?"

She looked over to Kalen before she turned her attention to her brother. He needed help now if he had any chance of survival. "I trust you," she whispered before she pulled her hand away which was quickly replaced by Torbin's.

As Torbin began to inspect Xandyr's injury, Kalen gently took Rexah by the waist and helped her to her feet, guiding her away from them.

"Let's give Torbin some room," he said softly into her ear.

Rexah didn't speak. She watched as Torbin reached into a small pouch on his belt, pulled out what looked like dried, crushed up petals, and smeared them into the laceration. Xandyr moaned in agony and squirmed, trying to get away from the pain. She took a step forward, but Kalen's grip on her waist tightened.

"It's okay. He's okay," he whispered.

More tears fell from Rexah's eyes as she watched them. Xandyr relaxed a little as Torbin whispered words in the language of the fae, and it was then she noticed his fingertips were glowing a faint green colour.

She'd read about the fae power of healing during her studies. She knew not every fae possessed the ability; it truly was a gift and a beautiful thing to witness.

Kalen gently turned her to face him. "We need to get you both back to the cottage. Torbin will carry Xandyr. Are you able to walk back with me, or do you want me to carry you too?"

Rexah nodded softly. "I can walk." She waited until Torbin confirmed Xandyr was stable enough to be moved before she headed back to the cottage with them.

Amelia was distraught by the time they walked through the front door, but she pulled herself together enough to get medical supplies out of one of the top kitchen cupboards and take them into Xandyr's room.

With Oliver's help, Torbin laid Xandyr down on his bed – Torbin's fae strength rendered him more than capable of doing so on his own, but Rexah knew he would not deny a father the chance to help his son.

Rexah sat down on the settee, shaking like a leaf with the hit of surging adrenaline.

Kalen kneeled down in front of her, a look of worry in his sapphire eyes. Her eyebrows knitted together in a frown as she noticed him holding a damp cloth.

"Can I?" he whispered gesturing to her hands.

She looked down at herself and found the blood that stained her hands, Xandyr's blood. Bile rose to the back of her throat, but she managed to hold herself together, the gentleness of his voice soothing her. She nodded her head and moved her hands closer to him.

"I know you're probably still in shock, but can you tell me what happened?" he asked as he began to wipe the blood from her hands.

"Venrhys," she whispered. "He took over Xandyr's body. I knew it was him. I could tell it was him from his eyes; they were as dark as the night sky. My dagger vibrated, almost like it was warning me."

"What did he say to you?"

She licked her dry lips. "He said a lot of things about killing me and how much he will enjoy it."

Kalen's whole body tensed, but a moment later he relaxed as he composed himself. "He won't get the chance to try. He won't get near you again."

A horrible sensation trickled down her spine when the realisation hit her.

Oh Gods.

"Kalen."

He stopped what he was doing, and his eyes met hers. The words died on her lips. She couldn't get them out.

"Rexah?" Kalen urged her to speak, his voice still soft.

She looked him dead in the eye. "He knows where I am."

30
KALEN

K alen gently took her hand, his other cupping her cheek. "Rexah," he whispered.

She didn't answer him; she couldn't. He watched the panic within her rise with each passing second and each breath she failed to make. The fear in her eyes and the way her body trembled sent an ache through him.

Kalen placed her hand on his chest. "Follow my breaths," he instructed as he began to breathe deeply. He watched her as his own chest rose and fell slowly beneath her hand, and it wasn't long before Rexah's own chest followed that same rhythm. "That's it, darling," he encouraged.

They sat like that for a few more moments; he was sure to give her all the time she needed to relax and ground herself.

"We can't stay here. We have to go," she whispered. "We must leave, but I cannot leave my family behind. The Dark Fae will come, and their beasts with them."

Torbin walked into the living area, wiping his hands on a cloth stained with Xandyr's blood.

Rexah rose to her feet. "How is he?"

"He's going to be all right," he confirmed with a nod. "We got to you both in time."

"How did he get the injury?" Kalen asked her as he stood up.

She licked her dry lips again, and it sent a wave of heat through his body which he quickly shoved away.

"When Venrhys took over his body he had a dagger in his hand, but I didn't see it until the last moment. I rushed over and grabbed his wrist to stop him from stabbing himself, but I wasn't quick enough."

Torbin's amber eyes softened as he put the cloth down on the dining table. "Rexah, that blade would have done a lot more damage if you hadn't grabbed hold of him. You saved his life."

"But Torbin, there was so much blood," she said, a

haunting look filling her eyes as though she was reliving it all over again.

"I know, but he hasn't damaged any vital organs; he more than likely would have if he'd stabbed himself," he told her as he walked closer to them.

"What were those flowers you pressed into his wound?"

"Lemisar," Torbin said as he sat down on the armchair. "A healing plant grown in Vellwynd. Their properties are well known for their aid in preventing infection and speeding up the healing process."

"Your fingertips were glowing. You have the power of healing," Rexah said. "I know how rare that is."

A soft smirk tugged on Torbin's lips.

"Don't flatter him, darling. He will end up becoming too cocky for his own good," Kalen told her.

Rexah ran her fingers through her raven-coloured hair as she sat back down. "Thank you for everything you've done for him."

"No need to thank me," he said, smiling softly.

Kalen sat down on the settee next to Rexah. "Everything's going to be okay, I promise you."

"We can't stay here," she said quietly. "But I can't leave my family. I've only just found them."

"No, Rexah, you have to go," Oliver's voice filled the room.

Rexah looked over to her father. "I won't leave you unprotected."

Kalen understood how she felt; all he'd wanted to do was protect his family and look how that had turned out. He watched as Oliver walked over to them, Amelia appearing from the hallway behind him.

"We will be okay. As much as I don't want to let you go again, you can't stay here," he said, his eyes already pleading his daughter's forgiveness.

"They will come here, and they won't spare anyone, not until they find out where we've gone. I won't have them hurt any of you because of me," Rexah argued.

Amelia's eyes were rimmed red from her tears. "Your father is right: you must go. We have protection here."

"What sort of protection?" Rexah asked her.

"There is a coven of witches that live here in Dorasa. They're known as the Water Witches. Their power comes from the sea, from Nadvika," Amelia explained. "They've protected Dorasa's shores and the town for thousands of years."

Oliver wrapped his arm around his wife's waist.

"The Water Witches have kept the Valfae and their masters at bay before."

Rexah's brows moved closer together. "When was the last time they attacked Dorasa?"

As soon as the question left her lips, Kalen instantly knew the answer, and it wasn't due to the look on her parents faces.

Rexah sucked in a breath. "They came here looking for me when I was born, didn't they?"

Oliver nodded. "They arrived two nights after both you and Xandyr were born. We knew the danger you would be in, but we didn't think they would come for you so quickly. You were only a few days old."

"The Water Witches protected the town from those monsters, drowned them on land," Amelia said. "And when the Dark Fae and what was left of their creatures fled, we spoke with the witches. They contacted the other elemental covens and asked them to keep you and your grandmother safe on your journey to Adorea."

There were covens scattered all over the realm that drew their power from the elements; air, fire, water, and earth; except for the Night Witches who lived closest to Adorea and drew their power from the moon.

Witches were born with magic in their blood thanks

to the goddess who blessed their bloodlines from the very beginning.

"They will keep you and every other living soul in this town safe?" Rexah asked, pulling Kalen from his thoughts.

Oliver nodded. "This is their home too, sweetheart. They won't stand by whilst it's destroyed by those monsters."

Kalen felt her sorrow and placed his hand on the small of her back.

"Then we will leave tonight by the cover of darkness," she said.

"I will ensure the horses are ready for our departure," Torbin said, standing up.

Kalen also rose to his feet. "I will go with him. We will replenish our supplies for the road too."

"Wait, we need to know where we are headed," Rexah said, her gaze moving from Kalen to Torbin. "Where will we go?"

"There are rumours of a man who lives in a village a few days ride from here who knows the sword's location," Oliver replied.

"If this man knows where the sword is, why haven't the Dark Fae gone straight to him first?" Rexah questioned him. "And why have you waited until now to tell us?"

"Like I said, it's only a rumour, stories that old wives liked to conjure up. But with our current situation we cannot afford to dismiss it as such," he replied.

Kalen looked at Oliver. "And where do we find this man? What's his name?"

"His name is Storglass. He lives in a village called Grimhollow," Amelia replied.

Torbin nodded. "I have heard of that village. It lives up to its name; a very grim place indeed."

Rexah nodded slowly. "Then it's settled."

Both were quiet as they made their way through the busy town.

"Are you okay?" Torbin asked him, finally breaking their silence.

"I am now I know she's alive," he replied.

He had known she was in trouble, felt inside him that she needed help. Kalen had felt her terror; it had hit him like an arrow to the chest, and he'd almost fallen to his knees with the sensation that gripped him. He'd thought the worst, and when he crested that hill and saw her, the relief he'd felt was indescribable.

"Are you going to tell her?" Torbin asked as they turned down towards the stables.

Kalen had almost told her so many times. It wasn't

something that could be said in casual conversation; it was a huge thing in fae culture, not something to be taken lightly.

"When the time is right, I'll tell her." He nodded. "But right now, things are too fragile, and I don't want to put her under any more pressure than she already is."

Torbin smiled at him. "I've never seen you like this about anyone before. It's refreshing."

Kalen glared playfully at his best friend. "Just wait until it's your turn," he said.

Torbin laughed. "I can't wait."

The stable hand promised to have their horses ready for them within the hour, and they soon arrived back at the inn to collect their things. When Kalen stepped into Rexah's room, her scent instantly surrounded him in a welcoming embrace. Closing the door behind him, he stepped further into the room.

She didn't have many possessions with her. The bag she carried lay at the foot of the bed, still fully packed. He crossed the room, picked up the bag and placed it on the bed before he gave the room a once over to make sure she didn't forget to pack anything.

He ran his hand through his dark hair as he pulled her bag over his shoulder. She'd been through so much, and it broke his heart each time he looked into those stunning eyes and saw pain. *I wish I could take it all away. I wish I could be the one to bare it all.*

The door creaked as he closed it behind him. Torbin was waiting for him in the hallway, a sympathetic look on his face.

"Don't," Kalen said before walking down the hallway.

Torbin was quick to catch up. "Don't what?"

"Don't look at me like that," he said.

"I'm sorry; I can't help it. You feel her pain, her sorrow. You feel it all, and I can only imagine what that's like," Torbin replied. "I just want you to know that I'm here if you ever need to talk about it."

Kalen stopped walking and looked at him. He sighed. "I know, Tor. I'm sorry."

Torbin patted his shoulder. "No need for apologies, Kal. We're with each other, no matter what."

Kalen nodded softly, placing his own hand on Torbin's shoulder. "No matter what."

"Now come on, let's go," he said. "The quicker we leave, the better."

Together they walked down to the bar and handed the keys back to the owner before they walked out.

"The journey ahead is going to be tough," Kalen said as he stepped outside. "Unlike anything we've ever faced before. It's not just the Dark Fae and Valfae – we're diving into some dark shit."

"If this is the part where you tell me I should go back to our people then you can save your breath," Torbin told him. "I'm not leaving your side. I made you a promise that day, and I intend to keep it."

"Do you need to be such a loyal asshole all the time?" Kalen asked.

Torbin laughed and nodded. "Oh yeah, I do."

Kalen couldn't help but chuckle too. "Fine, but don't say I didn't warn you."

"We've never run from a fight, and we aren't starting now," Torbin said.

"Promise me something," Kalen said, looking at him.

Torbin nodded softly. "Anything."

"If something happens to me, promise you'll keep her safe." Kalen watched him, searching his face for any doubt.

"Don't talk like that," he replied dismissively.

Kalen stopped walking and grabbed his arm. "Promise me, Tor."

Torbin looked down at the hand on his arm before looking into his friend's eyes. "You have my word."

Kalen nodded and released his arm before he continued walking. He was immortal, but not invincible; if anything was ever to happen to him, he had to know someone would be there to keep her safe when he couldn't, and the only person he trusted with that task was Torbin.

31
REXAH

Rexah sat on a chair beside the bed where her brother lay. He had been unconscious since they'd brought him back from the forest earlier in the day. Torbin had given him something to help him sleep, something that would help him recover quickly, and assured her he wasn't in any pain.

Xandyr's hand was warm in hers as she held it. She'd been sat by his bedside since Kalen and Torbin had gone to complete their tasks, talking to him about everything and anything. She wanted him to know that she was there by his side, that she didn't abandon him or their parents.

The sun was almost gone from the sky, the oranges

and pinks were slowly giving way to the night's dark blues, and the moon had begun its ascent.

"Torbin says you won't be awake until at least the morning. I won't be here. I'll be gone by then," she said quietly. "The night is almost upon us, and we need to go."

She knew he wouldn't answer her, but part of her hoped he could hear her words, and that was enough. "I wish I could stay here with you all forever, and I'm sorry we haven't been able to say goodbye properly. I'm so sorry you were hurt because of me, but I promise you, I will do everything I can to stop the Dark Fae from getting their hands on that sword, no matter the cost."

Xandyr's fingers twitched, almost like he was trying to squeeze her hand. Her eyes softened and her heart ached as she rose from her seat to sit on the edge of his bed, the mattress creaking under her weight. His hair was soft against her skin as she brushed it out of his eyes.

"It's an honour to have you as my brother. I didn't know I needed a sibling until I met you," she told him. "Promise me when you wake up, when you're stronger, you'll keep them safe."

This time when his fingers moved, his grip was strong enough to squeeze her hand.

Hot tears slid down her cheeks. "When this is all over, we will have our time together, as a family. I promise," she said, gently kissing the back of his hand.

Rexah could hear the muffled voices of her parents and fae companions in the living room. It was time to go.

"Until we meet again, brother," she whispered before she leaned down and pressed a gentle kiss to his forehead. "In a better world."

Rising to her feet, she looked over her shoulder to her brother one last time before she walked out of the room, the bottom of her black cloak sweeping along the floor behind her as she went.

Oliver and Amelia were standing in the living area, chatting quietly between themselves, and as soon as Rexah announced herself with a small cough, their hushed voices died down. Torbin stood by the front door and Kalen leaned against the fireplace, his strong arms crossed over his broad chest. The atmosphere was so thick you could cut it with a knife.

"Whatever anyone has to say, say it now," Rexah said, her eyes sweeping off each of them.

For a few long moments, nobody spoke, but then

her father stepped forward. "Your mother and I have talked, and we want you to consider all your options before you leave."

"No one is forcing you to follow in Riona's footsteps," her mother said quietly.

Rexah frowned at them. "You ... you want me to stay?"

"If she stays here, they will find her, they will take her blood, and they will kill her," Kalen said matter-of-factly. "There's no point in sugar coating it. If she decides to stay here, then she's signing her own death warrant."

It was the first time she'd ever heard Kalen speak so bluntly. No matter how much his words stung, they were truthful.

"Father—"

"The witches can protect you from them," Amelia interjected. "They did it before, they can do it again," she said, her eyes pleading with her.

Rexah looked to her father, and he stared back at her with pain in his eyes. The look on her father's face told her he'd tried to convince her mother that leaving was for the best, but she was clearly in denial.

"Mother, I understand. Trust me, if I could stay here I would, but I can't and you know it," she said as she closed the distance between them and took her mother's hands in hers, tears burning in her eyes. "The Dark Fae will never stop coming for me, no matter how powerful those witches are. They will stop at nothing until they have me in their grasp, and they will kill you if that's what it takes. I already lost my grandmother, I can't … I can't lose you too; I won't."

Tears escaped her mother's eyes and cascaded down her face – there was no changing her daughter's mind. "Oh, my beautiful girl. My beautiful, brave girl."

Rexah gently pulled her mother into her arms, hugging her. They held each other close, and soon her father's arms wrapped around them both.

Feeling her father's arms around them finally made the tears fall down Rexah's face, and they didn't stop. Oliver's grip on them only tightened as he too shed his tears.

I promise this won't be our last embrace. We will see each other again. We will have more time. I will make sure of it, make sure for not only our family, but for the families of every living soul in the realm. The Dark Fae will pay, she swore to herself.

"We are so proud of you. No words will ever describe just how proud," Oliver said as they pulled away.

"We haven't had as much time together as I'd hoped, but knowing you are alive, that I have a brother, fills me with so much happiness that words can't describe," she said, looking from her mother to her father. "I will be forever grateful to the gods who brought us back together."

Oliver met his daughter's eyes. "You are more powerful than you know. You are the light in this world full of darkness, and I will be forever grateful to the gods who chose to give you to us as our daughter. I am filled with joy that I got to see you grown, to see your beauty outside and within."

"We love you, Rexah," Amelia said quietly as if she was trying not to cry any harder than she already was. "May the Gods light your path in darkness; may they give you strength in your weakest moment; and may the Gods keep you safe."

Rexah gave them both a sad smile, trying to stop her tears from flowing. "Until we meet again."

Amelia kissed her cheek and Oliver kissed her head.

"Until we meet again, my love," her father whispered against her hair.

Rexah forced herself to pull away from their embrace, and it felt like a thousand knives piercing her heart all at once. She slid her gaze to Torbin and Kalen who each gave her an understanding nod.

She was ready to go.

Torbin and Kalen said their goodbyes to her parents, the former opening the front door and walking out without a second glance. Kalen held out his hand to Rexah. She looked down at it before looking at her parents one last time, taking note of every little detail – every little greying hair, every little wrinkle starting to form in their skin.

Kalen's hand was soft and warm as she took it. She slowly turned away from her mother and father and walked to the front door before they both stepped outside.

Rexah didn't stop walking out of fear she wouldn't start again if she did. Kalen gave her hand a gentle squeeze as they passed through the small gate at the end of the garden and stepped out onto the dirt path.

Rexah didn't speak as they made their way through the town, and Kalen never let go of her hand as they followed Torbin who lead the way a few paces ahead.

The town was still alive with folk going about their business, some heading home from a long day's work, others heading out to the tavern for a night of drinking. It wasn't long before they reached the stables that the grief Rexah had been attempting to keep at bay threatened to rear its ugly, consuming head.

"Hey, look at me," Kalen whispered softly to her. "Everything will be okay I promise you. I've got you darling."

Rexah shifted her gaze to meet his, and her bottom lip wobbled slightly as tears threatened to fall once more, but she blinked them back. Giving him a sharp nod, she turned to the horse and hoisted herself up onto it.

Kalen swung up onto the horse, taking his place behind her. Torbin gave the stable hand some extra coin for the excellent job he'd done before he mounted his own horse.

As they passed through the gates of Dorasa, Rexah sank back into Kalen's strong and comforting embrace. His scent surrounded her, reminding her that she wasn't alone. The next part of their journey would be difficult, and she would be lying if she said she wasn't afraid. Closing her eyes, she let herself bask in Kalen's warmth and let the rest of the world fade away.

32

*S*moke from glowing embers of broken and charred
wood filled the air with a misty haze. The sound of
crows echoed from all different directions. Ash
drifted past her like the falling of a light snow, and with each
step she took, her black boots became dirtier with the
remnants of destruction.

The light breeze made her raven-coloured hair dance
lightly as she walked through what remained of the castle
that she once called her home. The place she grew up in was
now nothing but cinders, smoke, and destruction, the scent of
death in the air.

It wasn't safe. She shouldn't be here, she knew, but something was drawing her to where the last remaining part of
the once magnificent palace stood.

The main door stood tall, but the stone walls around it were covered in black soot and crumbling in areas. Her steps came to a halt when the door drifted open, pieces of wood flaking off as it creaked loudly, and someone she didn't think she would ever see again, at least not in this life, stepped through it.

Aurelia Ravenheart looked exactly like Rexah remembered. Her long, dark grey hair flowed down to her waist, gently swaying in the breeze. She wore a white dress, a night gown that fell to just above her ankles, and she was barefoot.

"Hello, my darling," Aurelia said, her voice echoing.

"Grandmother," Rexah whispered, her own voice resounding. "It's not safe. We shouldn't be here. Those monsters are still out there; they'll find us."

A reassuring smile spread across the Queen's face. "The monsters cannot reach us here. We are protected."

Rexah frowned. "Here?"

"No one can change their own destiny. Fate will catch up no matter how hard you try," Aurelia replied as she slowly stepped towards her granddaughter. "I only wanted to protect you. Instead, I failed you, and for that I am so very sorry."

Rexah shook her head. "No; none of what happened was your fault. I met my mother and father, my brother too. They explained everything to me. You did what you thought was right to keep me safe, and I don't blame you for what happened."

Aurelia halted a few feet away from her. "Things will only get harder from here. The fae you travel with will not be enough to keep you from the clutches of darkness."

"I don't need anyone to protect me, Grandmother. You of all people should know that," Rexah replied.

Behind them, a howling screech pierced the air. Rexah spun on her heel and scanned her surroundings, but the fog was so thick. "We must leave. They are close."

"The sword must be found. It must not fall into the wrong hands; if it does, the consequences will be catastrophic," Aurelia said, ignoring her granddaughter's warnings.

Rexah turned to her again, her eyebrows knitting together in a frown. "I won't let that happen."

"Fate has already written your path, and just like my own fate, it is one you will not be able to change. No matter what you do, destiny will intervene, and all you will be able to do is watch it unfold before your very eyes."

Aurelia closed the distance between them as the sound of the Valfae grew louder and louder behind her. Rexah watched as Aurelia approached, her gaze never faltering as she took in every detail of this moment with her grandmother.

The dead queen stopped in front of Rexah and pulled her into her arms, hugging her gently. Rexah's arms slowly *wrapped around her, the burning pressure of unshed tears stinging her eyes. Her grandmother's arms tightened around her.*

Over Aurelia's shoulder, Rexah watched as dark shapes passed through the smoke, their red eyes bright with hunger and the promise of agonising death.

"Oh, my darling," Aurelia whispered. "You're already dead."

The words sliced through her soul like a knife. But it wasn't the words alone that sent a grave, chilling shiver through her, it was the voice that spoke them – a voice that wasn't her grandmother's.

Rexah pulled away slowly, and as she looked up she was met with Venrhys's menacing face, his black eyes hungry and his lips stretched into a wicked, evil grin.

"Darling! Darling, open your eyes!" a familiar voice begged her, bringing her back.

Rexah's eyes snapped open. It was then she could feel how hard her heart was thumping against her chest, how her lungs burned at the speed of her breathing, and how Kalen was pressed on top of her.

They were tangled in one another: Rexah's legs wrapped loosely around his waist while Kalen's elbow rested on the ground above her left shoulder, his hand pinning her right wrist to the ground. Her panic escalated as she felt her fingers squeezed tightly around the knife he'd given her.

Rexah turned her gaze to his once again, confusion and fear masking her features. "K-kalen?"

"You're okay. You're safe, but darling, I need you to let go of the dagger," he said calmly. "Can you do that for me?"

She did as he asked, and the blade slid from her trembling fingers onto the ground. Her eyes never left his as she felt him release her wrist.

"Easy," he whispered as he peeled himself off her and eased her into a sitting position.

Rexah took a moment to take in her surroundings. The last thing she remembered was being on the horse with Kalen as they left Dorasa. Now she sat on a bedroll surrounded by thick trees, in what looked like a makeshift camp. A small fire burned not too far from her. Torbin sat on his own bedroll, his eyes on them and his hand on the hilt of his own dagger.

"Where are we?" she asked quietly, her voice a little hoarse.

"We stopped to rest. We rode for a few hours; you fell asleep on me not long after we set off from Dorasa," Kalen told her. "You were having a nightmare."

Venrhys's black eyes and his wicked smirk appeared

in her mind, and she swallowed the lump in her throat. "Yes. How did you end up pinning me to the ground?"

Kalen sat back and leant against the tree behind him. "We'd both been sitting by the fire when you started fitting in your sleep."

"We tried to wake you," Torbin said. "You grabbed the dagger, and before you could harm us or yourself, Kalen had to restrain you."

"Oh Gods," she whispered, looking between the two of them, embarrassment staining her cheeks red. "I'm so sorry."

"What were you dreaming about?" Kalen asked her.

Taking a deep breath, she began to tell them about her dream, or rather her nightmare. She told them about the castle, about her grandmother, and about Venrhys and what he'd said to her. "He's inside my head."

"He's not, Rexah. He wants you to think he is, but he's not," Torbin assured her. "That's what the Dark Fae do; they try to weaken you from the inside out, so that when they are ready to make their killing blow you're already at their mercy."

Rexah couldn't find the words to reply as his words sent a chill through her. Instead, she focused on controlling her breathing – the harsh panting did nothing but make her insides burn, and she had to keep her head in the game.

"The sun will be up in a few hours; try to rest as much as you can," Torbin said, his amber eyes soft with an apology. His words had clearly affected her, and it was equally clear from the sadness brewing in his eyes that he felt responsible.

She didn't think she could rest at all after that, and the look on her face must have given her away as Kalen opened his arms to her.

"Come here."

Rexah slowly crawled over to him and let him pull her close. She lay her head on his chest, his legs bent slightly at either side of her. When his arms wrapped around her, she felt that instant familiar feeling of safety spread through her.

"Sleep, Rexah. I'm here," Kalen whispered to her soothingly, running his fingers gently through her hair. "Torbin and I will keep watch until the sun comes up."

They travelled for what felt like an eternity. Torbin had told her that it would take them around three or four days to get to Grimhollow, and on the third night, she stood on the edge of their makeshift camp with her arms folded across her chest as she gazed up at the twinkling stars. They winked at her as if they could feel her pain and her sorrow and they wanted her to know that she wasn't alone in the world, no matter what. That was the thing she loved most about stars; they would always be there.

The feeling of soft material snaked its way around her shoulders, and she looked up to find Kalen standing behind her, wrapping his cloak around her. "I thought you might be cold."

Smiling weakly, she pulled the cloak further around herself. The smell of cedarwood, bergamot and a hint of sage engulfed her senses and made the blood in her veins tingle with excitement. "Then you thought correctly."

"What secrets are the stars whispering to you?" he asked as his arms gently slid around her waist from behind.

She couldn't stop her smile from widening as

butterflies fluttered in her stomach. "If I told you then they wouldn't be secrets any longer."

"That's true," he said, chuckling softly. "Okay, I won't pry any further, star secret keeper."

Rexah huffed a laugh as she shook her head. She leaned back into him, savouring his warmth. "I used to love looking up at the stars. Late at night I would sneak out of my room and go to my favourite spot in the forest by the lake and watch them. I'd take my book with me, and I'd get lost in the story with them."

"I used to watch them too. It was like they could hear me, hear my worries and my fears. They didn't judge," he said.

Her heart pounded in her chest. "I thought so too. I would share my secrets and my worries with them, and somehow I knew they listened."

"They know us better than we know ourselves," he said, his gaze towards the sky, the moon sparkling in his deep blue eyes.

All she could do was nod. The stars in the sky were the only thing in this world that wouldn't be swayed by evil. Even in darkness they would shine bright.

"I didn't know your grandmother, but I have a feeling she would be extremely proud of you," he said softly.

"What would she have to be proud of? The fact that I hardly fought back, or how I'm running like a coward rather than standing my ground?" she asked. Nothing she had done since the attack was something to be proud of.

"I believe she would be proud of the fact that you survived, despite everything, and you did what you had to. Not to mention how you found your parents and your brother with little to no guidance," he said before he slowly turned her in his arms to face him. "Or how about the fact that you're not running away? You're on your way to search for an ancient weapon of power that will aid you in ridding this world of darkness."

"What if we don't find it, Kalen?" she asked. The question had been burning in her mind since they left Dorasa, and she was terrified of the answer. "What if it doesn't exist, or what if it's too godsdamned late?"

"You could be right, but it's up to us to make sure either way. Could you live with yourself if you gave up now and the Dark Fae somehow got their claws on it?"

"You know I couldn't," she whispered, looking away from him.

"I know you're scared. It's completely understandable and natural that you are, but there is something you need to understand," he said, the tone of his voice demanding her attention once again.

Rexah's violet eyes met his. The moonlight shone down on the side of his face, illuminating the line of his jaw and his cheekbone.

"There will be times when all hope seems lost. The feeling of complete terror will consume you, and the darkness will feel never ending – but I will be there," he said. "I will be the shoulder you need to cry on. I will be the weapon to strike down your enemies, and I will be your shield to protect you from dark."

Letting his words sink in, Rexah searched his eyes and all she found was pure, indisputable truth. They hadn't known each other long, but she couldn't deny the connection they had, the pull she felt towards him. It was a feeling that no words could ever describe, one that she'd never felt before in her life, and she loved it.

"And I will be yours," she whispered. "I cannot promise you the journey will be easy, and I cannot guarantee that our outcome will be a positive one, but what I can promise is that I will do everything I can to keep you safe."

Kalen gazed into her eyes so deeply she swore he attempted to find her soul.

"All my life I never truly believed, not until I met you," he whispered.

Rexah frowned softly as she looked at him curiously. "You never truly believed what?"

"That I would find you," he answered gently. "My—"

"Kalen?" Torbin's voice asked, cutting Kalen off.

Rexah stepped back and looked over to where Torbin stood holding broken branches and twigs in his arms.

"Would you mind helping me with the fire?" Torbin asked.

Kalen nodded before looking back down at Rexah. "Excuse me, darling."

She watched as Kalen walked away before turning her gaze back up to the stars. Feeling the chill more with his absence, she pulled Kalen's cloak further over her shoulders as a gentle, cold breeze brushed by.

Their conversation replayed over and over in her head, but there was something specific Kalen had said that stuck out like a sore thumb; it made the stars shine a little brighter, almost like they too acknowledged the significance of the words.

"That I would find you.

33

Grimhollow certainly lived up to its name: it was a small village, but still certainly larger than Oakhaven, with single-storey homes made of dark grey stone that stood – or more accurately, leaned – either side of the muddy road. The buildings were derelict, the roofs in places non-existent, and the walls crumbled like stale sponge cake.

The streets were quiet, hardly any villagers out and about, and Rexah wondered if that was due to the rain or the fact that not many people lived here.

Night had fallen quickly upon their approach to the village, the moon hidden by rain clouds making it difficult for Rexah to see where she was placing her feet.

She wasn't blessed with good night-vision like her companions were, and navigating the streets quickly became a stressful endeavour.

Mud squelched beneath their boots with each step they took, and Rexah stumbled into Torbin when the terrain became unstable beneath her feet. He caught her with ease and grace thanks to his fae strength, and Kalen chuckled softly as he witnessed it.

"Is there an inn or at least a tavern around so we can get out of this horrible weather?" Rexah asked, her voice shaking and her teeth chattering as she pulled the hood of her soaked cloak further over her head.

The rain had been battering down on them for at least an hour, and it was only getting heavier, with no signs of it easing up any time soon. Rexah's clothes clung to her skin and made the howling wind cut through her like broken glass.

"There's a tavern just up ahead. I don't know if it has rooms available though," Torbin answered, pulling his own cloak closer as the cold wind began to bluster.

Rexah didn't care if a room was available; she'd sleep on a bench if she had to; all she wanted was to be indoors, huddled next to a roaring fire to warm herself up and dry her sodden clothes. Her wish was soon granted when they stopped outside a larger, stable looking building at the end of a row of less stable looking homes.

The wooden door to The Hollow House groaned and creaked as Kalen pushed it open. Inside the tavern was just as dreary as the rest of the village; a few dirty tables were scattered around, some vacant and others occupied by customers, and the sconces along the cracked walls were lit but provided little light.

Torbin closed the door behind him once they were all inside. "For the love of the Gods," he mumbled quietly.

Rexah couldn't help but agree with his reaction.

"Let's get some rooms sorted," Kalen said to them before he made his way through the room towards the bar, Rexah and Torbin in tow.

A few customers looked in their direction as they passed, some murmuring inaudibly about them, no doubt. She couldn't blame them though – two fae and a human walk into a tavern in Grimhollow sounded like the start of a bad joke.

An older man stood behind the bar with a fatigued look on his face; his eyes were tired, his head hairless, and his skin showed the sagging signs of aging. The sleeves of his dark shirt were rolled up to reveal tattoos on his weathered skin, a wolf on his right arm and a skull on his left, both surrounded by red roses. A dirty rag hung over his shoulder, the stale stench of it sticking to the back of Rexah's throat, but it was his right eye that drew her attention. It was made of glass, disorientating swirls of blue shimmering within.

"Your parents ever tell you it's rude to stare at folk, girl?" he asked, his voice rough and deep. She swore she saw the blue swirls in his glass eye darken as he took her in.

"Pardon me," she said quietly.

Kalen moved closer to her, his body touching the side of her torso. It sent a delicious wave of need through her – if nothing else, she was grateful for the warmth the sensation granted throughout her body.

"Do you have any rooms for rent?"

The man slid his gaze to the fae. "I might."

Torbin rolled his eyes, and a bag of coin thudded against the bar when he threw it down. "That should more than cover whatever rooms you have available, supper, and breakfast tomorrow morning."

The innkeeper snatched up the bag of coin like a starved man stealing a loaf of bread and placed it behind the bar. He turned and limped to a board behind him, and with a violent sniff, he lifted a key off one of the many hooks within it before turning back to the bar. "Second door to the right on the second floor," he grumbled, slamming the key onto the bar and sliding it across to them. "Enjoy."

All three of them looked at the single key on the bar then looked at each other before turning their attention back to the innkeeper. The man looked at them with the same weary expression on his face he'd worn when they'd first walked in.

"One room?" Kalen asked, his eyebrow rising.

"One room," the innkeeper confirmed, folding his arms over his chest.

"How busy do you get with travellers?" Torbin asked him.

The man shrugged his shoulders. "We don't get many folks passing through our village, so I don't need many rooms. I have three rooms, but two are currently occupied. Take it or leave it."

Rexah snatched up the key before either Kalen or Torbin could say anything else. "Thank you; one room will suffice."

The innkeeper nodded before he moved further

down the bar to wipe it with the dirty rag on his shoulder.

Rexah looked between Kalen and Torbin. "Are you okay with us all sharing a room?"

"Well, it's a little late for that question don't you think, darling?" Kalen asked as that flawless smirk spread across his perfect lips. He knew exactly how to push her buttons, but she would be damned if she gave him the reaction he was looking for.

"We are fine with it as long as you are." Torbin smiled softly at her.

Rexah nodded. "I am. It won't be forever, a day or two at most. I don't want to spend any more time here than is necessary. This place is already giving me a bad feeling."

She looked around the room and the feeling of unease settled deep into her bones. Not judging a book by its cover was going to be a difficult task in this village.

"You two go on up to the room; I'll get us sorted with some supper," Torbin said.

Rexah didn't want to leave him down here alone, but Kalen didn't give her much of a choice as he gently guided her towards the stairs with his hand on her shoulder blade.

Torbin was a warrior – he could take care of himself.

The room was tiny with only one bed that looked neither comfortable nor inviting. Dust covered the furniture, which consisted entirely of a small table and a chair by the small window and a wooden chest of drawers.

"You can have the bed," Rexah told him before she crossed to the other side of the room and set down her bag.

"I'd happily let Torbin take it," he replied as he scanned the room. "We would have been better sleeping in the stable with the horses."

Rexah laughed softly. "How dare you speak ill of this tavern. You best be sure the innkeeper doesn't hear you or else you may end up in tomorrow's stew."

Kalen's hearty laugh filled her with warmth, and she came to realise that his laugh was a sound she would never grow tired of hearing, much like his voice.

"Like you said, we won't be here for long. We find Storglass, find out what he knows, and then we are out of here," he said. "You're not the only one this place gives the creeps."

"Do you really think he knows where it is?" she

asked him. It was one of the many questions that had been eating away at her.

Kalen's strong shoulders shrugged as he pulled his bedroll from his bag. "Who knows? If he doesn't, maybe he knows someone who does."

"I like your positive outlook on all of this," she said as she peeled off her soaked cloak that had begun to stick to her like a second skin.

There was a small fireplace next to the window that looked as though it hadn't been used in a while, and the firewood, stacked neatly in a basket next to it, was covered in a thick layer of dust.

"Positivity is good for the soul," Kalen replied as he smoothed out his bedroll along the floor near the door. "My mother used to tell me that all the time."

Rexah looked over to him. It was the first time he'd spoken to her about his mother without her asking first. She sat down by the unlit fireplace. "What was she like?"

Kalen sat down on his bedroll, leaning his back against the wall next to the set of wooden drawers. "She was the most caring and loving person I've ever met. She raised me and my younger brother by herself and never needed or wanted help. We never wanted for anything. She made sure we were fed before she was and that we had everything we wanted."

"What about your father?" she found herself asking before her eyes opened wide in panic. "I'm sorry, I shouldn't have asked that. You don't have to answer. It's none of my business."

"He doesn't deserve to be called father. When he found out my mother was pregnant with Niken, he took off like the coward he was," he told her, gritting his teeth. "In human years I was around five years old. I remember the day he left as if it were yesterday. He told my mother that I wasn't his, and neither was the *brat* in her womb."

Rexah's eyes filled with sadness. She could only imagine what that must have felt like to hear, especially being as young as he had been. "Oh, Kalen, I'm so sorry."

"Don't be – I'm not," he replied sharply. "We never needed him. We were better off without."

She could almost feel the sorrow and anger flowing from him, and her heart ached in her chest.

"Then my mother and Niken were killed right in front of me, and I did nothing to save them," he continued before his voice broke. "I was the coward then."

Rexah couldn't recall the moment she decided to crawl over to him, but there she was by his side. He didn't stop her as she lifted his arm and nestled into his side, her head resting on his shoulder.

"You weren't a coward. You fought so hard to save them, but those monsters stopped you. I've been under their influence; I understand how impossible it is to escape their grasp," she said quietly. "Don't you dare blame yourself for what happened."

Kalen wrapped his arms around her, holding her close to him, his scent completely engulfing her.

"Once we have the sword, we will hunt every single one of those beasts down, and we will end them," she promised him. "Together."

His fingers hooked under her chin and raised it gently. Those deep ocean eyes poured into her violet ones. "Together."

The door suddenly opened with a bang, and they flinched away from each other.

"Don't get too excited about this, the food isn't very —" Torbin halted when he saw the two of them. "Apologies, did I just interrupt something?" he asked, a smirk on his lips.

Kalen rolled his eyes. "What have we got for eating?"

"It's mashed potato and gravy," he replied, kicking the door closed with his foot.

Rexah rose to her feet and took one of the plates. "Thank you, Torbin. Would you by chance be able to light the fire?"

Torbin nodded and smiled. "Of course."

He handed one of the plates to Kalen before walking over to the fireplace. Rexah took a seat on the edge of the bed, sinking deeper into it than she thought she would and almost spilling her food as a result.

"What's the plan then? How do we find Storglass?" Rexah asked, stirring her food with her spoon to make it look more appetising.

A whooshing sound filled the room as the fire roared to life in the fireplace, filling the space with a warm glow.

"Well, it's like the innkeeper said, they don't get many travellers or newcomers to the village, so I'd bet my last coin that he will know where our friend lives," Kalen said before tucking into his food.

"And if he doesn't know, which is highly unlikely, then we ask someone else," Torbin said, sinking further against the wall.

"Do we want everyone to know we are looking for him? I mean, what if the Dark Fae have spies or something?" Rexah asked. "What if they overhear and go straight to them? Should I start taking the potions again?"

Kalen licked his lips. "It's a chance we're going to have to take, princess. As for the potions? Venrhys already knows where you were, and I don't think the potion will do much to disguise you from him. He can smell the magic in your blood."

"I know, but I…" She trailed off and sighed. "I have this horrible feeling in the pit of my stomach."

Rexah was scared; she didn't want to admit it to them, but she was. She didn't want them to think her weak. If she admitted it and heard the words out loud, she wasn't sure if she could do this anymore. She was no fool. She knew what would happen once they had the sword – she would have to kill the Dark Fae's master – and that fact alone terrified her beyond measure.

"We'll take it one step at a time, Rex," Torbin said softly. "Right now, all we need to do is eat and rest. Tomorrow is a new day."

She took a deep breath and nodded; he was right. They chatted quietly throughout their supper, and when Rexah was done she placed the empty bowl on top of the drawers, coughing at the disturbed dust as she did so. After rolling out her bedroll next to the fire, she lay down and accepted the heat from the flames as it seeped into her bones. She prayed to any of the Gods who might be listening, asking for their guidance. They would need all the help they could get.

In the morning, they would start their search for Storglass.

One step at a time.

34

"Where do we start our search?" Rexah asked, keeping her voice low. She didn't want anyone overhearing their conversation which was difficult when the silence in the room was almost deafening.

Kalen sipped his drink and waited until he'd set the cup back down on the wooden table before he replied. "If our friend – the innkeeper – has no knowledge of where he is, then we will head outside and explore, maybe ask a few of the locals. Someone has got to know him, or at least of him."

Rexah gazed over her shoulder and watched the man limp around the bar and place the dishes into the sink. "Sounds good to me."

They'd ordered porridge for breakfast, and Rexah had eaten it without complaint. It wasn't the best food she'd tasted, but her stomach had ached with hunger so painful that she didn't care. She'd finished it within minutes, and it had gained her a smirk from Kalen.

"I will never complain about food in any other town or village ever again after tasting this," Torbin said under his breath, pushing his almost empty bowl away with a look of disgust on his face.

"Well, the quicker we find Storglass the quicker we can get out of here and find some tastier food," Kalen said as he finished off his own bowl. "But for now, you'll just have to deal with it."

Torbin nudged him with his elbow causing Kalen to chuckle.

"Both of you stay here. I'll go ask the innkeeper," Rexah said, rising from her seat. "Wish me luck."

"Good luck, darling, not that you'll need it though." Kalen smiled at her.

Rexah managed to stop her cheeks from reddening as she turned and walked up to the bar. The innkeeper sighed in annoyance when he spotted her making her way over.

She gave him a friendly smile. "Good morning," she said.

"What do you want, girl?" he said and grunted.

Dismissing his rudeness, she was sure to keep her voice low when she spoke. "My friends and I are looking for someone. He goes by the name of Storglass. Do you happen to know where we might find him?"

The innkeeper let out a harsh laugh that sent him into a coughing fit. "What do you want with Storglass?" he asked when he recovered.

"Our business is our own," she replied. "Do you know where he is or not?"

"He's right over there," he told her, pointing over her shoulder.

Rexah looked around and saw a man sitting at a table tucked away in the corner, almost hidden in the shadows. From a distance it was hard to make out any distinctive features; all she could see were puffs of smoke that drifted lazily from the darkness that enshrouded him.

"You're sure that's him?" Rexah asked as she turned back to the innkeeper.

"Aye I am, girl. Like I told you last night, we don't have many residents. Storglass is a regular of mine," he said, picking up a tankard and pouring ale into it for a customer further down the bar.

"Thank you. Oh, one last thing," she said before

placing her palms flat on the bar and leaning closer to him. "If you call me *girl* again, I'll cut your balls off and make you one, understood? Manners don't cost anything, try using them now and again."

She didn't wait for a response and headed back over to her table. Her companions studied her with raised eyebrows as she sat down.

"Storglass is in the corner behind you," she said in a hushed tone, indicating his whereabouts with a small nod of her head as she pulled her seat closer to the table.

"What did you say to the innkeeper?" Kalen asked, a small smirk playing on his lips.

"Nothing," Rexah replied, straightening her spine. "Just a reminder that manners cost nothing, that's all."

Kalen chuckled. "He's as white as a sheet."

"It serves him right," she said matter-of-factly. She wasn't a *girl*; she was a fierce, independent woman. The events of the past month or so had certainly shaken her, but she would find her way back to herself, and it started with the innkeeper. "What happens now? Do we approach him and say, 'hello, we are complete strangers to you, but we need your help with something of the utmost importance'?"

"That's one option," Torbin said, sitting back in his

chair. "Or we could wait outside and catch him as he's leaving."

"Or you could simply ask whatever it is you require of me," a voice said beside them.

Rexah almost hit the ceiling; her entire body jolted in fright. Her head snapped to the side to find a man sitting in the seat beside her – a man she hadn't seen walk over or even sit down. From the looks on Kalen and Torbin's faces, they hadn't either.

Shaggy brown hair touched the top of his shoulders, and his deeply tanned skin made his hazel eyes stand out like a candle in the dark. The pipe in his hand was no longer lit as he set it down carefully on the table in front of him.

Rexah looked over to the now empty table she'd seen Storglass sitting at before she turned her attention back to him. "How ... how did you get here so fast?"

"You're a warlock," Kalen said before Storglass had the chance to answer. His deep blue eyes studied the man like he could see inside him and access his thoughts.

Rexah's jaw hung open. He'd used his magic to get here.

Storglass smirked and nodded. "I am. Now, would you be so kind as to enlighten me to the reason why a human and two fae wish to speak to me? Why have you sought me out?"

"Is there some place a little more private we could talk?" Rexah asked, looking around the room that was steadily filling with customers.

Storglass slid his gaze to her, studying her for a moment. "There is, but tell me, why should I trust any of you?"

"Because if you don't then the world as we know it will end," Rexah replied, her gaze steady on his. "This is a very important matter. We need your help."

The warlock was quiet as he swept a scrutinizing gaze over them, and Rexah could have sworn she saw his eyes flash green for a split second.

"Very well," he said after long consideration. "We may converse in my abode. Let's get going, shall we?"

Rexah looked to Kalen who gave her a soft nod. Their chairs scraped against the wooden floor as they rose to their feet, the sound amplified in the quiet space, and they followed Storglass out of The Hollow House.

Rexah pulled the hood of her cloak over her head. Thankfully it had stopped raining, but the less attention she drew to herself, the better – a difficult task in a village where newcomers stood out like a sore thumb.

Storglass led the way with Torbin by his side, and Kalen walked behind the warlock, his hand resting on the hilt of his sword. Rexah could see Kalen was on edge, ready for anything, and she remained loyal to his side, just in case.

Grey clouds blocked the sun and painted a gloomy picture in the sky, the threat that it would begin to pour with rain at any moment looming over them. A few villagers went about their daily tasks as they passed. Some gave the group a curious look, others scowled, and one man went as far as to spit at their feet.

"Charming," Rexah muttered to Kalen under her breath as they walked.

"I wouldn't take offense, my lady; none of the villagers particularly like newcomers. Think of it as their way of welcoming you to their home whilst suggesting you keep your visit short," Storglass said, keeping his gaze forward. "And maybe your hand on your coin purse."

Rexah looked at Storglass, burning a hole in the back of his head with her gaze when he called her "my lady".

"Oh yes," Storglass said as if he'd read her thoughts, looking at her over his shoulder. "I know who you are."

Her heart pounded in her chest and her mouth

gaped open, but before she could speak, Storglass came to a halt outside one of the small stone homes. It looked in better shape than the others; a few cracks snaked through the stone here and there, but at least his home was still in one piece.

"Here we are," he said, pulling a brass key from his pocket and unlocking the dark blue door. The hinges squealed when he pushed it open. He motioned to Rexah. "Ladies first."

The smell of incense and herbs instantly filled her nostrils, reminding her of Merin's home. Paintings hung upon deep red walls, so many that the colour underneath only peaked through between frames. A dark-brick fireplace was built into the wall on the left side of the room, a red settee and two armchairs placed by it. A kitchen area sat to the right of the room where plentiful pots and pans hung from hooks on the wall.

As she stepped further into the large room, glass cabinets filled with jars came into view along the back wall. A workbench was bolted to the floor in front of the cabinets, books and parchment littering it. Dried candlewax was set mid-drip off the edge of the workbench; some had dripped onto the floor leaving hardened splotches on the wood.

It was then she noticed chalk marks on the floor.

Frowning, she looked to her feet and tried to make sense of it, twisting her gaze to connect the lines.

It hit her all at once: she was standing in the centre of a perfectly drawn pentagram, but it looked different from the drawings she'd seen in her magic study class. Filled with runes and arcane symbols, it was far beyond her magical knowledge skill to decipher what each of them represented.

Gasping, she lurched backwards out of the arcane circle, her hood falling.

Storglass laughed from the other side of the room. "Don't be so dramatic, my dear," he said as he closed the door. "They are harmless unless they have been activated."

Rexah glanced at the warlock sheepishly before shifting her eyes to Kalen. He stood in the doorway, his arms crossed and an amused smile across his face.

"Tea anyone?" Storglass asked as he walked into the kitchen area and picked up the teapot.

"Sounds lovely, thank you," Rexah replied. "As long as you don't bewitch it."

Storglass chuckled. "Of course not. Please have a seat whilst I conjure up my best brew."

"I like him," Kalen whispered to Rexah as he passed her and walked over to the settee.

Rexah rolled her eyes before following them. She sat down beside Kalen while Torbin opted for standing by the fireplace.

"You know who I am, but I'd like to introduce you to my companions, Kalen and Torbin," Rexah said, motioning to them.

"Well met," Storglass nodded his head to them before he continued with his tea brewing.

"And you," Torbin replied politely.

"You aren't like the other villagers," Rexah said. "I mean no offense, but you don't seem like you belong here."

"No offense taken. You're right. Grimhollow isn't where I envisioned settling down, but it's quiet and I can carry out my arcana studies in peace."

"How long have you lived here?" Torbin asked.

"Almost five years now," he replied, busying himself around the kitchen.

A few moments later, Storglass walked over with a tray of cups filled with steaming hot tea and set it down on the small table between the settee and armchair. Rexah noticed a plate filled with various biscuits and cakes, and her stomach responded loudly with a grumble.

"Please, help yourself," Storglass said as he caught her eyeing the plate hungrily.

Kalen reached forward and grabbed a plain biscuit. "Thank you," he said, biting off a piece.

"Now, let's get down to business. What can I help you with?" Storglass asked as he lifted one of the steaming cups.

Rexah took one of the cups and held it between her hands, enjoying the heat that seeped into her chilled skin. "We are searching for a weapon, and we are led to believe you know its whereabouts."

"I see, and what weapon would that be?" he asked, sitting back in the armchair.

"The Shadow Star," she replied, her eyes narrowing slightly. "But you already knew that."

Storglass simply nodded. "Yes. I was at The Hollow House when you arrived. It wasn't your beautiful hair that I recognised – it was your blood. I sensed the magic in your veins before you even crossed over the threshold."

Rexah felt a chill slide down her spine like a raindrop on a window. "Do you know where the sword is?"

"No," he replied before taking a small sip of the hot liquid. "I don't know it's whereabouts, and those who lived before us never documented it, trust me – I've looked on more than one occasion."

Rexah tried to hide the disappointment on her face but failed miserably. "Are you sure?"

He nodded. "I have searched every book in the realm. There was no mention of the sword's location or if it is still in existence."

Torbin folded his arms across his chest and sighed.

Rexah considered mentioning the book she'd acquired from Dorasa, but there was no point; it didn't hold any information that would help in their search. Only Rexah could find it, but she would need all the help she could get.

"I'm sorry I brought you both here for nothing," Rexah said quietly to her companions.

"Hold on, Your Highness," Storglass said. "I said *I* didn't know it's whereabouts."

"Spit it out, Storglass. What do you know?" Kalen asked, a hint of impatience in his voice.

Storglass sat forward and placed the cup down on the table. He leaned his elbows on his knees and said, "I know someone, a very good friend of mine, who may be able to help you."

"How do we know this isn't another dead end?"

Torbin asked. "How do we know you're not trying to throw us off the scent?"

"I know the horrors that await in the shadows. I am not naive to what will happen if they get their hands on that sword," Storglass said. "We are all soldiers of the Gods, and I will protect this world and every creature of light within it, no matter what it takes."

Witches and warlocks weren't evil beings, but Rexah had heard of them being taken by the darkness. As it had with the fae who had been taken, it resulted in more of their kind, Valfae, and sometimes Dark Fae.

A horrible realisation settled within her. "When my kingdom was attacked, the Valfae that almost killed me seemed stronger, more intelligent than the others. Is there a possibility that Valfae could have been a witch or a warlock?" she asked Storglass.

His hazel eyes saddened, and he nodded. "The more magic in a witch or warlock's blood the more intelligent and powerful the Valfae will be. For reasons we don't fully understand yet, witches and warlocks are deadlier than fae if they are turned."

The cup of tea suddenly felt cold in her grasp. She set it down on the table with trembling hands. "Gods," she whispered.

Torbin stood and paced with obvious agitation

before he returned to his seat. "Who is this friend you speak of?"

"Her name is Arelle. She is more powerful than I am," he told him.

"Why haven't you gone to her before about this?" Rexah asked him.

"As I grew older, I realised the sword didn't want to be found," he replied. "It's clearer to me now more than ever: the sword cannot be found without the Chosen One, without you."

Rexah shifted slightly in her seat. "You are certain she will be able to help us?"

Once again, Storglass sat back in his chair, his lips failing to resist a grin. "Of course, Seers are exceptional at what they do."

A Seer.

Seers were powerful and extremely rare. They had the ability to look into both the past and future, and the legends say they were blessed by the Goddess of Destiny, that she was the one who bestowed her power on them.

"I haven't heard of any Seers still existing in the realm, not since …" Torbin trailed off.

Rexah looked at him. "Since what?"

His amber eyes met hers. "Since the Battle of Adorea."

Her breath caught in her lungs and her mouth went dry.

"You are correct, Torbin; there have been no other Seers since Arelle was born," Storglass said.

"You're saying that Arelle was on the battlefield, that she met my ancestor?" Rexah asked once she found her voice again.

Storglass nodded. "Precisely."

"How old is she?" she asked.

"It's not polite to ask a lady her age," Storglass replied with a playful smile. "But I will say she looks *very* good for her age."

"Seers have similar lifespans to the fae," Kalen told her quietly. "They live for hundreds, sometimes thousands of years."

Rexah nodded softly. "So where can we find her?"

"You don't find her. She went into hiding after the battle, and I made her a promise that I would never share her location with any soul, living or dead," Storglass said.

"So, you know the location of the only person that can help us, and the realm, but you won't tell us? What good is that to anyone?" Kalen asked angrily.

Without thinking, Rexah put her hand on Kalen's thigh to calm him down. Instantly, blood rushed to her cheeks, and she moved to pull her hand away, but Kalen stopped her with his own, placing it delicately on top of hers.

"That is exactly what I'm saying, but don't fret my fae friend," Storglass said, a mischievous look in his eyes. "I will bring her to us."

35

A Seer. Never in her lifetime did Rexah think she would ever meet one. They were so rare that many believed they didn't exist, that they were only a bedtime story for children – a myth.

Rexah would be lying if she said she didn't feel anxious about what was going to happen, but when she felt Kalen's comforting hand on her shoulder leading her to the edge of the circle, she felt her anxiousness ease. She stepped back and pressed herself against him for a moment, savouring the familiar feel of him.

Torbin stood on the edge of the circle opposite Rexah and Kalen. They all shared a look, and with it Rexah knew they would be ready for anything and would keep each other safe.

"How do we know you aren't about to summon the Dark Fae?" Kalen asked Storglass. "For all we know this could be a trap."

The warlock rolled his hazel eyes. "Stop being so melodramatic, Kalen. I am not summoning the enemy; I give you, my word."

"Forgive me for being a little cautious," Kalen muttered under his breath.

Storglass stood at his workbench grinding herbs with a pestle and mortar before grabbing a small vial filled with a shimmering, light green liquid. Rexah considering asking him what it was, fascinated with the process and eager to know more, but she didn't want to disturb him.

"Now then, let us begin," he said as he walked around the table and over to join them around the arcane circle.

Storglass set the small bowl down on the wooden floor and began to quietly chant in a language Rexah didn't recognise. He poured the liquid from the vial along the outer lines of the pentagram, slowly circling it until he was back at Rexah's side.

Lowering himself to his knees, he picked up the mortar, scooping up the crushed herbs with his fingers. "Come forth wise one, come forth."

With a flick of his wrist, he sprinkled the herbs over the circle and they sparkled like specs of dust caught in moonlight. The arcane markings on the floor began to glow a shade of deep green, smoke filled the air, and a loud boom resounded throughout the room.

Rexah winced at the ringing in her ears, twisting her neck to relieve the ache that lingered in her head. Kalen and Torbin coughed quietly as the smoke tickled their throats, and Storglass rose to his feet once again. The warlock took a step back as the smoke began to disperse, the shape of a figure gradually coming into view.

A woman now stood within the circle; she stood not in her physical form but as a translucent, ghost-like figure. A light grey dress covered the woman's thin frame, pinching her waist perfectly. Teal-coloured locks flowed in waves to her waist, complimenting her stunning, mint green eyes that shone brightly. Her eyes weren't the only thing that demanded Rexah's attention though, it was the markings on her forehead and cheekbones that grasped her focus. Arelle had delicate double lines underneath her eyes, one longer than the other, and two smaller lines ran over the bridge of her nose between her beautiful eyes. From those lines, intricate dots rose between her brows and were crowned by a tiny upturned crescent moon, its edges pointed upwards like horns. As Rexah studied them, she realised they weren't tattoos but scars that marked her flesh, a shade darker than her skin tone.

If Rexah had to guess, this was some sort of astral projection.

"Welcome, wise one," Storglass said, nodding his head respectfully. "Thank you for answering my call. We are honoured to have you in our presence."

"Storglass, I don't have time for your silly games, what do you ..." she trailed off when her gaze fell upon Rexah who stood at his side.

Arelle's face became clouded with confusion and heartrending grief as she looked at her. "Riona?" she whispered in disbelief.

As soon as her ancestor's name left Arelle's lips, Rexah's knees almost buckled. She thought that she was the long dead queen.

"I-I'm sorry, but I am not Riona," Rexah said quietly once she composed herself a little.

Arelle's eyes saddened, and she blinked away her tears. "Yes, of course. Forgive me, it's just you look exactly like she did."

The Seer observed her for a long moment, taking in

every single detail with wonder and awe. No one spoke as she did this, not even Storglass.

"What is your name?" Arelle asked, her voice echoing softly.

"My name is Rexah," she replied. "Rexah Ravenheart."

The name made Arelle's eyes brighten, and a wonderous expression filled her face. "Rexah, it is an honour and a privilege to meet you. I am Arelle, Seer of the realm."

"Now that the formalities are out of the way," Storglass interrupted, "this young lady and her fae companions are in need of your assistance, and I'm afraid it is rather urgent."

Anger flashed in Arelle's eyes as her head snapped to him. "Do not interrupt me again, warlock."

Rexah swore she saw Storglass flinch before he apologised profusely to her. It had been the first time she'd ever seen him uncomfortable.

"He speaks the truth, Arelle. We are looking for a weapon," Rexah explained. "One that can save the realm."

"The Shadow Star," Arelle said, turning her attention back to Rexah. "Riona knew there would be another Chosen, and she knew it would be you – as did I."

Rexah's heart pounded fiercely in her chest. "You were by her side."

Arelle nodded sadly. "I was. Riona was my best friend. In all my years I've never met anyone quite like her. She broke the rules and made new ones, and she fought for those who couldn't fight for themselves. For her, being queen wasn't about power or wealth, it was about the duty to protect her people, and that's exactly what she did, right to the very end."

It was a surreal feeling hearing someone speak so familiarly about her ancestor. Her grandmother spoke of her often, yes, but Arelle *knew* her.

"You were on the battlefield?" Rexah asked, wanting, *needing* to know more.

"Yes, I was by her side. She passed into the other world whilst in my arms," Arelle replied, her voice breaking. "The battle was one of the worst I've ever seen. So many lives were lost, so much destruction."

Rexah could see in her face that she was reliving it as if it had happened only yesterday. It was clear she carried the events of that day even now and would continue to do so for the rest of her life.

"The Dark Fae and their beasts were ruthless,

relentless, and stopped at nothing to ensure the fall of the kingdom," she said. "Their master came, the Elder Fae, and he held power none of us could ever have anticipated or prepared for."

"When the Elder Fae was defeated, what was left of the Dark Fae and Valfae retreated." Arelle's face then turned sombre. "Riona let out a cry of victory, and the Adorian army and the fae who fought by their side echoed it. A few moments later, Riona collapsed."

Rexah's heart sank, and hot tears spilled down her cheeks. She knew Riona had died from her wounds in the battle, but as Arelle explained the details, she felt like she was there experiencing it first-hand.

"When Riona passed, the Shadow Star disappeared," Arelle said.

"How did it disappear?" Kalen asked, his eyebrows knitting together in a frown. "Did someone take it?"

The Seer looked at him, shaking her head. "It vanished when Riona died, and no one has seen it since."

"Is it lost forever?" Torbin asked quietly. He seemed to be the only one in the room who was calm and at ease.

"No, the sword calls to the blood of the Chosen. Only they can find it again," Arelle replied. She turned her gaze to Torbin and took in the sight of him for a moment before she looked back to Rexah. "The Blood of the Raven is within you."

Rexah's skin tingled at her words; every hair on her body stood on end. Her father's voice echoed in her mind.

The power is known as the Blood of the Raven.

"Have you been having the dreams? The nightmares?" Arelle asked her.

Rexah's eyes widened as she nodded. "Yes, I have."

"When did they start?" the Seer asked.

"I've been having them for the last few months," she replied. "How did you know about them?"

Arelle's expression soured. "Riona had them too. Dreams filled with war and death, slaughter and storms. They were a warning of the upcoming war, the Battle of Adorea."

Rexah's stomach sank. "You think my dreams are connected? They are warnings of what's to come?"

"It's too coincidental not to be. I need you to write down from start to finish everything that happens in your nightmares, every single detail," Arelle replied.

Rexah nodded softly as flashbacks of what happened to her kingdom and every other incident with the Valfae filled her head. Each time, she noted, there had been thunder and signs of a storm, just like her dreams.

Kalen's posture stiffened, and he placed a firm hand on Rexah's shoulder blade. "How does she find the sword?" he asked, taking his turn to ask the question burning in Rexah's mind.

"Rexah will need to tap into the power that is lying dormant in her blood," Arelle told him before shifting her gaze to Rexah. "That is something I can help with, but in my current form it is impossible; we will need to meet face to face. It also means I can determine if your dreams are similar to Riona's – please remember to write it down for me."

"Are you sure that's wise? Giving away your location?" Storglass asked.

He'd been awfully silent throughout the conversation – Rexah hadn't known he was capable of being so quiet.

"The fate of the world hangs in the balance, and I'd say that's reason enough," Arelle said.

"Where shall we meet you?" Rexah asked softly. "Name a time and a place, and we will be there."

"My magic is at its strongest on a full moon," Arelle replied. "The next full moon is four days from now. That will give you plenty of time to travel. Meet me—"

Rexah frowned when the Seer stopped speaking, her eyes glazed over and her mouth slackened.

"Arelle?" Rexah whispered.

"What is it? What do you see?" Storglass asked, stepping closer to the circle.

Rexah looked up at Kalen worriedly. His jaw was clenched, and his eyes never left Arelle. Her eyes moved to Torbin, whose hands were curled into fists at his sides in anticipation.

Arelle's eyes became clear again and she gasped. "They are coming."

"They? Who are they?" Torbin asked.

Rexah didn't need her to answer. The chill oozing down her spine like spilled honey, and the heaviness in her stomach told her exactly who she meant.

The Seer looked into Rexah's eyes and said, "The Valfae."

36

Rexah's stomach dropped, and her body began to tremble. It would take those monsters seconds to destroy this village, kill every living soul within it, and they would find them without difficulty.

"How long do we have?" Torbin asked, switching to fight mode. "How many are there?"

"Five minutes at most. There are at least six of them," she replied, worry in her light green eyes. "You have to leave right now if you have any hope of losing them."

"We will come to you. Where will we meet you?" Rexah asked, rising to her feet.

"Fear not, Rexah; get yourselves out of here first,

and I will contact you. Now go!" Arelle said before her image shimmered and disappeared. The light emanating from the arcane circle died, plunging them back into the soft glow of the candles littered around the room.

"You heard her, five minutes – let's go," Storglass said as he made his way over to the cabinets at the back of the room.

Kalen frowned. "You're coming with us?"

"Damn right I am. I'm not staying here to be slaughtered when the Valfae arrive," he replied, grabbing jars and other trinkets and throwing them in a bag Rexah hadn't seen him pick up. "I rather enjoy being alive, thank you very much."

"We don't have time for this, let's go," Torbin said, heading towards the front door.

Rexah followed Kalen but stopped when Storglass grabbed her arm. "What are you doing?" she asked forcefully.

"I noticed the only weapons you carry are those daggers," he said. He nodded to the daggers in her belt. "If it comes to it and we need to fight, you need something that's going to pack more of a punch."

Rexah watched as he pulled a beautiful sword with

an emerald-encrusted hilt from underneath the workbench.

"This is your weapon. I cannot take this from you."

Storglass smirked at her. "I have many weapons, Your Highness, don't worry about me. Now, take it before your fae companion kills me with his stare alone."

Rexah looked over to see Kalen watching them like a hawk, his gaze dark. The look in his eyes made the muscles low in her stomach tighten. Ignoring the feelings flaring within her, she turned back to Storglass and took the sword from him. It was solid and heavy in her hand, but she would manage. "Thank you."

He nodded before he ushered her along and out of the door.

All was calm and eerily quiet as usual, but Rexah could feel the air was charged as she fixed the sword to her belt, it's weight heavy on her hip. "What's the plan?" she asked as they began walking at a fast pace. "Where do we go?"

"We need to get as far away from here as possible first, then we can decide where to go," Torbin said, his eyes everywhere.

Rexah looked at Storglass. "You know where Arelle lives. Stop being all mysterious about it and tell us. We can head to her location, and it means she'll be closer to us too."

The warlock looked ready to argue, but with another look of warning from Kalen, he sighed. "Very well. I will lead the way, but I won't risk saying her location out loud; too many spies could be lurking, especially with the Valfae so close."

Rexah rolled her eyes. "Fine, come on."

With that, they all broke out into a run through the village, heading for the forest. Guilt for abandoning the villagers ate away at Rexah as they fled; they had no idea what was about to befall them. She had to swallow the feeling down and force her legs to keep going, because if she didn't she would turn back and evacuate the village.

The forest came into view, but a dark shape dropped from the sky and landed at the treeline with a loud thud. They halted, and Rexah heard Torbin curse.

"Back to the village. *Now!*" Kalen ordered as he grabbed Rexah's hand, and with that they turned, racing back in the direction they came.

Once they arrived at the centre of the small village, Rexah noticed a few of the villagers looking out of their windows, some even stepping outside their doors to see what all the commotion was about.

Rexah breathed heavily. "Okay, now what?"

Before anyone could answer her a horrifyingly familiar screech filled the sky. Lifting her gaze to the heavens she saw numerous dark shapes, their batlike wings flapping furiously.

This is bad.

One by one the Valfae landed on the ground with a deafening thud, surrounding them and cutting off any chance of escape.

We are trapped.

The only way they could get out of this was to fight their way out. Torbin unsheathed his short swords at the same time Kalen pulled out his own weapon, their blades singing as they did. Storglass mumbled to himself, and seconds later emerald swirls of magic came to life in his hand, the power licking up his fingers like flames.

Rexah unsheathed the sword Storglass had given her, gripping it tightly in her hand. She took a deep, steadying breath, and when she felt hands grab the tops of her arms, she looked up to be met with Kalen's stunning dark blue eyes.

"You know how to use that?" he asked.

She scoffed. "Seriously?"

"Don't try and be a hero, okay? Kill every single one

of these bastards you can, but save yourself if you must," he said, his tone serious.

Kalen wasn't joking around; she could see the severity and fear in his eyes.

"Right back at you." She nodded softly.

Kalen cupped her cheek with his warm hand. "We leave here alive, together."

Her heart ached in her chest, tears burning in her eyes. "Together."

Kalen leaned down and captured her lips with his. She wasted no time in kissing him back, her hand resting on his chest, her sword at her side. The kiss was full of passion and love, and when her tears fell Kalen gently wiped them away with his thumb.

Rexah didn't want their moment to end, but they had monsters to kill. She slowly pulled away. "Let's do this," she whispered.

With difficulty, they pulled away from each other. Torbin's soft smirk didn't go unnoticed, but she shrugged it off – they had more important matters to deal with.

"Stick as close together as possible. Don't let your guard down. Don't give these beasts any opportunity to strike or you'll be dead before you know it," Storglass said.

Standing back-to-back with one another, they readied themselves for what was to come, and a shift in the air made Rexah's skin pebble with goosebumps. Torbin murmured in the language of the fae, and his swords lit up with familiar fae fire and his amber eyes began to glow. He spun the blades in his hands a few times, preparing himself.

Turning her gaze over her shoulder she saw a glowing, dark blue aura surrounding Kalen's hands. The aura travelled up his sword in magical flames, engulfing the sharp blade.

As if feeling her eyes on him, he looked at her over his shoulder, and like Torbin's, Kalen's eyes were glowing the same colour as his power.

Growling pulled her attention back to the Valfae. The beasts snarled and snapped, hungry for a piece of them. With red eyes gleaming and maws dripping with drool, they attacked.

Rexah's grip on her sword tightened as she braced herself, just like Zuko had taught her. A razor-sharp claw swiped the air making an obvious effort for Rexah's head; anticipating the blow, she ducked out of the way and brought the blade down, cutting the creature's arm clean off. The creature howled in pain which sent a rush of adrenaline through her, and she kicked it hard enough in the side to send it to the ground. With all her strength, she pinned the Valfae down with her foot and drove her sword through its heart.

Taking a quick breath, she spun on her heel to find another fast approaching. Rexah dove forward and rolled out of the brute's way, bouncing back to her feet just as quickly. With a cry she brought the sword back and stabbed through the Valfae like butter. Black blood sprayed from the wound as she removed the blade from its back, covering the muddy ground and her hand.

All the training Zuko had given her was flooding back.

Green flame shot past her and hit a Valfae she hadn't noticed dangerously close. It crumpled to the ground in a heap, a gaping hole now smouldering in its chest. Rexah looked over and gave Storglass a nod in thanks.

Torbin and Kalen worked seamlessly together. They fought by each other's sides as if they were performing a dance, one they had done many times before. The blue and orange magic of their weapons merged as they took down one of the beasts together – it was a beautiful thing to witness.

We can do this.

The hope and belief were instantly ripped away

when a Valfae slammed into her side and sent her flying through the air; she smashed through the window of a nearby home, and searing pain spread through Rexah's forearm and head upon impact with the glass.

She landed on the wooden floor of a living room, glass falling like rain around her. Groaning, she dragged herself up onto her feet and walked towards the closest door, glass crunching beneath her boots. She lifted her hand to her head and winced at the sting. As she removed her hand, she saw her fingers were stained with blood.

Shit.

The pain in her forearm burned; the sleeve of her top had been sliced open and the wound beneath it was oozing blood. Cursing, she quickly ripped a piece of her shirt and wrapped it tightly around the bleeding wound, wincing at the pressure.

Suddenly, the front door was smashed to pieces as one of the Valfae crashed through it. The beast's red eyes fixated on her, and it snarled, drool sliding through is jagged teeth and dripping down its chin. Rexah's heart jolted in her chest as she turned, hoisted herself up onto the windowsill, and jumped out through the now broken window.

Outside, the scene before her was one of utter

chaos. Villagers stumbled by her in a hurry to flee for their lives, screaming as they went. Three Valfae lay dead on the ground, one missing its head, but more of the monsters had joined the fight.

Not good.

The odds were heavily stacked against them, but she wouldn't give up, she couldn't.

Rexah spotted her sword lying a few feet away; she hadn't been able to keep hold of it when she was sent through the window; and she rushed over, picked it up, and turned in time to see a Valfae charging straight for Torbin who was midbattle with another.

Rexah raced towards the Valfae, her feet moving before she could even think. Raising the sword above her head in both hands, she jumped and drove the blade through the creature's back. It screeched and howled in pain as it collapsed face down in the mud. Rexah kneeled on the small of its back as she twisted the sword, and a sickening crack resounded as she severed its spinal cord. With that, the Valfae stopped moving.

"Thanks, Rex!" Torbin groaned as he dealt a killing blow to the brute he'd been fighting. He didn't look too bad; his face was splattered with dirt and Valfae blood, but other than a tear in his fighting leathers from what looked like a close call, he thankfully looked fine.

"How many are left?" Rexah asked as she looked around.

Torbin did the same. "At least another six or seven. They just keep coming."

"We have to get out of here," Rexah said. "They're toying with us."

Kalen appeared at her side, concern in his deep blue eyes. "Darling, you're bleeding."

"I'm okay." Rexah looked up at him, scanning him for injuries. Apart from a scrape to his left cheek, like Torbin, he was fine.

Kalen gently held her close and opened his mouth to speak, but he was interrupted by a snarl. A Valfae had picked up a broken piece of wood and hurled it straight at them. Rexah's eyes widened in surprise, and she moved to duck out of its path, but Kalen's grip on her waist tightened. He threw his other hand up and brilliant blue energy exploded from his palm, halting the debris in mid-air before he thrust his hand forward and shot it straight back at the creature. The Valfae hadn't the time to avoid it; the wood struck the creature in the throat, and it made a pained whimpering noise and choked violently before it fell to the ground, dead.

It was one of the most incredible things she'd seen

in her life. She'd never seen Kalen use his magic before, and it was something she would never forget or tire of seeing.

Storglass appeared from around the corner, his hand still illuminated with green magic, panting as he grew closer. "There's too many of them for us to deal with. If you have any chance of surviving, you need to leave right now."

"And how do you propose we do that? We're surrounded," Kalen said, annoyance thick in his voice.

Rexah looked at Storglass as the realisation hit her.

You need to leave.

She shook her head. "No, absolutely not."

"It's the only way," Storglass said. "I will lead them away as a distraction whilst you flee."

"They'll kill you," Rexah said softly.

Storglass smirked at her. "Don't be so quick to underestimate me, Your Highness. Arelle will find you, just keep running as far as you can from here. There is one last thing I require from you, if I may?"

Rexah slowly nodded and watched as he approached her. He ripped a piece of his cloak before slowly untying the scrap of clothing from the wound on Rexah's arm. Quickly, he replaced it with the fresh piece before stepping back.

"This will draw them to me," he said, lifting the cloth soaked with her blood.

"You don't have to do this," Rexah said as howling and screeching filled the air.

Storglass smiled at her. "It's been an honour to fight by your side, Rexah Ravenheart. Now, go."

She didn't want to go. She didn't want to leave him with those monsters, but Kalen didn't give her a choice as he gripped her arm and began to pull her away.

Stumbling slightly as she sheathed her sword, Rexah looked back at Storglass and watched as he turned to face the Valfae who rounded the corner. The warlock faced a pack of at least six of them.

"Run, Rexah, come on!" Kalen shouted as they broke out into a run.

With difficulty, she pulled her gaze away from the warlock, pulled her arm from Kalen's grip, and pushed her legs to move as fast as they could.

Don't turn around.

The trees at the opening of the forest drew closer and closer with each hurried step they took, the village behind them now. All that remained was a small no-man's-land between the village and the forest. Rexah's lungs were burning but she couldn't stop, they had to keep going or they would be dead.

Both Kalen and Torbin groaned behind her. She looked at them over her shoulder, frowning when she saw they'd come to a complete stop. Suddenly, Rexah collided with something hard, almost falling to the ground, and cried out softly at the pain radiating up her forearm. She looked up, and her heart dropped into her stomach.

"No … no …" she chanted as she struggled, ignoring the fiery pain in her arm.

Venrhys smirked down at her, his black eyes almost glowing with excitement. "Hello, Little Raven."

37

"How wonderful it is to see you again. I will admit, I rather enjoyed the game of cat and mouse we played, but the time for games is now over," Venrhys said, his grip on her arm tightening. "It's time to fly, Little Raven."

Rexah's heart was in overdrive, and tears burned in her eyes as she struggled against him. "Get your hands off me!"

"Let her go, Venrhys," Kalen growled behind her. "Or I'll tear your fingers off and shove them down your throat until you choke."

Venrhys focused his black eyes on Kalen as he turned Rexah to face him, her back squirming against his chest. "Brave words, Kalen Vidarr, but you are in no position to command me to do anything."

Rexah could hear the threat in his voice, and brought the heel of her boot down hard on his foot. Venrhys groaned, annoyed more than anything, and grabbed her around the neck, his other hand tightly wrapped around her waist.

"Careful now, Rexah," Venrhys warned, his breath hot in her ear. "I won't stand for disobedience of any kind."

Rexah looked to Torbin and Kalen and wondered why they hadn't advanced, before she remembered how Venrhys liked to play with his victims. Nausea sat heavy in the bottom of her stomach.

Venrhys has used his power on them, just like he did that day Vellwynd was destroyed. Just like he did to me when I tried to kill Kalen...

The realisation made her knees shake.

The group of Valfae stood a few feet behind Kalen and Torbin, four or five of them at least. The look in their eyes told her they were hungry, and this was only just the beginning.

"I will send you back to the pit you crawled out of," Kalen said through gritted teeth. "I will make sure you can't escape."

Venrhys chuckled, the vibration of it spreading through his chest against Rexah's back. "This situation must give you a case of déjà vu, Kalen. My fellow general still talks about your mother and brother to this very day."

Rexah's heart ached at the look of grief in Kalen's eyes. How dare this monster talk about his family like that.

As hard as she could, she thrust her elbow into his stomach. Venrhys groaned in pain, but it wasn't enough to make him release her from his hold. Instead, Venrhys tightened his grip on her neck, pulling her head back against his shoulder whilst his other arm wrapped around her torso and pinned her arms to her sides.

"Now, now – play nice," he said before he leaned down and ran his tongue along the cut on her head, licking up the blood still oozing from it. His body shuddered with pleasure from the taste, and Rexah almost brought up the contents of her stomach right there and then.

"Absolutely divine," Venrhys groaned softly. "I can taste the power in your blood, Little Raven. It's a shame I can't have it all for myself."

"I won't let you or anyone have it," she said, gritting her teeth.

The Dark Fae chuckled, a piece of her hair fluttering with his breath. "You speak as though you have any choice in the matter."

Torbin's eyes flashed as he tried his hardest to break free of the dark magic, but his efforts were in vain. For a moment, Kalen's power came to life in his hands but was soon snuffed out by the malevolent sorcery holding him captive, the veins in his neck straining as he battled for control. The look on his face was enough to tell her he wouldn't give up, not without a fight.

"No matter how it warms my blood to see you both," he said to her fae companions. "Rexah and I must take our leave. My master has waited long enough, and he grows more impatient by the second."

She couldn't move much, he gripped her too tightly, but her fingers itched with free movement. Rexah let Venrhys talk; as he droned on and on about his master, she managed to slip her dagger from the pocket of her trousers. Her eyes moved to meet Kalen's gaze, and with a slight tilt of the head, she winked.

Kalen's eyes flashed with a warning not to do it, but she'd already decided; this was the only lifeline any of them had, it was the only chance they had to get away.

The handle of the blade began to vibrate as she gripped it tightly in her sweaty hand. She gritted her teeth, and with all the strength she could muster she brought it down hard, stabbing it through the Dark Fae's thigh, lightning crackling down the steel and into his leg.

Venrhys cried out in pain, and his grip on her slackened enough for Rexah to shove him away from her. Venrhys collapsed on the ground, holding the handle of the dagger still embedded in his leg, blood soaking the material of his trousers. Lightning continued to spark along the handle causing the Dark Fae to curse and groan in pain.

The power holding Kalen and Torbin at bay wavered, and they both fell to their knees with a groan. Rexah unsheathed her sword and sliced it down in time to cut through the Valfae who'd attempted to take her down. The creature fell to the ground with a gaping wound in its neck, and it did not rise again.

Kalen and Torbin drew their swords and joined in the fight, working in sync once again. Rexah moved closer to them as she jumped out the way of a Valfae that threatened to grab her with its outstretched claws. Spinning, she brought her sword up in a sweeping motion and took the beast's arm clean off. Swinging her blade back around, she made the finishing blow and sliced into its chest with minimal resistance. The creature fell to the ground, and Rexah left it there, clinging to life – death would come quick to claim it.

She made a step towards Kalen, ready to run to him when she was slammed into the mud. Her sword went flying from her grasp and landed just out of her reach as she hit the ground heavily. Pain shot through her shoulder and her breaths came out in gasps as the wind was knocked out of her. Looking up her eyes were met with an extremely pissed off Venrhys.

Before he could do anything, Rexah kicked out, swiping his legs from beneath him. As he fell to his knees, his fist connected with Rexah's jaw, smacking her head to the side; she fell to the ground, blood from her lip spilling into the mud.

Venrhys rose to his feet, kicking her onto her back, and a moan of pain escaped her as the air left her lungs a second time.

"I underestimated you, I'll admit it, but my patience with you is growing extremely thin," he said, twirling Rexah's dagger in his hand. "It's time we were on our way, but first, you need to be taught a lesson in obedience."

Rexah's eyes widened as he gripped the dagger, lifting it high above his head. Before he could bring it down, a flash of brilliant blue energy came flying through the air and hit him square in the chest, knocking him off his feet and into the trunk of a tree a few feet away.

Twisting her head in the direction the energy came from, she saw Kalen with his arm outstretched, the beautiful blue power that matched his eyes swirling around his hand like the mists of Kaldoren. His chest rose and fell heavily as he gulped down deep breaths.

Rexah rolled onto her stomach before slowly bringing herself up onto her knees. Her head and arm ached from her wounds, and now she could add her split lip to that list.

Before she could try and stand, a cry of agony pierced Rexah's ears, and she turned her head in time to see a Valfae rake its claws through the flesh of Torbin's side.

"NO!" she screamed as she scrambled to her feet.

Torbin collapsed on the ground, clutching the wound, his swords discarded at his sides, and his face twisted with pain.

Kalen killed the beast who'd delivered the blow to his friend, showing it no mercy for what it had done. The Valfae dropped to the ground in two separate pieces.

"Torbin, look at me," he said, kneeling to his fallen

companion. "We will get you out of here; you will live. Just hold on, and keep your eyes open, brother. Keep your eyes on me."

The sound of splintering bark caught Rexah's attention. Snapping her head to the sound behind her, she watched as Venrhys pulled himself free from the tree's embrace. Its trunk had caved in from the force of Venrhys's body hitting it, and broken pieces of bark fell from him as he rolled his shoulders.

Venrhys limped forward, black blood still oozing from his thigh. Scratches marked his skin here and there from the bark of the tree, but nothing was slowing him down.

"The Shadow Star's location may be buried deep inside your mind, but fear not, Little Raven, I shall help you remember," Venrhys said, a sadistic grin spreading across his face and a predatory look filling his black eyes.

Before she could decide her next move, a Valfae appeared as if from nowhere and knocked her through the air. She hit the ground with a hard thud, a groan of pain leaving her lips.

A conflicted look filled Kalen's face for a moment; it was clear he was reluctant to leave his friend's side, but rage took over him as he watched Rexah hit the ground. Blue energy danced through his fingers, and he gripped his blade tightly as his legs carried him forward towards the Dark Fae.

Venrhys's black eyes shifted, and a sadistic smirk spread across his face as he focused his attention on Kalen and baited him with a menacing laugh.

Time itself seemed to slow as Rexah lifted herself onto her elbows and watched as Kalen charged for Venrhys who braced himself, waiting like a predator for its prey.

No ... no ... NO! Rexah forced herself onto her unsteady feet, her jelly-like legs almost giving out. As she moved, she picked up her dagger that had been inches from where she was thrown, the handle a comfort in her grasp.

In the blink of an eye, Kalen's sword was on the ground, and he was frozen in place, his muscles straining as he tried to regain control.

"You don't mind if Kalen and I go for a little trip, do you, Rexah?" Venrhys asked, his eyes never leaving Kalen's face.

Taking a few steps forward, her heart began to pound in her chest. "Let him go! Take me instead! You wanted me!"

Those soulless darkened pits of Venrhys's eyes

moved to her. "Oh, but this is much more fun," he said, his smirk growing more sinister.

With a flick of the Dark Fae's wrist, Kalen spun to face her. His face was strained as he fought against the compulsion, but that only seemed to make it worse. The blue magic in his fingertips petered out. "Rexah, darling, run!"

"Let us strike a bargain," Venrhys said, stepping closer to Kalen.

She glared at him. "No, I know better than to make a bargain with someone like you."

"Not even if Kalen's life depended on it?" he asked almost innocently, but that twisted, evil smirk on his face gave him away.

"N-no ..." A weak groan came from behind her. Looking over her shoulder, she saw Torbin lay on his back, his eyes on her. "R-rex ..."

"Torbin," Kalen said through gritted teeth.

Rexah turned her attention back to Kalen and Venrhys. Torbin was hurt, and if his wound wasn't healed soon then he would die. She had to do something. "Fine! I'll bargain with you, just let him go."

"I think not, he will serve as collateral. Bring me the Shadow Star, and you shall have Kalen returned to you – unharmed I cannot guarantee, but alive, nonetheless,"

Venrhys said, his black eyes connecting with hers across the space.

"I cannot bring you the weapon if I don't know where it is," she said, tightening her grip on the dagger, sparks of lightning flashing in her fingertips.

"Then you better start looking," he replied as he placed his hand on Kalen's shoulder. "The full moon is almost upon us. I will give you until the next full moon to deliver the sword. Do we have a deal?"

Rexah kept her eyes trained on the Dark Fae. "Kalen isn't to be harmed."

"That I cannot promise, but I will do my best to keep him whole. You give me the sword and he will be returned to you alive," Venrhys replied. "Do you accept?"

Defeat washed over her in pummelling waves, and her eyes flickered to Kalen.

"It's okay, darling," he whispered, his ocean eyes pouring into hers. "Everything's going to be okay."

Tears filled her eyes as she looked to Venrhys once again. "We have a deal."

"The clock is ticking, Little Raven." Venrhys winked at her.

The wind began to pick up, thrashing her dark hair around her face. The space around Kalen and Venrhys shimmered, and black magic that threatened to suffocate her filled the air as it swirled around her.

Rexah's blood drained from her face. "No, no wait!" she cried out as she ran towards them.

Kalen's eyebrows rose in shock, his mouth dropping open. "REXAH!" he screamed.

His eyes filled with pure, undiluted terror were the last thing she saw before the darkness consumed them. All that remained was the remnants of dark magic dissipating into nothingness, like black smoke rising from an inferno and getting lost in the wind.

They were gone.

He was gone.

38

The roaring of flames sounded behind Rexah. She turned to see Torbin use his power to fend off three Valfae who were stalking towards him, hungry looks in their red eyes as they closed in on their prey.

Torbin's amber flames weren't enough to deter the creatures. His power waned and sparked in his bloody hand as he tried to call upon it once more, but he was too weak.

Rage filled Rexah's blood as her feet carried her forward towards the Valfae advancing on her friend. Before she got close enough to take out her anger on the beasts, green flame exploded over the creatures and sent them shooting off in different directions. They howled and whimpered in pain; some dropped to the ground with a thud, instantly dead, while others managed to take to the sky and flee.

Rexah spotted Storglass limping towards them. His head and nose were bleeding, and his clothing was ripped to shreds in places, but he was alive.

"They're gone. We're safe now," Storglass said, breathing heavily as he stopped beside them.

Rexah rushed to Torbin's side, dropping to her knees. "Keep your eyes open, Torbin."

Torbin's heavy amber eyes met hers, his lips tugging upwards in a weak smile. "You ... you won't be getting r-rid of me that ... e-easily."

"Where is Kalen?" Storglass asked as his eyes scanned the area.

Rexah looked up at the warlock. "Venrhys took him he's ... he's gone."

Storglass blanched. "Well, this isn't good."

"Instead of standing there saying things that are painfully fucking obvious, in case you haven't noticed, Torbin is dying and could use your help," Rexah snapped.

"You're right, apologies. I don't do well in situations like this; I tend to ramble on a bit," he said. "Like right now."

"STORGLASS!" Rexah roared.

The warlock flinched and limped over to them, wincing in pain as he got to his knees. He examined Torbin's wound and cursed quietly. "This is beyond my healing capabilities."

"I won't let him die," Rexah said. "There's got to be something you can do."

"The poison from the Valfae's claw is spreading already. I will do what I can to slow it down, but we *need* to get him to Arelle," Storglass said, green energy flickering to life on his fingertips.

Rexah frowned. "She's a Seer."

"Yes, but she is extremely powerful, and she has the herbs needed for this type of wound," he told her as he began focusing his power on Torbin's bleeding side. "I'll put him to sleep to limit his pain."

Torbin moaned weakly in pain as Rexah took his hand. "We're going to get you the help you need. Storglass will do what he can for you until then. Sleep Torbin, I'm right here."

Torbin's eyes slowly closed, and his body relaxed.

"That will do for now; we have to get moving," Storglass said. "I will carry him."

"Are you sure? What about your injuries?" Rexah asked.

Storglass dismissed her concerns with a wave of his hand before reaching down and lifting the injured fae. "Let's go, Your Highness, or should it be Your Majesty?"

"Enough of that, Storglass. Now isn't the time," she said as she picked up Torbin's twin blades. She scanned the ground before her eyes fell on the sword the warlock had given her. Once the blade was secure at her hip, she turned back to Storglass who nodded to her.

They walked in silence. The only sounds were those of twigs snapping and cracking beneath their feet as they made their way through the forest. Storglass walked a few steps ahead as Rexah's eyes scanned their surroundings, keeping a look out – more of those monsters could be lurking.

Kalen's scream echoed in her mind; she'd never heard such a gut-wrenching sound in all her life. The look of pure horror on his face was one she would never forget.

Grief threatened to rip through her courage and tear her apart, but she couldn't crumble, not now. Breaking down would be the easiest thing in the world, but he needed her – Torbin needed her.

Rexah shifted her tear-filled gaze to the dark, gloomy sky and silently prayed to any of the gods or goddesses who would listen; she prayed that she would reach Kalen in time, and that she would find the Shadow Star before it was too late.

EPILOGUE

All was quiet as he watched the realm they'd all created shimmer within the iridescent scrying pool. There was only one person who had his undying attention – his chosen.

"You may be a God, but even you need to rest," a familiar voice echoed behind him.

He didn't turn to her. "I will rest when our realm is at peace once more."

She stood beside him, gazing down into the pool. "You truly believe she has what it takes? You thought the last one did and look what happened."

"That will not happen again," he replied, a hint of anger in his voice.

"Really? Is that why you sent that lightning bolt straight

through the beast's chest when it was about to kill her?" she asked.

He moved his gaze to meet hers. "She is my Chosen, and I will do as I wish. She didn't have nearly as much of a chance as Riona did. It would have been unfair."

"Renvian, what will you do if she fails?" she asked as she held his stare.

"She will not fail," he replied.

Her eyes saddened. "You cannot intervene again."

"I won't need to. She is different, Tella," he said as he shifted his gaze back to the pool, to Rexah. "I can feel it."

"This is our last chance. For all our sakes, I hope you are right," Tella said before she turned and left the room.

Rexah was strong and resilient, and once she tapped into her power, into his power, she would be a force to be reckoned with.

ACKNOWLEDGMENTS

It's such a surreal feeling writing this. It's been a dream of mine since I was a little girl to share my writing with the world. It's been an incredible journey writing the first book in the Ravenheart series and I have some amazing people I would like to thank.

First off I'd like to thank my mum. You have supported me through this process from the very beginning and I wouldn't be where I am today if it wasn't for you. Thank you from the bottom of my heart. I am so lucky to have you as my mum and I love you so much!

To my dad. Even though you're not here in person to see my achievement, I know you've been here helping me through the tough chapters and the self-doubt. I know you'll be proud of me. I'll be sending a few copies up there for you and the rest of the family to enjoy.

To my sister, Christine, who insisted she get one of the first copies. Who has always been there for me growing up. Who watched Buffy the Vampire Slayer with me every Thursday night and encouraged my creativity.

Linzi Westwood, where would I be without you? You've been my best friend for so many years I've lost count! My Alpha reader! Thank you for reading countless chapters and drafts of Heir of Ravens and Ruin. Thank you for helping me through the tough times and laughing with me through the best times. I love you dude, till the end of the line.

To the writing group, every single one of you helped make this possible. Your advice kept my head above the water, and I will be forever grateful to you all!

To Danielle for designing the STUNNING cover! It's beyond anything I could ever have imagined!

To my editor, Amy. Thank you for sorting through the final draft and enhancing the story. Thank you for fixing my grammar and punctuation. You are the absolute best!

To my beta-readers and hype team. You have been my rock throughout this process. Lifting my spirits when I've been down. Giving me the confidence that the world, the characters, and the story I'd created was worth publishing.

Finally, to my husband Nicky. The Kalen to my

Rexah, my soulmate. Thank you for listening to me go on about my book baby, even when you had no idea what I was talking about. Thank you for all the love and support you've given me through this journey. I love you so much, my sun and stars.

CPSIA information can be obtained
at www.ICGtesting.com
Printed in the USA
BVHW041027271022
650472BV00005B/44

9 781739 712624